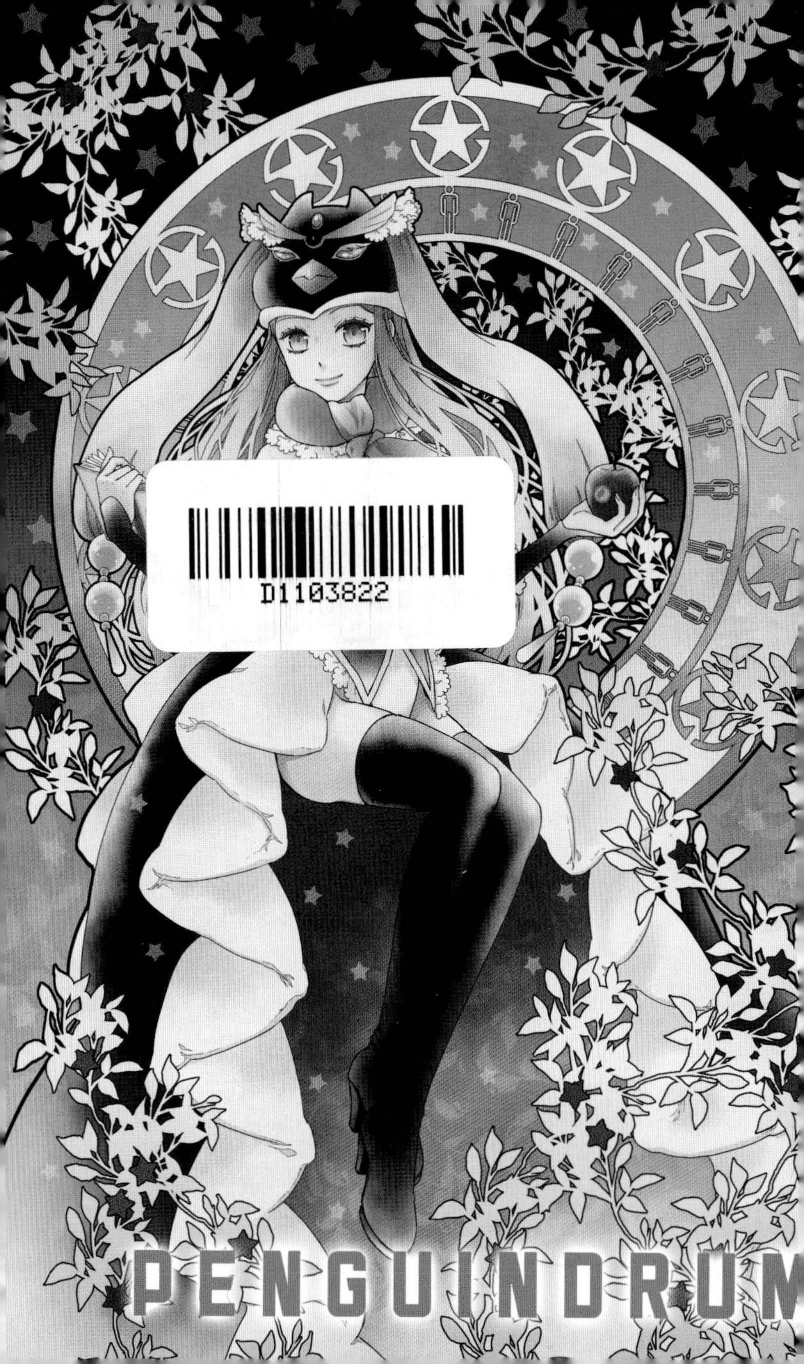
PENGUINDRUM

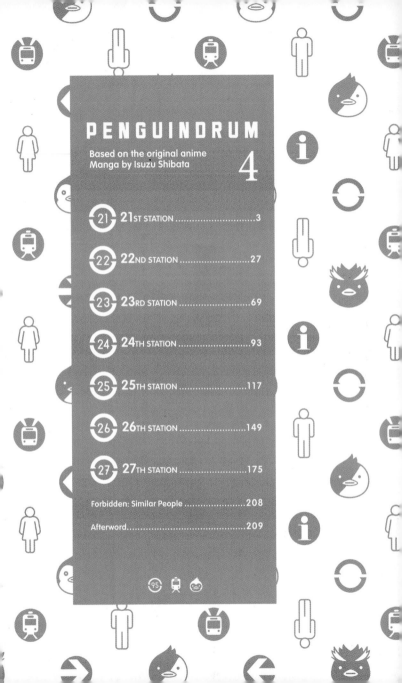

PENGUINDRUM

Based on the original anime
Manga by Isuzu Shibata

4

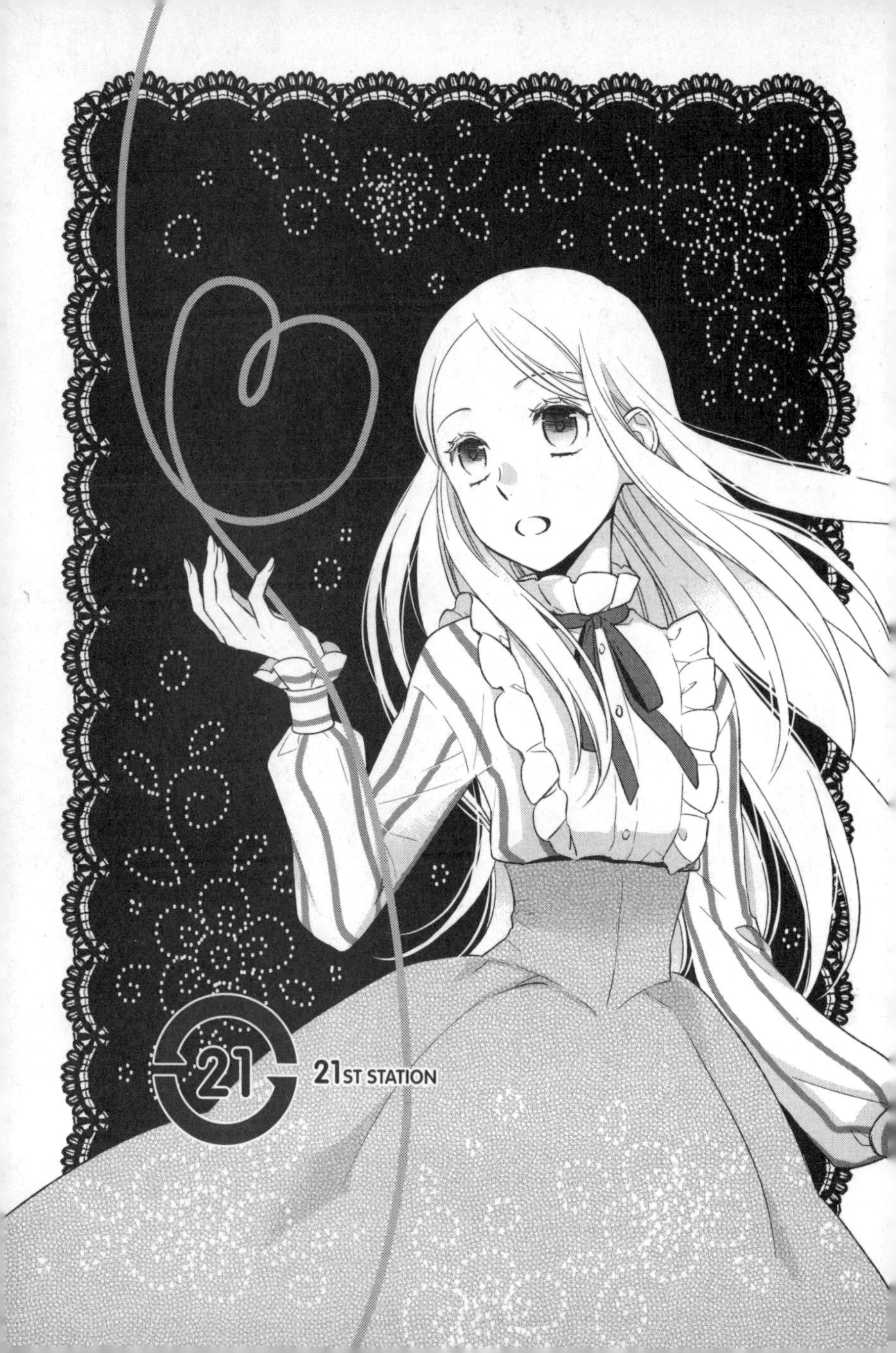

21
21ST STATION

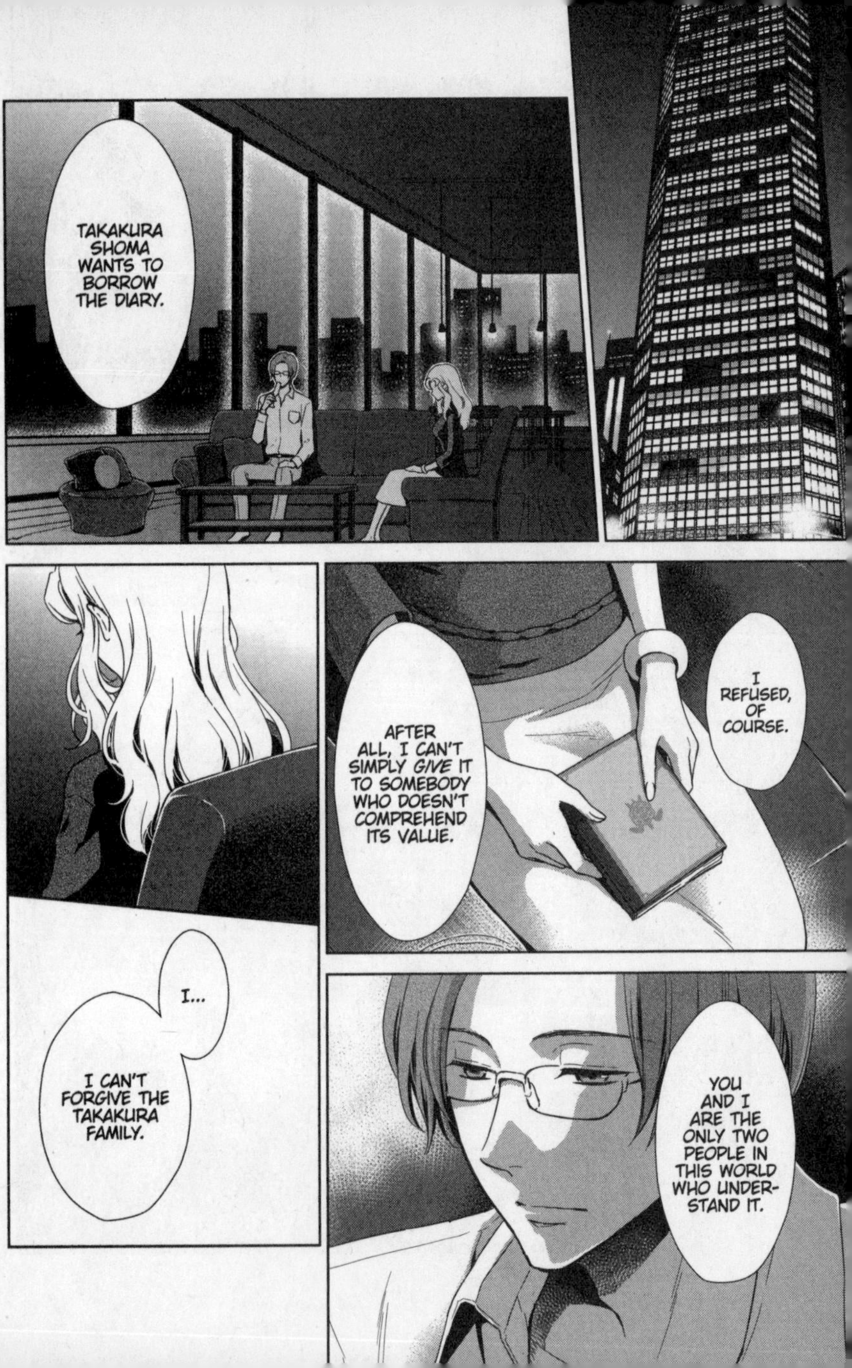
TAKAKURA SHOMA WANTS TO BORROW THE DIARY.
I REFUSED, OF COURSE.
AFTER ALL, I CAN'T SIMPLY *GIVE* IT TO SOMEBODY WHO DOESN'T COMPREHEND ITS VALUE.
YOU AND I ARE THE ONLY TWO PEOPLE IN THIS WORLD WHO UNDER-STAND IT.
I...
I CAN'T FORGIVE THE TAKAKURA FAMILY.

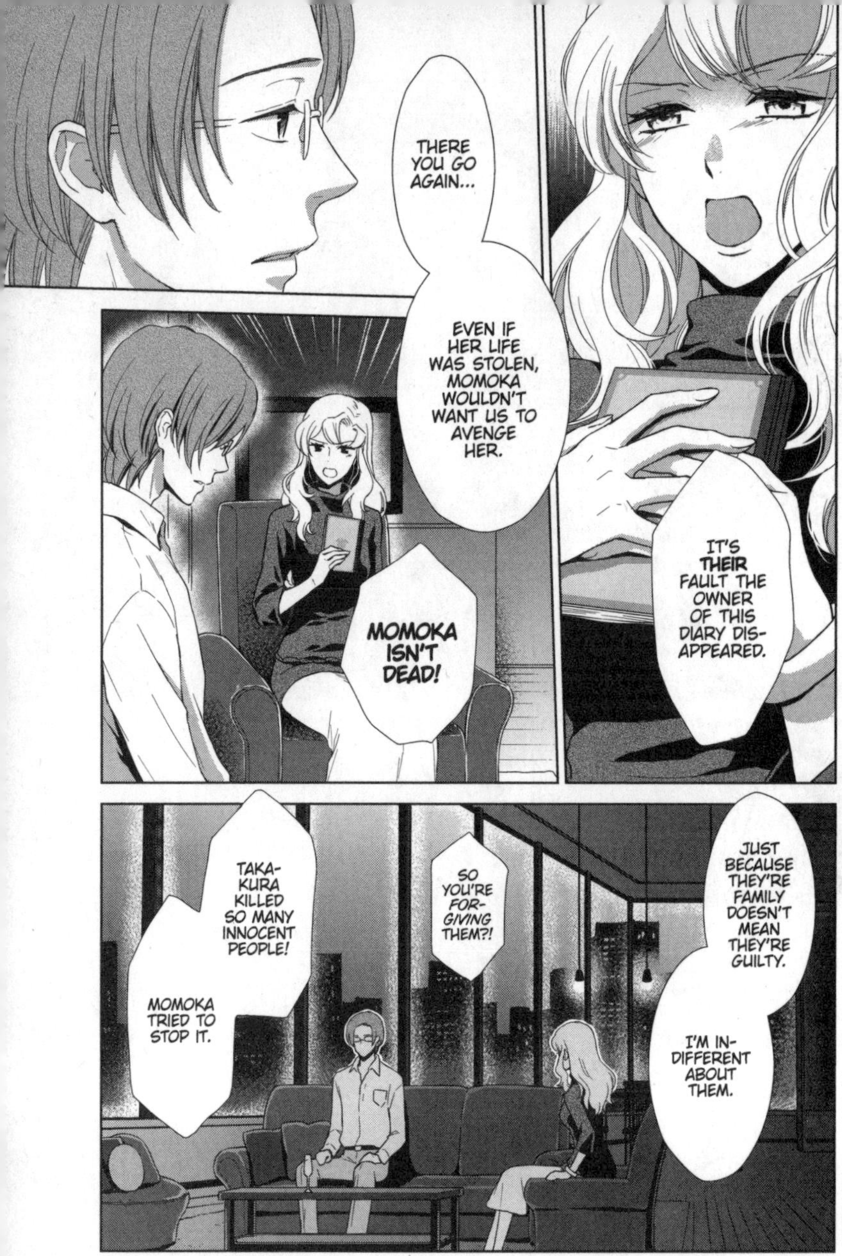
IT'S **THEIR** FAULT THE OWNER OF THIS DIARY DIS-APPEARED.
THERE YOU GO AGAIN...
EVEN IF HER LIFE WAS STOLEN, MOMOKA WOULDN'T WANT US TO AVENGE HER.
MOMOKA ISN'T DEAD!
JUST BECAUSE THEY'RE FAMILY DOESN'T MEAN THEY'RE GUILTY.
I'M IN-DIFFERENT ABOUT THEM.
SO YOU'RE FOR-GIVING THEM?!
TAKA-KURA KILLED SO MANY INNOCENT PEOPLE!
MOMOKA TRIED TO STOP IT.

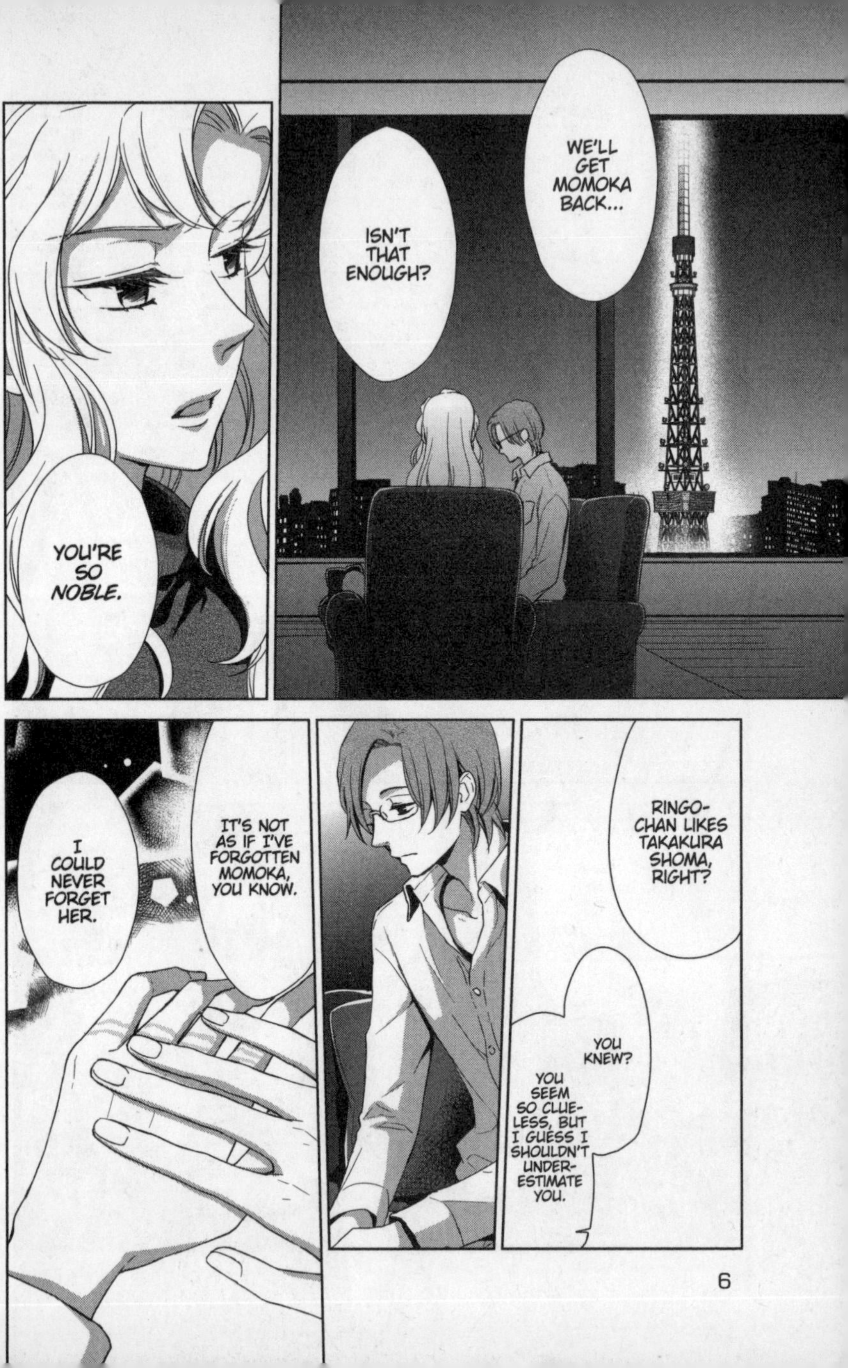
WE'LL GET MOMOKA BACK...
ISN'T THAT ENOUGH?
YOU'RE SO NOBLE.
RINGO-CHAN LIKES TAKAKURA SHOMA, RIGHT?
YOU KNEW?
YOU SEEM SO CLUE-LESS, BUT I GUESS I SHOULDN'T UNDER-ESTIMATE YOU.
IT'S NOT AS IF I'VE FORGOTTEN MOMOKA, YOU KNOW.
I COULD NEVER FORGET HER.

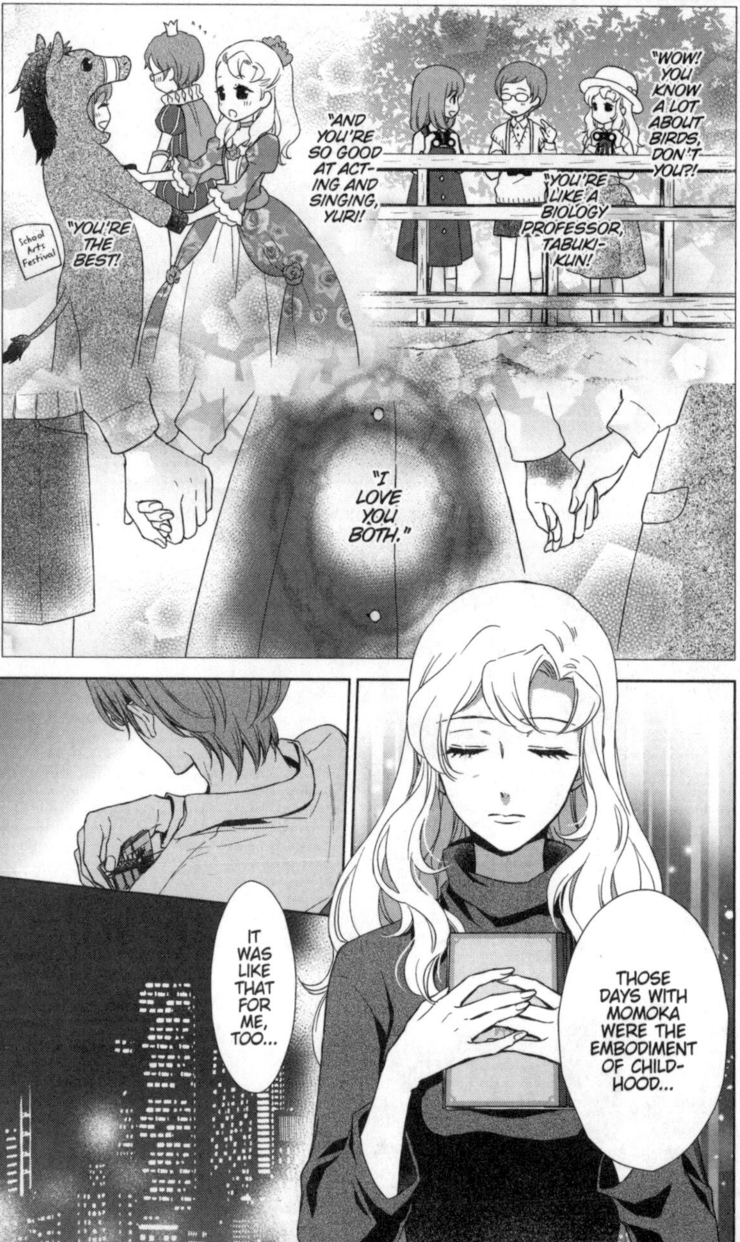
"WOW! YOU KNOW A LOT ABOUT BIRDS, DON'T YOU?!
"YOU'RE LIKE A BIOLOGY PROFESSOR, TABUKI-KUN!
"AND YOU'RE SO GOOD AT ACTING AND SINGING, YURI!
School Arts Festival
"YOU'RE THE BEST!
"I LOVE YOU BOTH."
THOSE DAYS WITH MOMOKA WERE THE EMBODIMENT OF CHILDHOOD...
IT WAS LIKE THAT FOR ME, TOO...

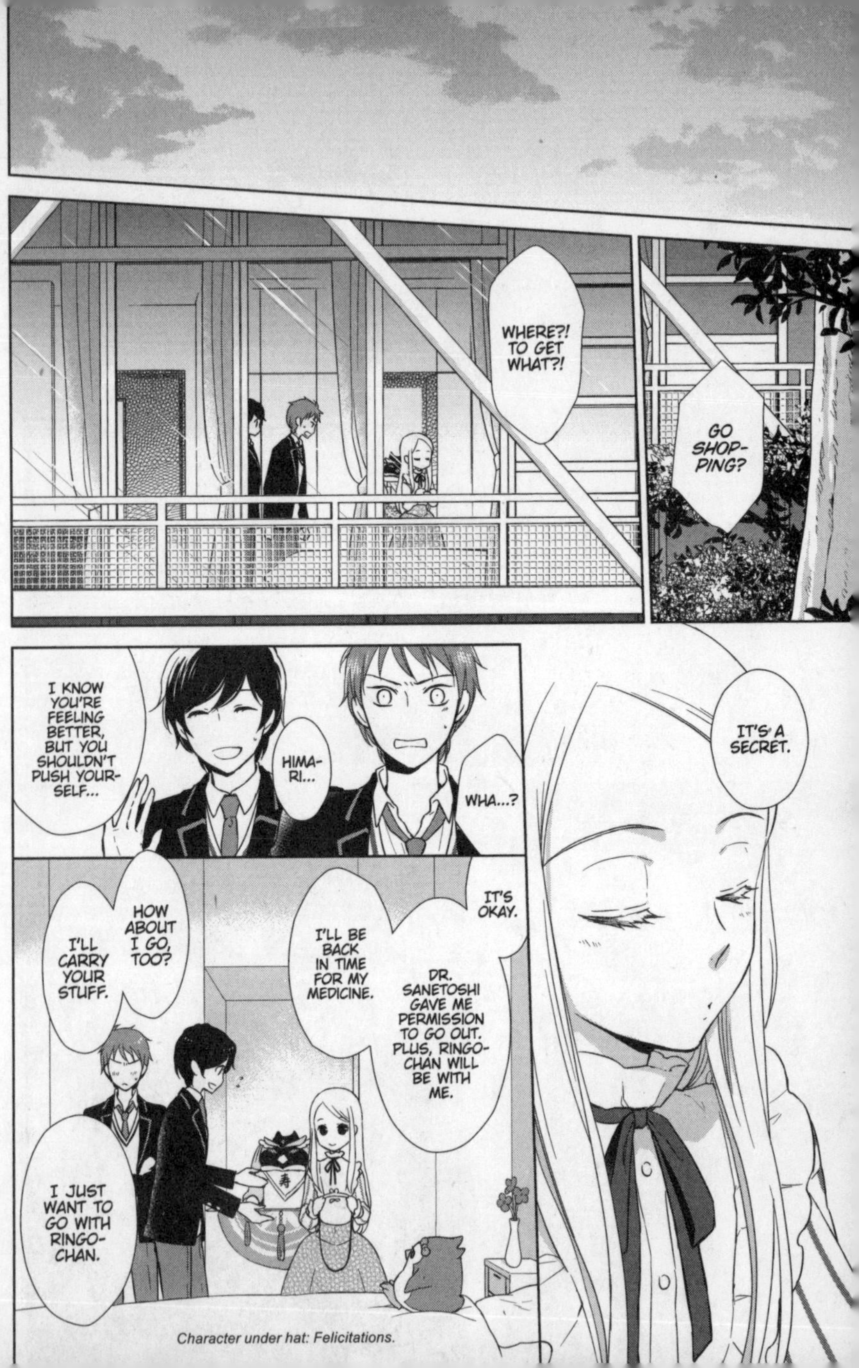
GO SHOPPING?
WHERE?! TO GET WHAT?!
IT'S A SECRET.
WHA...?
HIMARI...
I KNOW YOU'RE FEELING BETTER, BUT YOU SHOULDN'T PUSH YOURSELF...
IT'S OKAY.
I'LL BE BACK IN TIME FOR MY MEDICINE.
DR. SANETOSHI GAVE ME PERMISSION TO GO OUT. PLUS, RINGO-CHAN WILL BE WITH ME.
HOW ABOUT I GO, TOO?
I'LL CARRY YOUR STUFF.
I JUST WANT TO GO WITH RINGO-CHAN.

Character under hat: Felicitations.

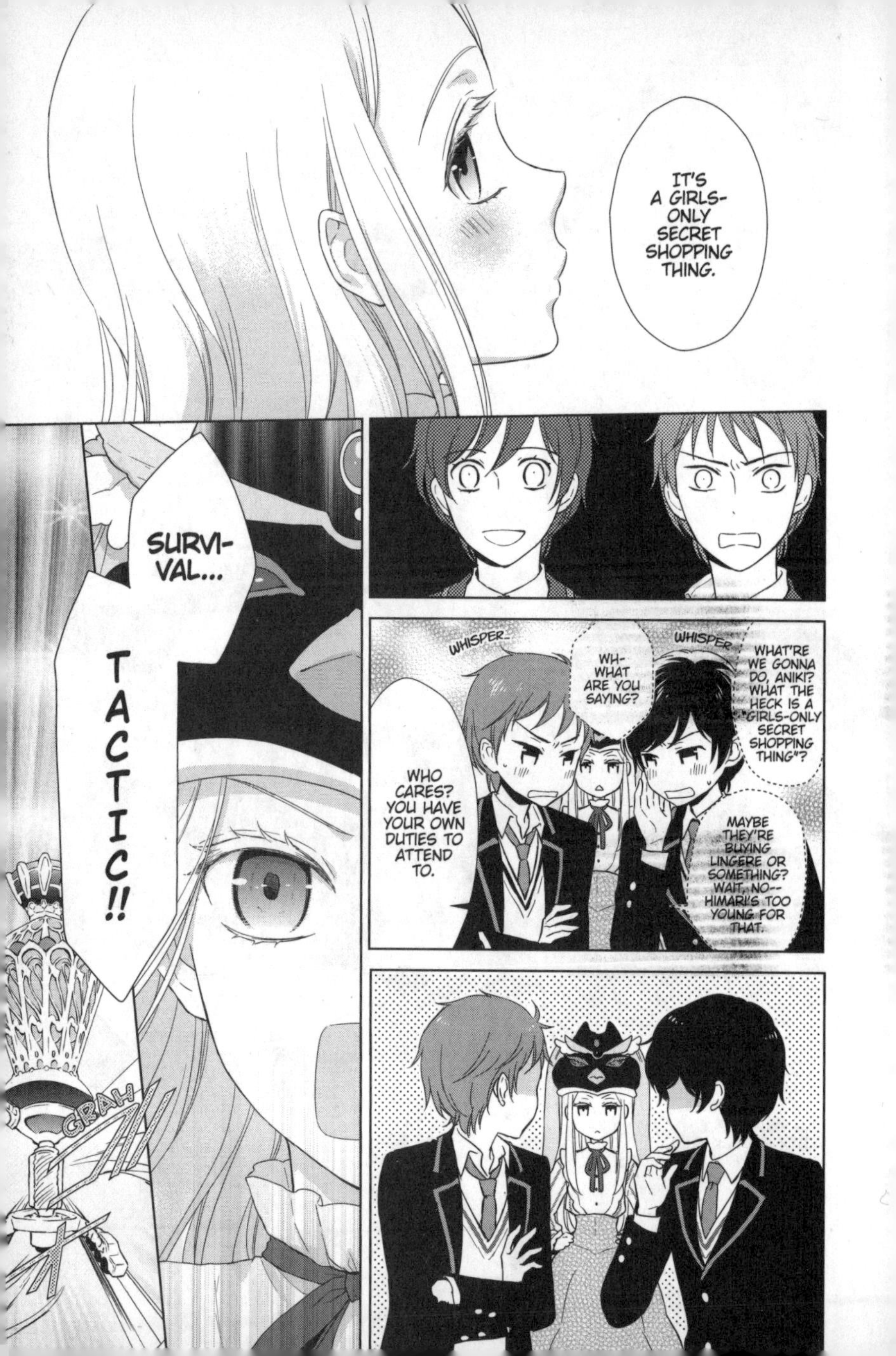
IT'S A GIRLS-ONLY SECRET SHOPPING THING.
WHISPER
WHAT'RE WE GONNA DO, ANIKI? WHAT THE HECK IS A "GIRLS-ONLY SECRET SHOPPING THING"?
WH-WHAT ARE YOU SAYING?
WHISPER
MAYBE THEY'RE BUYING LINGERE OR SOMETHING? WAIT, NO--HIMARI'S TOO YOUNG FOR THAT.
WHO CARES? YOU HAVE YOUR OWN DUTIES TO ATTEND TO.
SURVIVAL...
TACTIC!!
GRAH

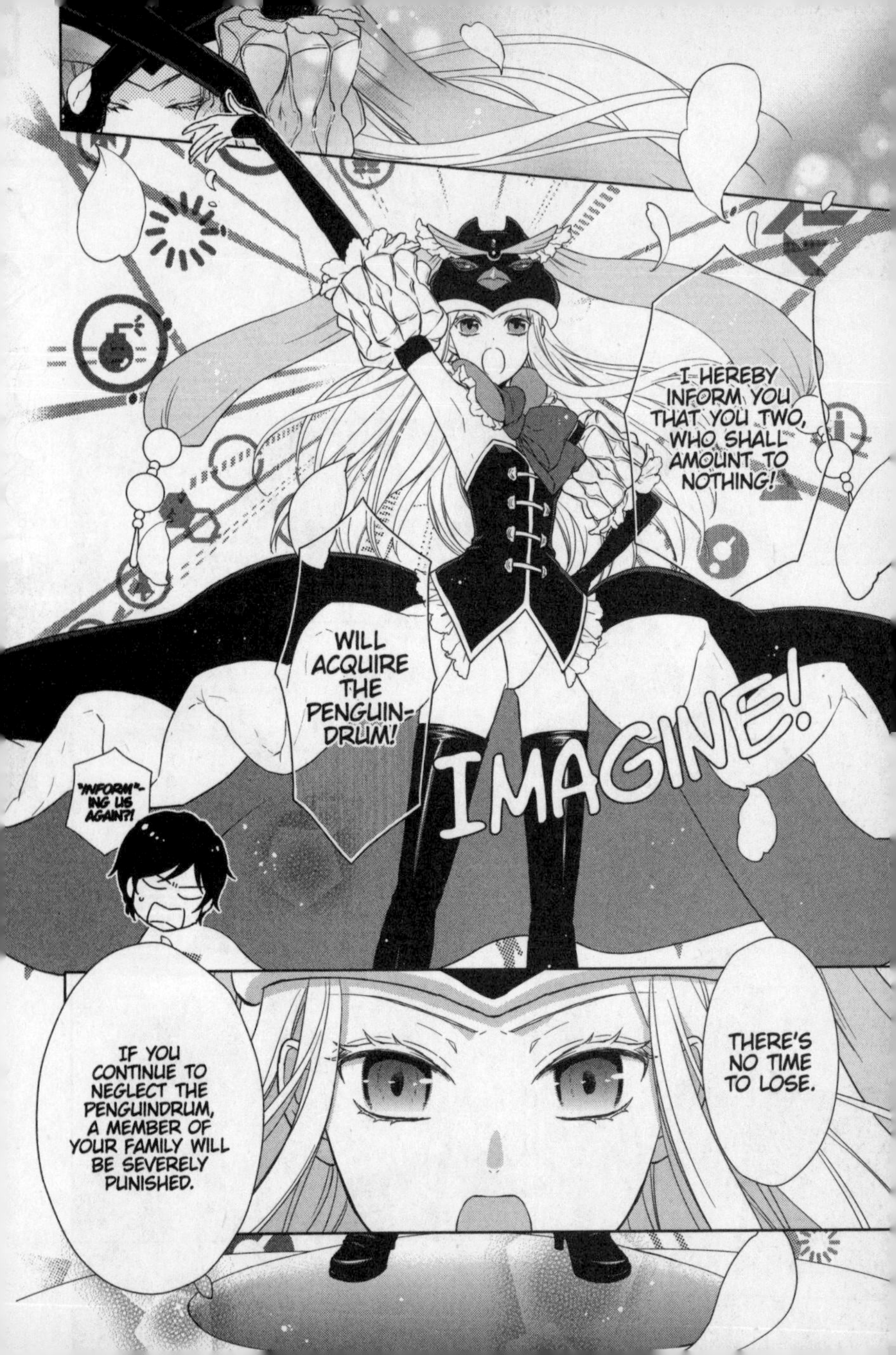
I HEREBY INFORM YOU THAT YOU TWO, WHO SHALL AMOUNT TO NOTHING!
WILL ACQUIRE THE PENGUIN-DRUM!
IMAGINE!
"INFORM"-ING US AGAIN?!
THERE'S NO TIME TO LOSE.
IF YOU CONTINUE TO NEGLECT THE PENGUINDRUM, A MEMBER OF YOUR FAMILY WILL BE SEVERELY PUNISHED.

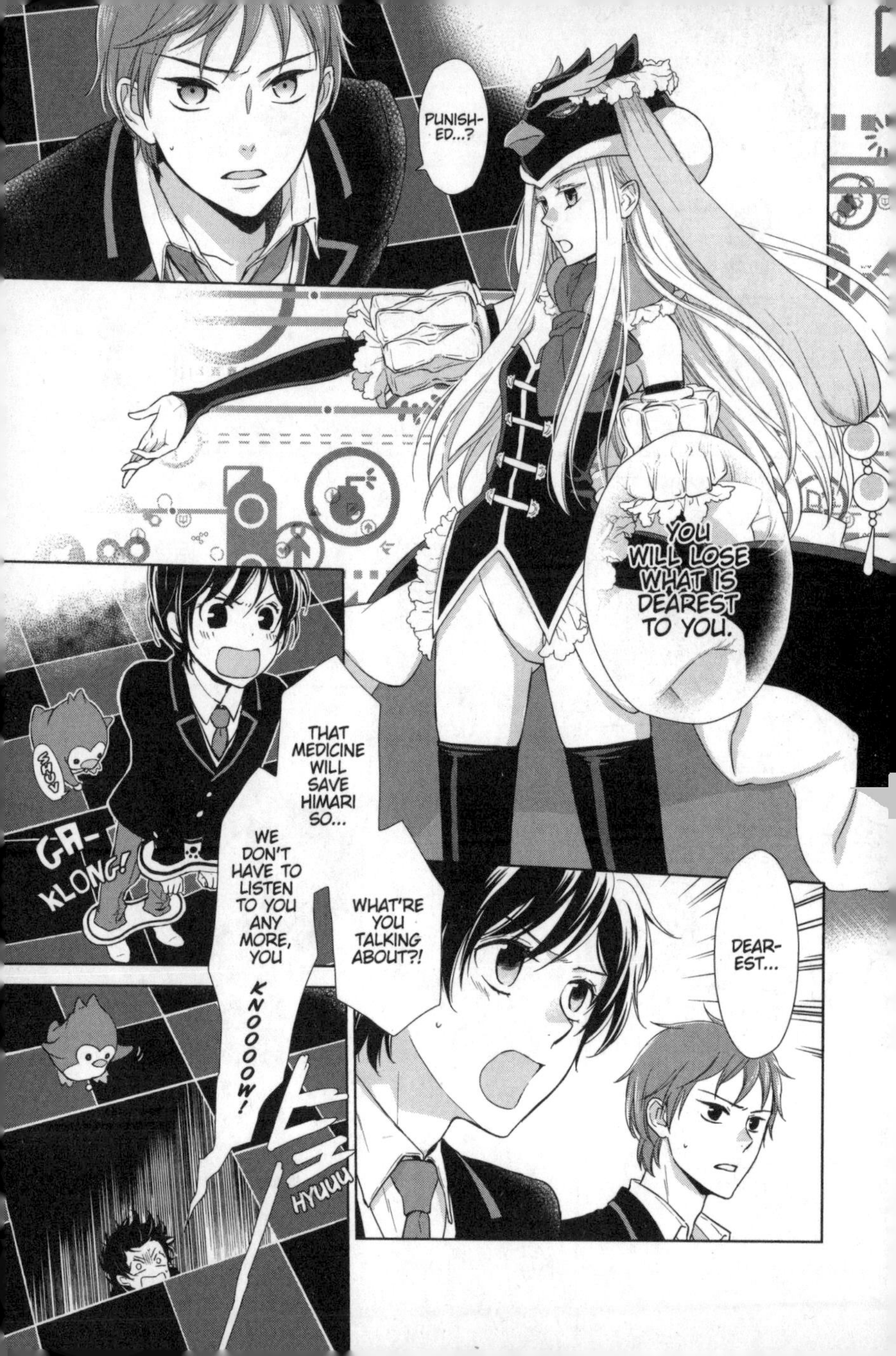
PUNISH-ED...?
YOU WILL LOSE WHAT IS DEAREST TO YOU.
DEAR-EST...
WHAT'RE YOU TALKING ABOUT?!
THAT MEDICINE WILL SAVE HIMARI SO...
WE DON'T HAVE TO LISTEN TO YOU ANY MORE, YOU KNOOOOOW!
GA-KLONG!
HYUUU

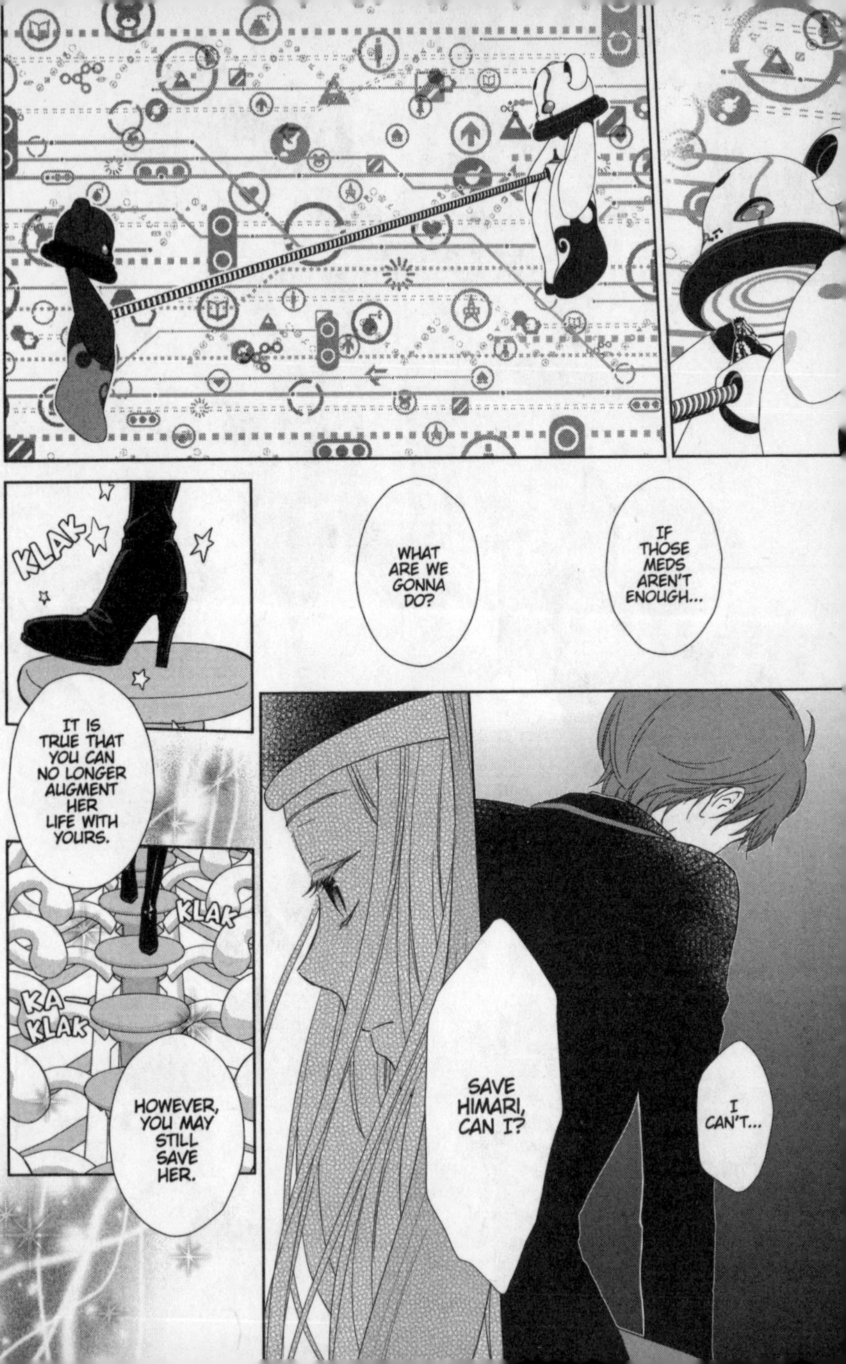
IF THOSE MEDS AREN'T ENOUGH...
WHAT ARE WE GONNA DO?
KLAK
IT IS TRUE THAT YOU CAN NO LONGER AUGMENT HER LIFE WITH YOURS.
I CAN'T...
SAVE HIMARI, CAN I?
KLAK
KA-KLAK
HOWEVER, YOU MAY STILL SAVE HER.

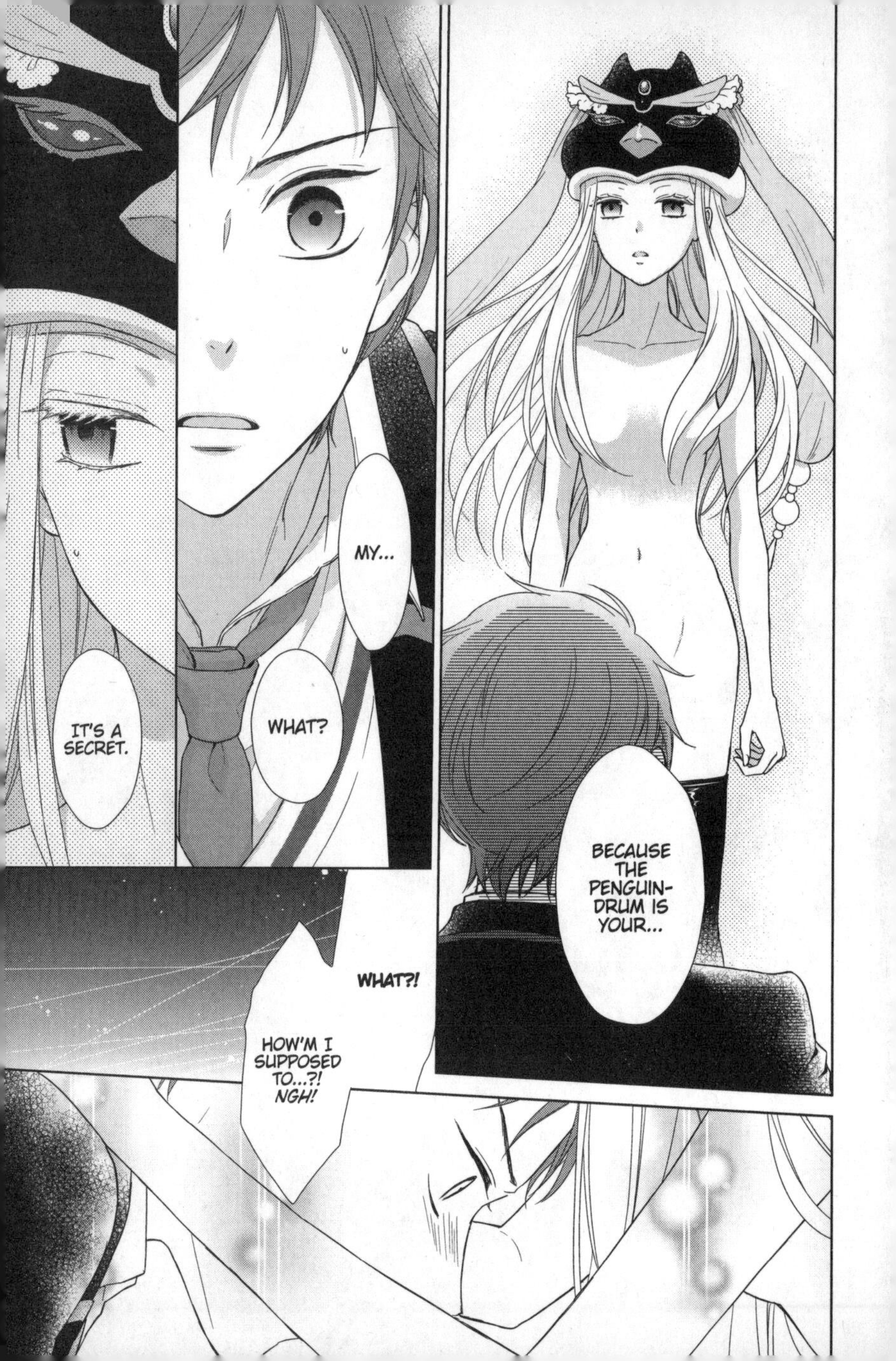
BECAUSE THE PENGUIN-DRUM IS YOUR...
MY...
WHAT?
IT'S A SECRET.
WHAT?!
HOW'M I SUPPOSED TO...?! NGH!

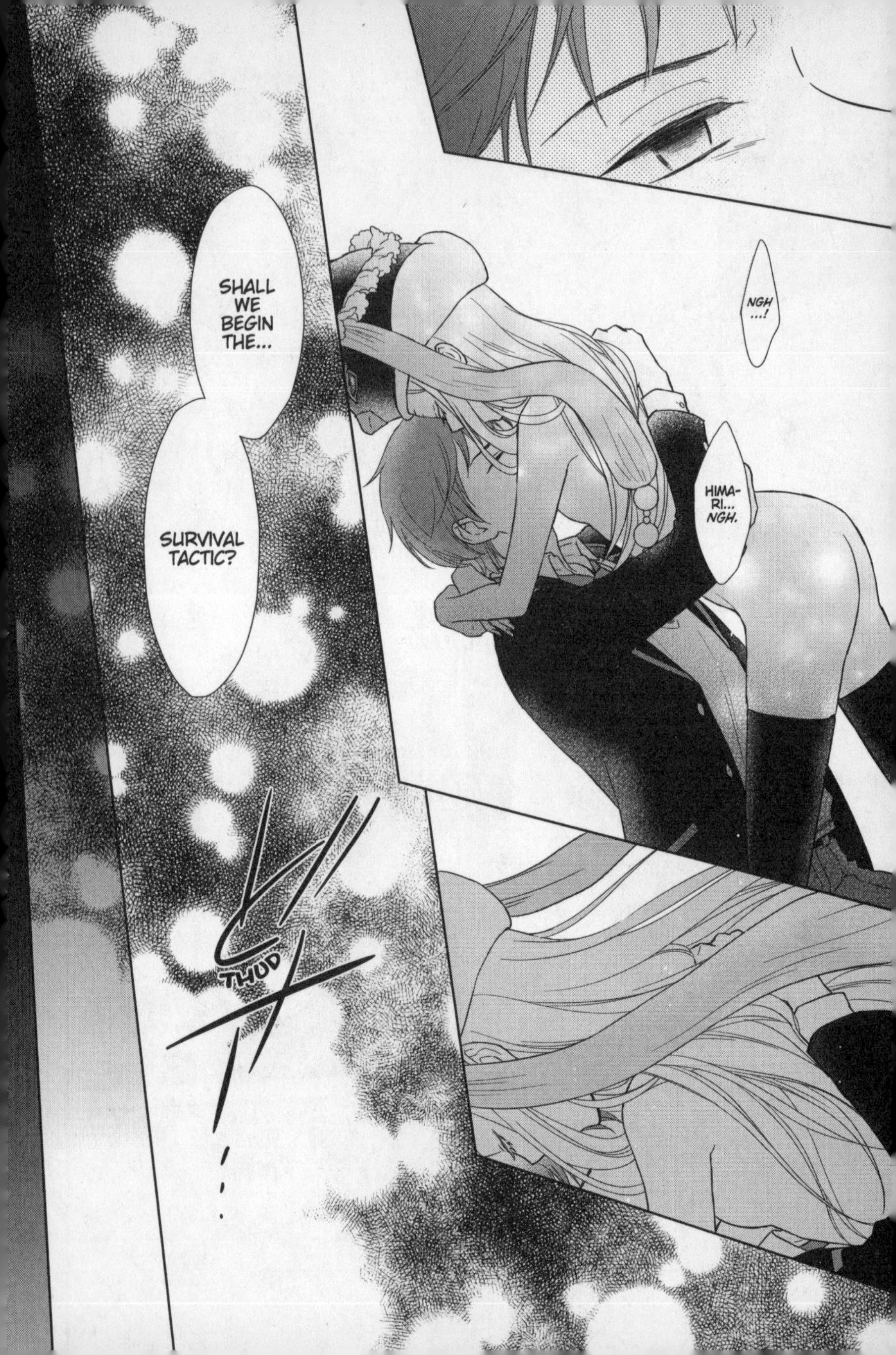
NGH ...!
HIMA-RI... NGH.
SHALL WE BEGIN THE...
SURVIVAL TACTIC?
THUD
...

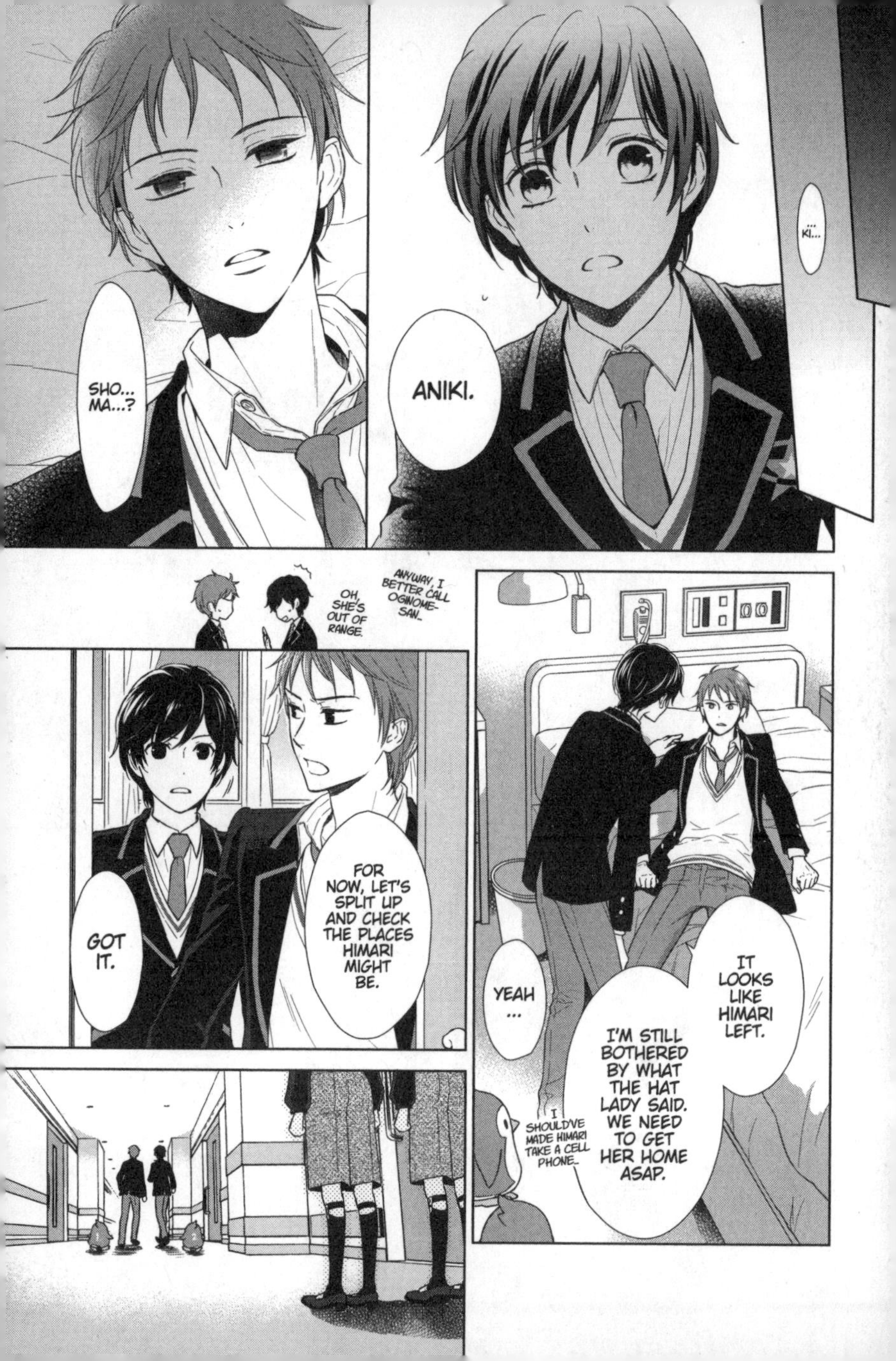
...KI...
ANIKI.
SHO... MA...?
IT LOOKS LIKE HIMARI LEFT.
YEAH...
I'M STILL BOTHERED BY WHAT THE HAT LADY SAID. WE NEED TO GET HER HOME ASAP.
I SHOULD'VE MADE HIMARI TAKE A CELL PHONE..
ANYWAY, I BETTER CALL OGINOME-SAN..
OH, SHE'S OUT OF RANGE.
FOR NOW, LET'S SPLIT UP AND CHECK THE PLACES HIMARI MIGHT BE.
GOT IT.

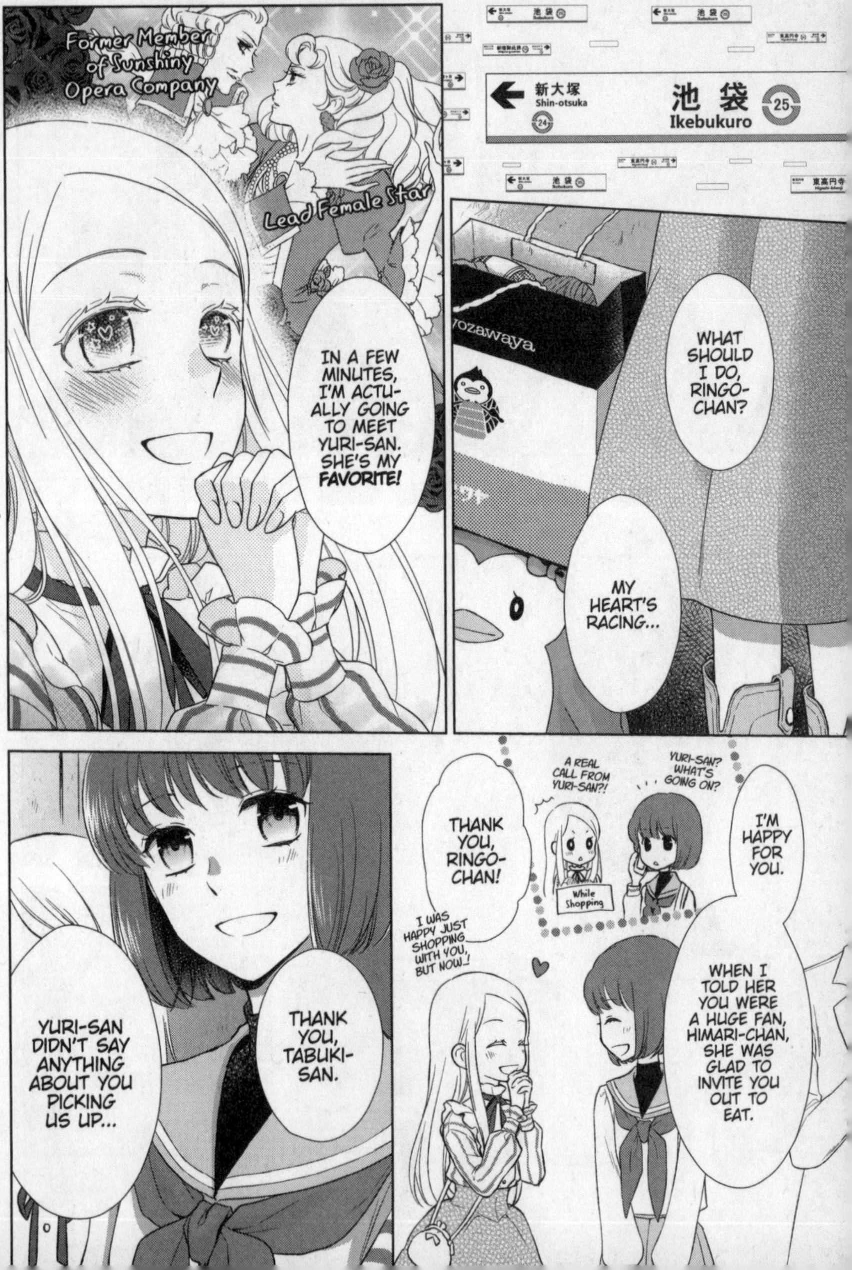

新大塚
Shin-otsuka
24
池袋
Ikebukuro
25
WHAT SHOULD I DO, RINGO-CHAN?
MY HEART'S RACING...
Former Member of Sunshiny Opera Company
Lead Female Star
IN A FEW MINUTES, I'M ACTUALLY GOING TO MEET YURI-SAN. SHE'S MY **FAVORITE!**
I'M HAPPY FOR YOU.
YURI-SAN? WHAT'S GOING ON?
A REAL CALL FROM YURI-SAN?!
While Shopping
THANK YOU, RINGO-CHAN!
WHEN I TOLD HER YOU WERE A HUGE FAN, HIMARI-CHAN, SHE WAS GLAD TO INVITE YOU OUT TO EAT.
I WAS HAPPY JUST SHOPPING WITH YOU, BUT NOW..!
THANK YOU, TABUKI-SAN.
YURI-SAN DIDN'T SAY ANYTHING ABOUT YOU PICKING US UP...

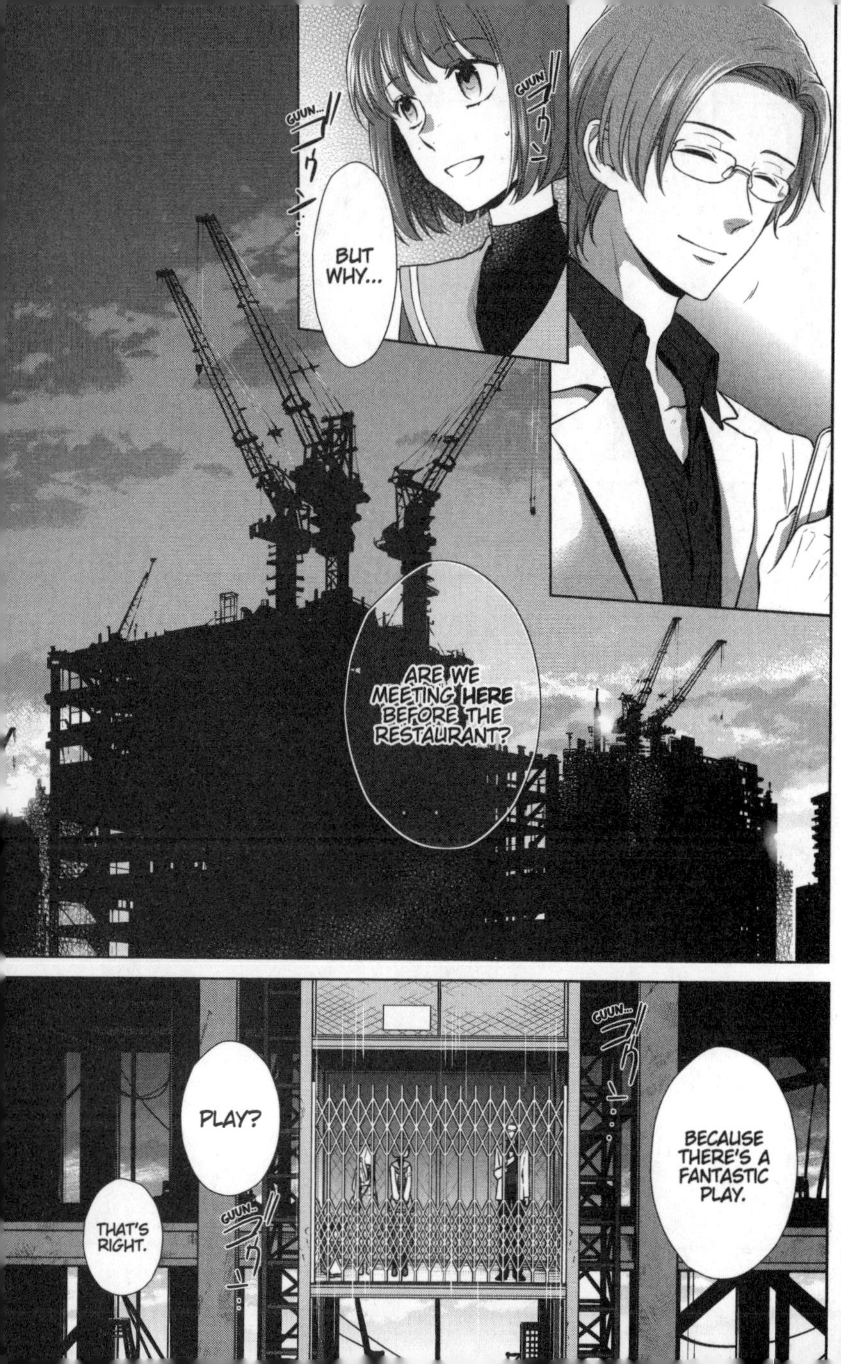
GUUN
GUUN...
BUT WHY...
ARE WE MEETING HERE BEFORE THE RESTAURANT?
GUUN...
BECAUSE THERE'S A FANTASTIC PLAY.
PLAY?
GUUN..
THAT'S RIGHT.

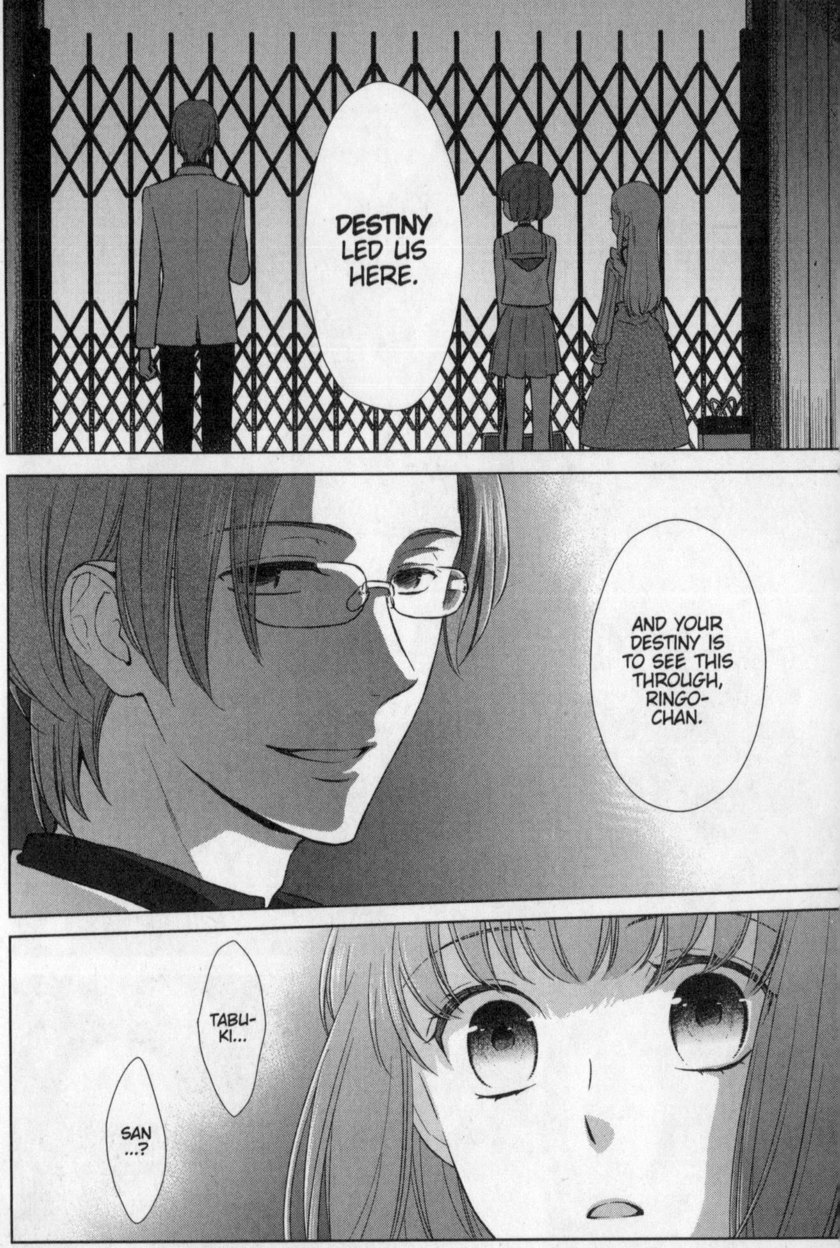
DESTINY LED US HERE.
AND YOUR DESTINY IS TO SEE THIS THROUGH, RINGO-CHAN.
TABU-KI...
SAN ...?

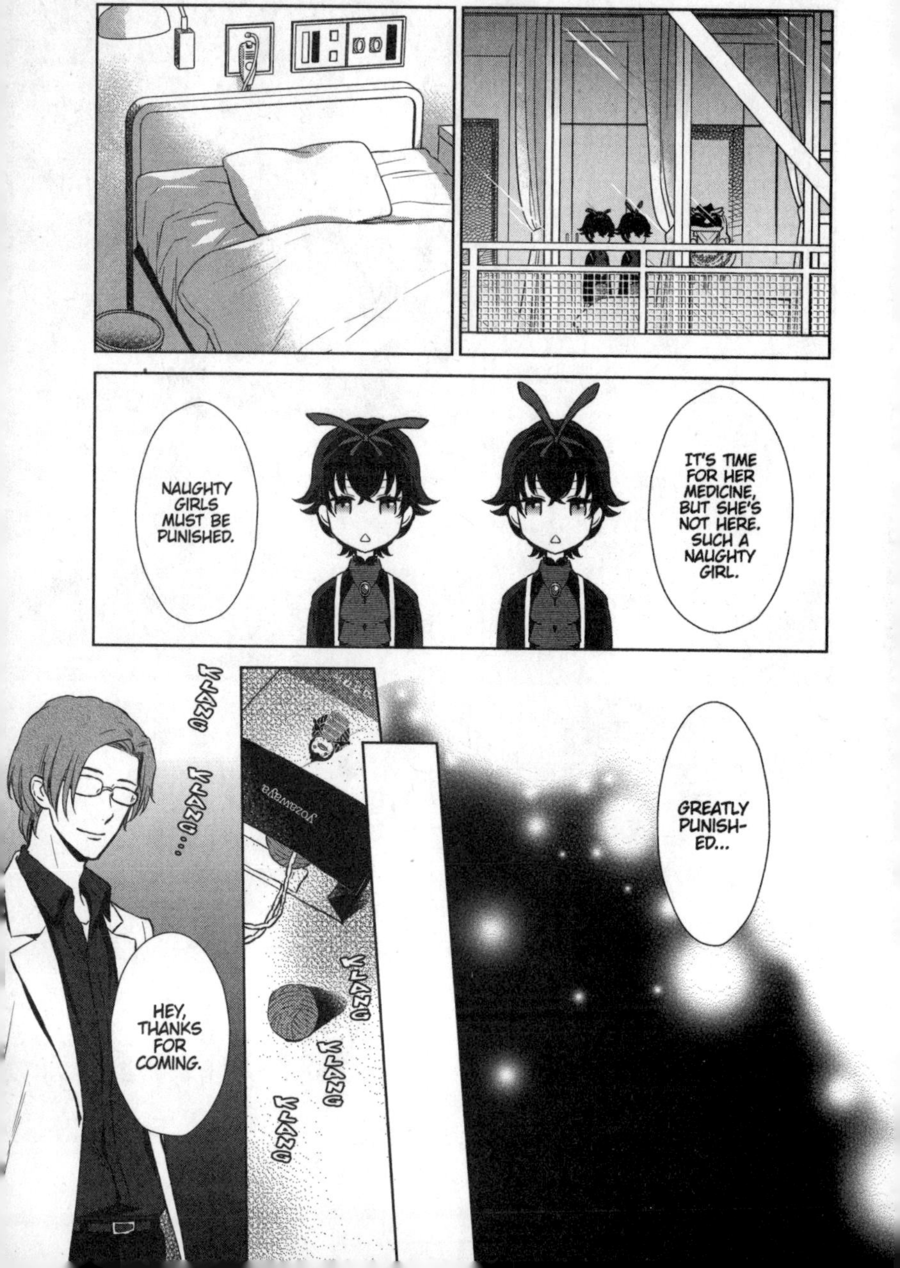
IT'S TIME FOR HER MEDICINE, BUT SHE'S NOT HERE. SUCH A NAUGHTY GIRL.
NAUGHTY GIRLS MUST BE PUNISHED.
GREATLY PUNISH-ED...
KLANG
KLANG
KLANG
Yozawaya
KLANG
KLANG...
HEY, THANKS FOR COMING.

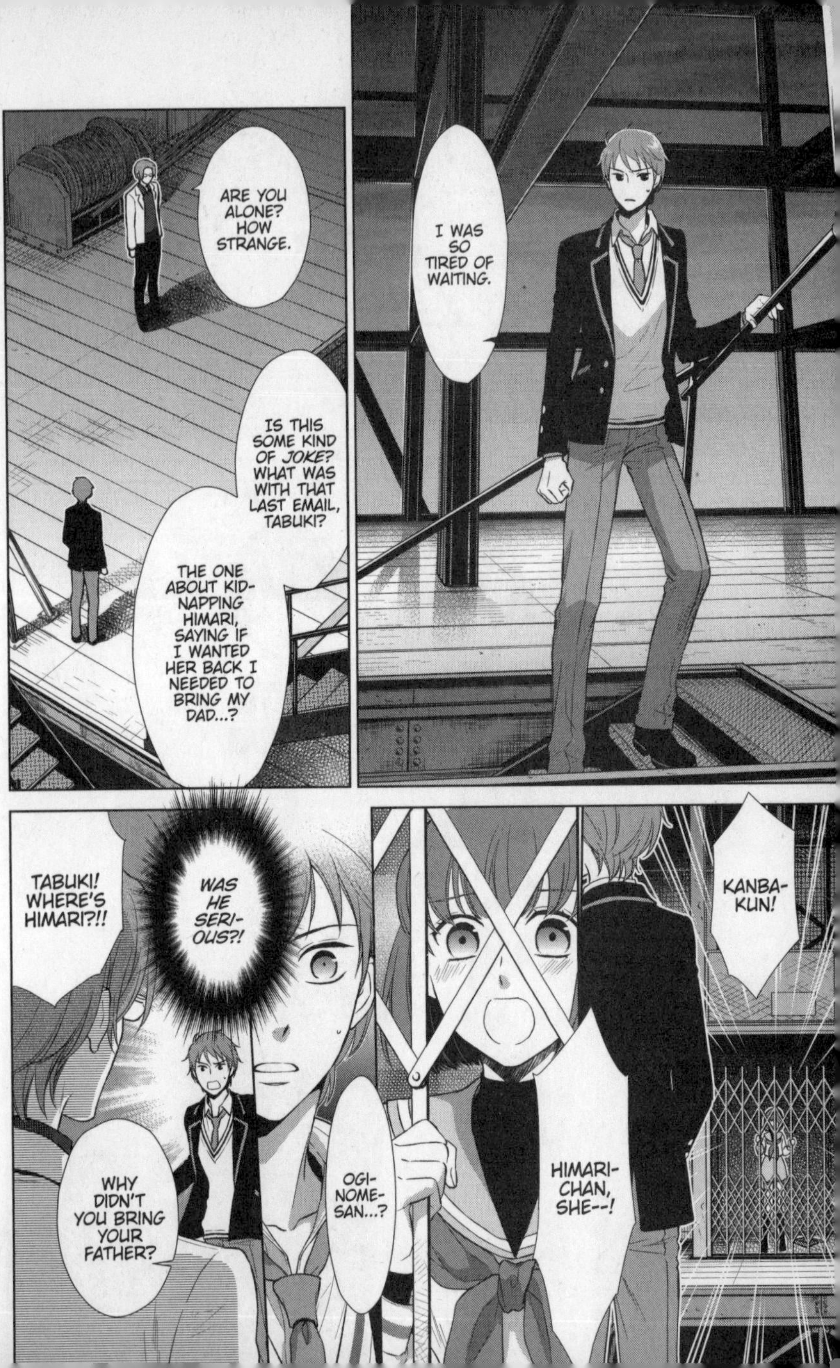
I WAS SO TIRED OF WAITING.
ARE YOU ALONE? HOW STRANGE.
IS THIS SOME KIND OF *JOKE*? WHAT WAS WITH THAT LAST EMAIL, TABUKI?
THE ONE ABOUT KID-NAPPING HIMARI, SAYING IF I WANTED HER BACK I NEEDED TO BRING MY DAD...?
KANBA-KUN!
HIMARI-CHAN, SHE--!
OGI-NOME-SAN...?
TABUKI! WHERE'S HIMARI?!!
WAS HE SERI-OUS?!
WHY DIDN'T YOU BRING YOUR FATHER?

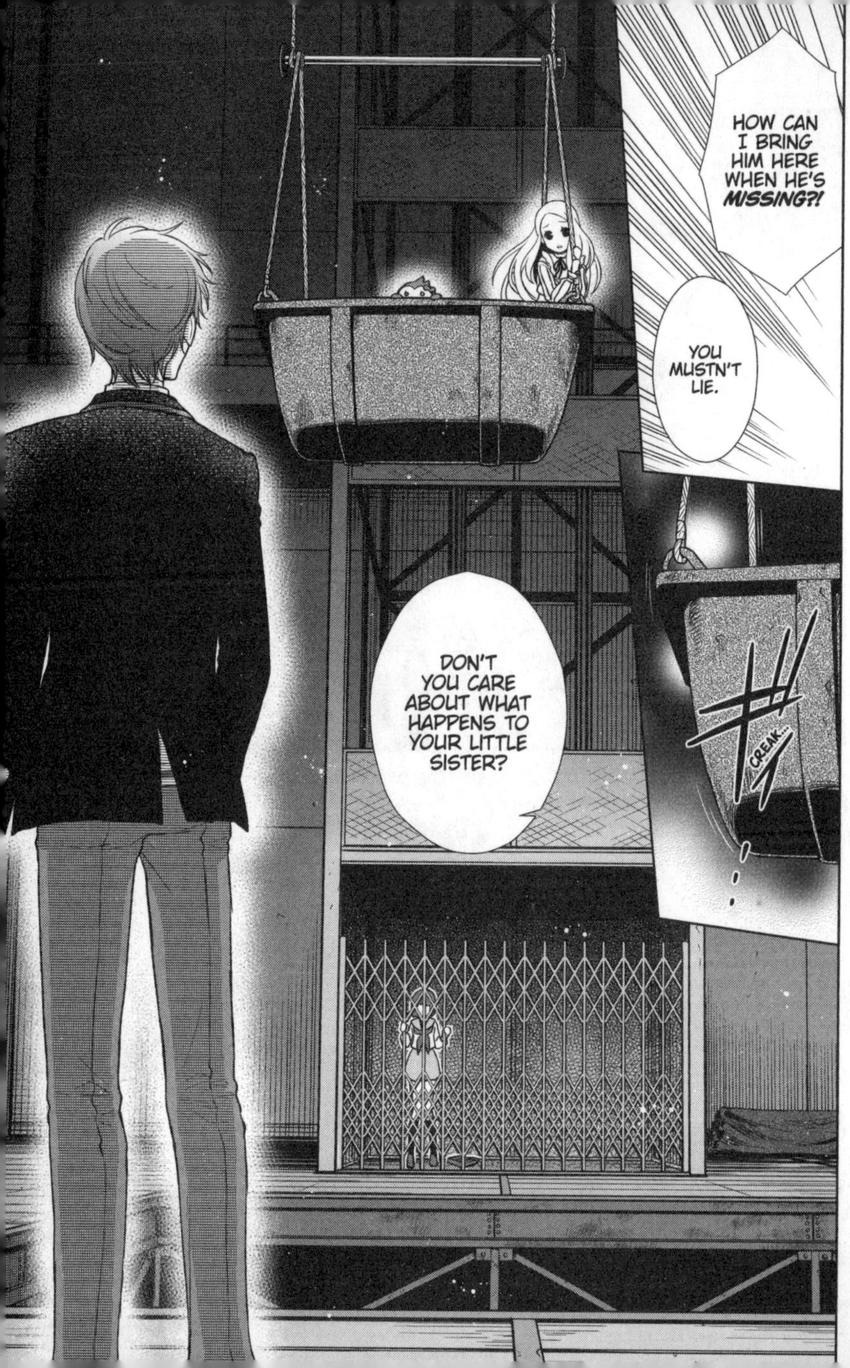
HOW CAN I BRING HIM HERE WHEN HE'S ***MISSING?!***
YOU MUSTN'T LIE.
CREAK...
DON'T YOU CARE ABOUT WHAT HAPPENS TO YOUR LITTLE SISTER?

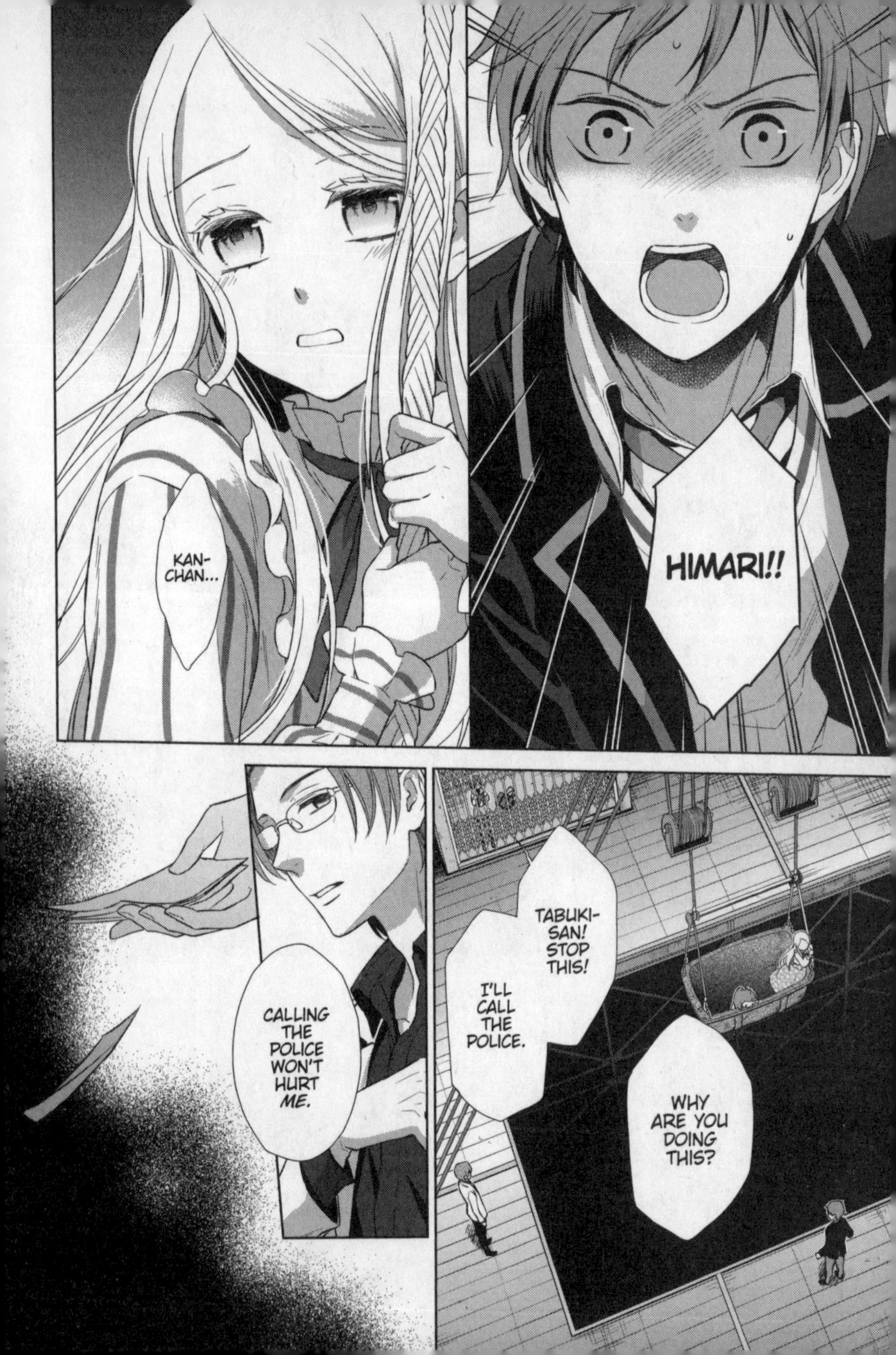
HIMARI!!
KAN-CHAN...
TABUKI-SAN! STOP THIS!
I'LL CALL THE POLICE.
WHY ARE YOU DOING THIS?
CALLING THE POLICE WON'T HURT *ME.*

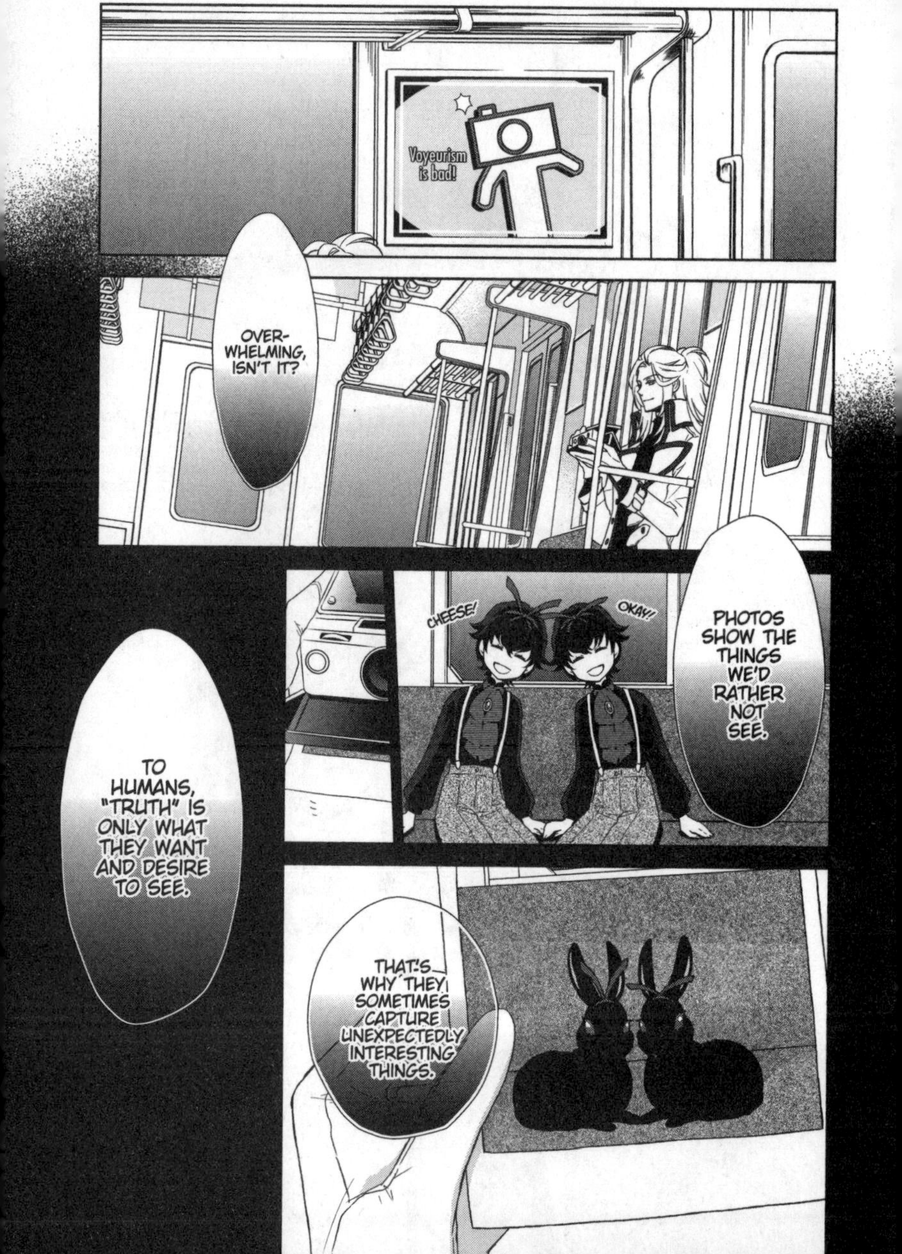
Voyeurism is bad!
OVER-WHELMING, ISN'T IT?
PHOTOS SHOW THE THINGS WE'D RATHER NOT SEE.
OKAY!!
CHEESE!
TO HUMANS, "TRUTH" IS ONLY WHAT THEY WANT AND DESIRE TO SEE.
THAT'S WHY THEY SOMETIMES CAPTURE UNEXPECTEDLY INTERESTING THINGS.

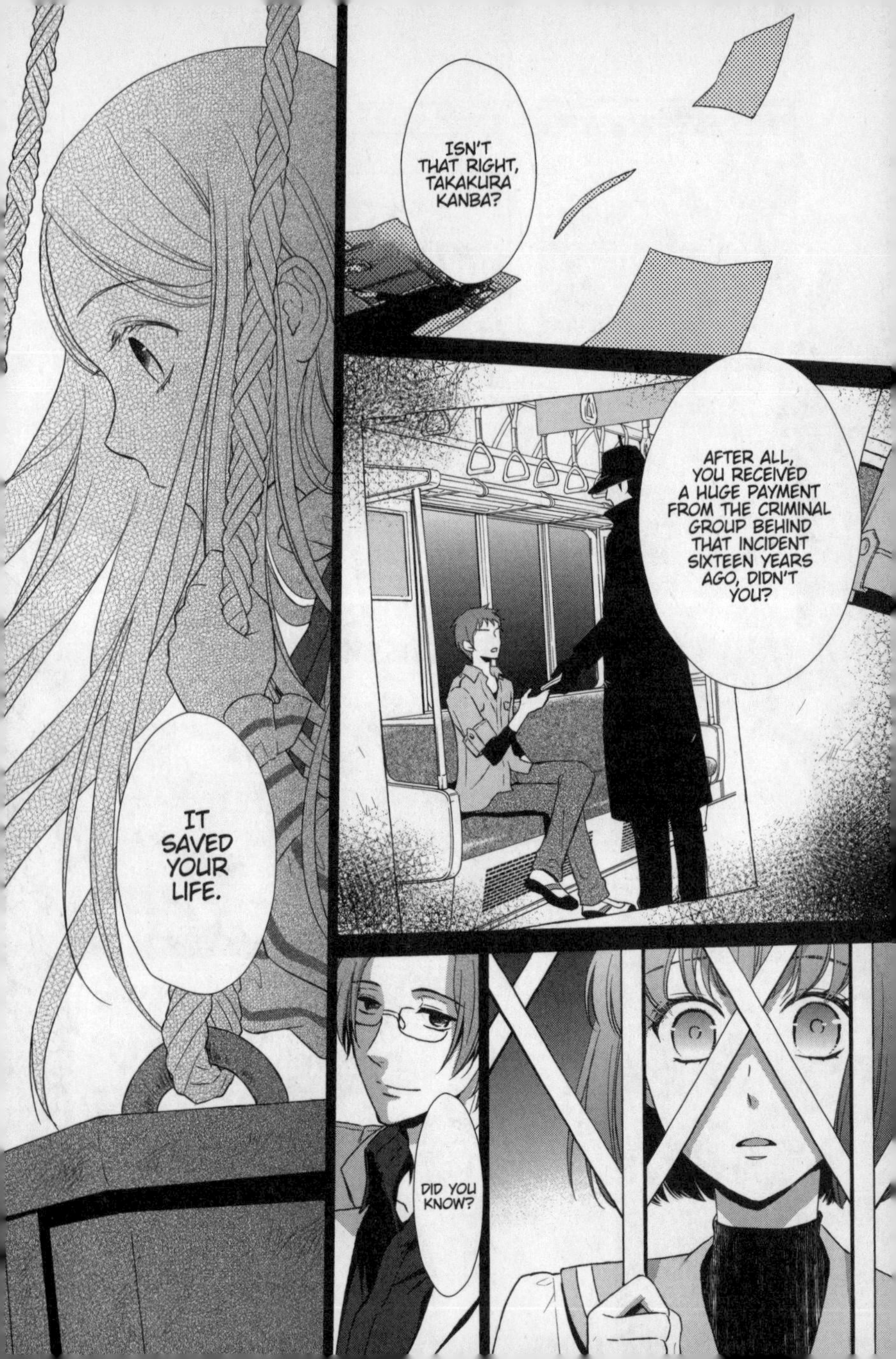
ISN'T THAT RIGHT, TAKAKURA KANBA?
AFTER ALL, YOU RECEIVED A HUGE PAYMENT FROM THE CRIMINAL GROUP BEHIND THAT INCIDENT SIXTEEN YEARS AGO, DIDN'T YOU?
DID YOU KNOW?
IT SAVED YOUR LIFE.

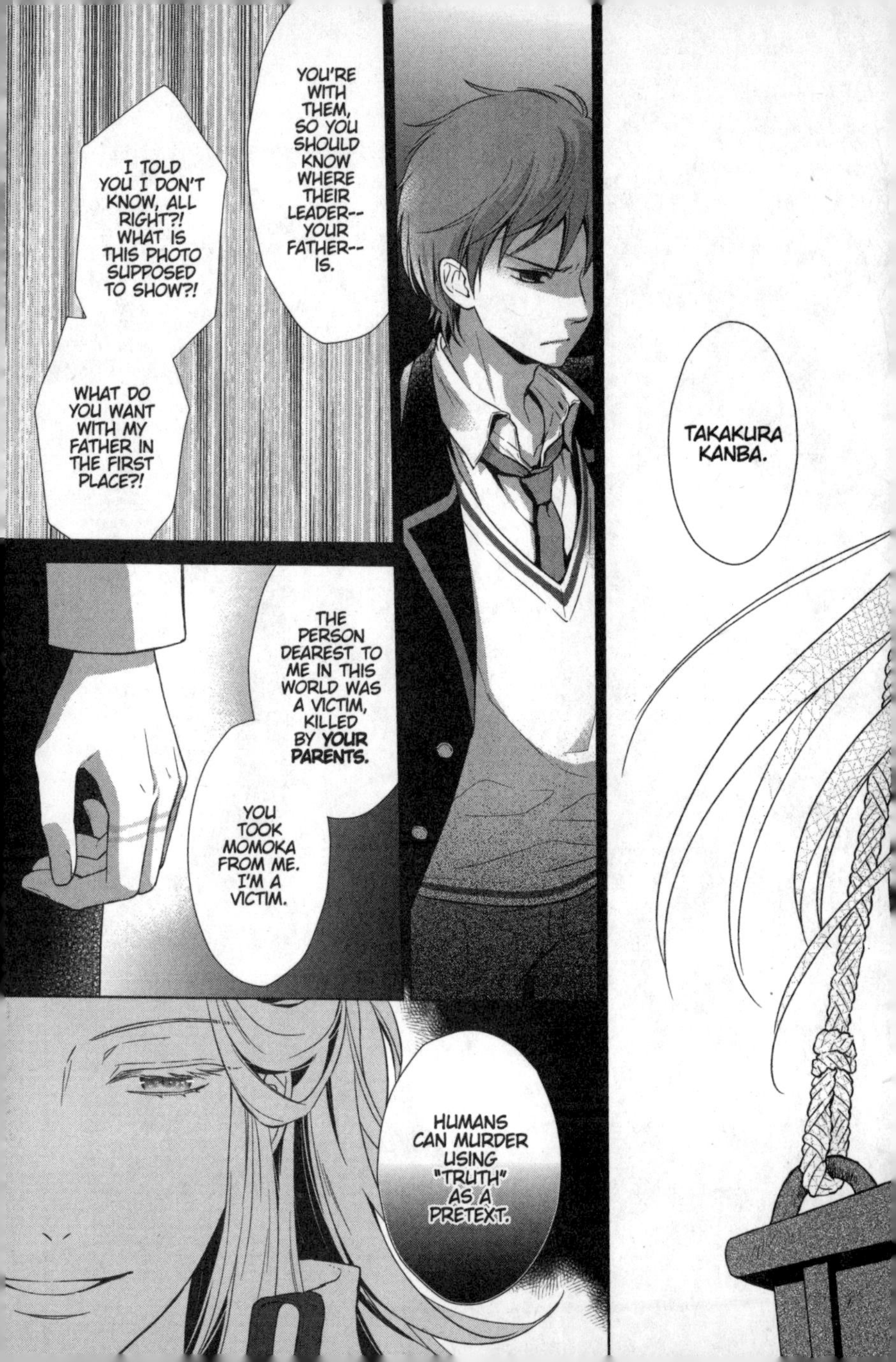
TAKAKURA KANBA.
YOU'RE WITH THEM, SO YOU SHOULD KNOW WHERE THEIR LEADER-- YOUR FATHER-- IS.
I TOLD YOU I DON'T KNOW, ALL RIGHT?! WHAT IS THIS PHOTO SUPPOSED TO SHOW?!
WHAT DO YOU WANT WITH MY FATHER IN THE FIRST PLACE?!
THE PERSON DEAREST TO ME IN THIS WORLD WAS A VICTIM, KILLED BY **YOUR PARENTS.**
YOU TOOK MOMOKA FROM ME. I'M A VICTIM.
HUMANS CAN MURDER USING "TRUTH" AS A PRETEXT.

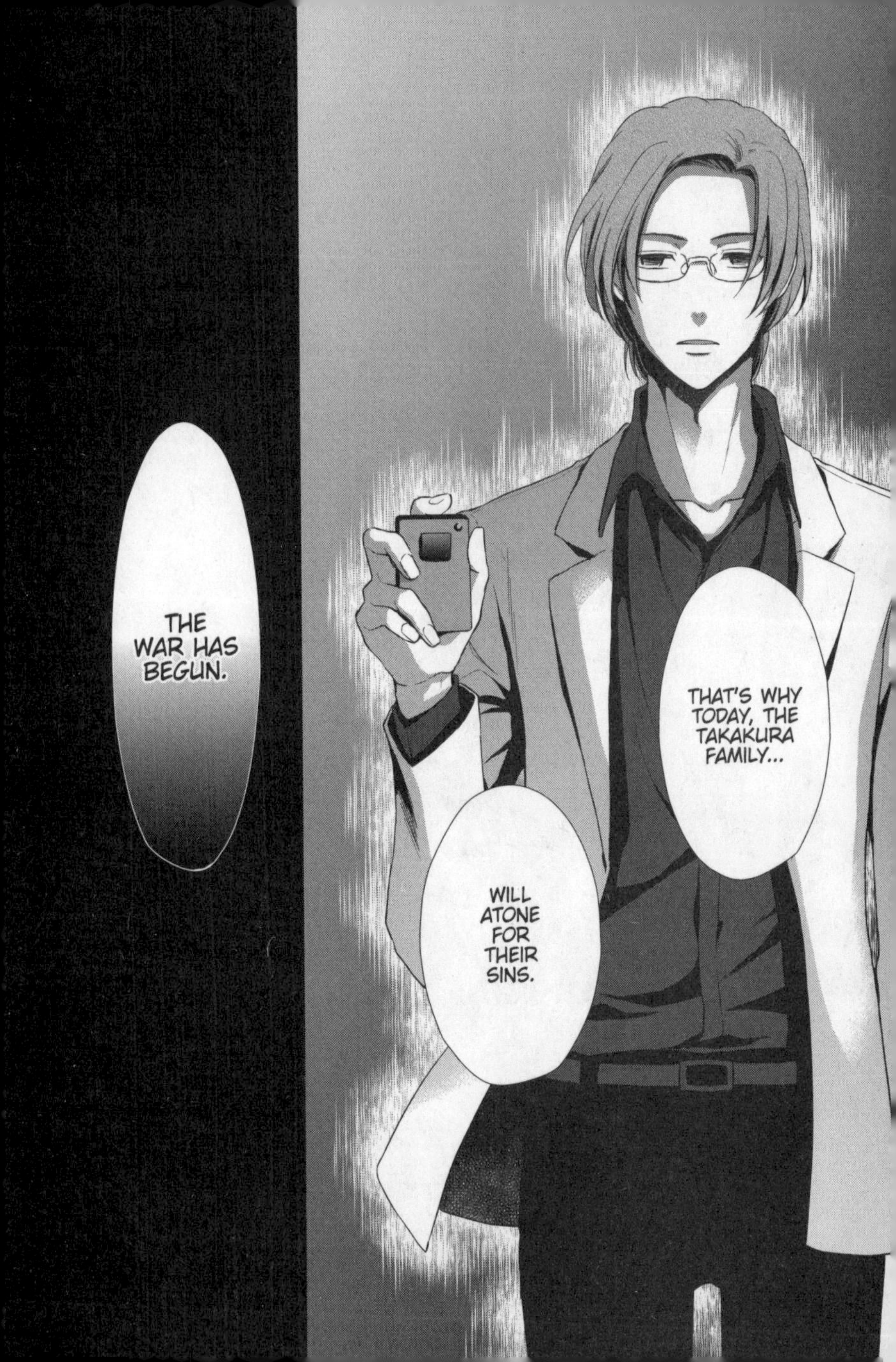
THAT'S WHY TODAY, THE TAKAKURA FAMILY...
WILL ATONE FOR THEIR SINS.
THE WAR HAS BEGUN.

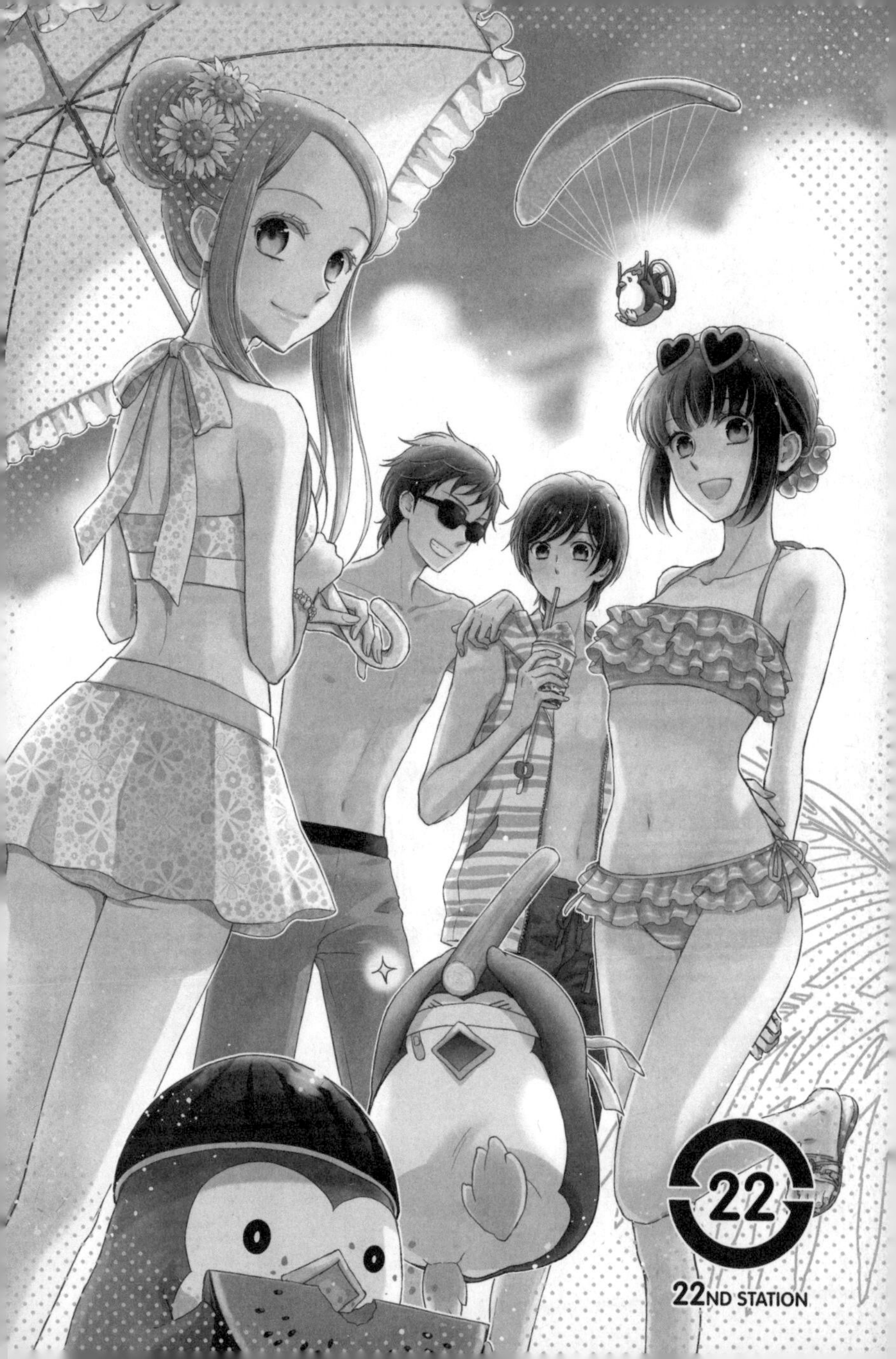
22
22ND STATION

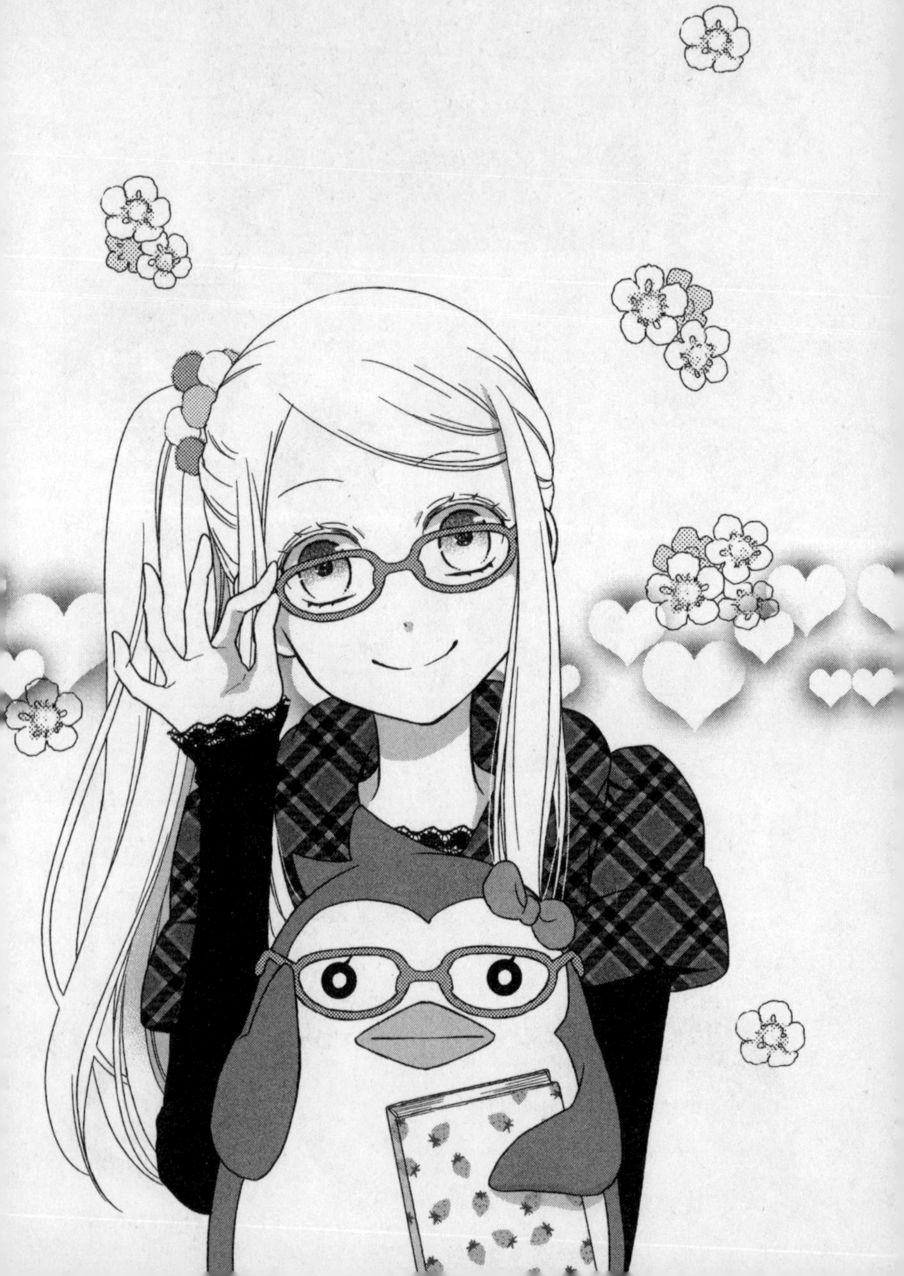

Flashback

Tabuki

Childhood

His mother likes the piano and his father is a pianist.

※ *His mother only loves talented people.*

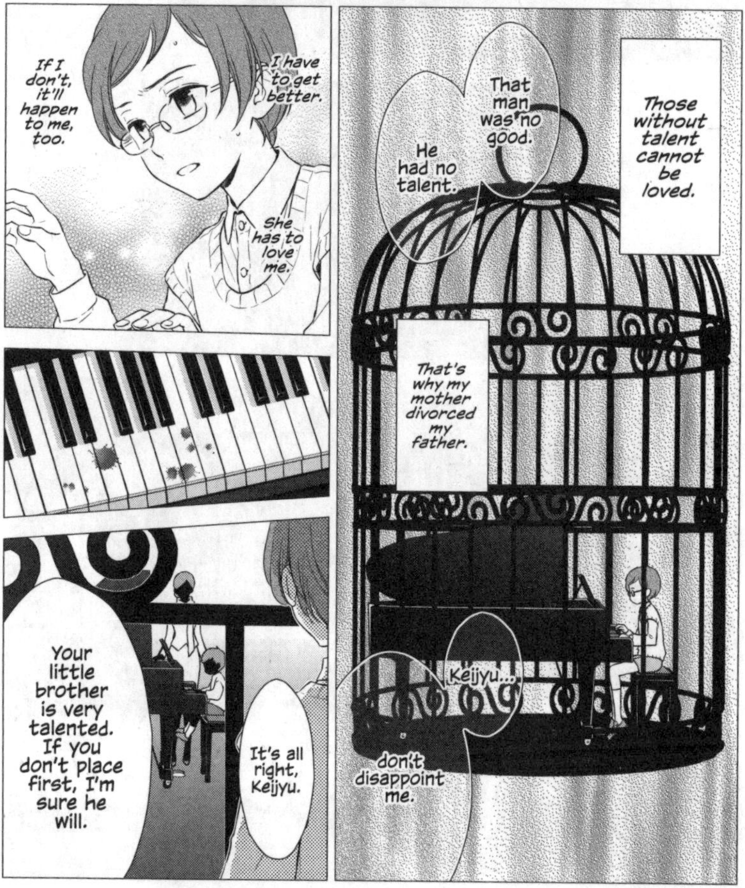
Those without talent cannot be loved.
That man was no good.
He had no talent.
That's why my mother divorced my father.
Keijyu...
don't disappoint me.
I have to get better.
If I don't, it'll happen to me, too.
She has to love me.
It's all right, Keijyu.
Your little brother is very talented. If you don't place first, I'm sure he will.

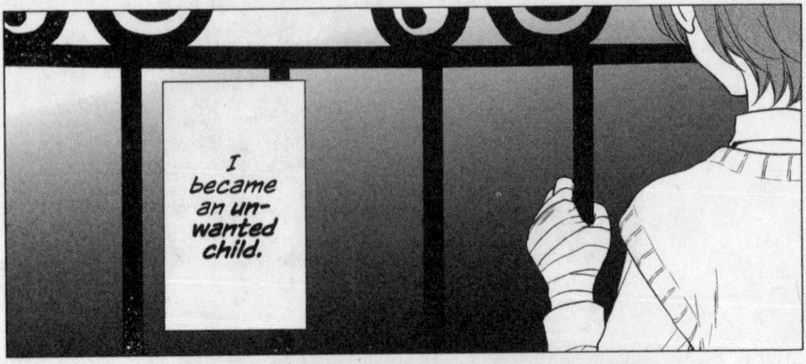
I became an un-wanted child.

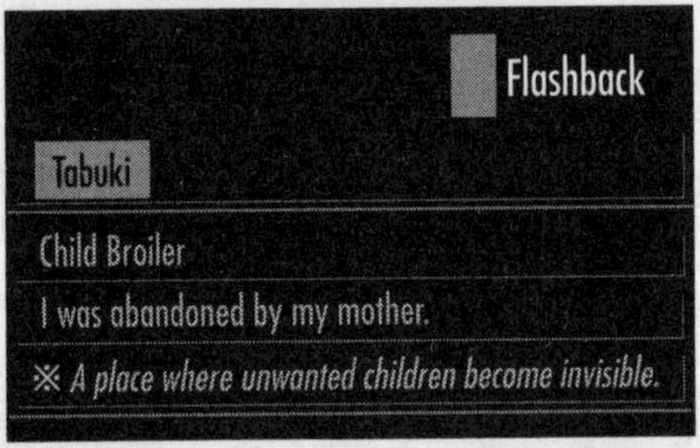
Flashback
Tabuki
Child Broiler
I was abandoned by my mother.
※ A place where unwanted children become invisible.

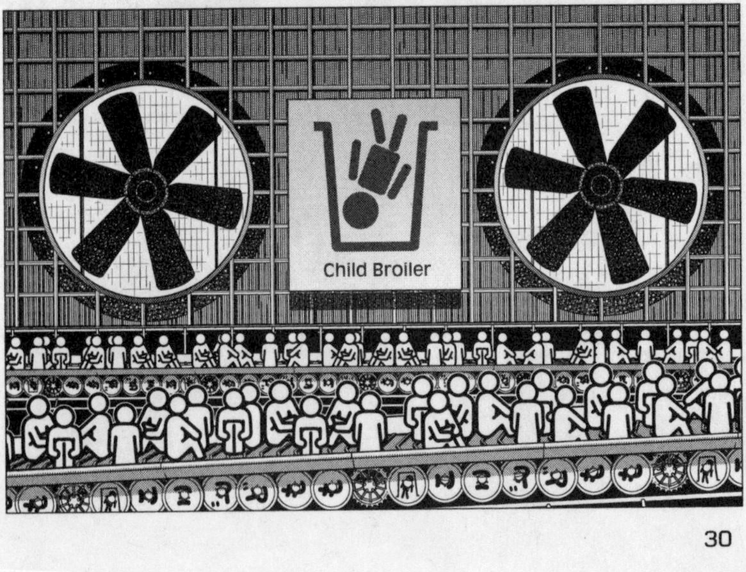
Child Broiler

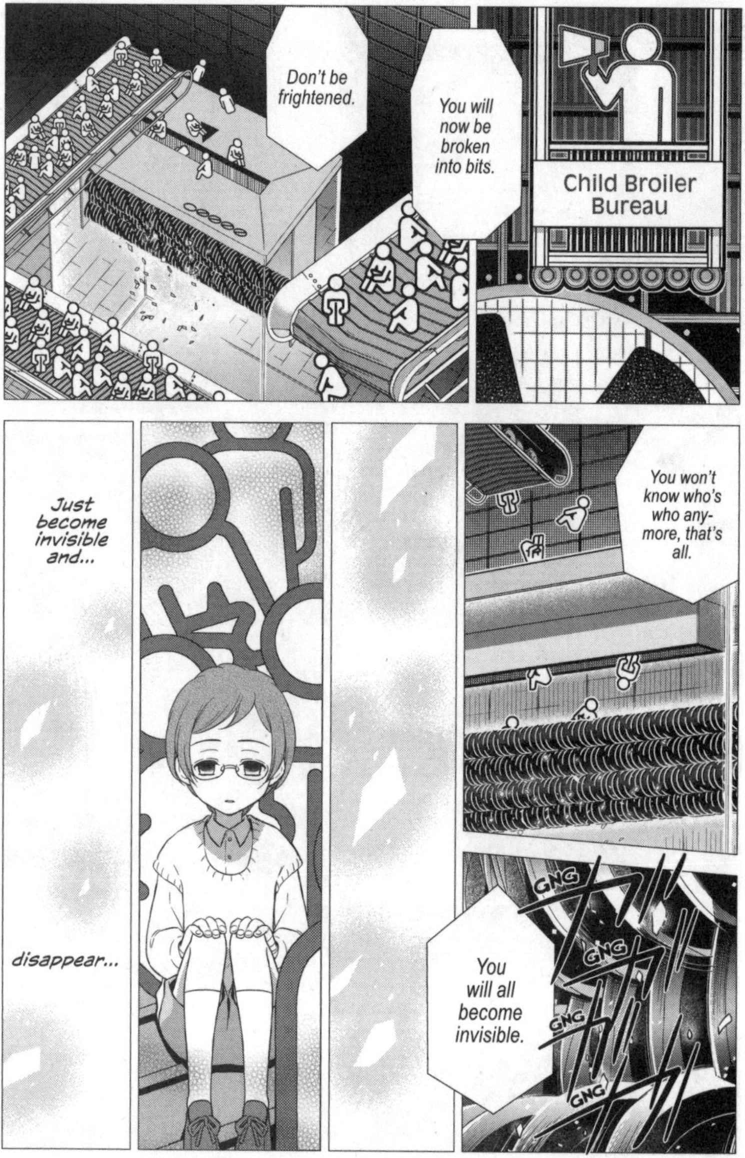
Child Broiler Bureau
Don't be frightened.
You will now be broken into bits.
You won't know who's who any-more, that's all.
GNG
GNG
GNG
GNG
You will all become invisible.
Just become invisible and...
disappear...

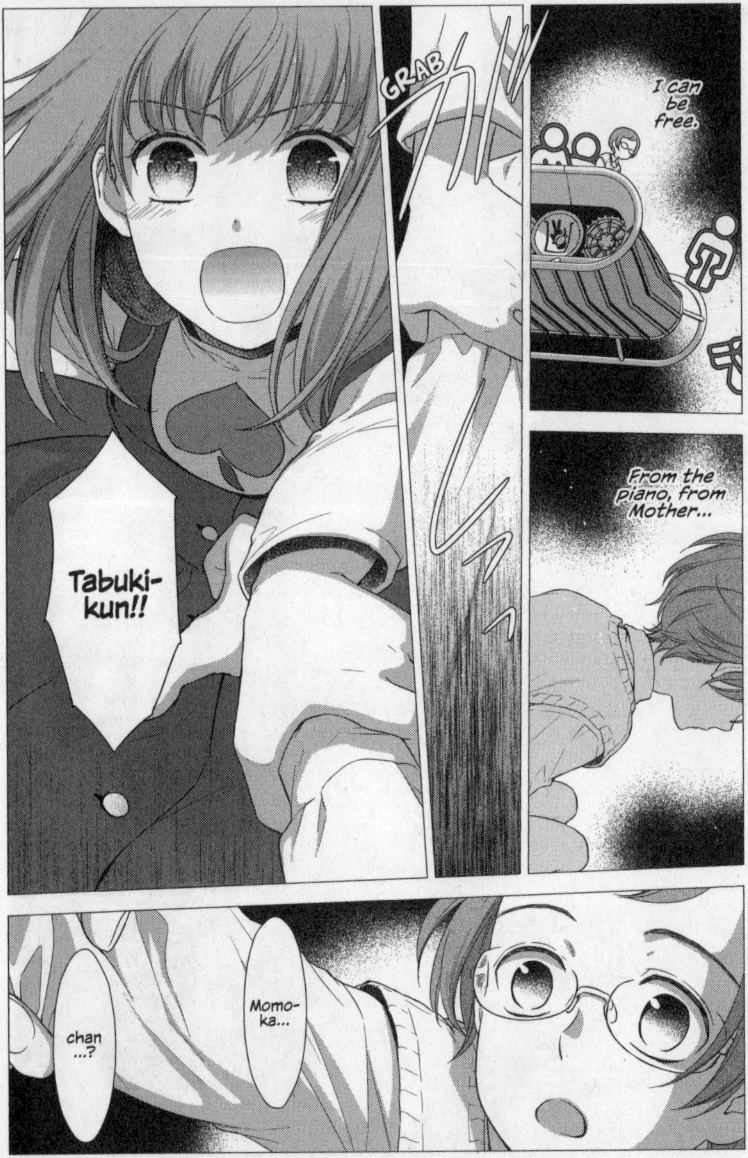
I can be free.
From the piano, from Mother...
GRAB
Tabuki-kun!!
Momoka...
chan ...?

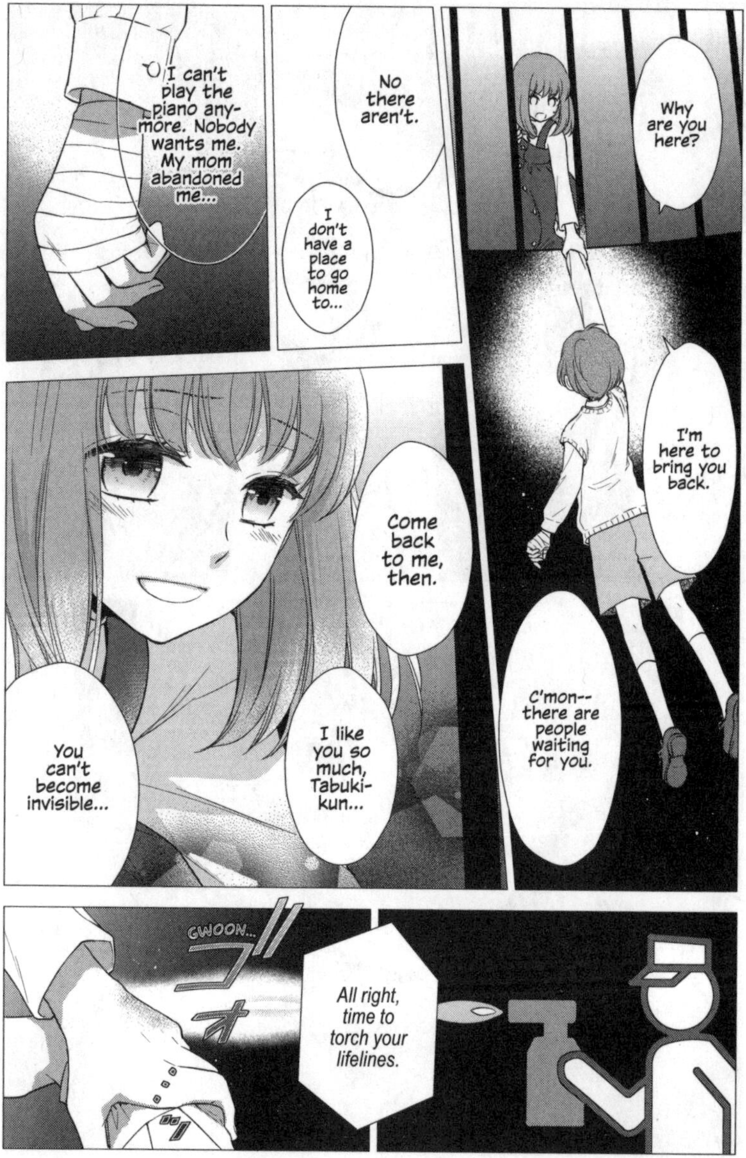
Why are you here?
I'm here to bring you back.
C'mon--there are people waiting for you.
No there aren't.
I don't have a place to go home to...
I can't play the piano anymore. Nobody wants me. My mom abandoned me...
Come back to me, then.
I like you so much, Tabuki-kun...
You can't become invisible...
All right, time to torch your lifelines.
GWOON...

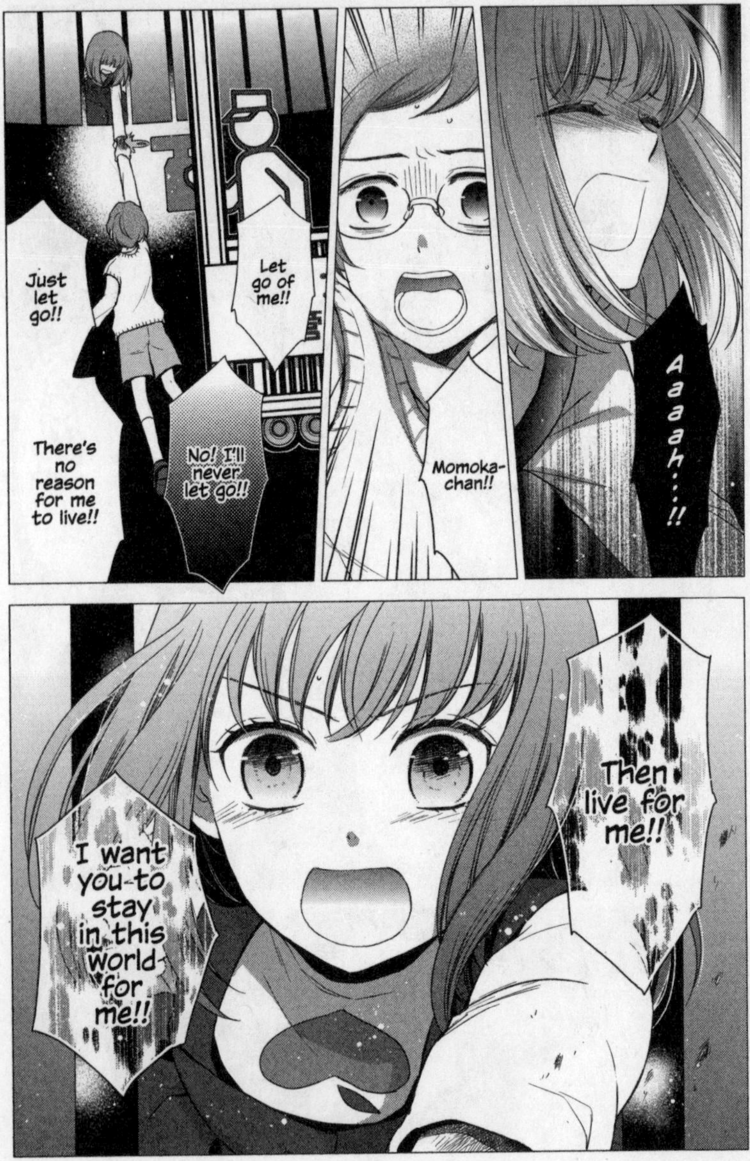

Aaaah...!!
Momoka-chan!!
Let go of me!!
Just let go!!
No! I'll never let go!!
There's no reason for me to live!!
Then live for me!!
I want you to stay in this world for me!!

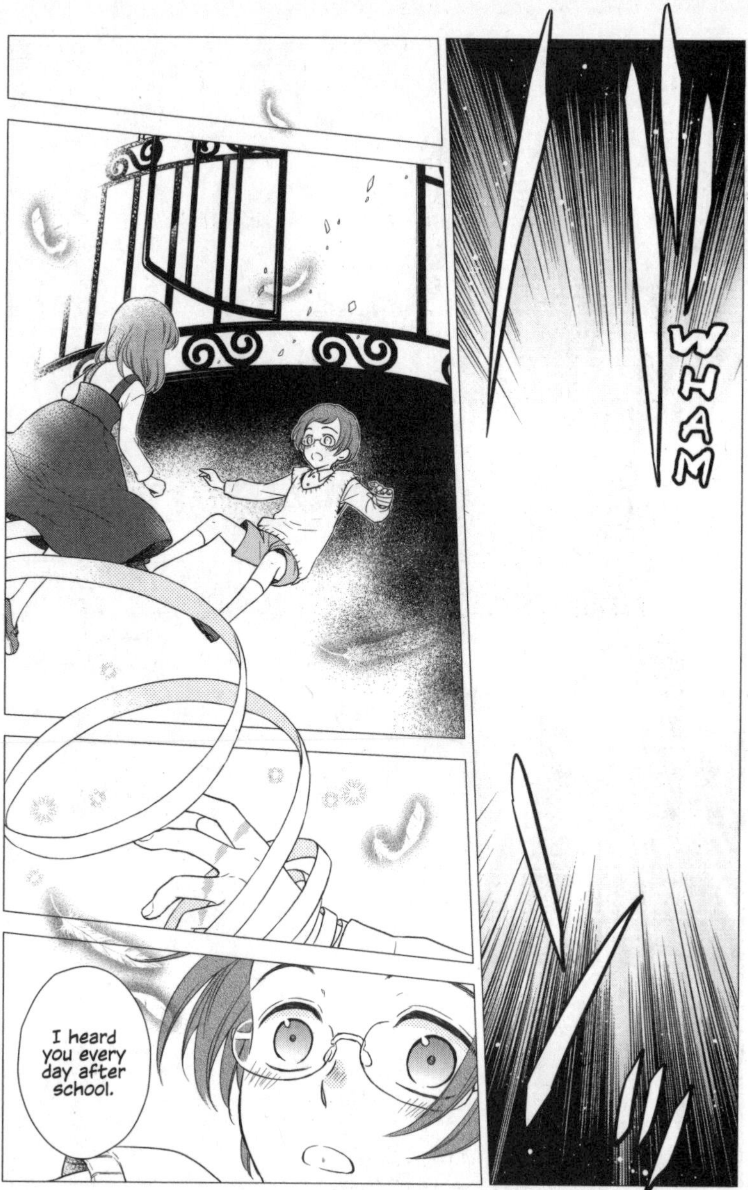
WHAM
I heard you every day after school.

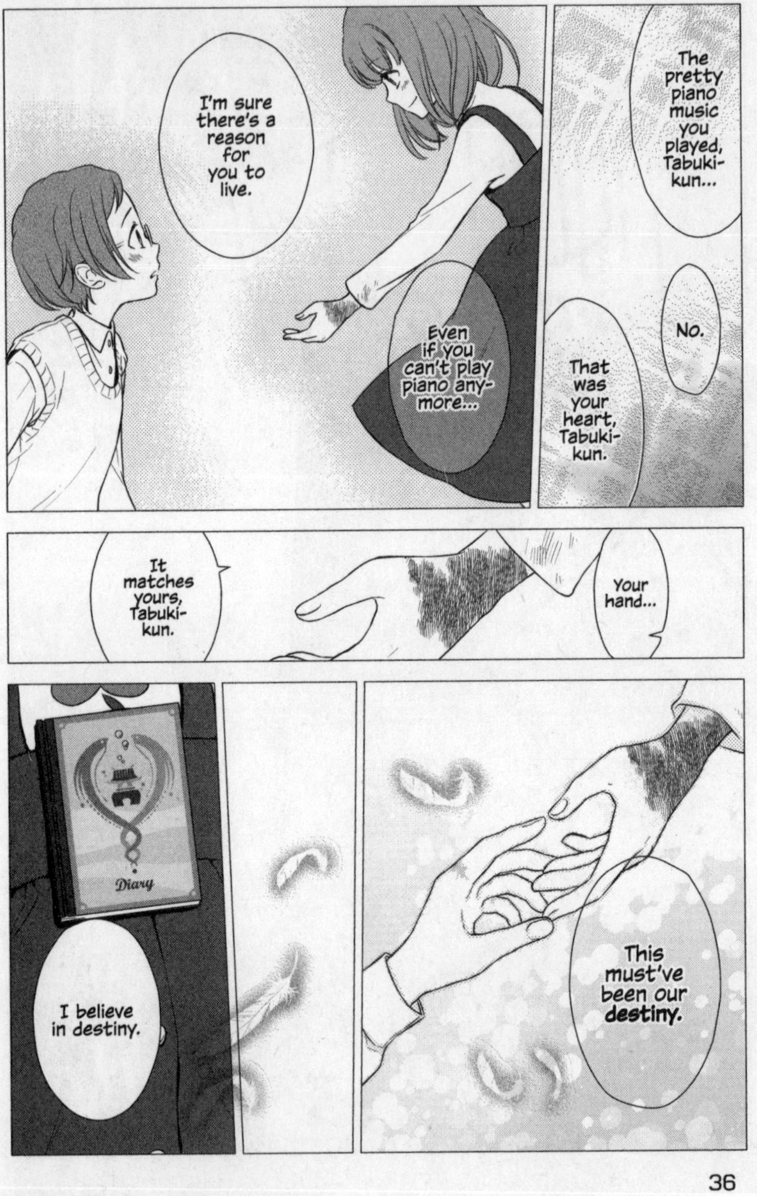

The pretty piano music you played, Tabuki-kun...
No.
That was your heart, Tabuki-kun.
I'm sure there's a reason for you to live.
Even if you can't play piano any-more...
Your hand...
It matches yours, Tabuki-kun.
This must've been our **destiny.**
Diary
I believe in destiny.

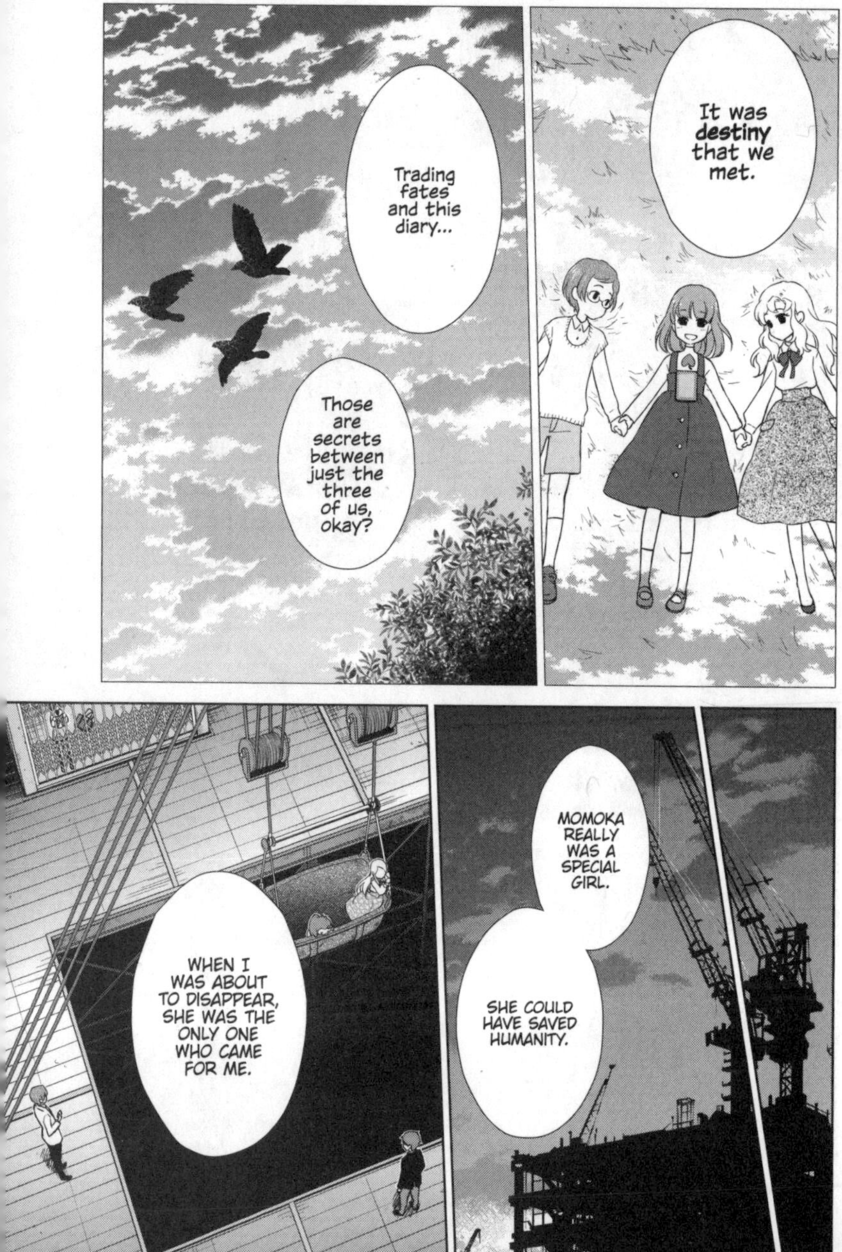
It was destiny that we met.
Trading fates and this diary...
Those are secrets between just the three of us, okay?
MOMOKA REALLY WAS A SPECIAL GIRL.
SHE COULD HAVE SAVED HUMANITY.
WHEN I WAS ABOUT TO DISAPPEAR, SHE WAS THE ONLY ONE WHO CAME FOR ME.

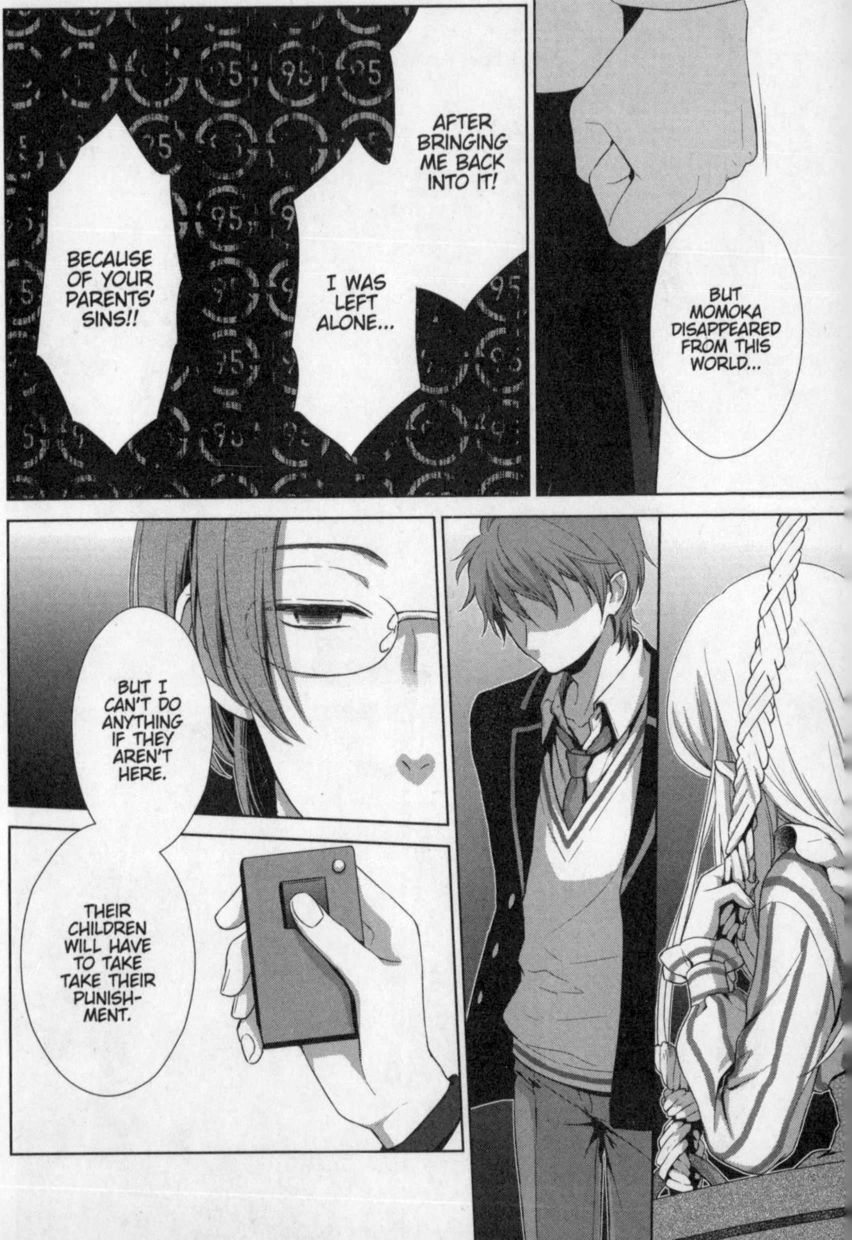
BUT MOMOKA DISAPPEARED FROM THIS WORLD...
AFTER BRINGING ME BACK INTO IT!
I WAS LEFT ALONE...
BECAUSE OF YOUR PARENTS' SINS!!
BUT I CAN'T DO ANYTHING IF THEY AREN'T HERE.
THEIR CHILDREN WILL HAVE TO TAKE TAKE THEIR PUNISH-MENT.

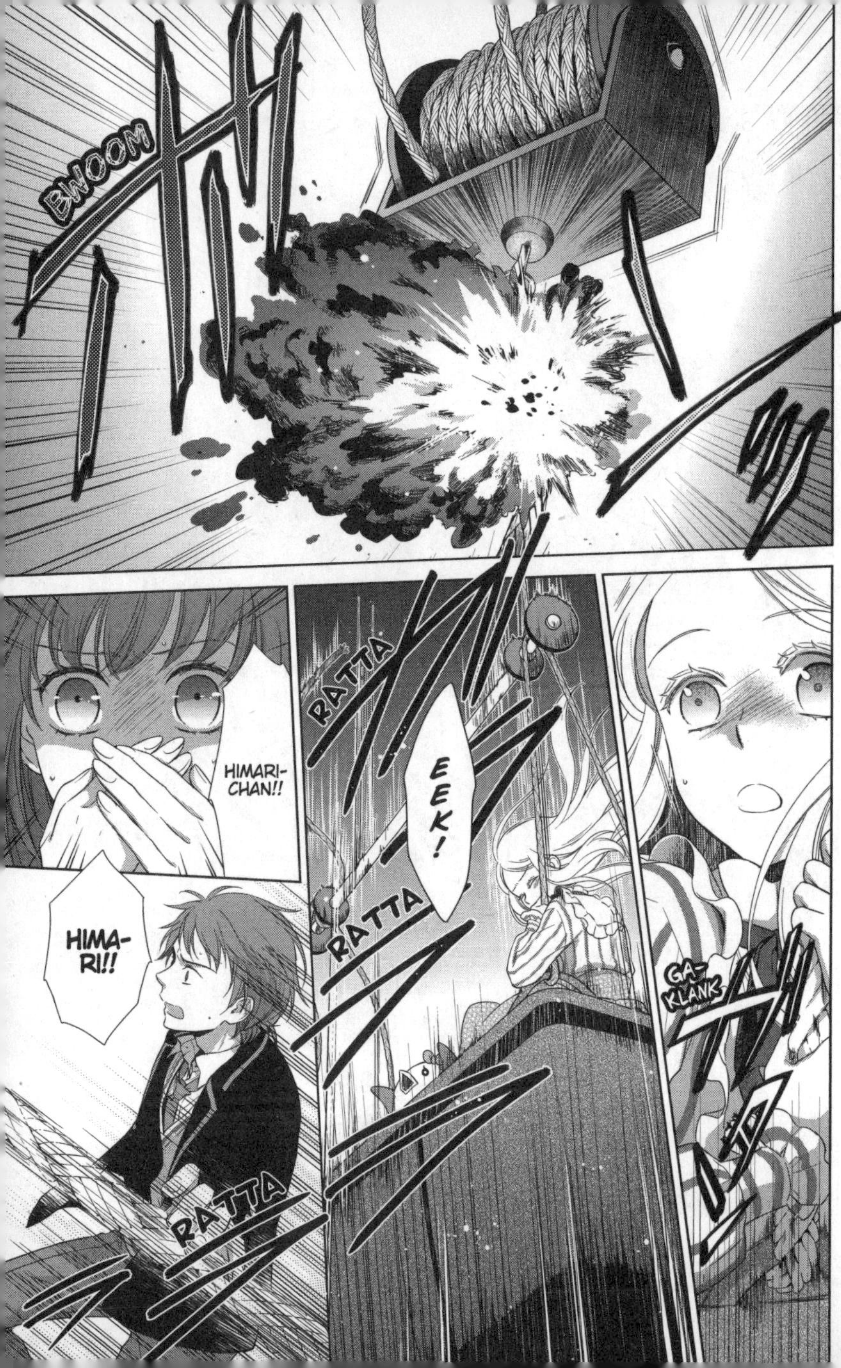
BWOOM
GA-KLANK
RATTA
EEK!
RATTA
HIMARI-CHAN!!
HIMA-RI!!
RATTA

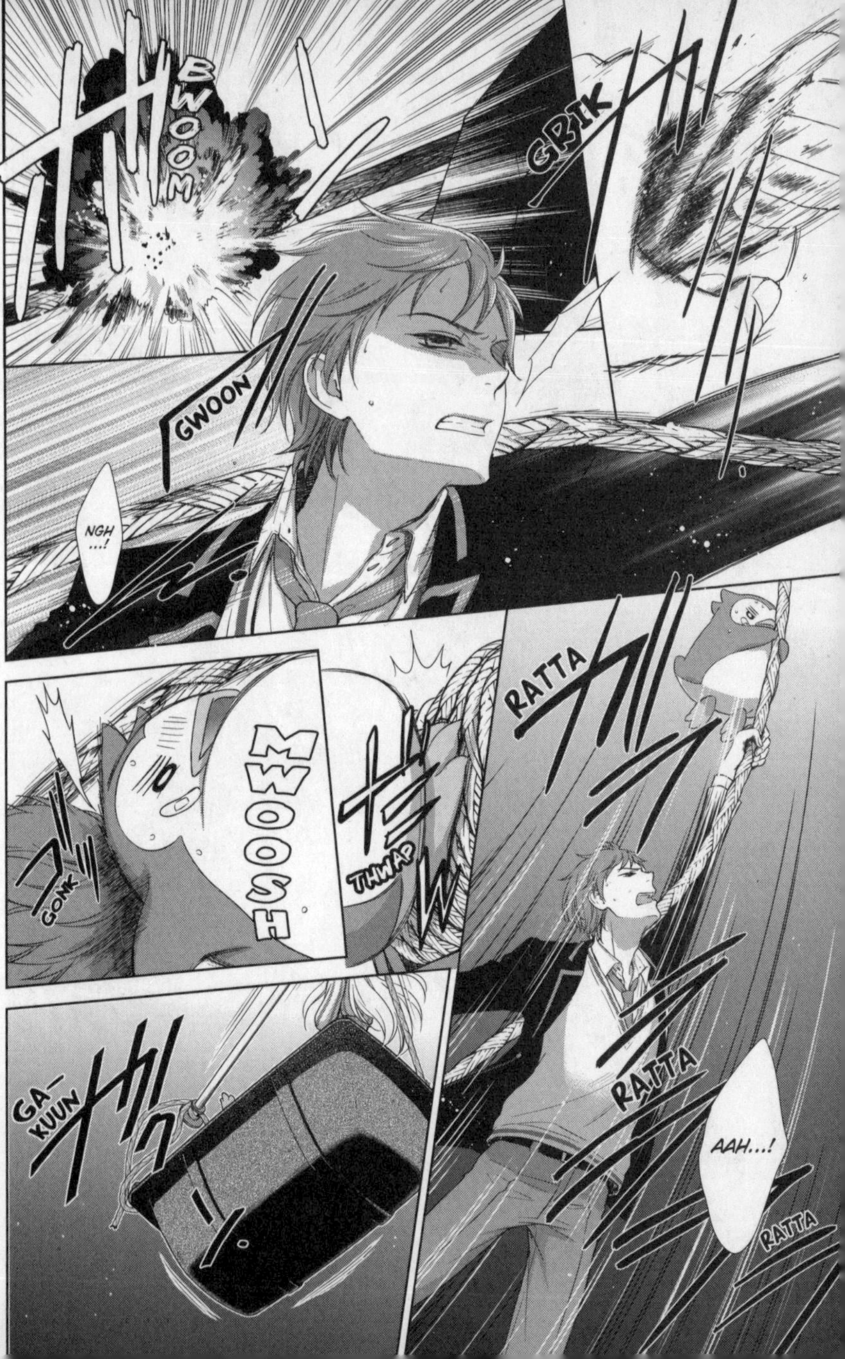
GRIK
BWOOM
GWOON
NGH ...!
RATTA
RATTA
AAH...!
RATTA
MWOOSH
THWAP
GONK
GA-KUUN

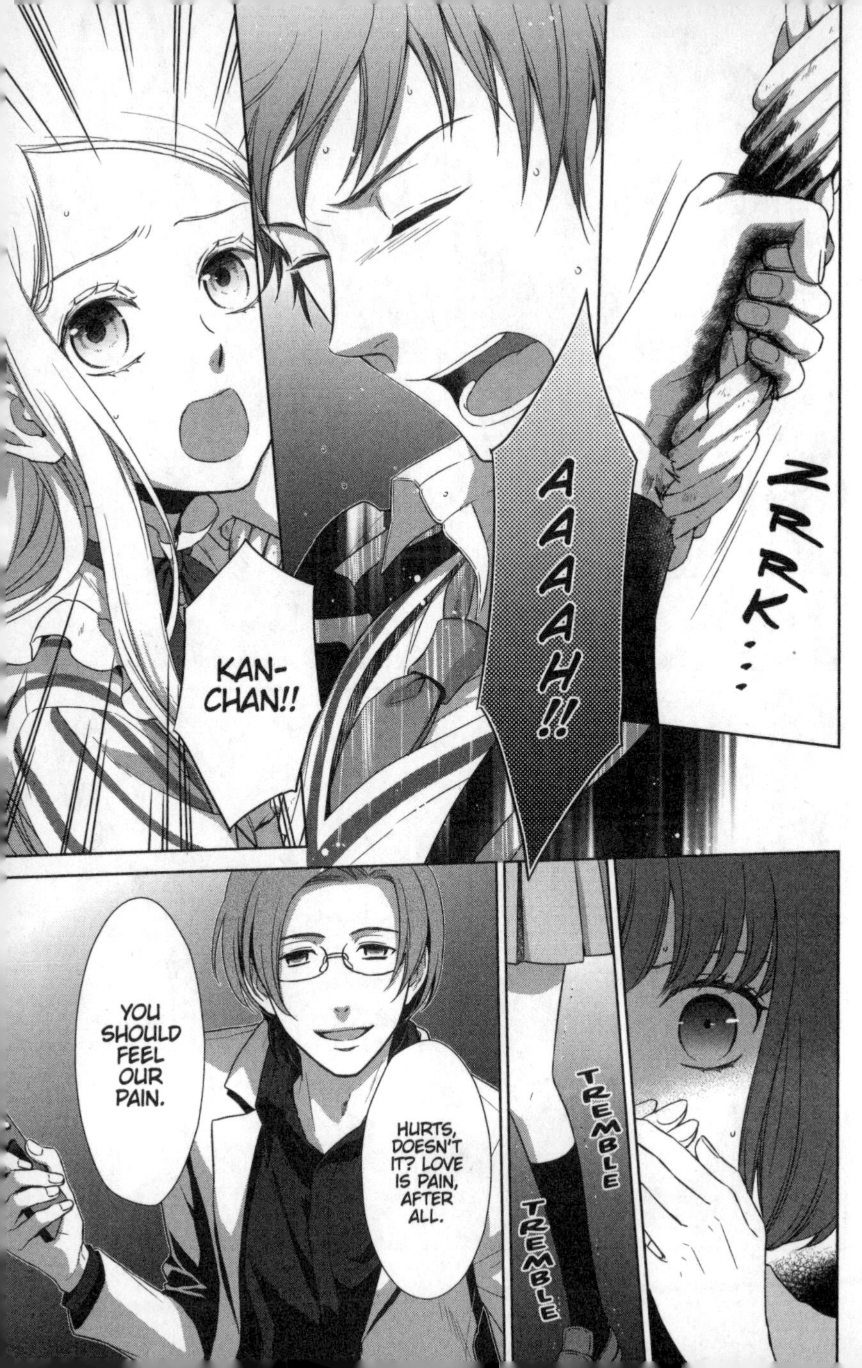
ZRRK...
AAAAAH!!
KAN-CHAN!!
TREMBLE
TREMBLE
HURTS, DOESN'T IT? LOVE IS PAIN, AFTER ALL.
YOU SHOULD FEEL OUR PAIN.

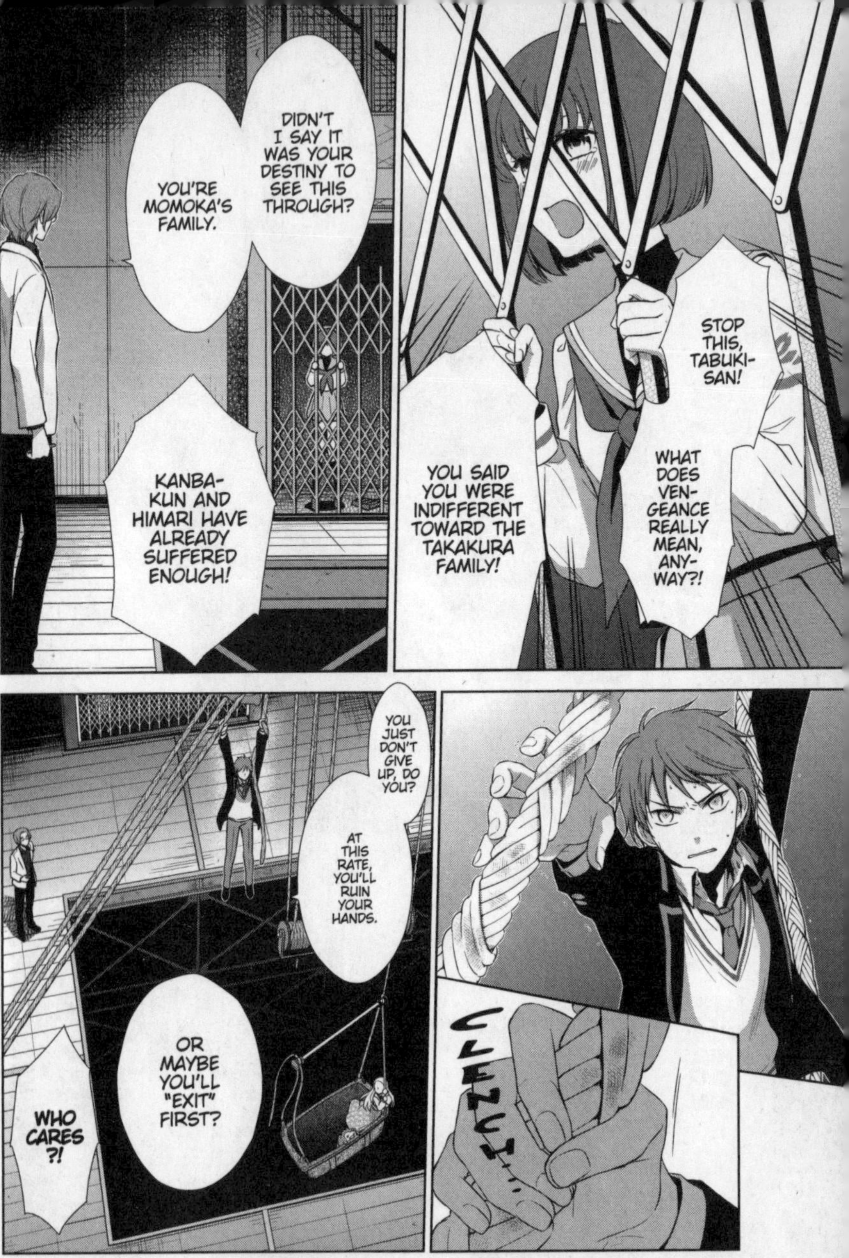

STOP THIS, TABUKI-SAN!
WHAT DOES VEN-GEANCE REALLY MEAN, ANY-WAY?!
YOU SAID YOU WERE INDIFFERENT TOWARD THE TAKAKURA FAMILY!
DIDN'T I SAY IT WAS YOUR DESTINY TO SEE THIS THROUGH?
YOU'RE MOMOKA'S FAMILY.
KANBA-KUN AND HIMARI HAVE ALREADY SUFFERED ENOUGH!
CLENCH...
YOU JUST DON'T GIVE UP, DO YOU?
AT THIS RATE, YOU'LL RUIN YOUR HANDS.
OR MAYBE YOU'LL "EXIT" FIRST?
WHO CARES?!

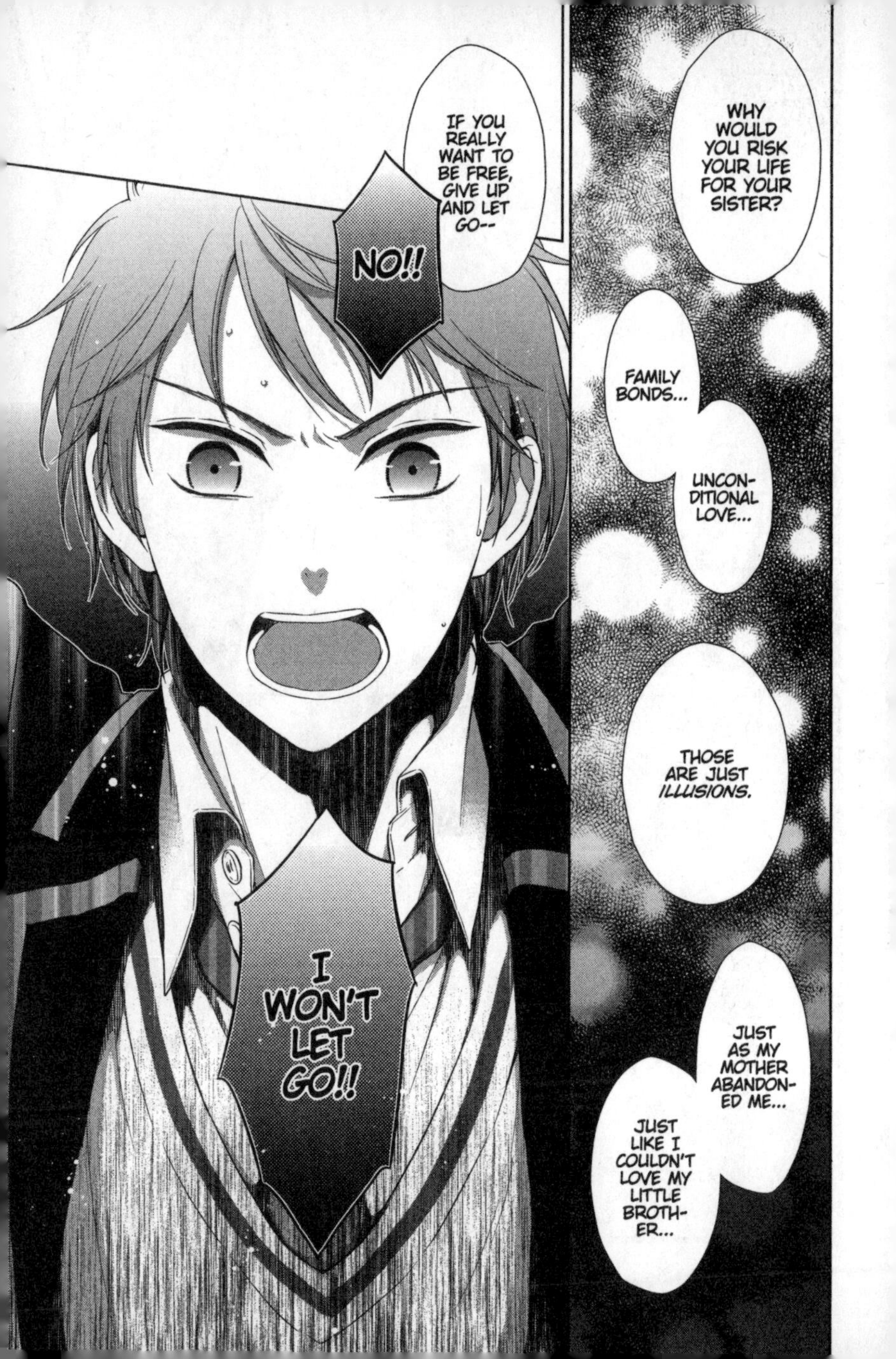
WHY WOULD YOU RISK YOUR LIFE FOR YOUR SISTER?
FAMILY BONDS...
UNCON-DITIONAL LOVE...
THOSE ARE JUST *ILLUSIONS.*
JUST AS MY MOTHER ABANDON-ED ME...
JUST LIKE I COULDN'T LOVE MY LITTLE BROTH-ER...
IF YOU REALLY WANT TO BE FREE, GIVE UP AND LET GO--
NO!!
I WON'T LET GO!!

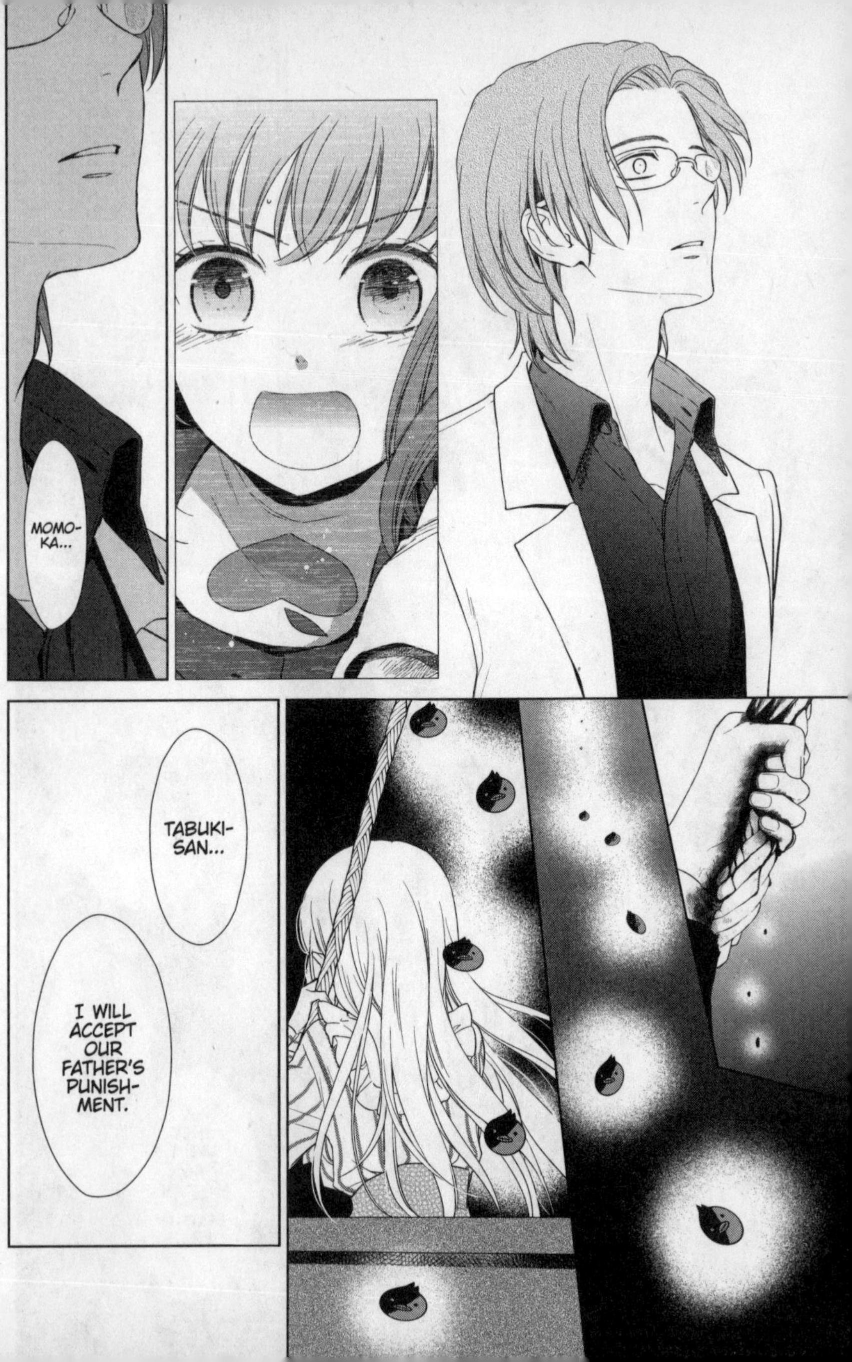
MOMO-KA...
TABUKI-SAN...
I WILL ACCEPT OUR FATHER'S PUNISH-MENT.

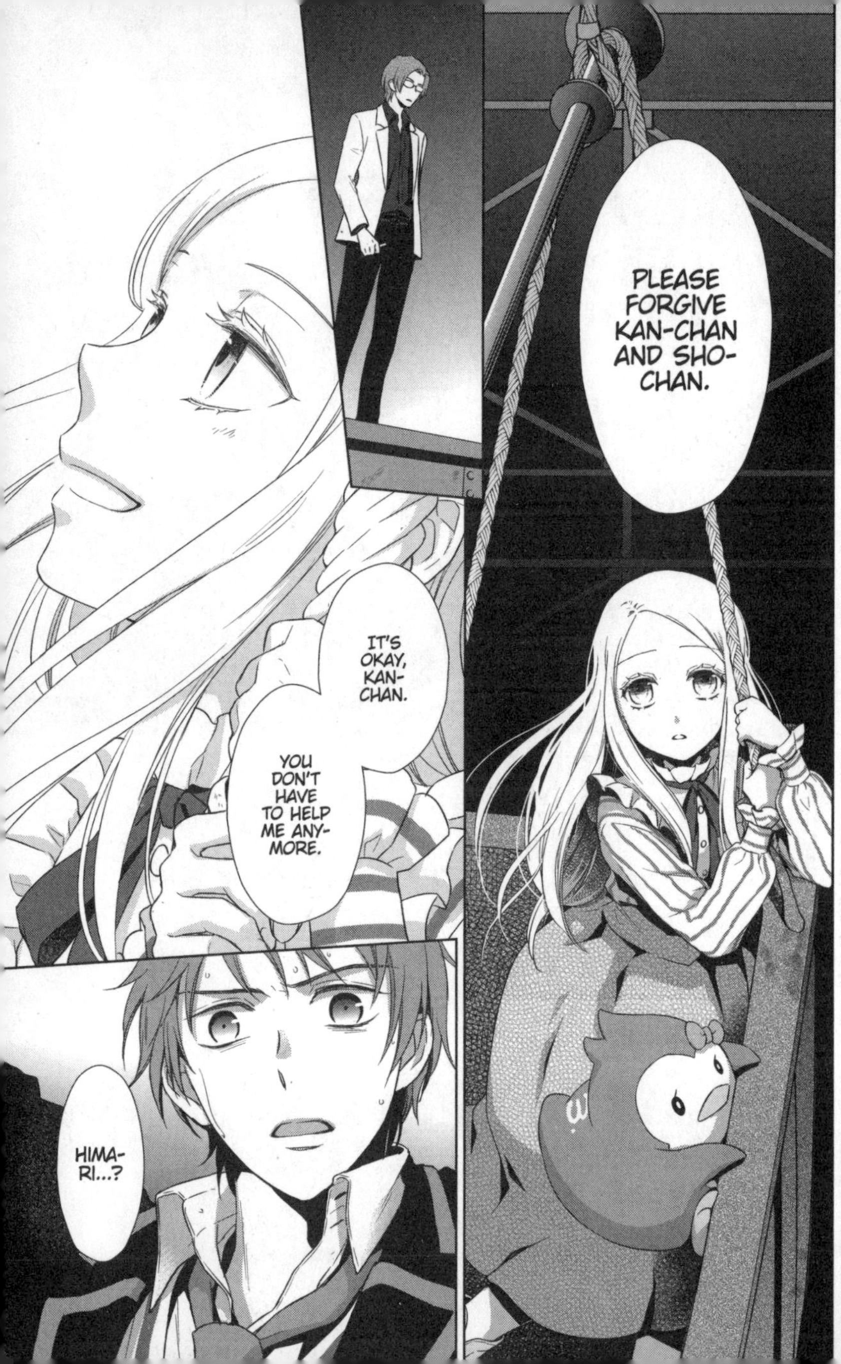
PLEASE FORGIVE KAN-CHAN AND SHO-CHAN.
IT'S OKAY, KAN-CHAN.
YOU DON'T HAVE TO HELP ME ANY-MORE.
HIMA-RI...?

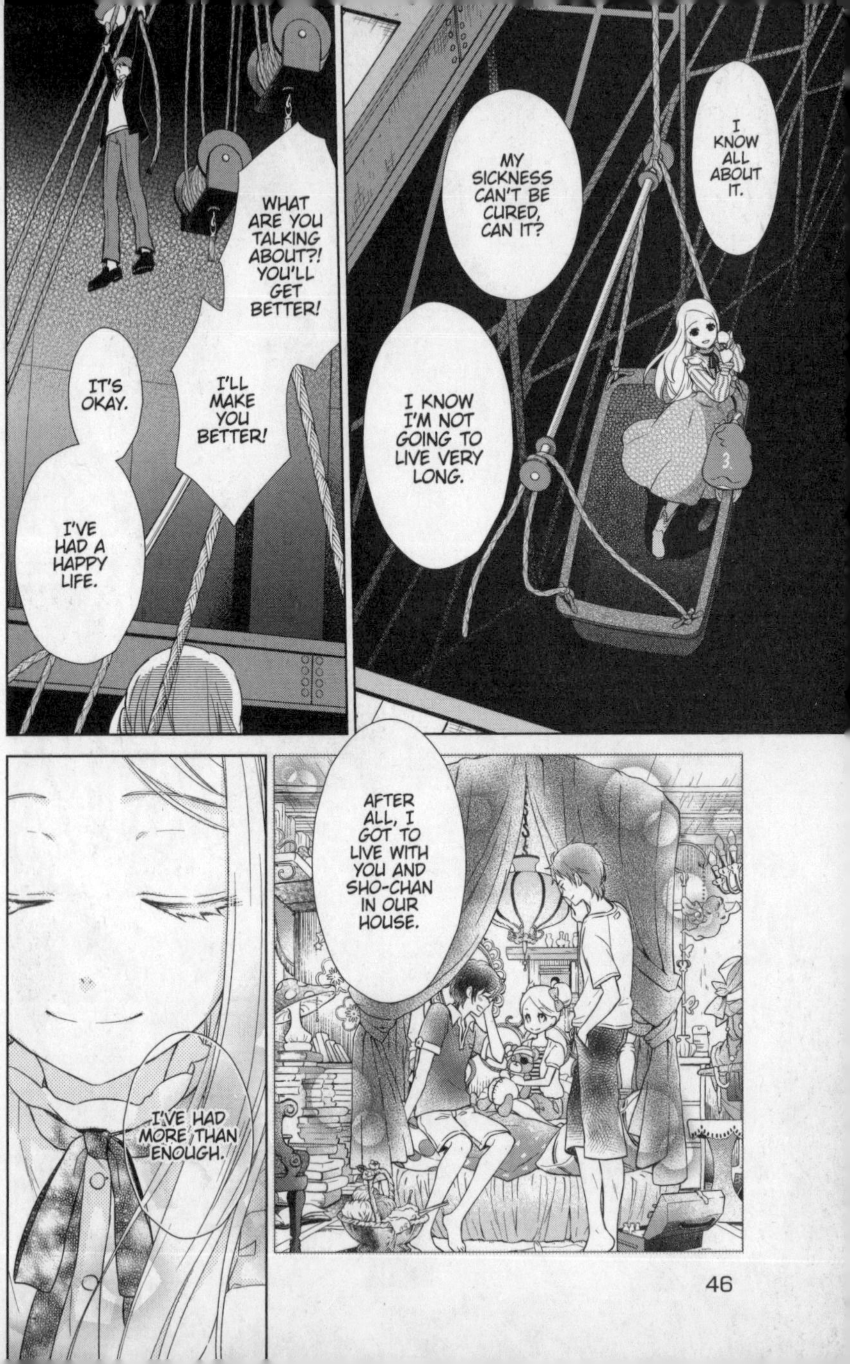
I KNOW ALL ABOUT IT.
MY SICKNESS CAN'T BE CURED, CAN IT?
I KNOW I'M NOT GOING TO LIVE VERY LONG.
WHAT ARE YOU TALKING ABOUT?! YOU'LL GET BETTER!
I'LL MAKE YOU BETTER!
IT'S OKAY.
I'VE HAD A HAPPY LIFE.
AFTER ALL, I GOT TO LIVE WITH YOU AND SHO-CHAN IN OUR HOUSE.
I'VE HAD MORE THAN ENOUGH.

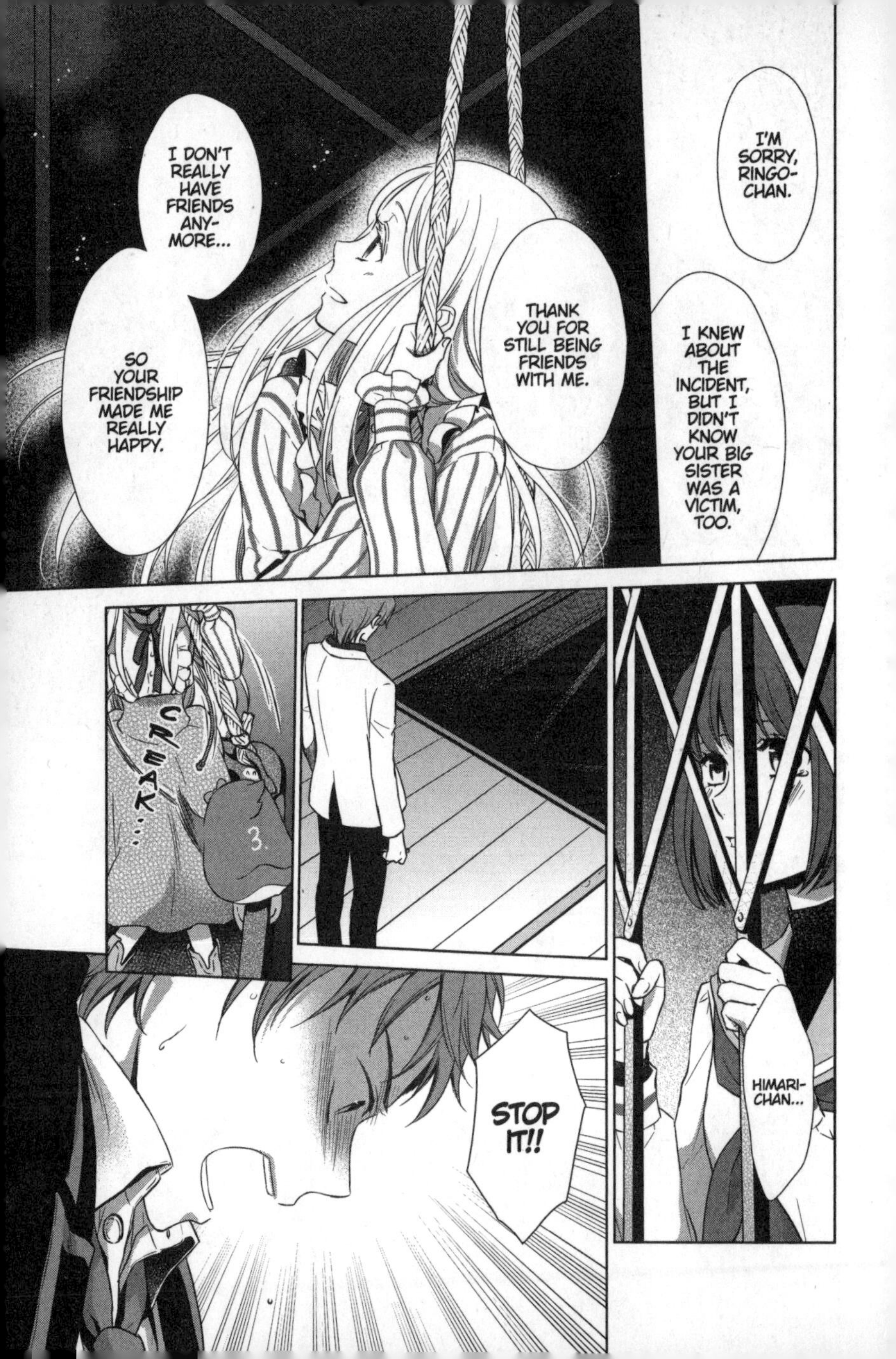
I'M SORRY, RINGO-CHAN.
I KNEW ABOUT THE INCIDENT, BUT I DIDN'T KNOW YOUR BIG SISTER WAS A VICTIM, TOO.
THANK YOU FOR STILL BEING FRIENDS WITH ME.
I DON'T REALLY HAVE FRIENDS ANY-MORE...
SO YOUR FRIENDSHIP MADE ME REALLY HAPPY.
HIMARI-CHAN...
CREAK...
STOP IT!!

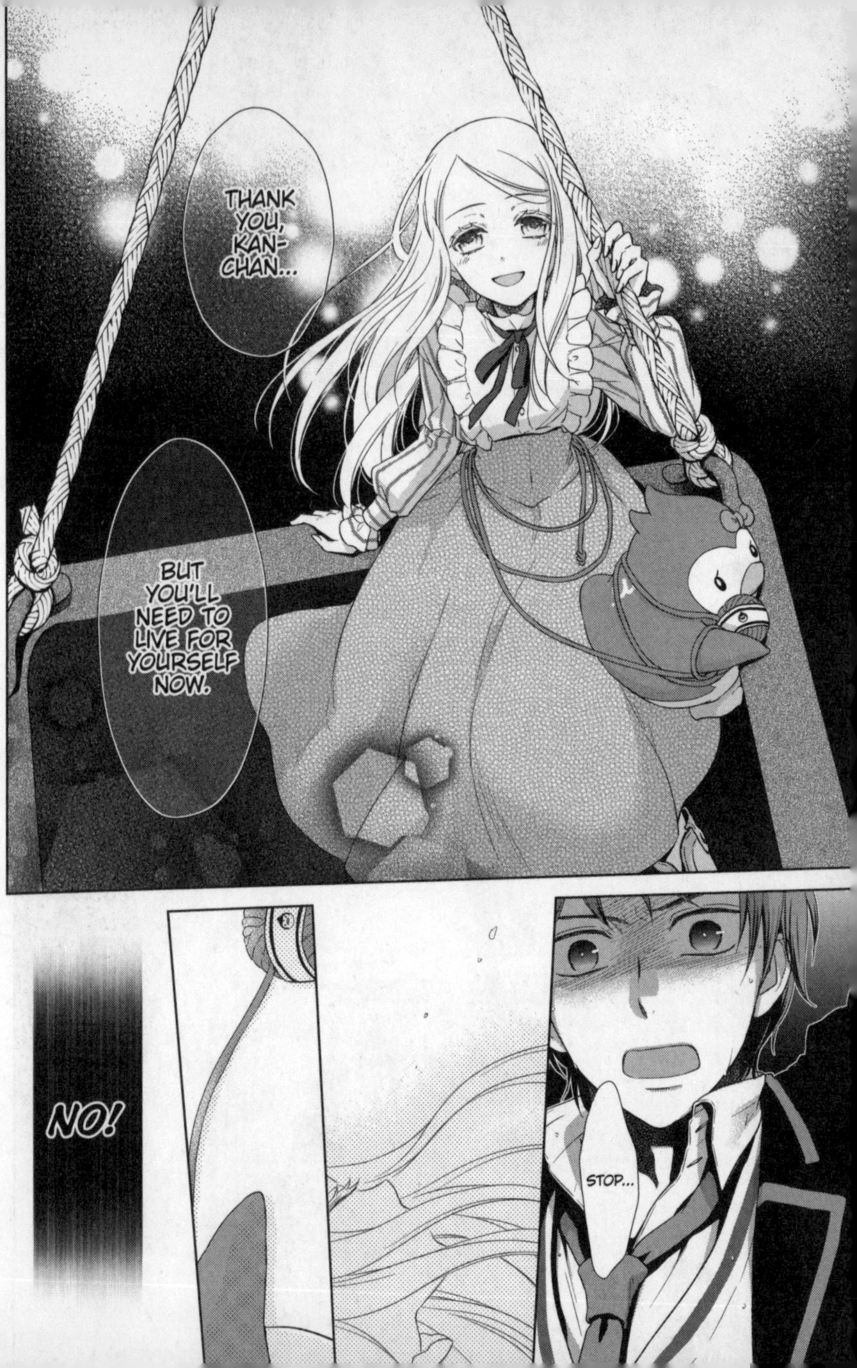
THANK YOU, KAN-CHAN...
BUT YOU'LL NEED TO LIVE FOR YOURSELF NOW.
STOP...
NO!

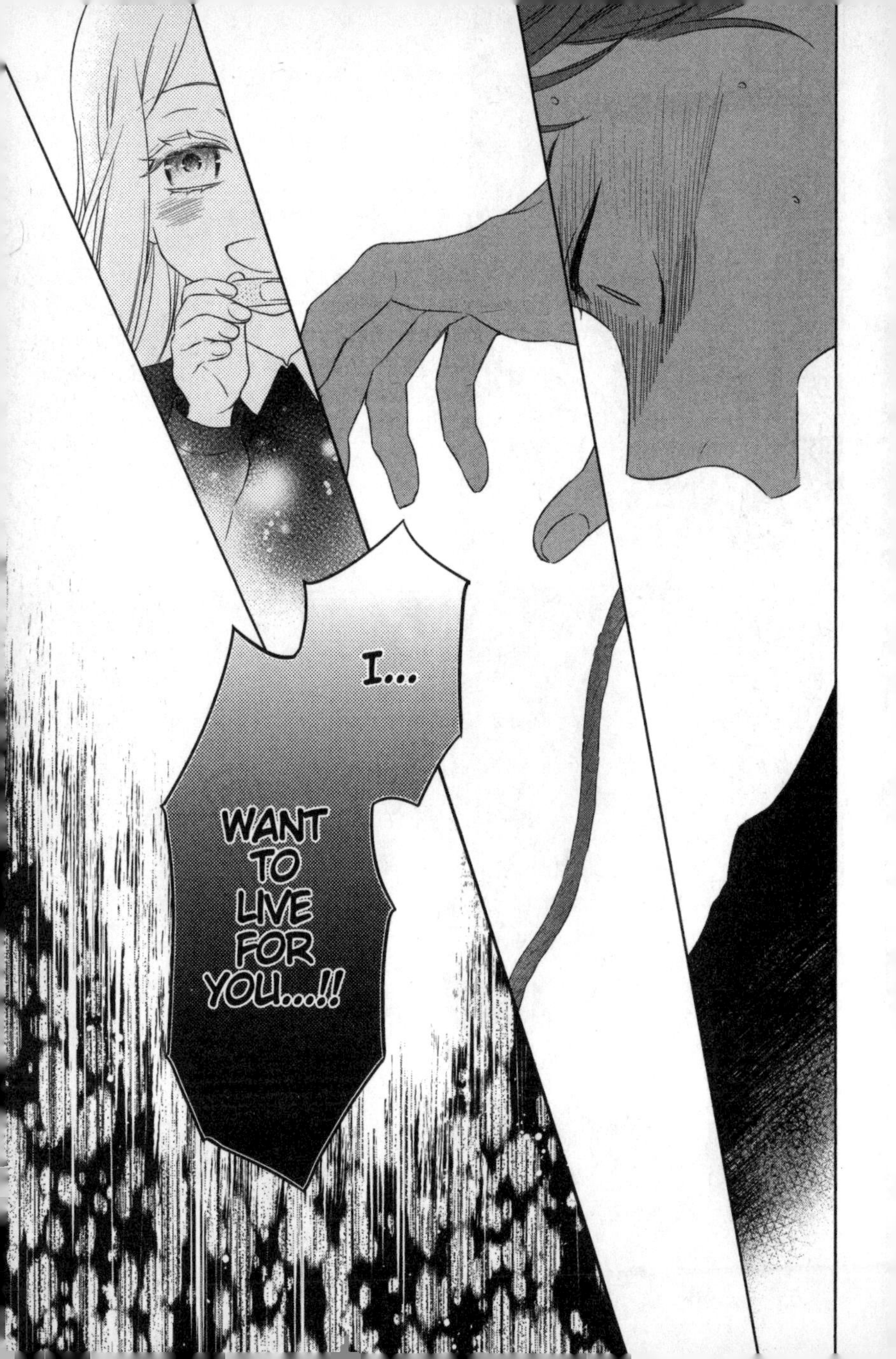
I...
WANT TO LIVE FOR YOU...!!

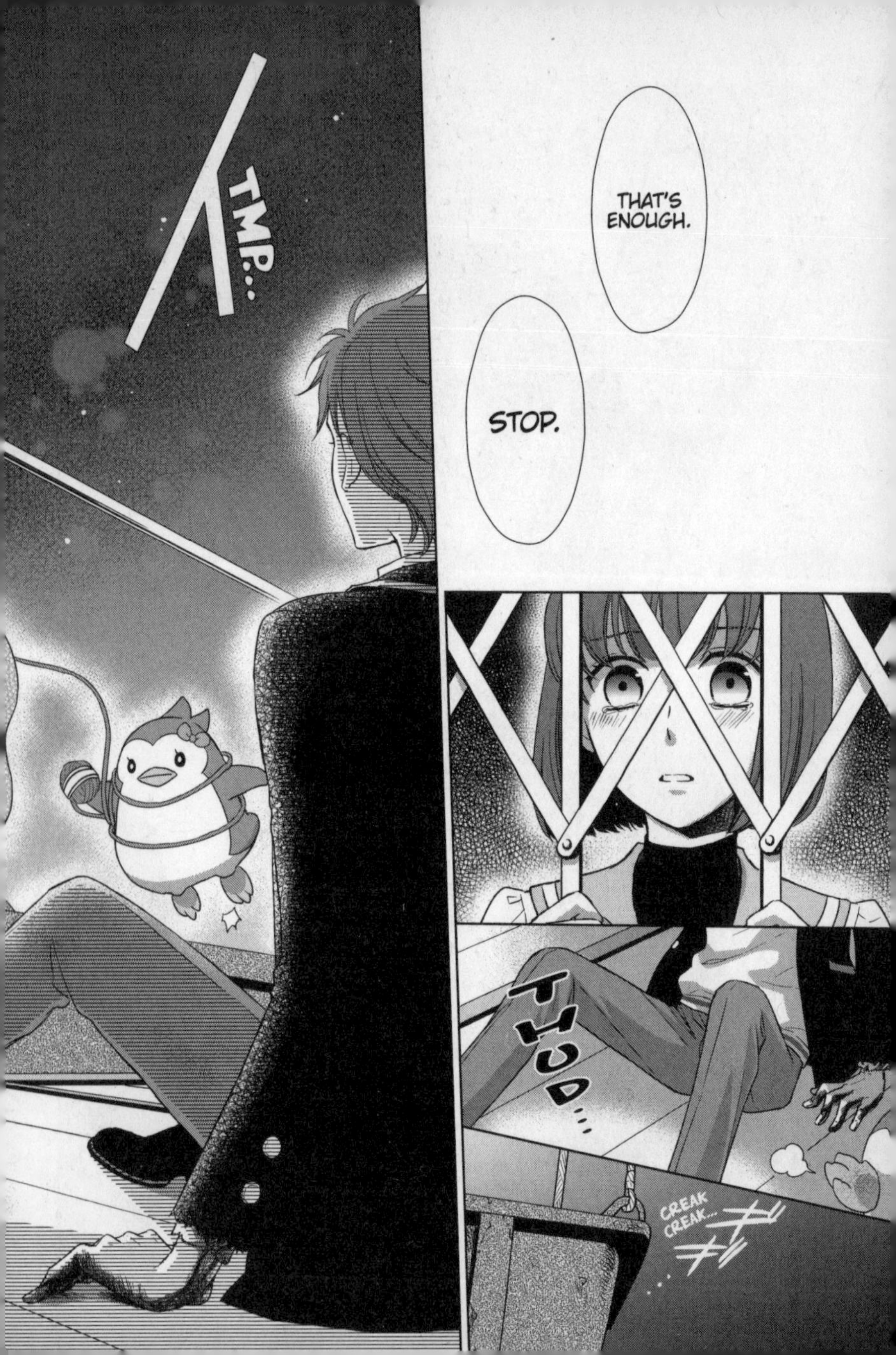
THAT'S ENOUGH.
STOP.
THUD...
CREAK CREAK...
TMP...

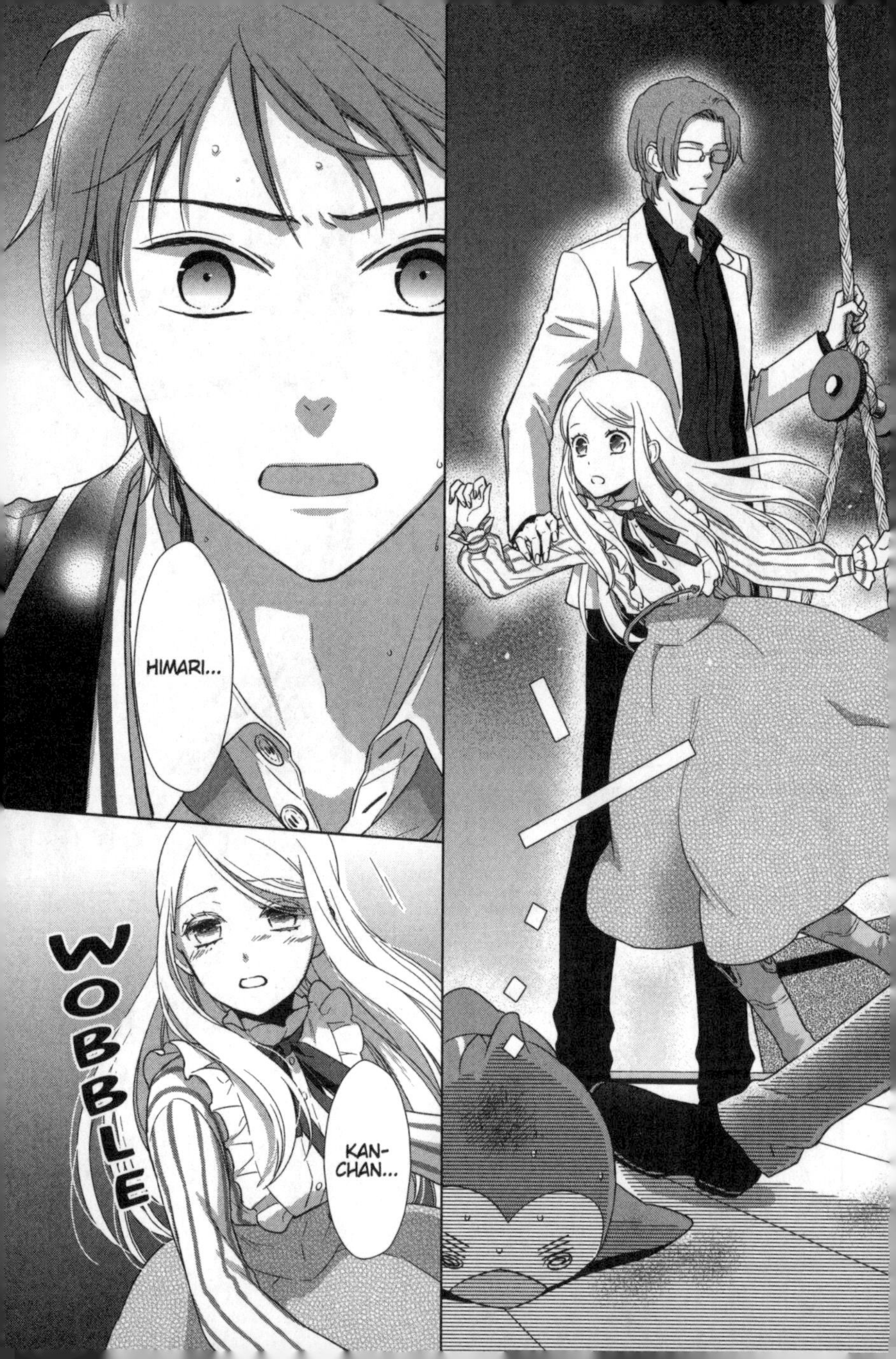
HIMARI...
WOBBLE
KAN-CHAN...

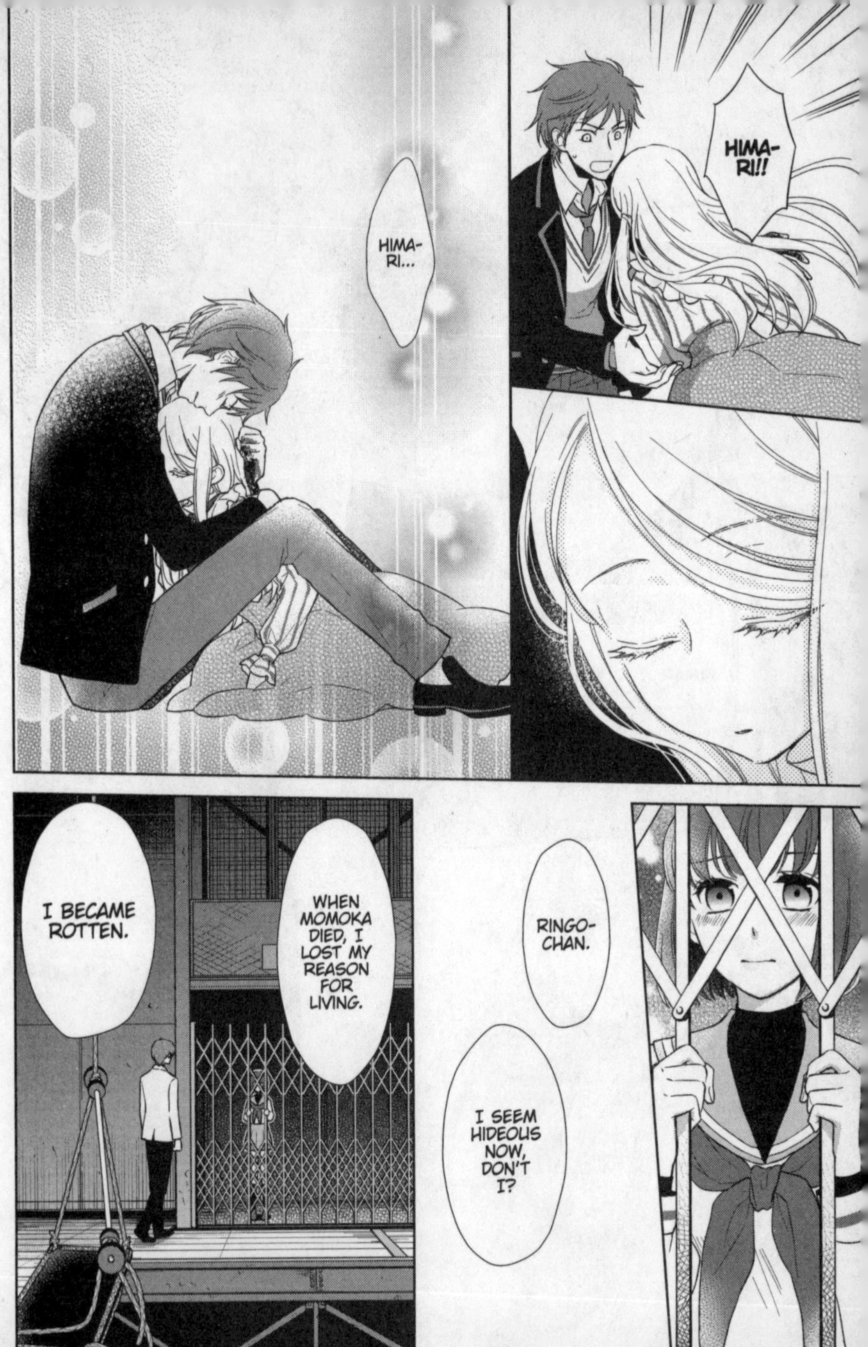
HIMA-RI!!
HIMA-RI...
RINGO-CHAN.
I SEEM HIDEOUS NOW, DON'T I?
WHEN MOMOKA DIED, I LOST MY REASON FOR LIVING.
I BECAME ROTTEN.

MOMOKA WAS SO DESPERATE TO SAVE ME, EVEN THOUGH WE WEREN'T FAMILY.

BECAUSE OF THAT TWIST OF FATE, THE BURNING DARKNESS BEGAN EATING ME ALIVE.

2	Sasaki
3	Kiyomizu Take
14	Senoo Sato
15	Takakura Kanba
16	Takakura Shoma
17	Tsukiyama Kyoko

Attendance Records

I WANTED TO FIND OUT WHAT WOULD HAPPEN'...

IF I CONFRONTED THAT SINNER, TAKAKURA KENZAN.

I DON'T KNOW...

WHY SHE ABANDONED ME.

TABUKI-SAN...

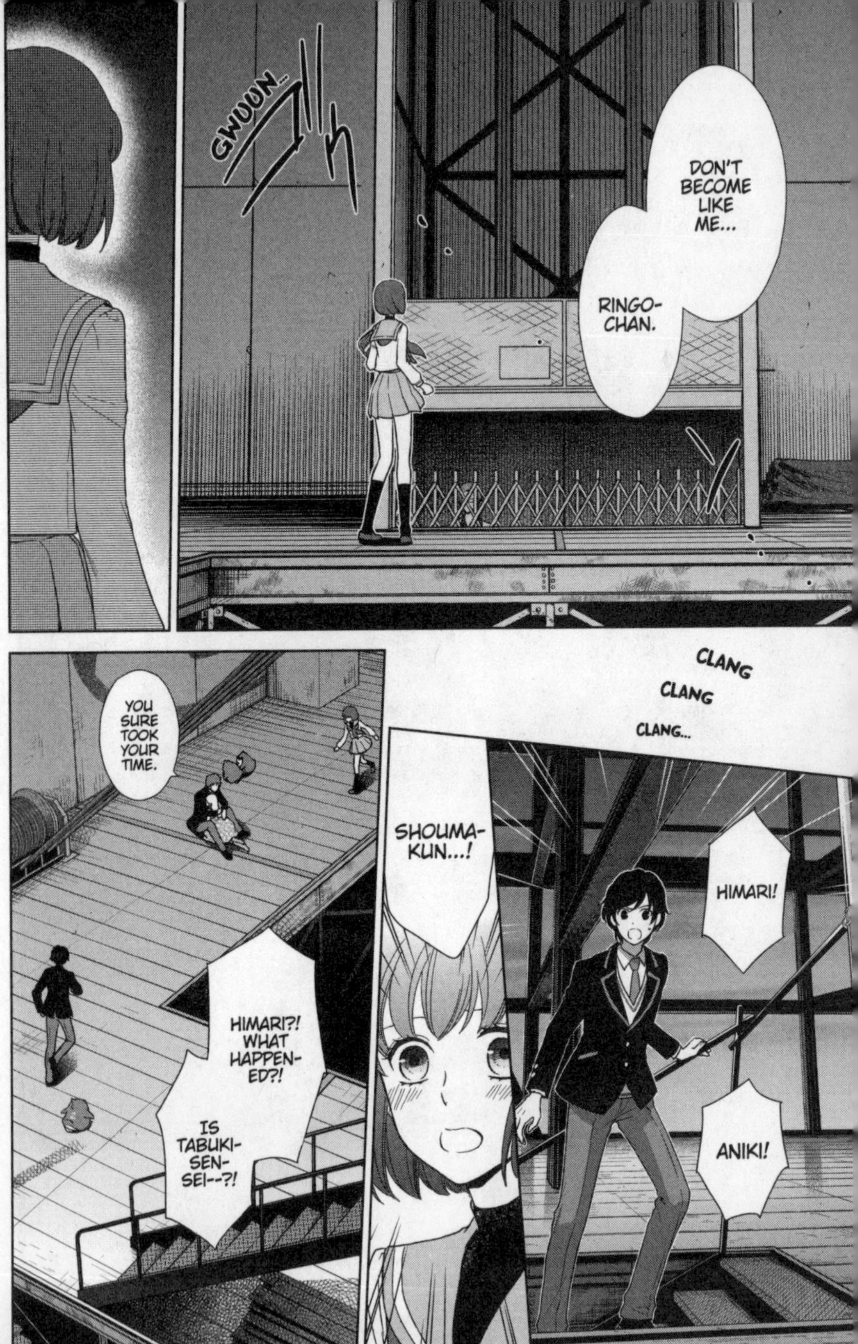

DON'T BECOME LIKE ME...
RINGO-CHAN.
GWUUN...
CLANG
CLANG
CLANG...
HIMARI!
ANIKI!
SHOUMA-KUN...!
YOU SURE TOOK YOUR TIME.
HIMARI?! WHAT HAPPENED?!
IS TABUKI-SENSEI--?!

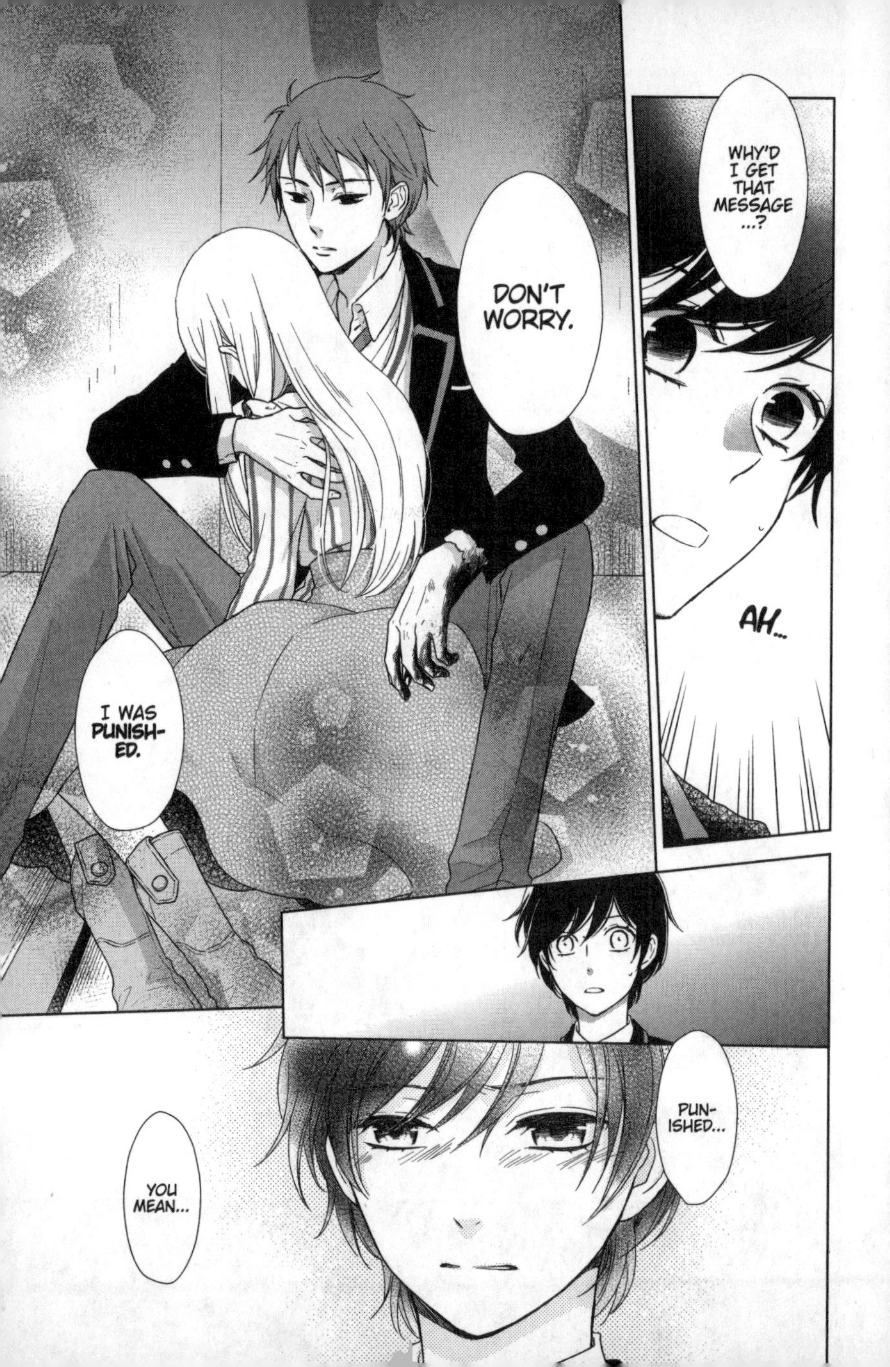
WHY'D I GET THAT MESSAGE ...?
AH...
DON'T WORRY.
I WAS PUNISH-ED.
PUN-ISHED...
YOU MEAN...

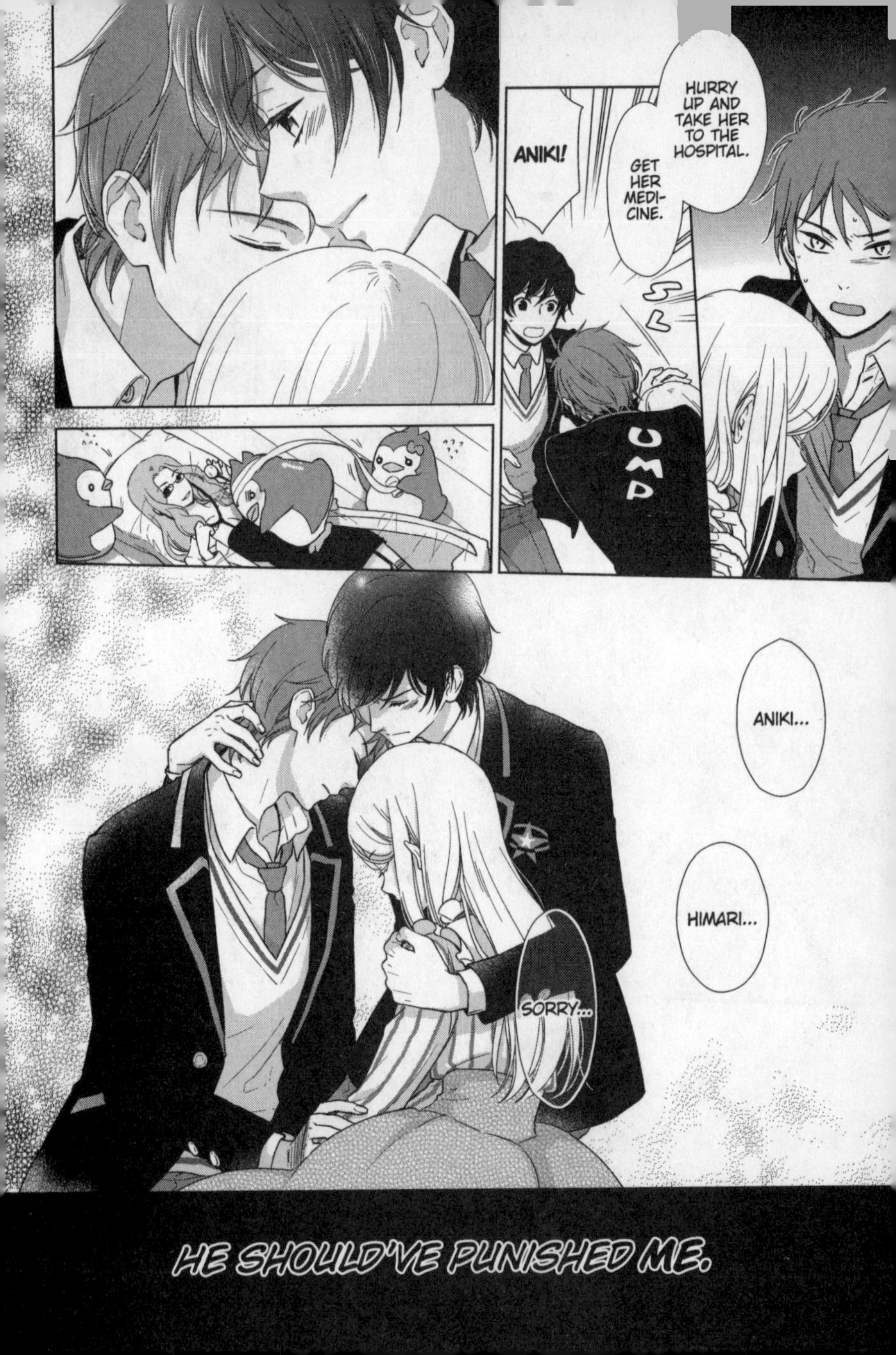
HURRY UP AND TAKE HER TO THE HOSPITAL.
GET HER MEDICINE.
ANIKI!
S
L
UMP
ANIKI...
HIMARI...
SORRY...
HE SHOULD'VE PUNISHED ME.

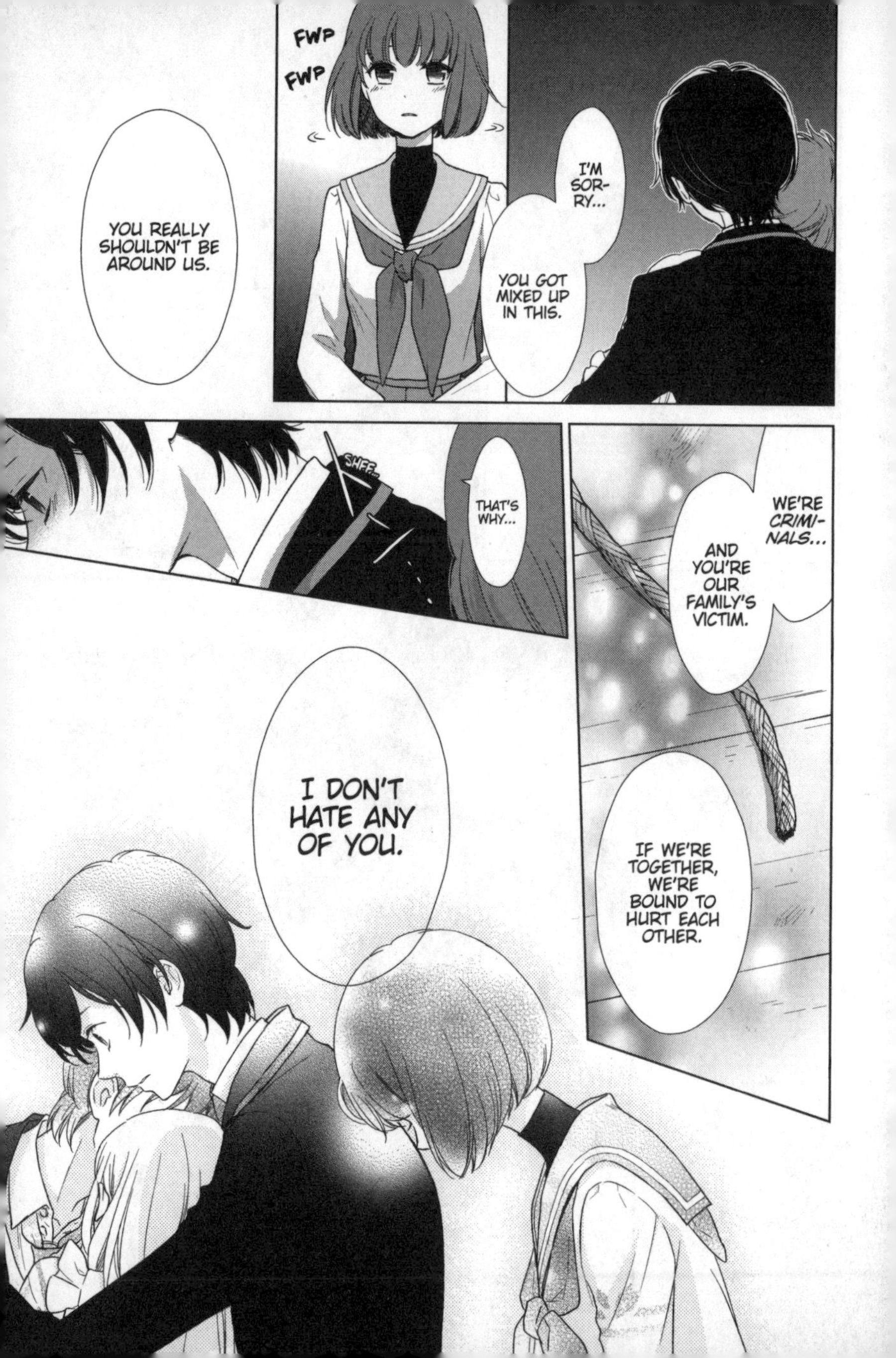
I'M SORRY...
YOU GOT MIXED UP IN THIS.
FWP
FWP
YOU REALLY SHOULDN'T BE AROUND US.
WE'RE CRIMINALS...
AND YOU'RE OUR FAMILY'S VICTIM.
IF WE'RE TOGETHER, WE'RE BOUND TO HURT EACH OTHER.
SHFF...
THAT'S WHY...
I DON'T HATE ANY OF YOU.

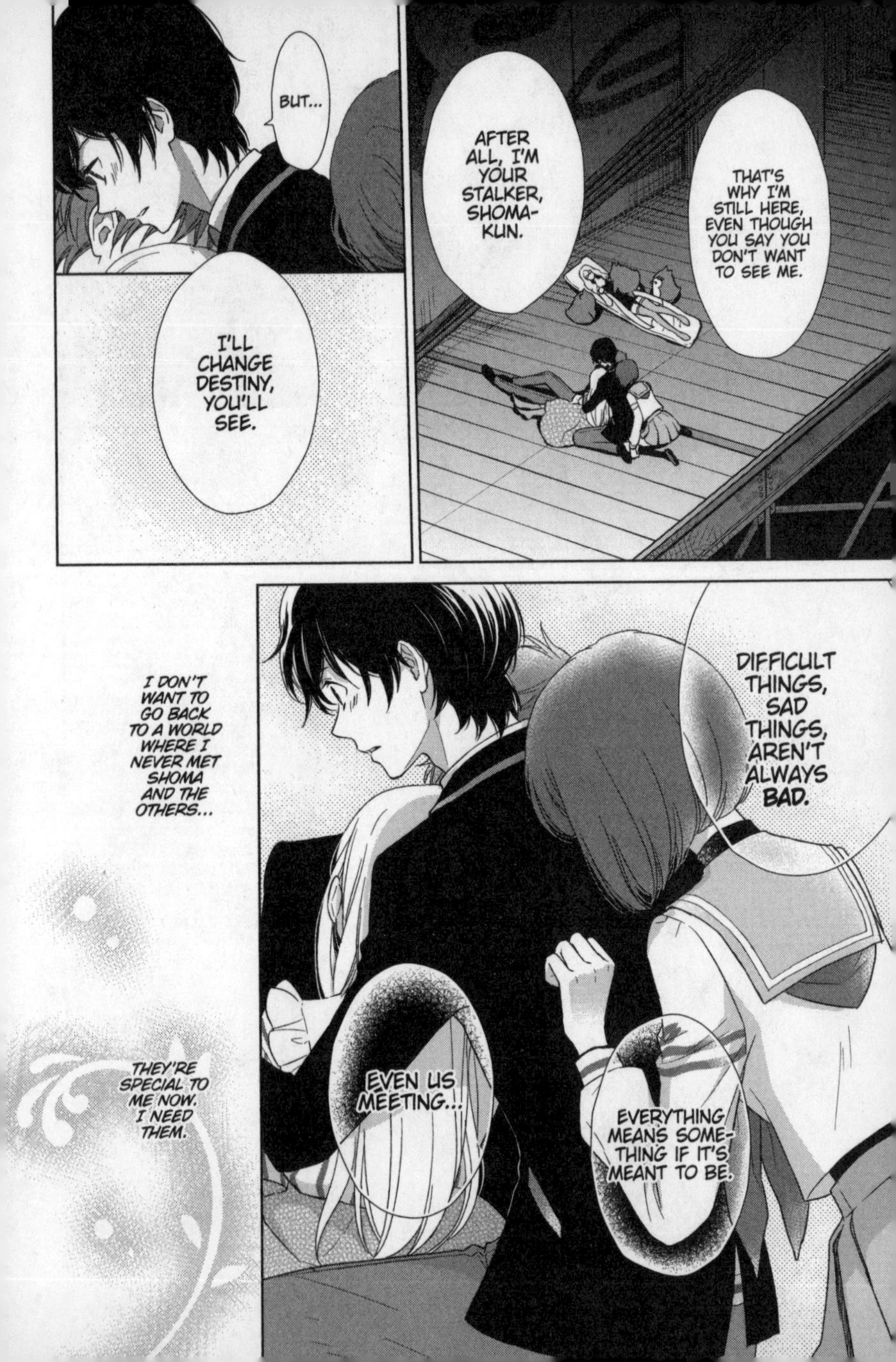
THAT'S WHY I'M STILL HERE, EVEN THOUGH YOU SAY YOU DON'T WANT TO SEE ME.
AFTER ALL, I'M YOUR STALKER, SHOMA-KUN.
BUT...
I'LL CHANGE DESTINY, YOU'LL SEE.
DIFFICULT THINGS, SAD THINGS, AREN'T ALWAYS BAD.
EVEN US MEETING...
EVERYTHING MEANS SOME-THING IF IT'S MEANT TO BE.
I DON'T WANT TO GO BACK TO A WORLD WHERE I NEVER MET SHOMA AND THE OTHERS...
THEY'RE SPECIAL TO ME NOW. I NEED THEM.

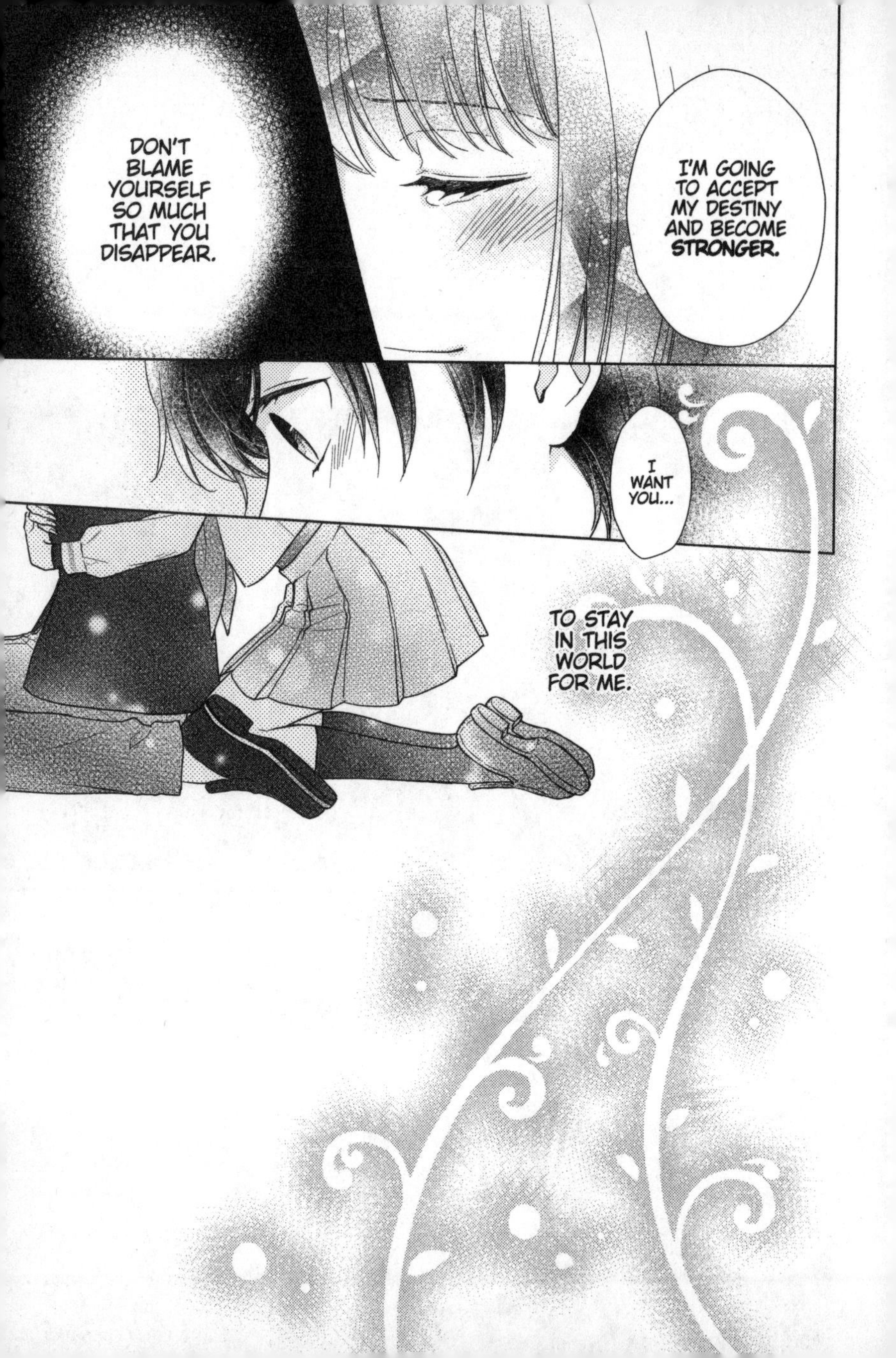
I'M GOING TO ACCEPT MY DESTINY AND BECOME STRONGER.
DON'T BLAME YOURSELF SO MUCH THAT YOU DISAPPEAR.
I WANT YOU...
TO STAY IN THIS WORLD FOR ME.

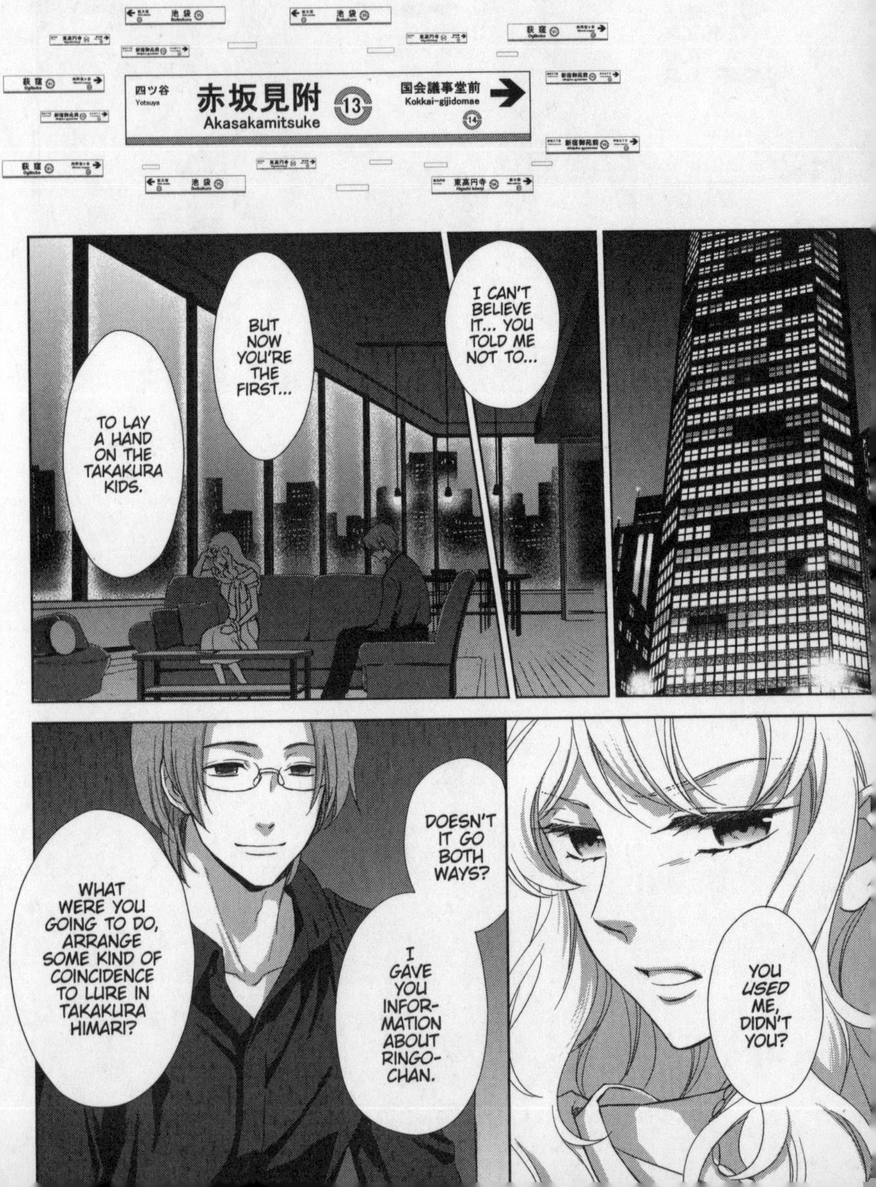
四ツ谷
Yotsuya
赤坂見附
Akasakamitsuke
13
国会議事堂前
Kokkai-gijidomae
14
I CAN'T BELIEVE IT... YOU TOLD ME NOT TO...
BUT NOW YOU'RE THE FIRST...
TO LAY A HAND ON THE TAKAKURA KIDS.
YOU USED ME, DIDN'T YOU?
DOESN'T IT GO BOTH WAYS?
I GAVE YOU INFORMATION ABOUT RINGO-CHAN.
WHAT WERE YOU GOING TO DO, ARRANGE SOME KIND OF COINCIDENCE TO LURE IN TAKAKURA HIMARI?

I KNEW WE COULDN'T BECOME A REAL FAMILY.

THIS FAMILY'S A SHAM. WE ONLY USED EACH OTHER FOR MOMOKA'S SAKE.

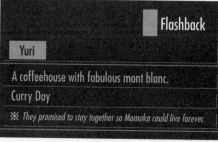

Flashback

Yuri

A coffeehouse with fabulous mont blanc.

Curry Day

※ They promised to stay together so Momoka could live forever.

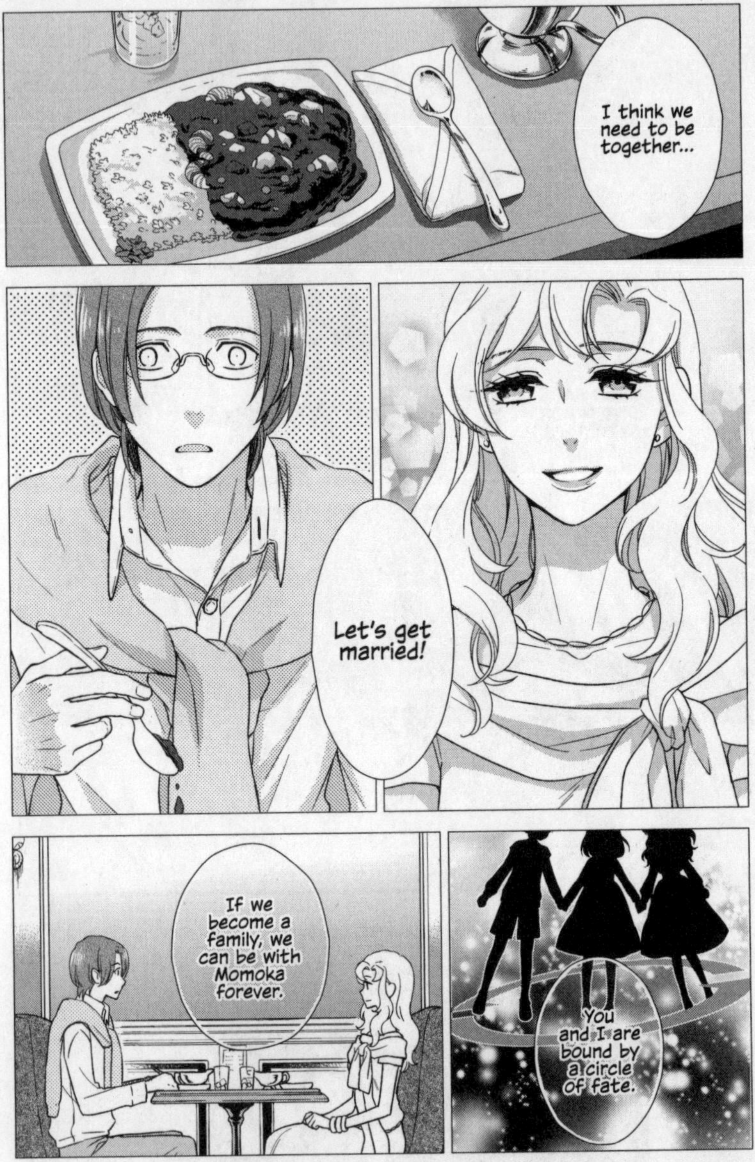
I think we need to be together...
Let's get married!
You and I are bound by a circle of fate.
If we become a family, we can be with Momoka forever.

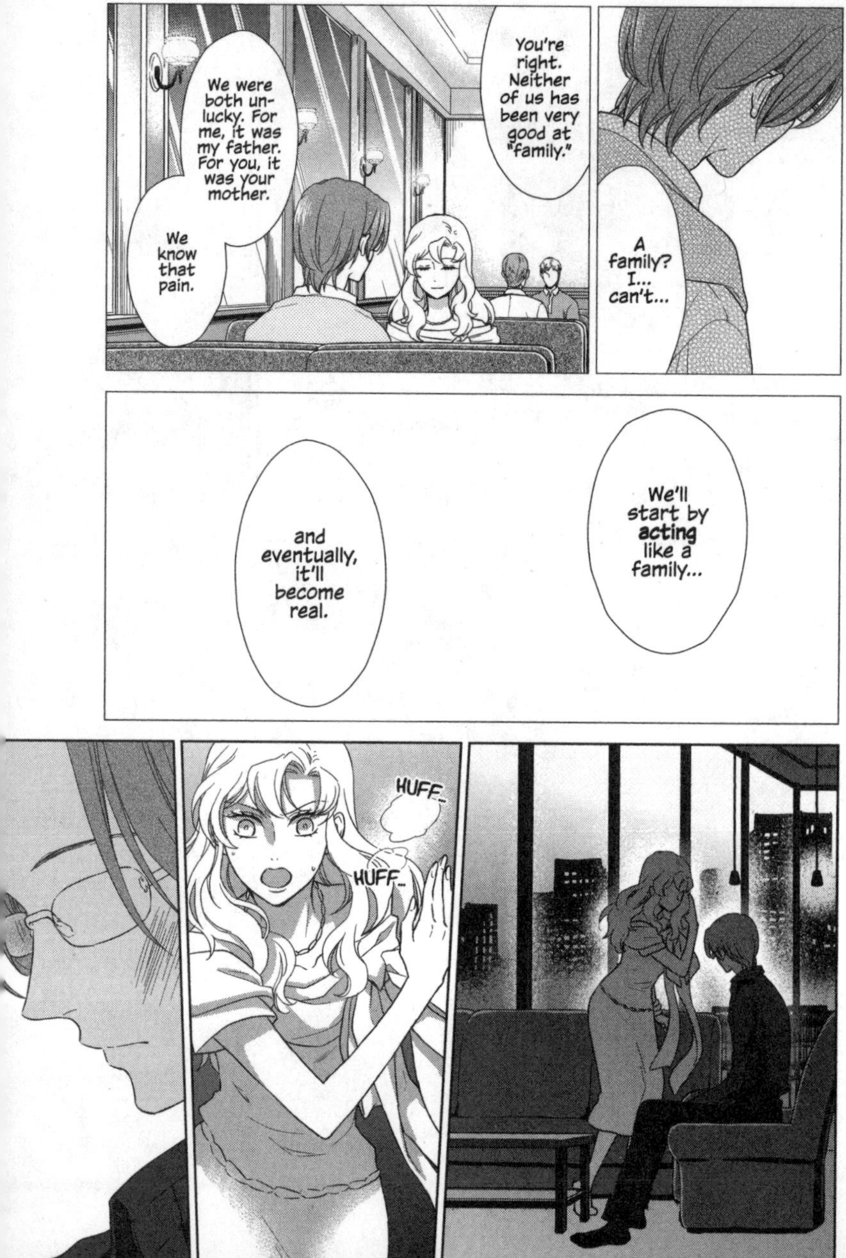
A family? I... can't...
You're right. Neither of us has been very good at "family."
We were both un-lucky. For me, it was my father. For you, it was your mother.
We know that pain.
We'll start by **acting** like a family...
and eventually, it'll become real.
HUFF...
HUFF...

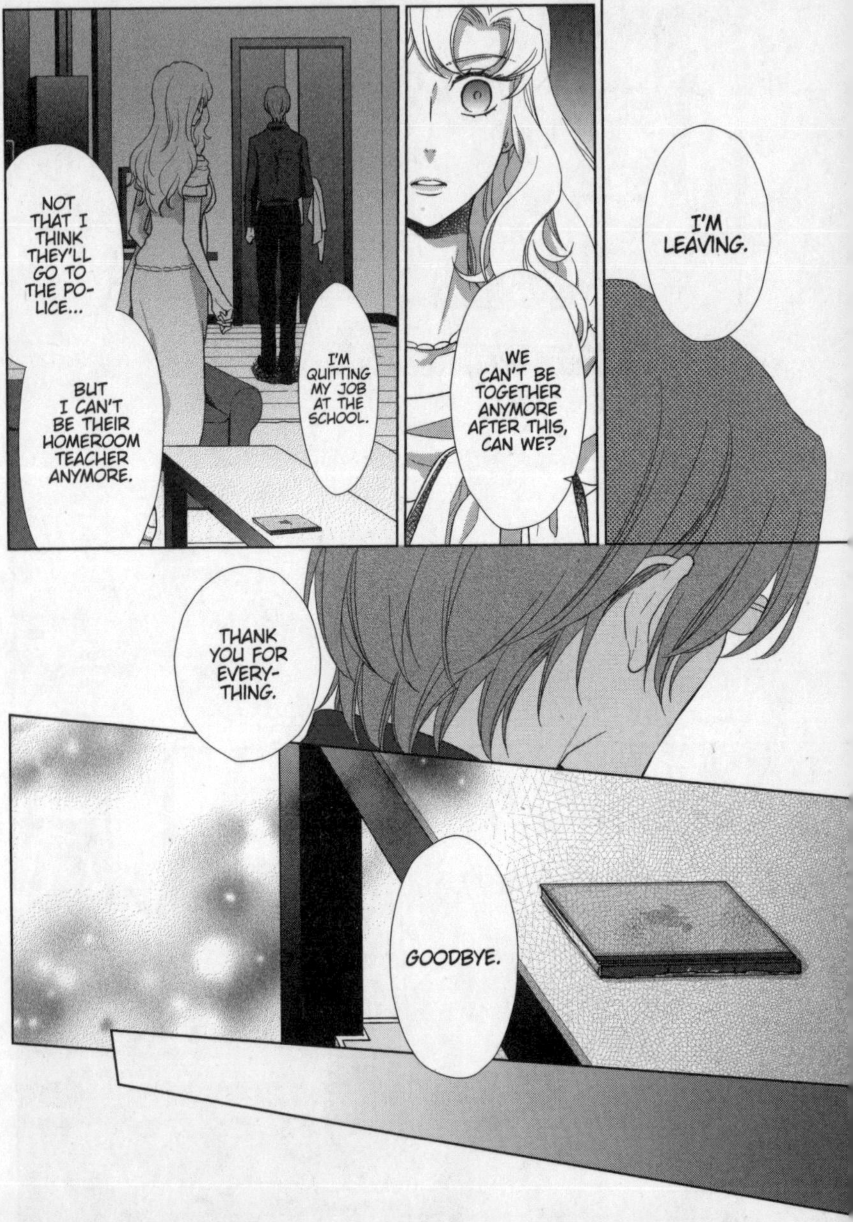
I'M LEAVING.
WE CAN'T BE TOGETHER ANYMORE AFTER THIS, CAN WE?
NOT THAT I THINK THEY'LL GO TO THE PO-LICE...
BUT I CAN'T BE THEIR HOMEROOM TEACHER ANYMORE.
I'M QUITTING MY JOB AT THE SCHOOL.
THANK YOU FOR EVERY-THING.
GOODBYE.

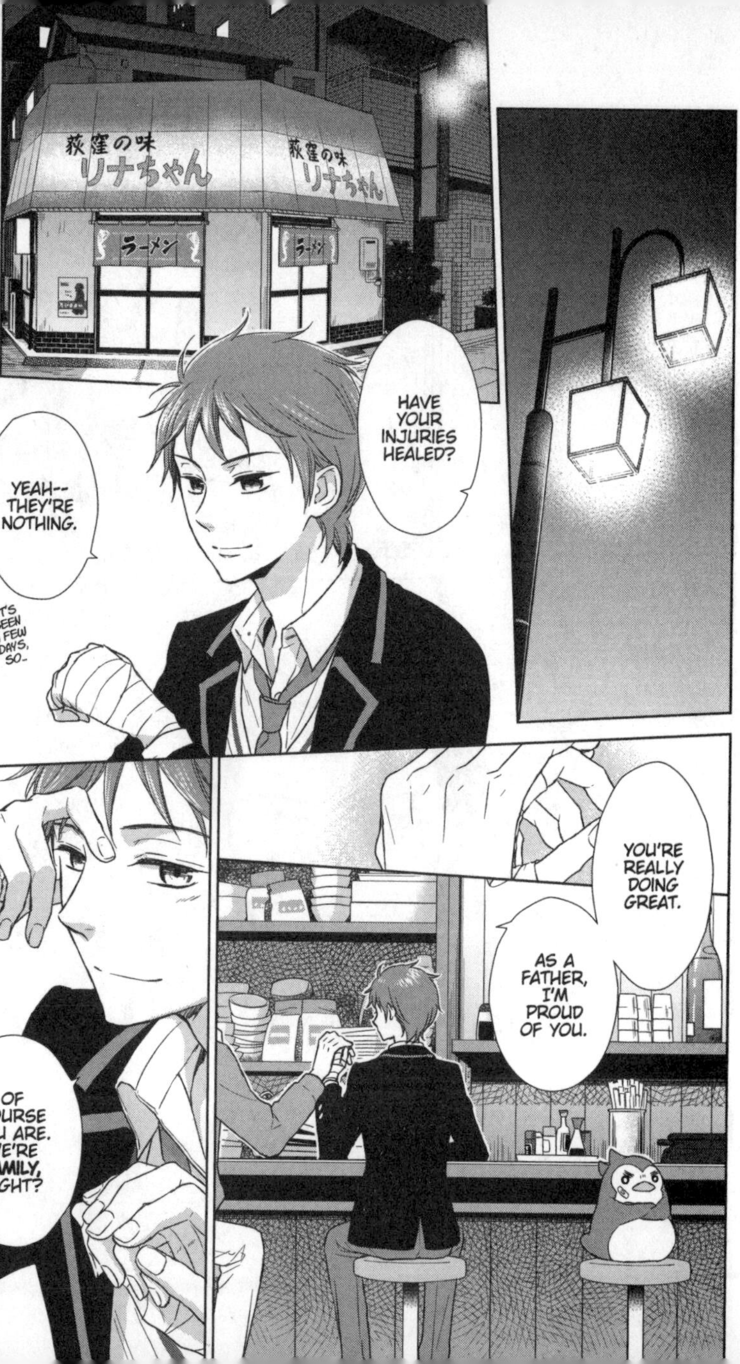
荻窪の味
リナちゃん
荻窪の味
リナちゃん
ラーメン
ラーメン
HAVE YOUR INJURIES HEALED?
YEAH-- THEY'RE NOTHING.
IT'S BEEN A FEW DAYS, SO--
YOU'RE REALLY DOING GREAT.
AS A FATHER, I'M PROUD OF YOU.
OF COURSE YOU ARE. WE'RE **FAMILY**, RIGHT?

Signs: The Flavor of Ogikubo, Rina-chan, Ramen

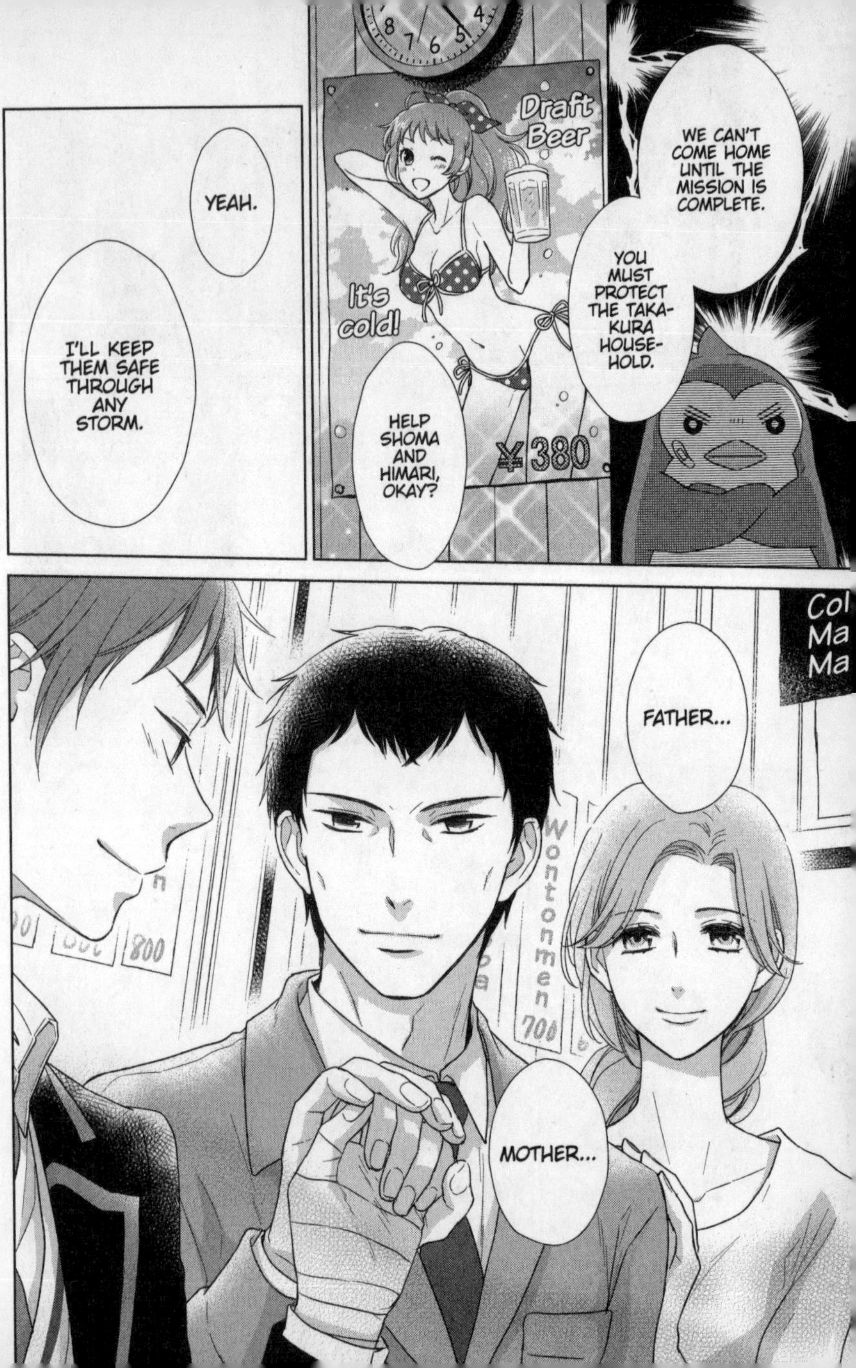
WE CAN'T COME HOME UNTIL THE MISSION IS COMPLETE.
YOU MUST PROTECT THE TAKAKURA HOUSEHOLD.
Draft Beer
It's cold!
¥380
HELP SHOMA AND HIMARI, OKAY?
YEAH.
I'LL KEEP THEM SAFE THROUGH ANY STORM.
FATHER...
Wontonmen 700
800
MOTHER...

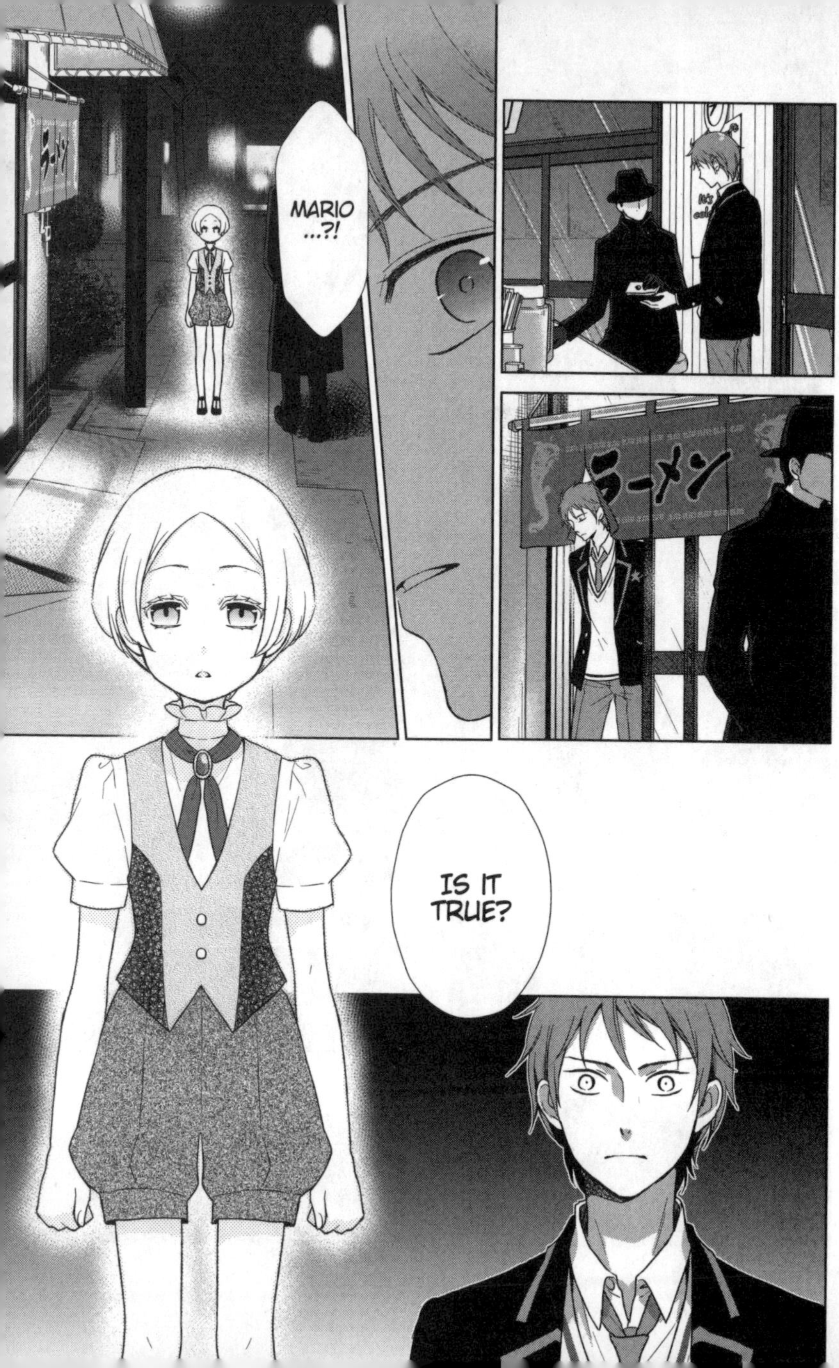
ラーメン
MARIO ...?!
IS IT TRUE?

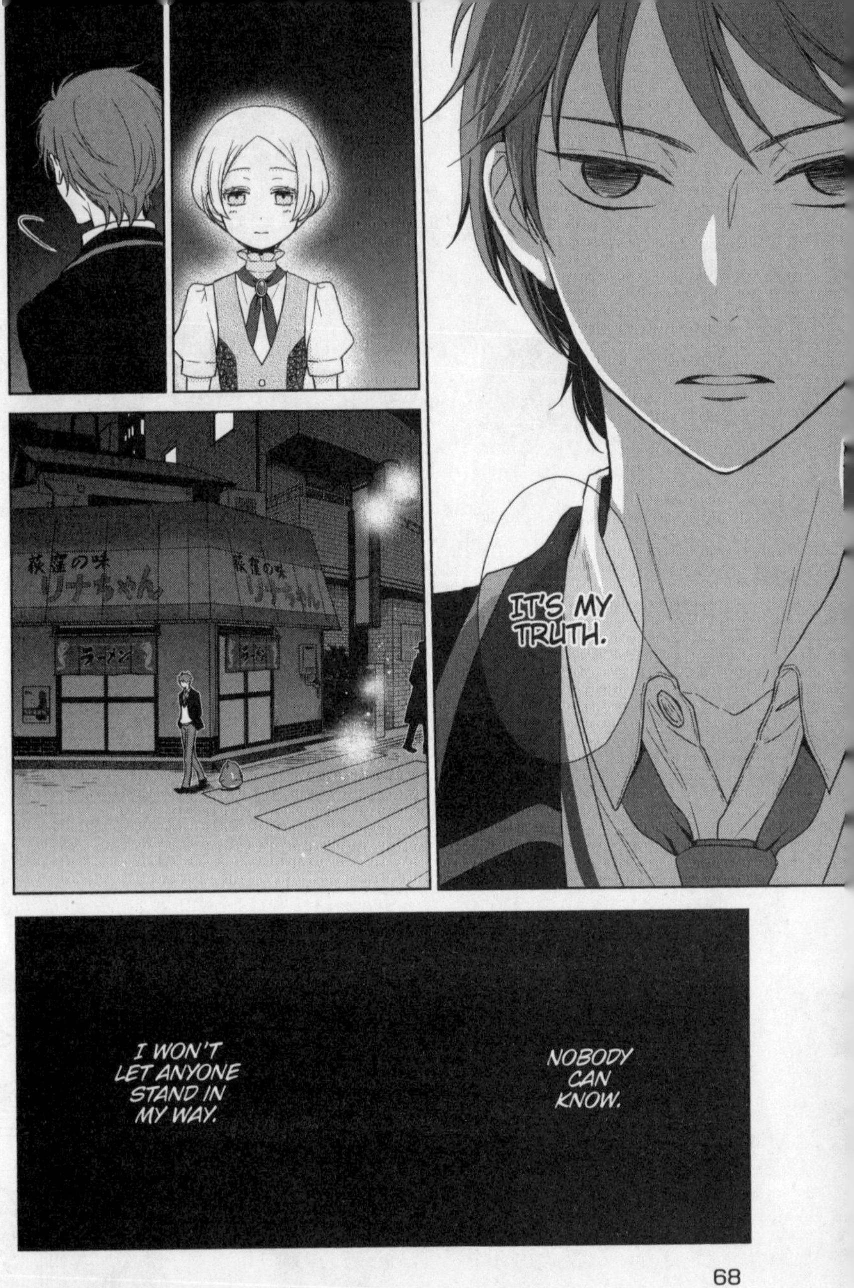
IT'S MY TRUTH.
荻窪の味
リナちゃん
ラーメン
NOBODY CAN KNOW.
I WON'T LET ANYONE STAND IN MY WAY.

23 23RD STATION

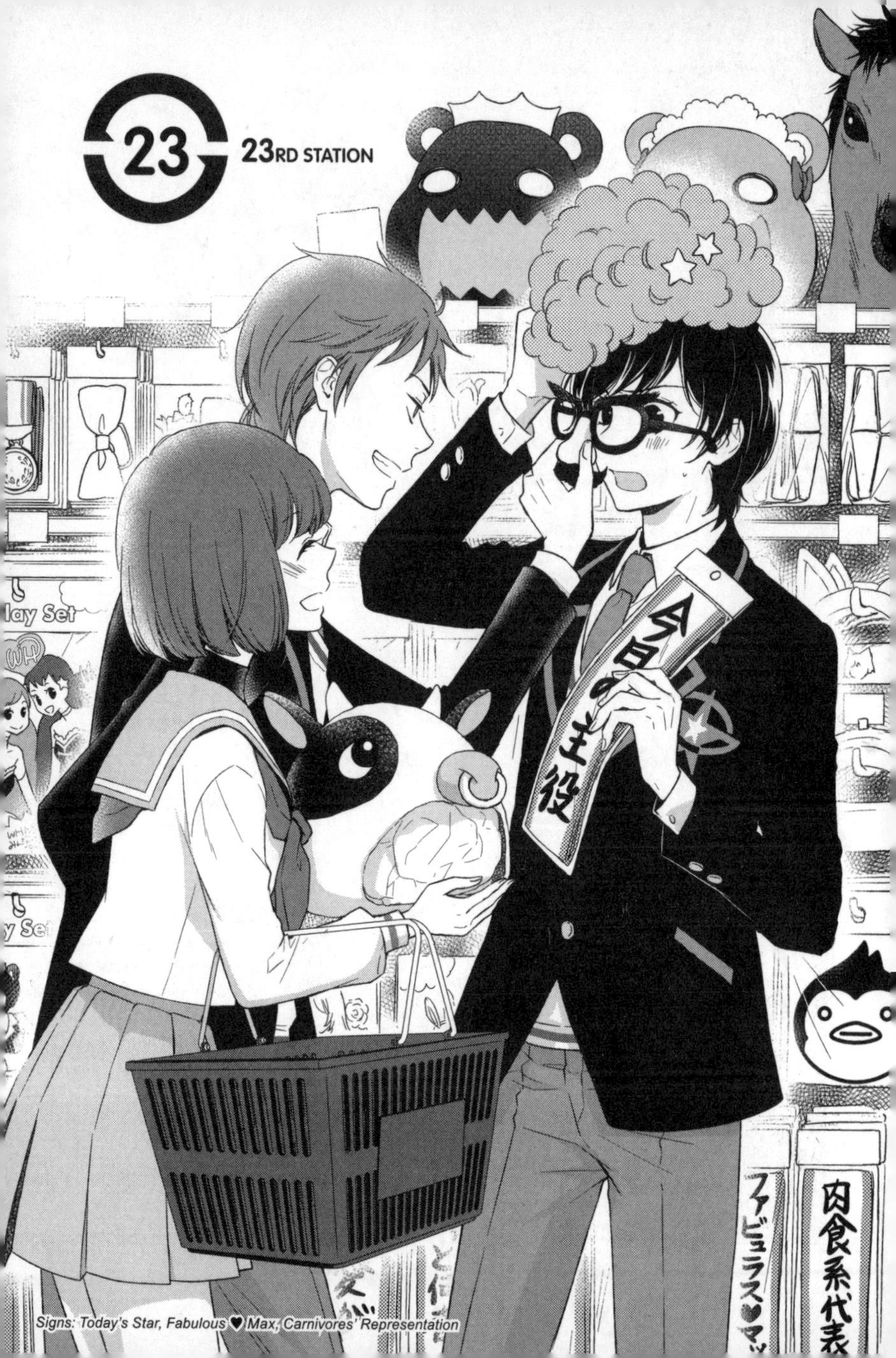
今日の主役
ファビュラス♥マッ
肉食系代表
lay Set
y Set

Signs: Today's Star, Fabulous ♥ Max, Carnivores' Representation

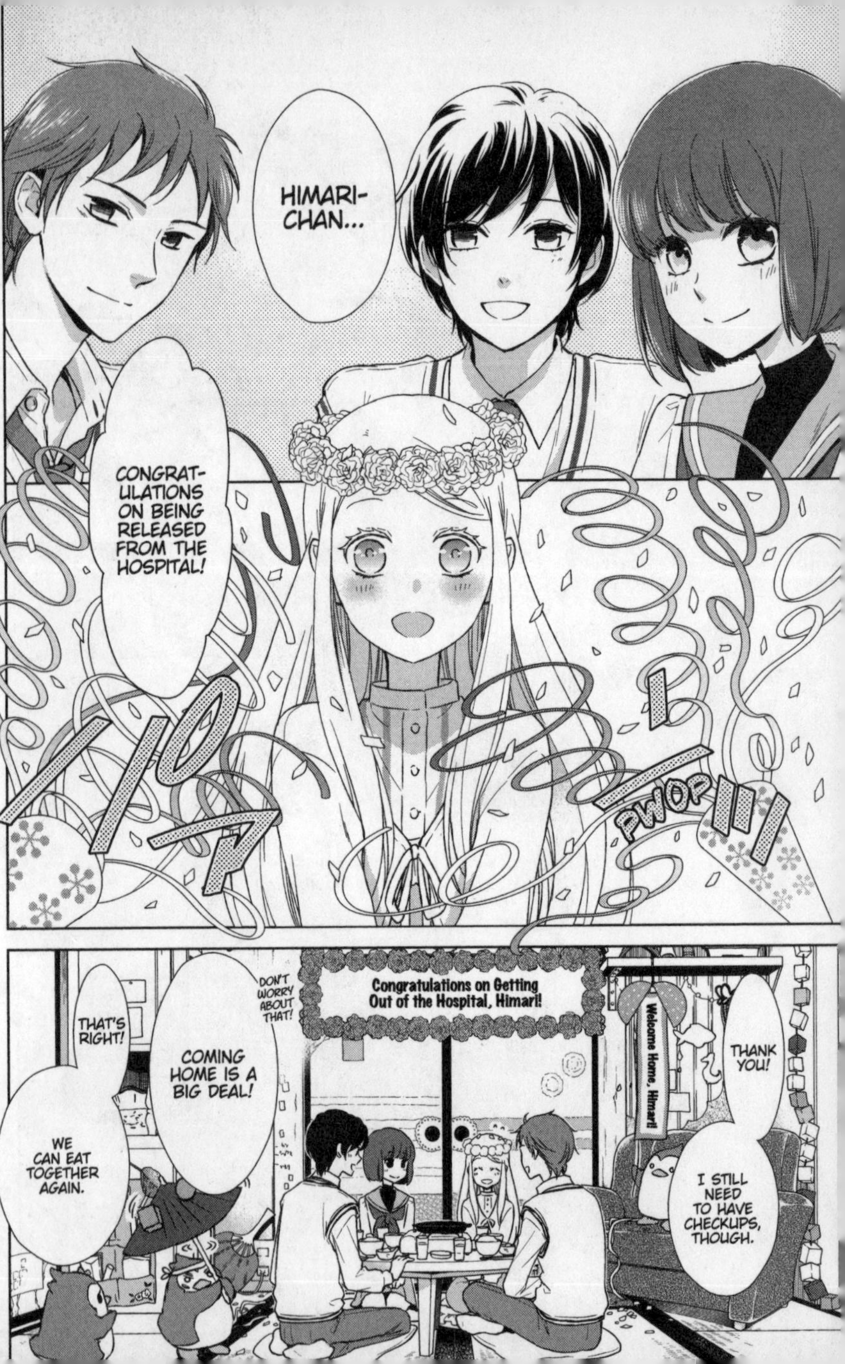
HIMARI-CHAN...
CONGRAT-ULATIONS ON BEING RELEASED FROM THE HOSPITAL!
PWOP!!!
THANK YOU!
I STILL NEED TO HAVE CHECKUPS, THOUGH.
Welcome Home, Himari!
Congratulations on Getting Out of the Hospital, Himari!
DON'T WORRY ABOUT THAT!
COMING HOME IS A BIG DEAL!
THAT'S RIGHT!
WE CAN EAT TOGETHER AGAIN.

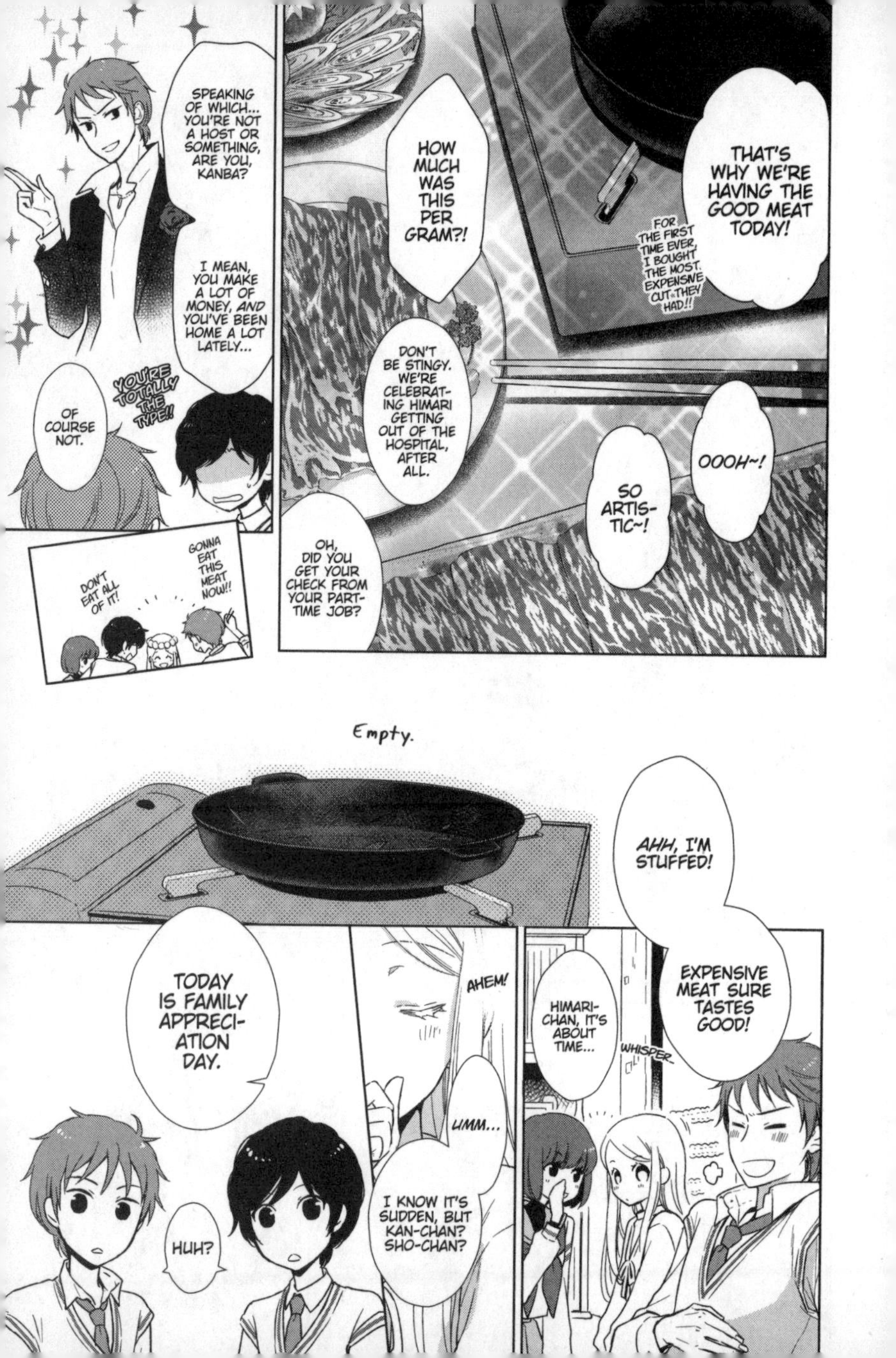
THAT'S WHY WE'RE HAVING THE GOOD MEAT TODAY!
FOR THE FIRST TIME EVER, I BOUGHT THE MOST EXPENSIVE CUT THEY HAD!!
HOW MUCH WAS THIS PER GRAM?!
OOOH~!
SO ARTISTIC~!
DON'T BE STINGY. WE'RE CELEBRATING HIMARI GETTING OUT OF THE HOSPITAL, AFTER ALL.
OH, DID YOU GET YOUR CHECK FROM YOUR PART-TIME JOB?
SPEAKING OF WHICH... YOU'RE NOT A HOST OR SOMETHING, ARE YOU, KANBA?
I MEAN, YOU MAKE A LOT OF MONEY, AND YOU'VE BEEN HOME A LOT LATELY...
OF COURSE NOT.
YOU'RE TOTALLY THE TYPE!!
GONNA EAT THIS MEAT NOW!!
DON'T EAT ALL OF IT!
Empty.
AHH, I'M STUFFED!
EXPENSIVE MEAT SURE TASTES GOOD!
HIMARI-CHAN, IT'S ABOUT TIME...
WHISPER
AHEM!
UMM...
I KNOW IT'S SUDDEN, BUT KAN-CHAN? SHO-CHAN?
TODAY IS FAMILY APPRECIATION DAY.
HUH?

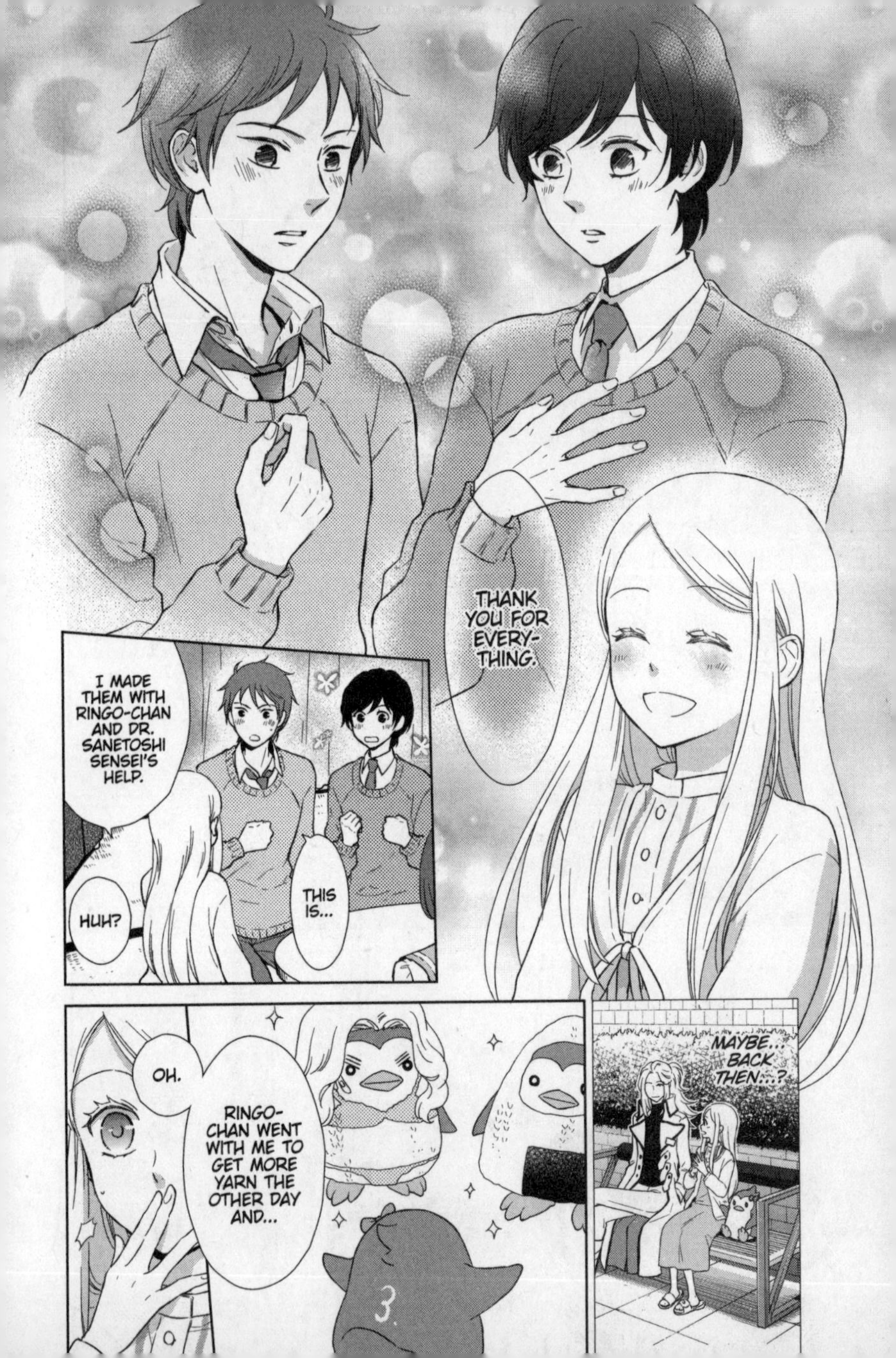
THANK YOU FOR EVERY-THING.
I MADE THEM WITH RINGO-CHAN AND DR. SANETOSHI SENSEI'S HELP.
THIS IS...
HUH?
MAYBE... BACK THEN...?
OH.
RINGO-CHAN WENT WITH ME TO GET MORE YARN THE OTHER DAY AND...

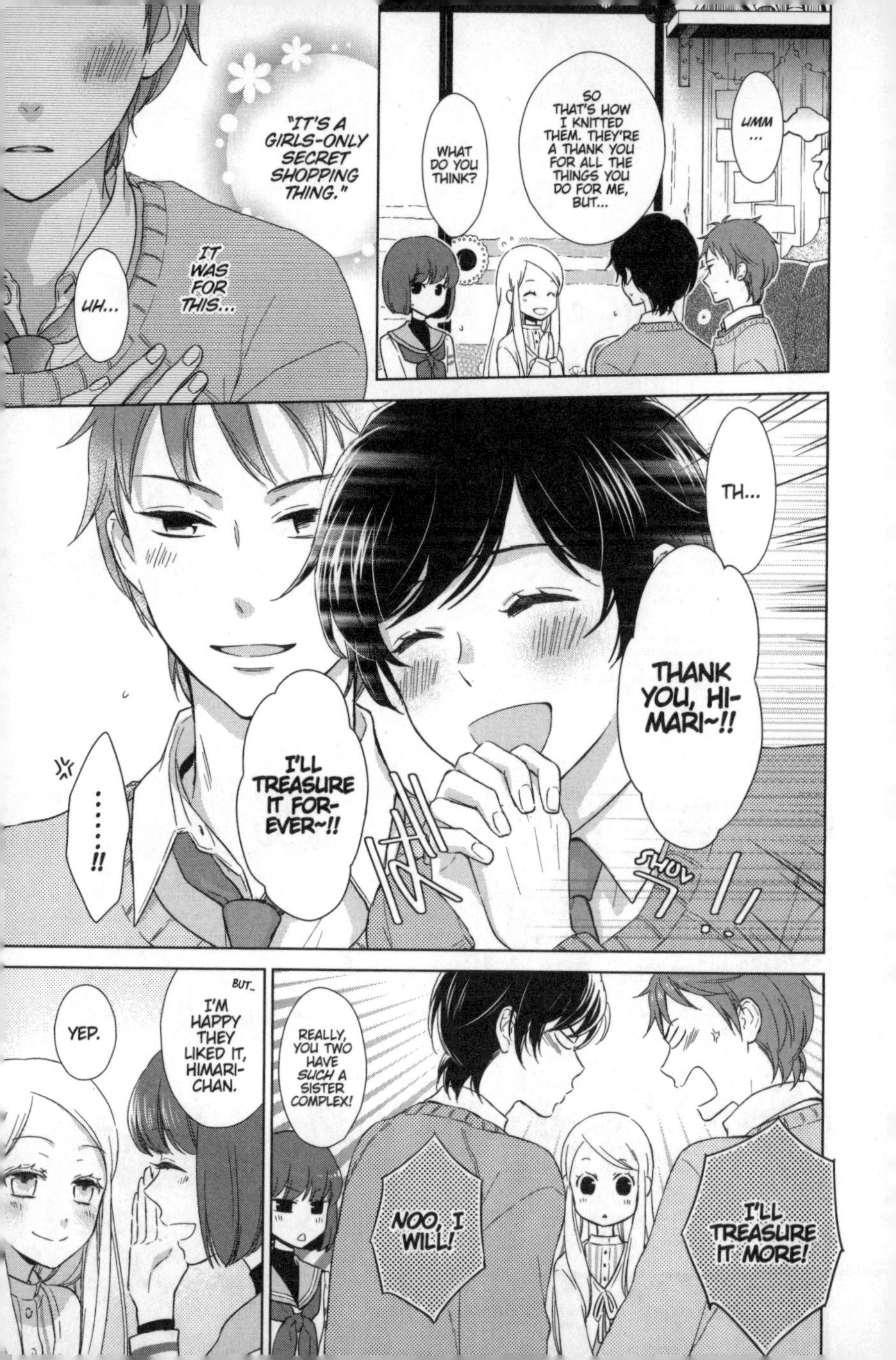
UMM...
SO THAT'S HOW I KNITTED THEM. THEY'RE A THANK YOU FOR ALL THE THINGS YOU DO FOR ME, BUT...
WHAT DO YOU THINK?
"IT'S A GIRLS-ONLY SECRET SHOPPING THING."
IT WAS FOR THIS...
UH...
TH...
THANK YOU, HI-
MARI~!!
SHUV
I'LL TREASURE IT FOR-
EVER~!!
......!!
I'LL TREASURE IT MORE!
NOO, I WILL!
REALLY, YOU TWO HAVE SUCH A SISTER COMPLEX!
BUT...
I'M HAPPY THEY LIKED IT, HIMARI-CHAN.
YEP.

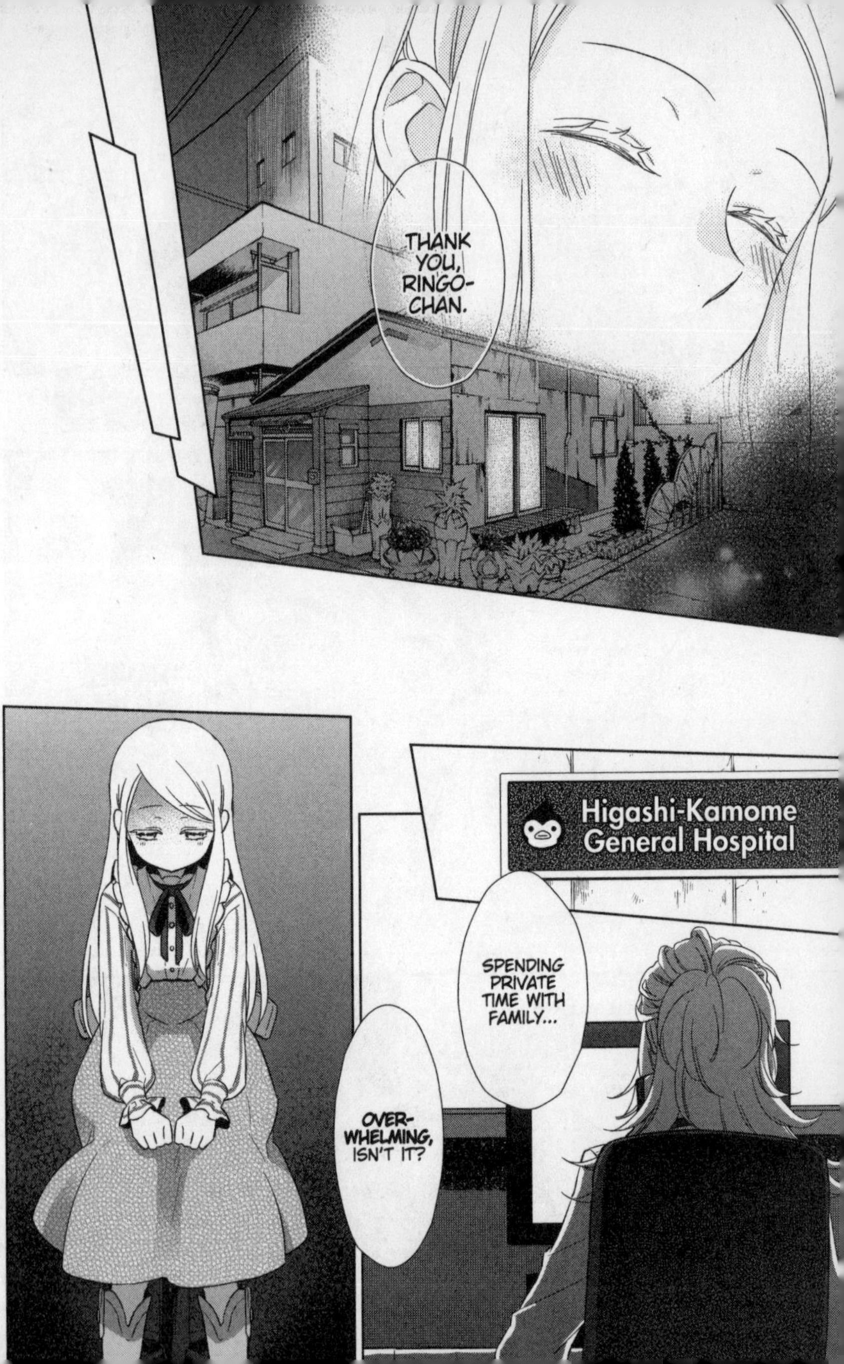
THANK YOU, RINGO-CHAN.
Higashi-Kamome General Hospital
SPENDING PRIVATE TIME WITH FAMILY...
OVER-WHELMING, ISN'T IT?

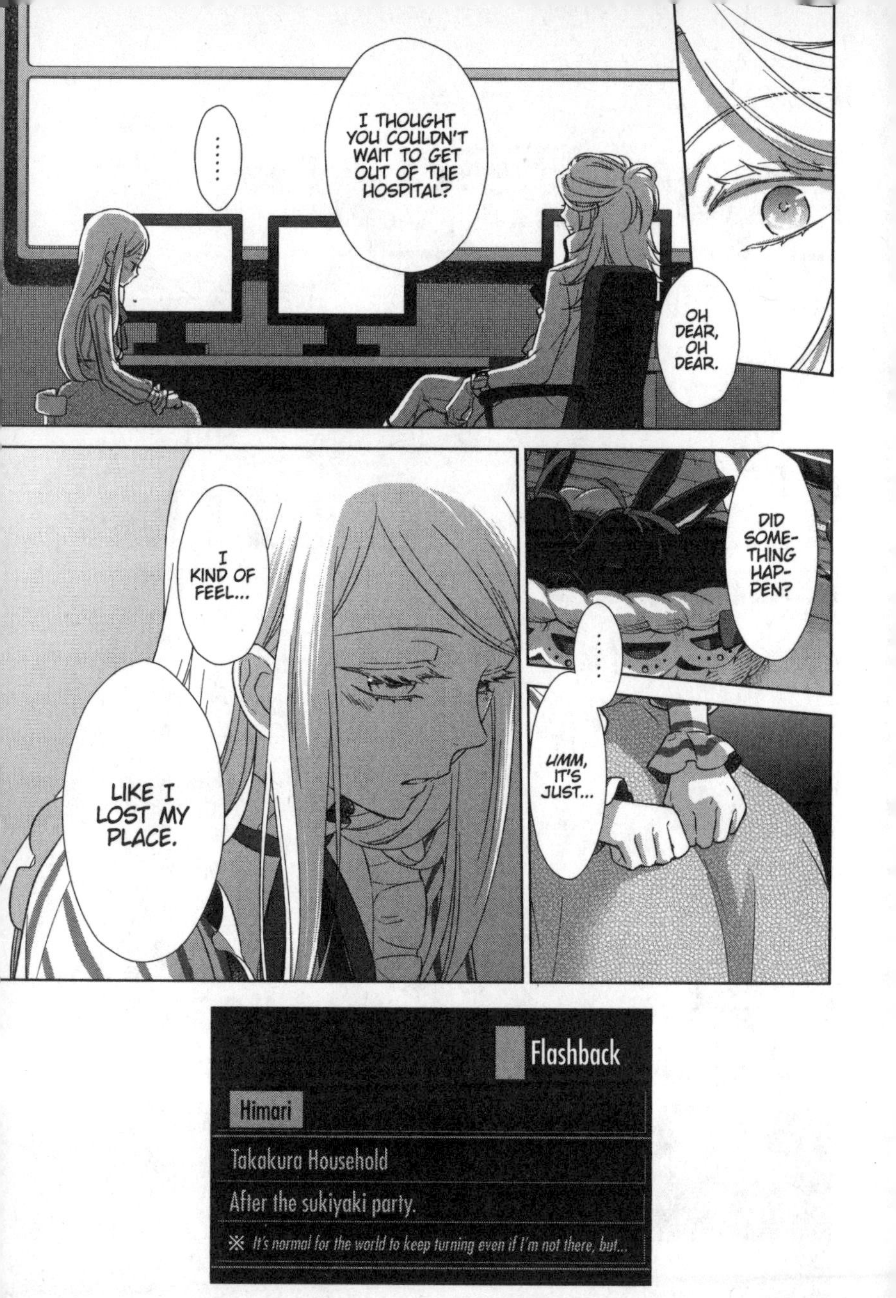
OH DEAR, OH DEAR.
I THOUGHT YOU COULDN'T WAIT TO GET OUT OF THE HOSPITAL?
......
DID SOMETHING HAPPEN?
......
UMM, IT'S JUST...
I KIND OF FEEL...
LIKE I LOST MY PLACE.

Flashback

Himari

Takakura Household

After the sukiyaki party.

※ *It's normal for the world to keep turning even if I'm not there, but...*

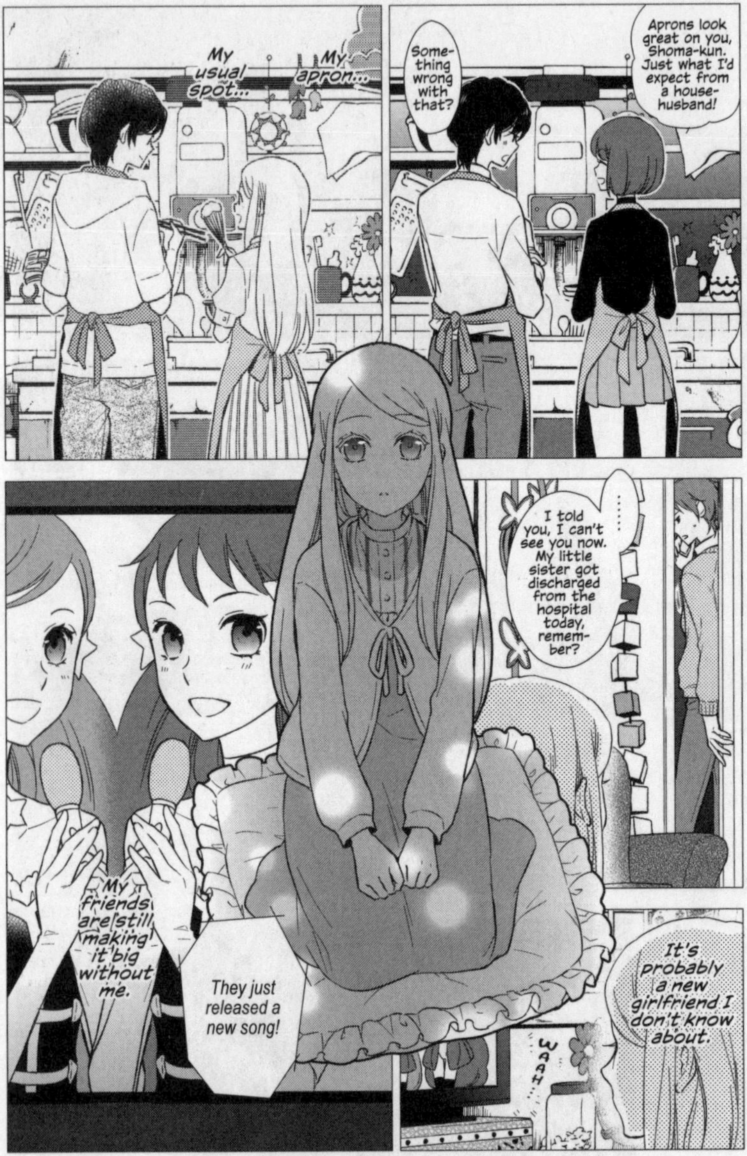
Aprons look great on you, Shoma-kun. Just what I'd expect from a house-husband!
Some-thing wrong with that?
My apron...
My usual spot...
......
I told you, I can't see you now. My little sister got discharged from the hospital today, remember?
It's probably a new girlfriend I don't know about.
WAAH...
My friends are still making it big without me.
They just released a new song!

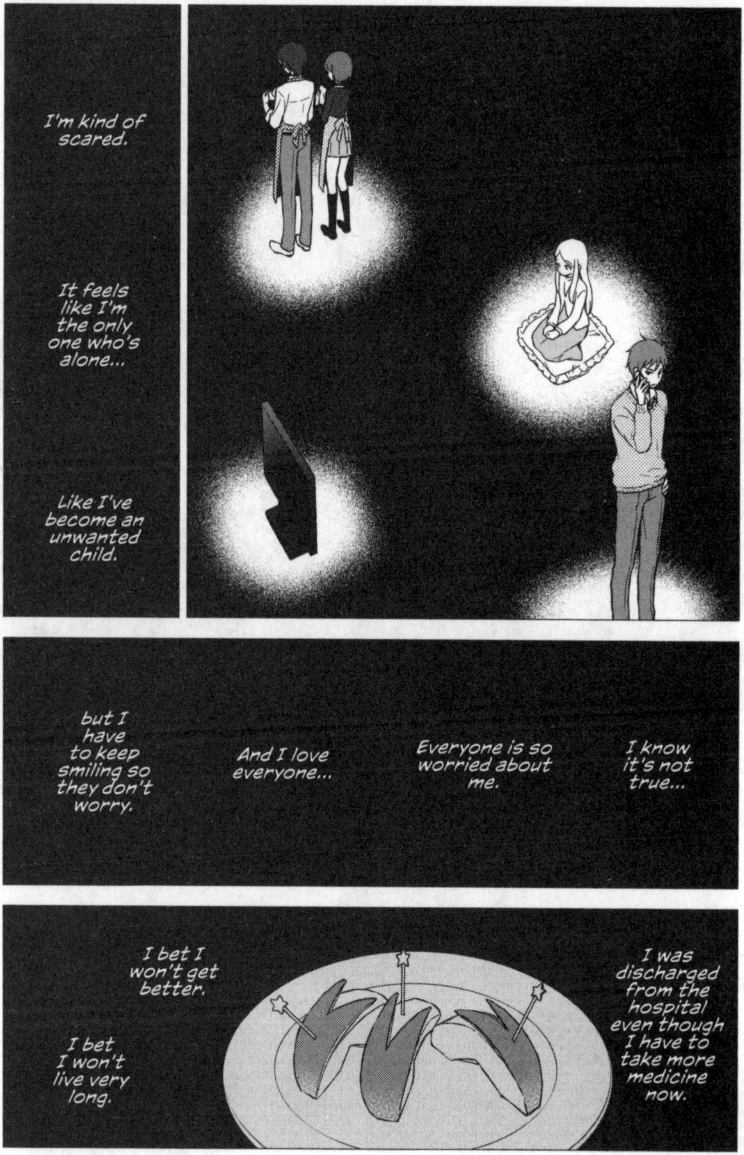
I'm kind of scared.
It feels like I'm the only one who's alone...
Like I've become an unwanted child.
I know it's not true...
Everyone is so worried about me.
And I love everyone...
but I have to keep smiling so they don't worry.
I was discharged from the hospital even though I have to take more medicine now.
I bet I won't get better.
I bet I won't live very long.

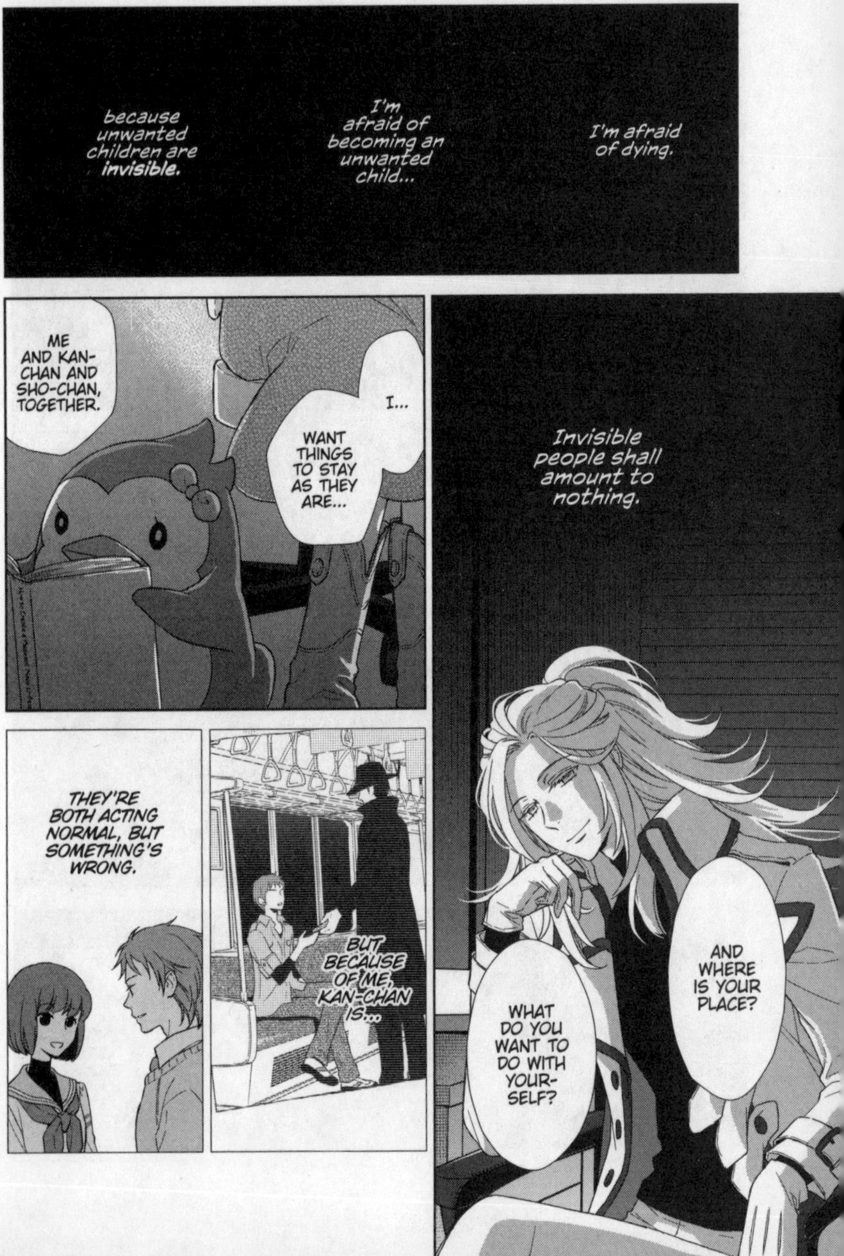
I'm afraid of dying.
I'm afraid of becoming an unwanted child...
because unwanted children are **invisible.**
Invisible people shall amount to nothing.
AND WHERE IS YOUR PLACE?
WHAT DO YOU WANT TO DO WITH YOUR-SELF?
I...
WANT THINGS TO STAY AS THEY ARE...
ME AND KAN-CHAN AND SHO-CHAN, TOGETHER.
BUT BECAUSE OF ME, KAN-CHAN IS...
THEY'RE BOTH ACTING NORMAL, BUT SOMETHING'S WRONG.

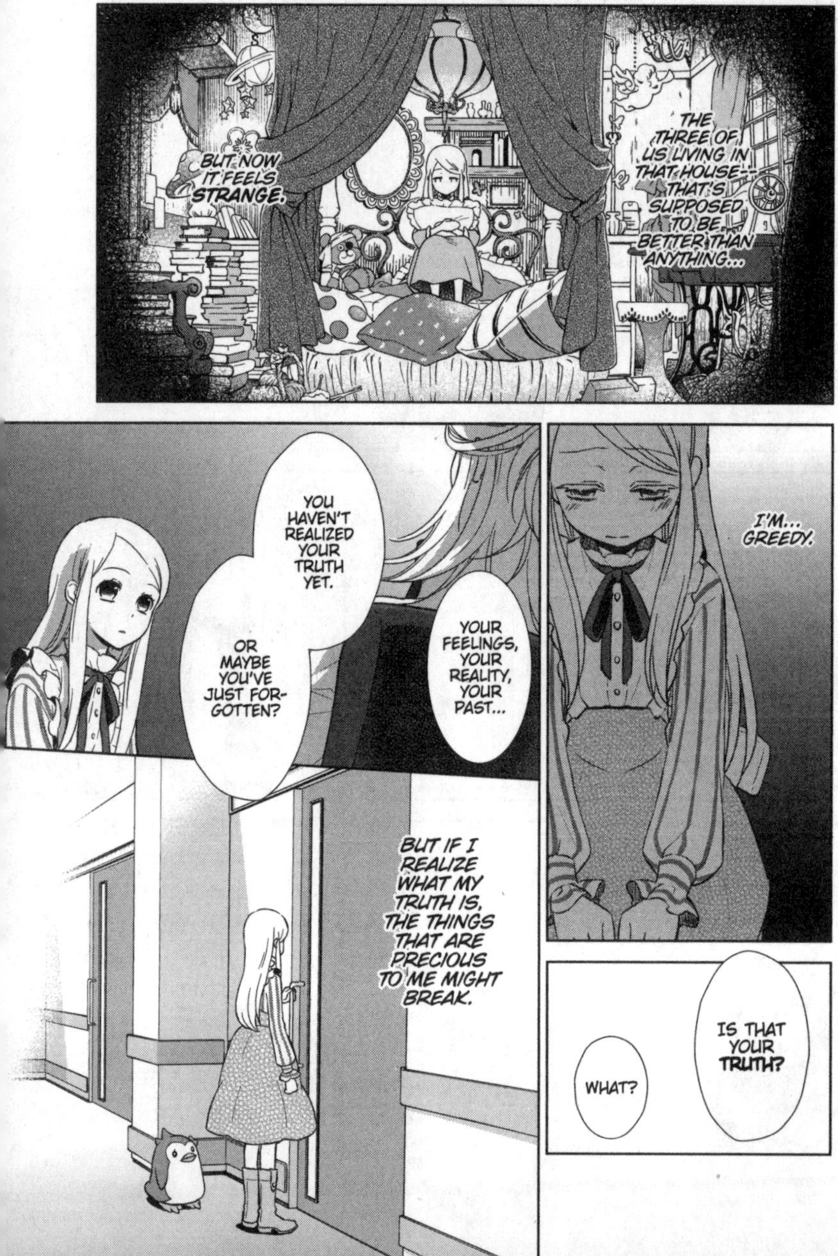
THE THREE OF US LIVING IN THAT HOUSE-- THAT'S SUPPOSED TO BE BETTER THAN ANYTHING...
BUT NOW IT FEELS STRANGE.
I'M... GREEDY.
YOU HAVEN'T REALIZED YOUR TRUTH YET.
YOUR FEELINGS, YOUR REALITY, YOUR PAST...
OR MAYBE YOU'VE JUST FOR-GOTTEN?
IS THAT YOUR TRUTH?
WHAT?
BUT IF I REALIZE WHAT MY TRUTH IS, THE THINGS THAT ARE PRECIOUS TO ME MIGHT BREAK.

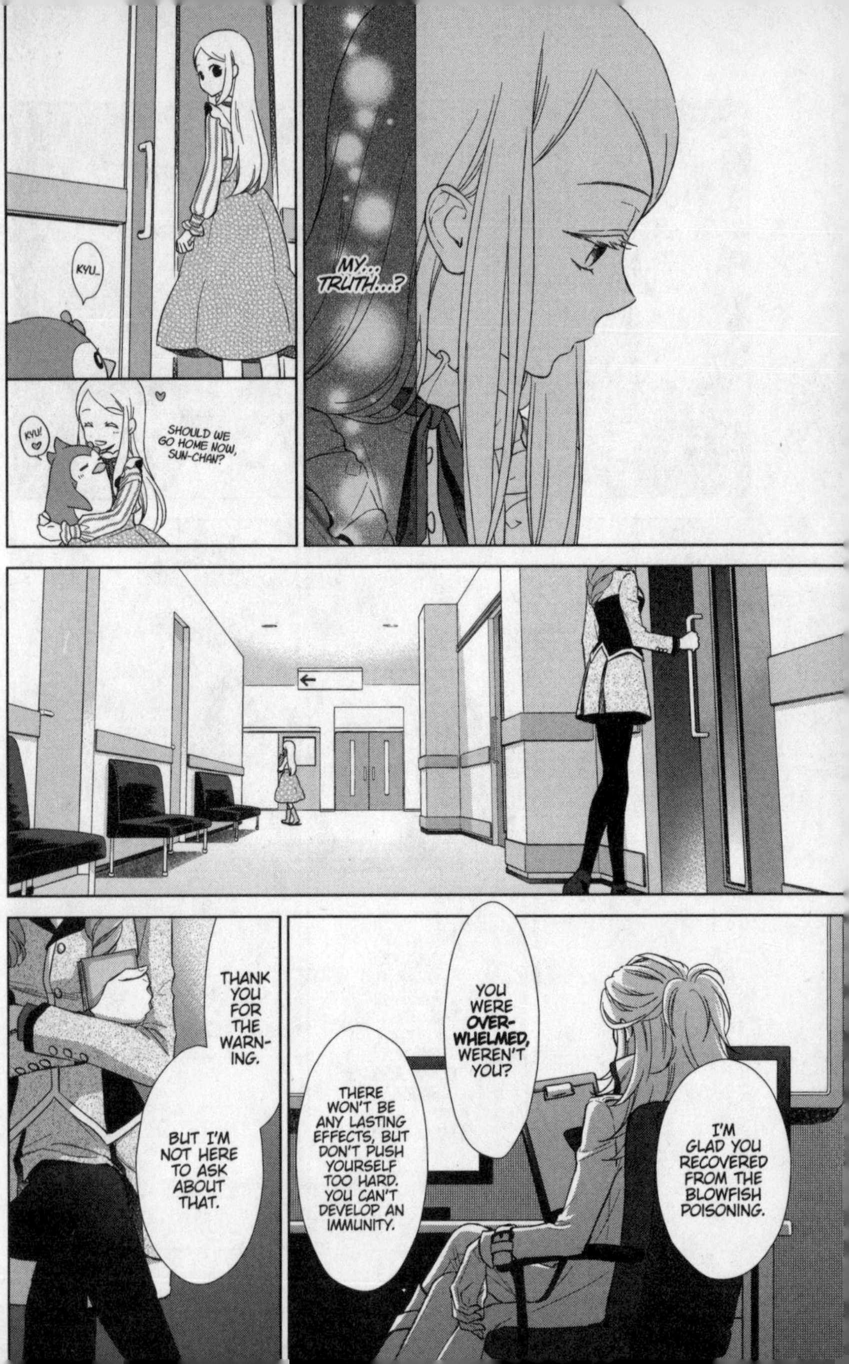
MY... TRUTH...?
KYU...
SHOULD WE GO HOME NOW, SUN-CHAN?
KYU!
I'M GLAD YOU RECOVERED FROM THE BLOWFISH POISONING.
YOU WERE **OVER-WHELMED,** WEREN'T YOU?
THERE WON'T BE ANY LASTING EFFECTS, BUT DON'T PUSH YOURSELF TOO HARD. YOU CAN'T DEVELOP AN IMMUNITY.
THANK YOU FOR THE WARN-ING.
BUT I'M NOT HERE TO ASK ABOUT THAT.

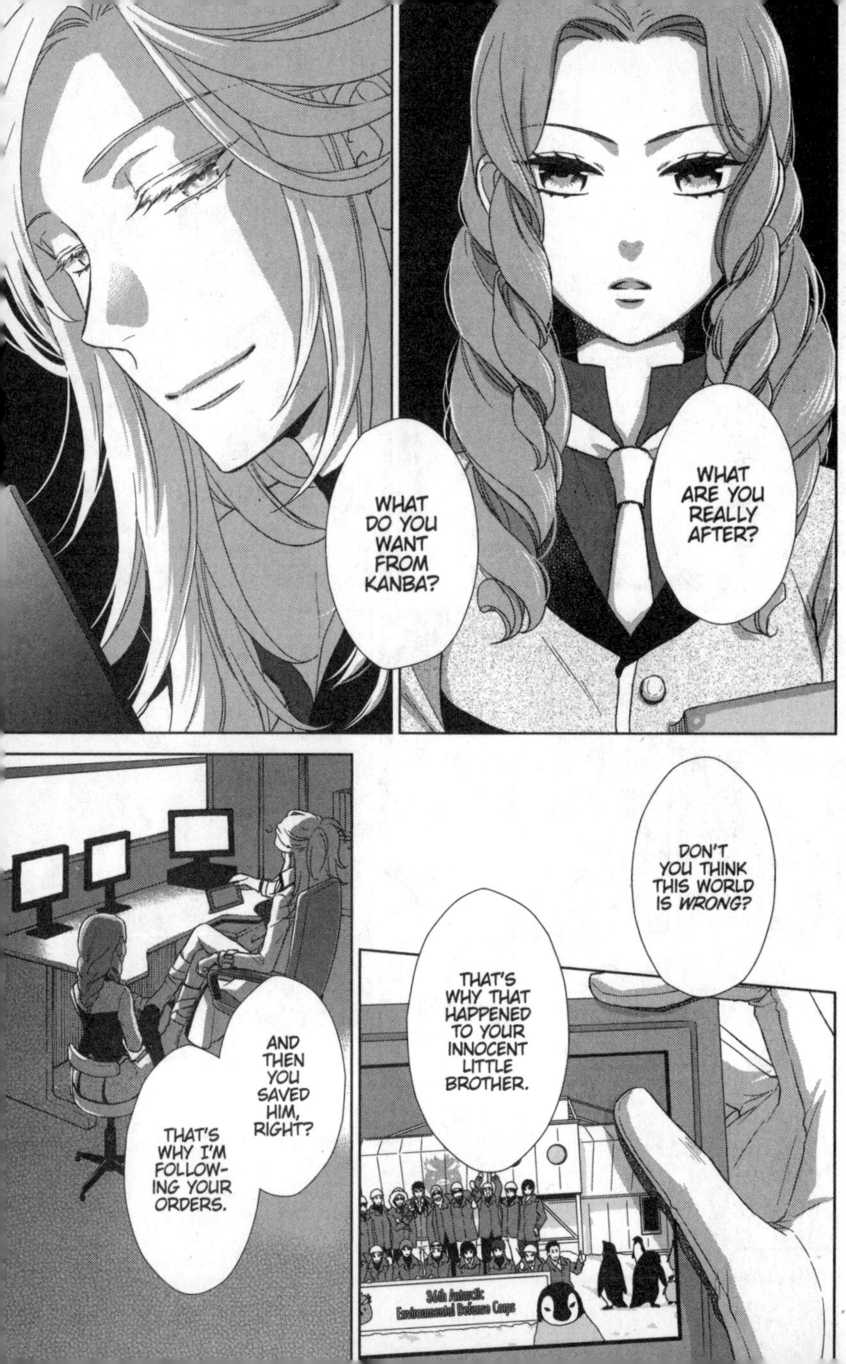
WHAT ARE YOU REALLY AFTER?
WHAT DO YOU WANT FROM KANBA?
DON'T YOU THINK THIS WORLD IS *WRONG*?
THAT'S WHY THAT HAPPENED TO YOUR INNOCENT LITTLE BROTHER.
36th Antarctic Environmental Defense Corps
AND THEN YOU SAVED HIM, RIGHT?
THAT'S WHY I'M FOLLOW-ING YOUR ORDERS.

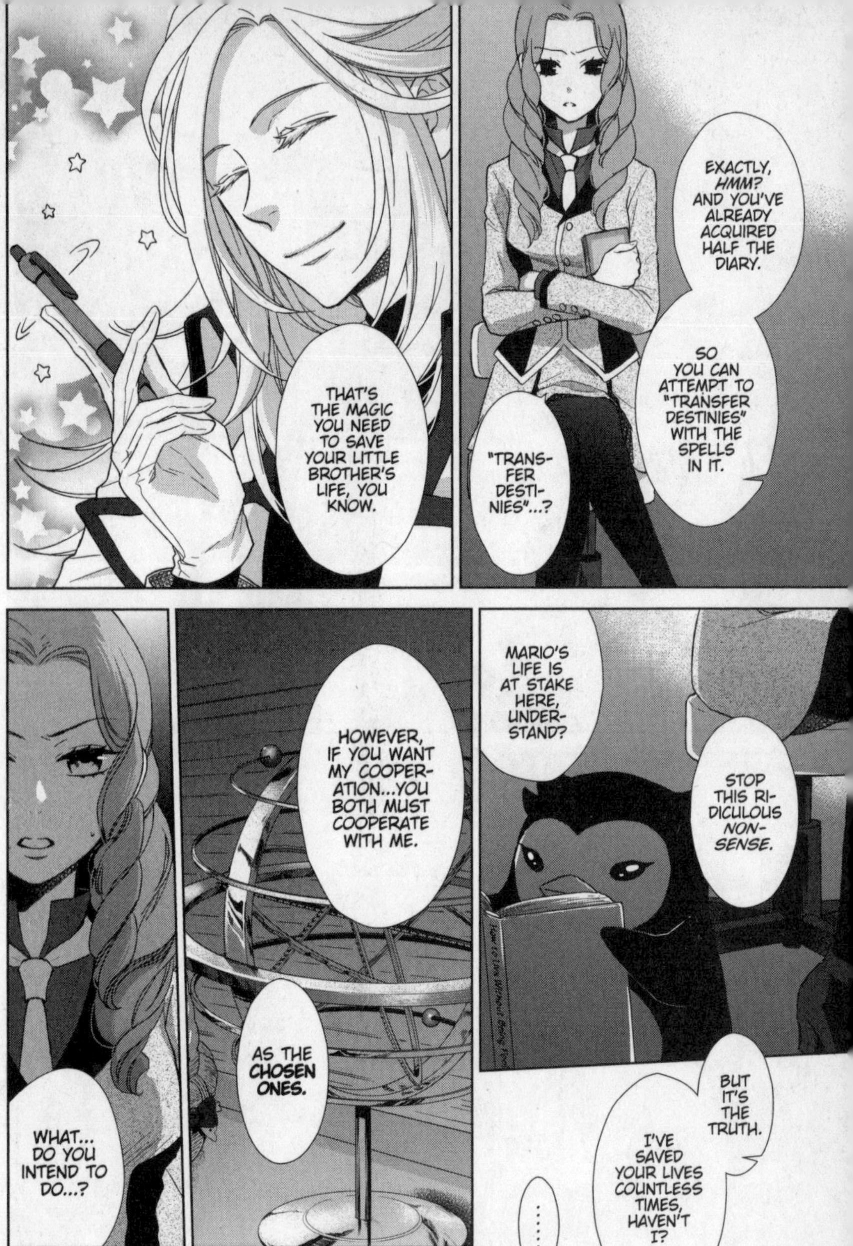
EXACTLY, *HMM?* AND YOU'VE ALREADY ACQUIRED HALF THE DIARY.
SO YOU CAN ATTEMPT TO "TRANSFER DESTINIES" WITH THE SPELLS IN IT.
"TRANS-FER DESTI-NIES"...?
THAT'S THE MAGIC YOU NEED TO SAVE YOUR LITTLE BROTHER'S LIFE, YOU KNOW.
MARIO'S LIFE IS AT STAKE HERE, UNDER-STAND?
STOP THIS RI-DICULOUS *NON-SENSE.*
BUT IT'S THE TRUTH.
I'VE SAVED YOUR LIVES COUNTLESS TIMES, HAVEN'T I?
......
HOWEVER, IF YOU WANT MY COOPER-ATION...YOU BOTH MUST COOPERATE WITH ME.
AS THE **CHOSEN ONES.**
WHAT... DO YOU INTEND TO DO...?

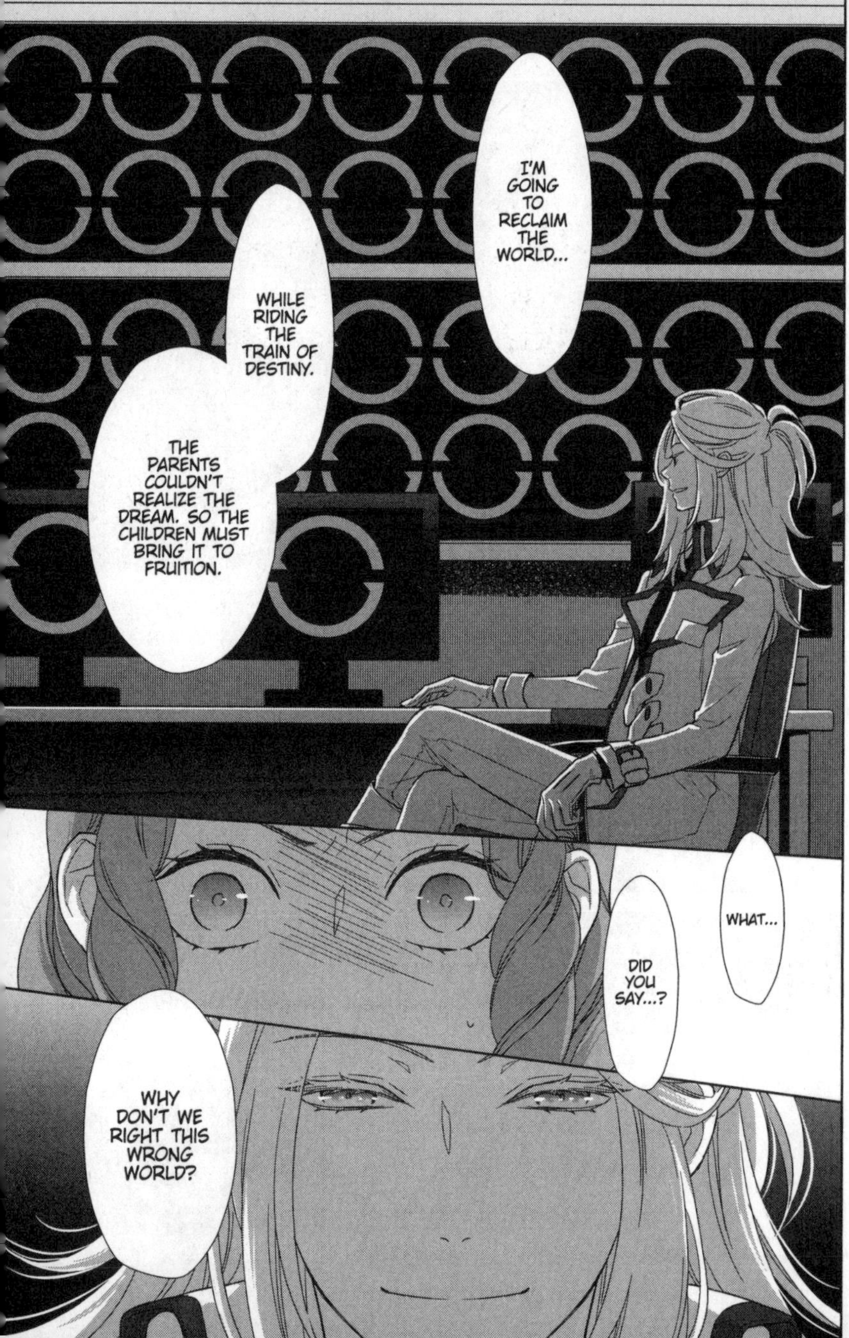
I'M GOING TO RECLAIM THE WORLD...
WHILE RIDING THE TRAIN OF DESTINY.
THE PARENTS COULDN'T REALIZE THE DREAM. SO THE CHILDREN MUST BRING IT TO FRUITION.
WHAT...
DID YOU SAY...?
WHY DON'T WE RIGHT THIS WRONG WORLD?

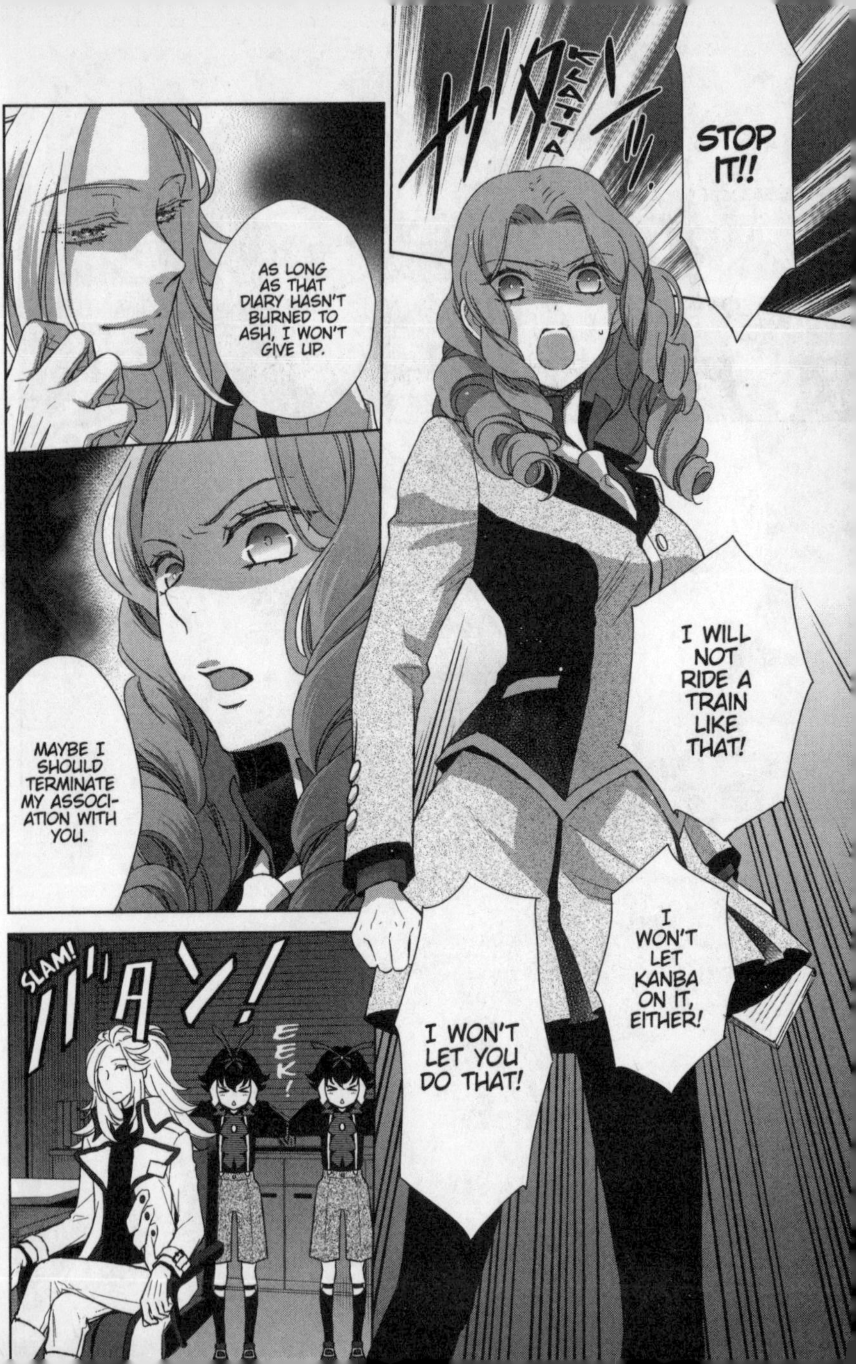
KLATTA
STOP IT!!
I WILL NOT RIDE A TRAIN LIKE THAT!
I WON'T LET KANBA ON IT, EITHER!
I WON'T LET YOU DO THAT!
AS LONG AS THAT DIARY HASN'T BURNED TO ASH, I WON'T GIVE UP.
MAYBE I SHOULD TERMINATE MY ASSOCIATION WITH YOU.
SLAM!
EEK!

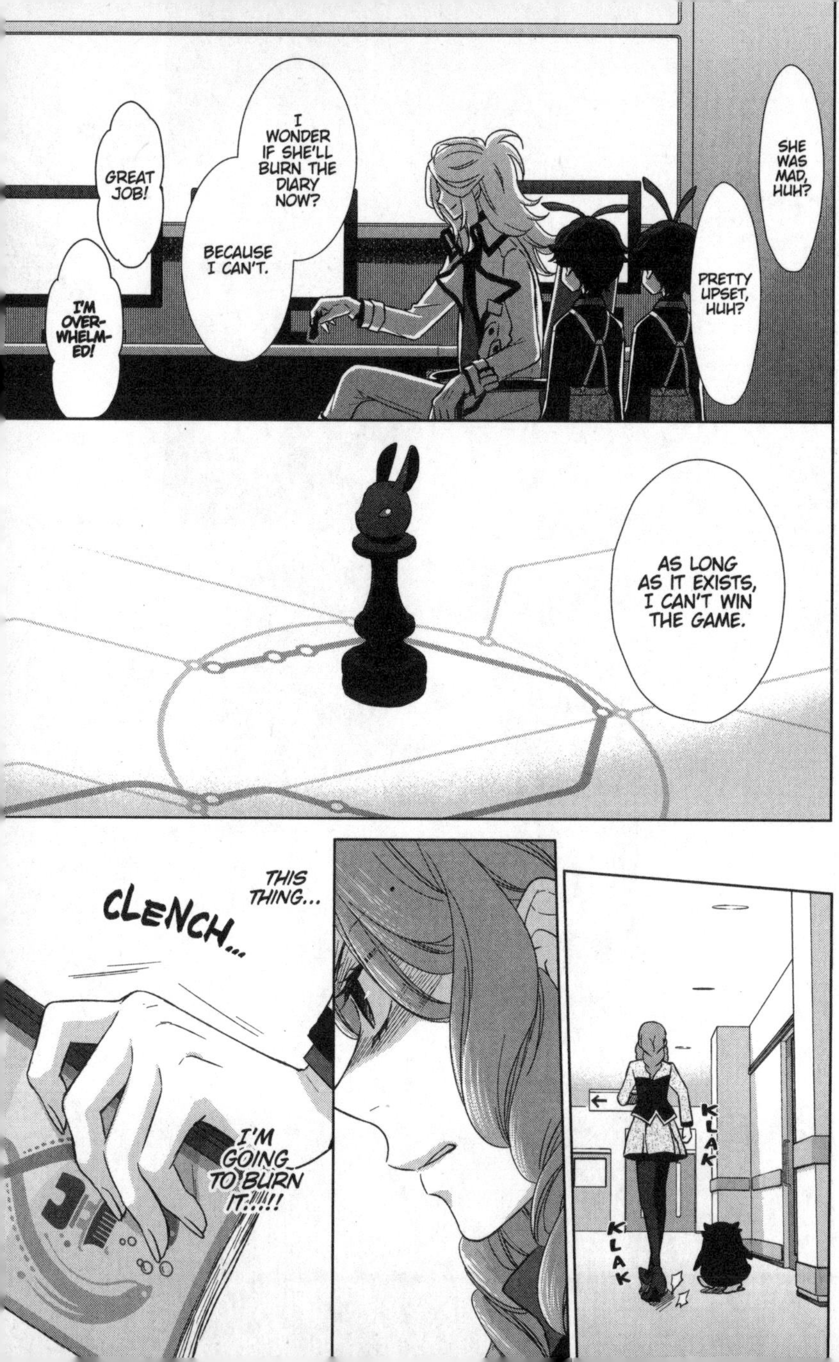
SHE WAS MAD, HUH?
PRETTY UPSET, HUH?
I WONDER IF SHE'LL BURN THE DIARY NOW?
BECAUSE I CAN'T.
GREAT JOB!
I'M OVER-WHELM-ED!
AS LONG AS IT EXISTS, I CAN'T WIN THE GAME.
KLAK
KLAK
THIS THING...
CLENCH...
I'M GOING TO BURN IT!!!!!!

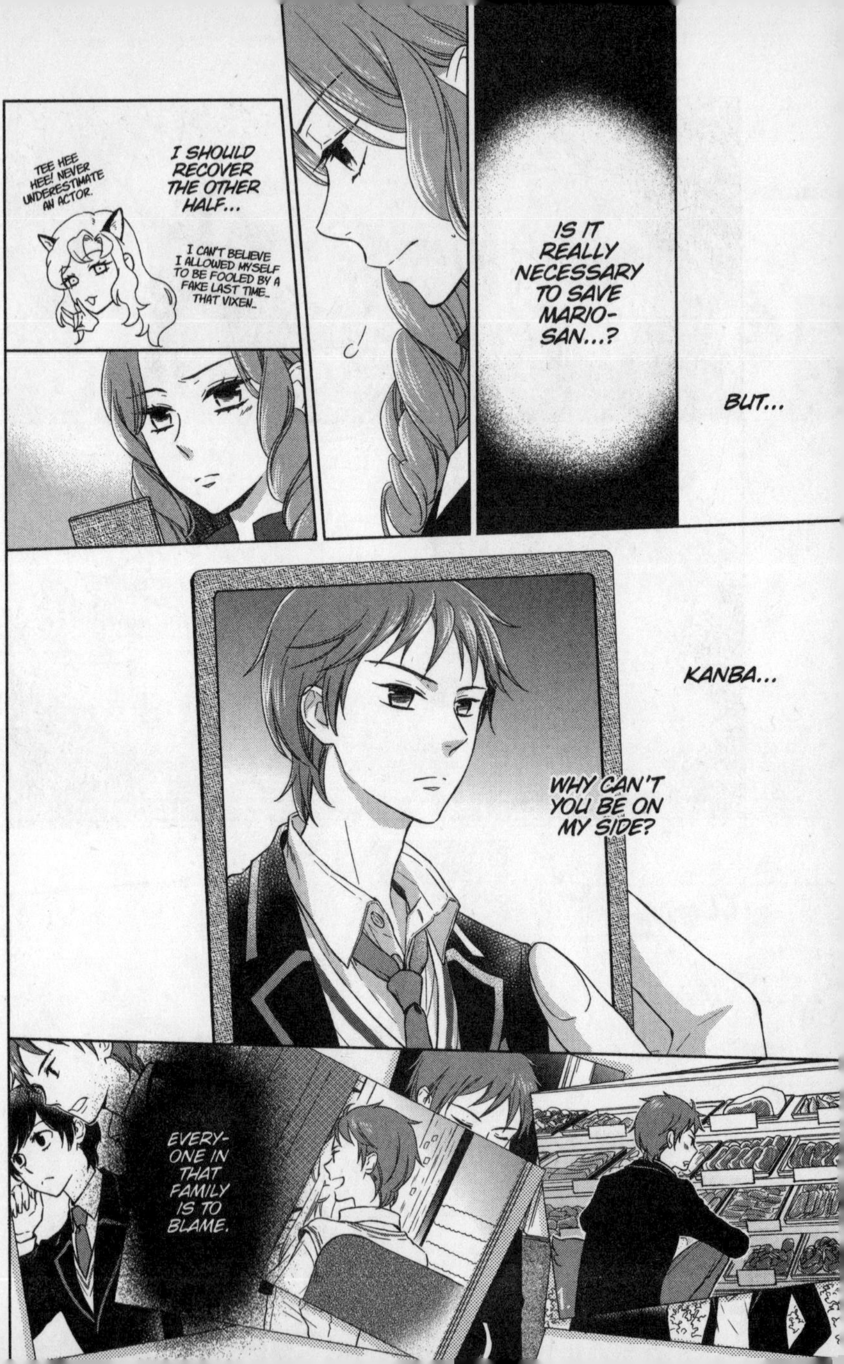

IS IT REALLY NECESSARY TO SAVE MARIO-SAN...?
BUT...
I SHOULD RECOVER THE OTHER HALF...
TEE HEE HEE! NEVER UNDERESTIMATE AN ACTOR.
I CAN'T BELIEVE I ALLOWED MYSELF TO BE FOOLED BY A FAKE LAST TIME.. THAT VIXEN..
KANBA...
WHY CAN'T YOU BE ON MY SIDE?
EVERY-ONE IN THAT FAMILY IS TO BLAME.

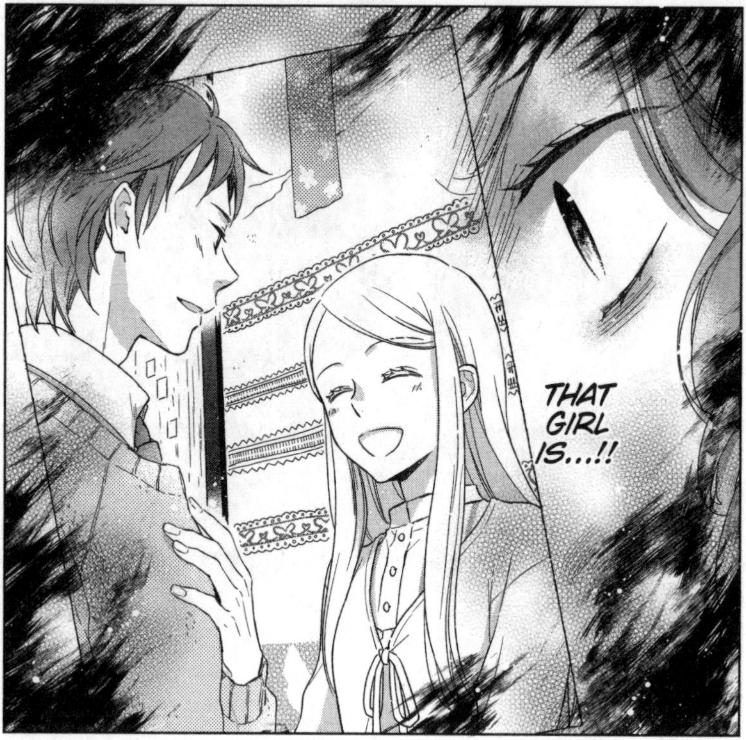
THAT GIRL IS...!!

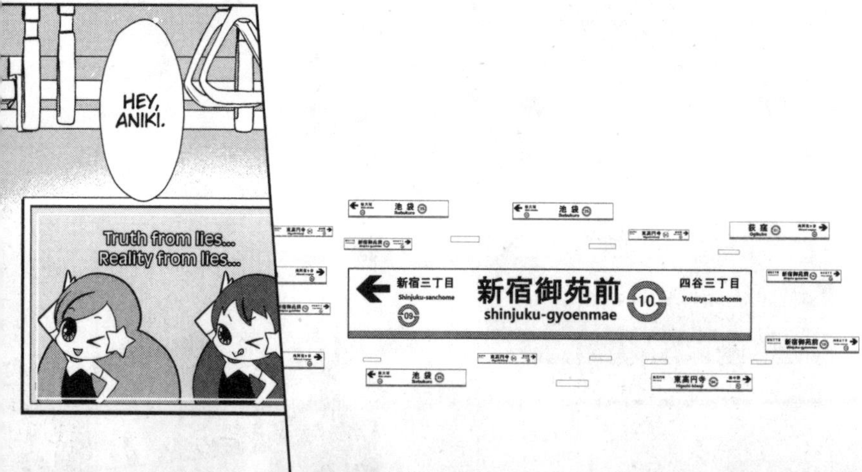
HEY, ANIKI.
Truth from lies...
Reality from lies...
新宿三丁目
Shinjuku-sanchome
09
新宿御苑前
shinjuku-gyoenmae
10
四谷三丁目
Yotsuya-sanchome

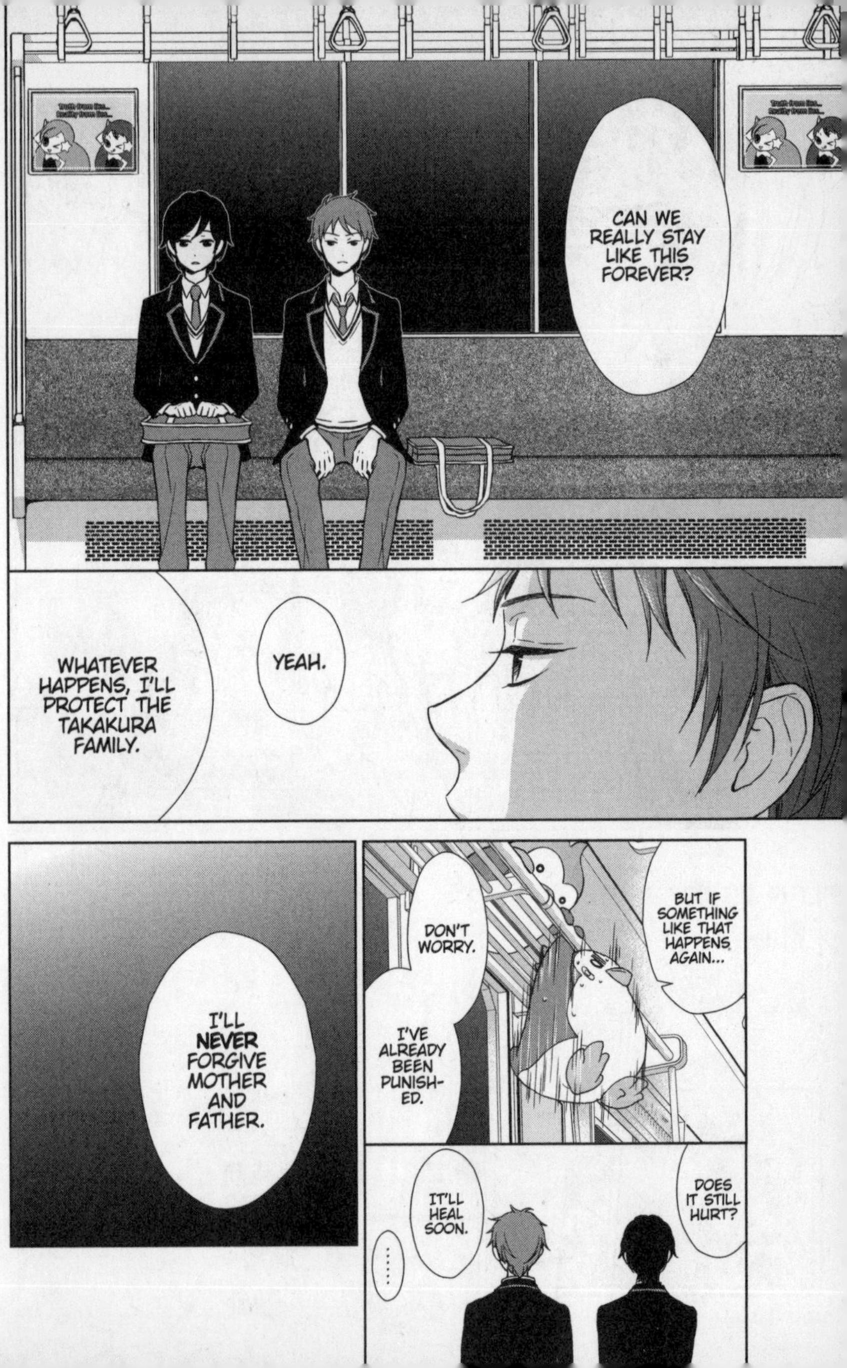
CAN WE REALLY STAY LIKE THIS FOREVER?
YEAH.
WHATEVER HAPPENS, I'LL PROTECT THE TAKAKURA FAMILY.
BUT IF SOMETHING LIKE THAT HAPPENS AGAIN...
DON'T WORRY.
I'VE ALREADY BEEN PUNISH-ED.
DOES IT STILL HURT?
IT'LL HEAL SOON.
......
I'LL **NEVER** FORGIVE MOTHER AND FATHER.

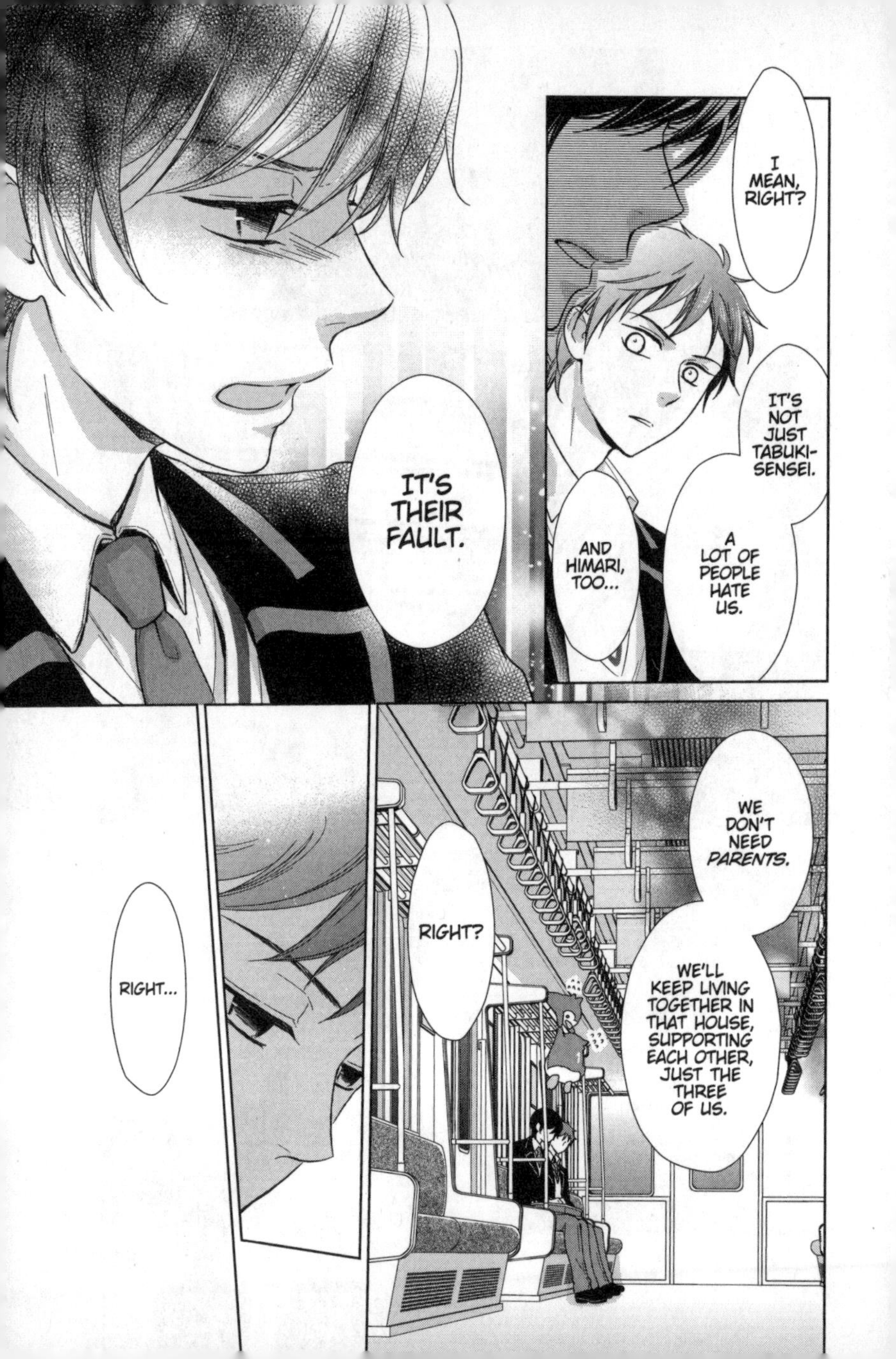
I MEAN, RIGHT?
IT'S NOT JUST TABUKI-SENSEI.
A LOT OF PEOPLE HATE US.
AND HIMARI, TOO...
IT'S THEIR FAULT.
WE DON'T NEED *PARENTS.*
WE'LL KEEP LIVING TOGETHER IN THAT HOUSE, SUPPORTING EACH OTHER, JUST THE THREE OF US.
RIGHT?
RIGHT...

Flashback

Day Before the Incident

Penguin Force Hideout

A room in an apartment complex.

※ *There were numerous identical doors there, all real. That's where it began.*

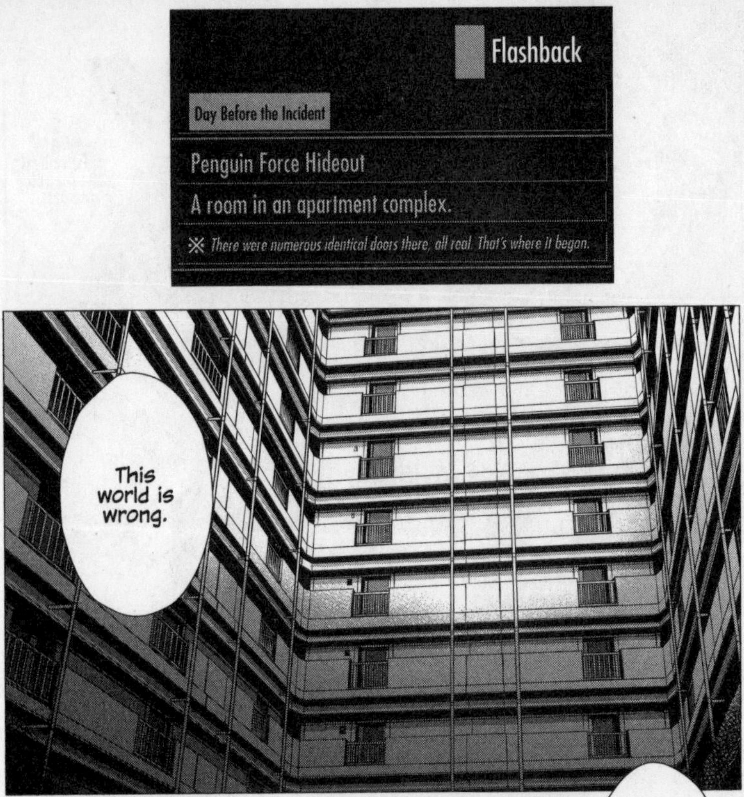
This world is wrong.

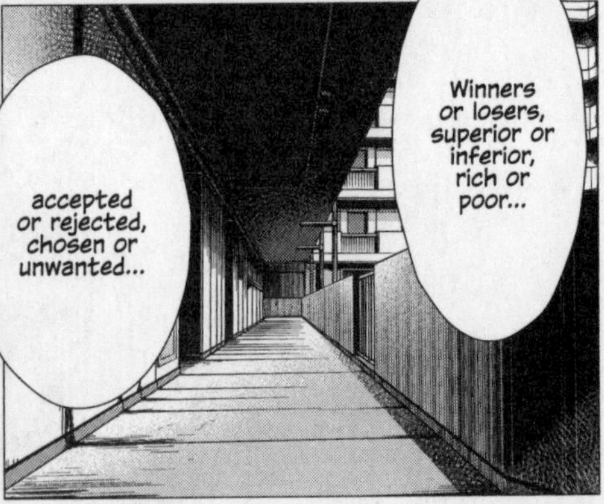
Winners or losers, superior or inferior, rich or poor...
accepted or rejected, chosen or unwanted...

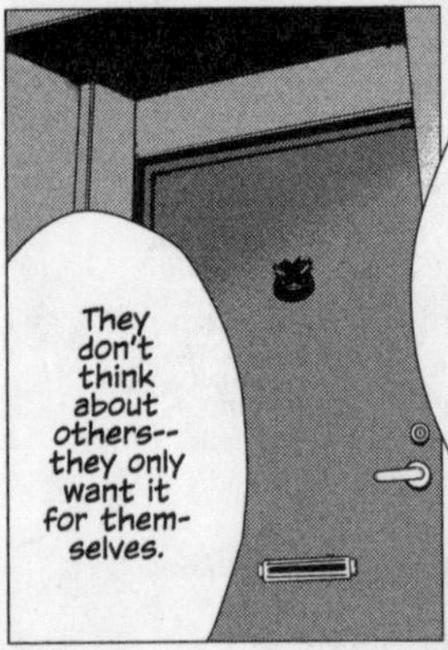
They don't think about others--they only want it for themselves.

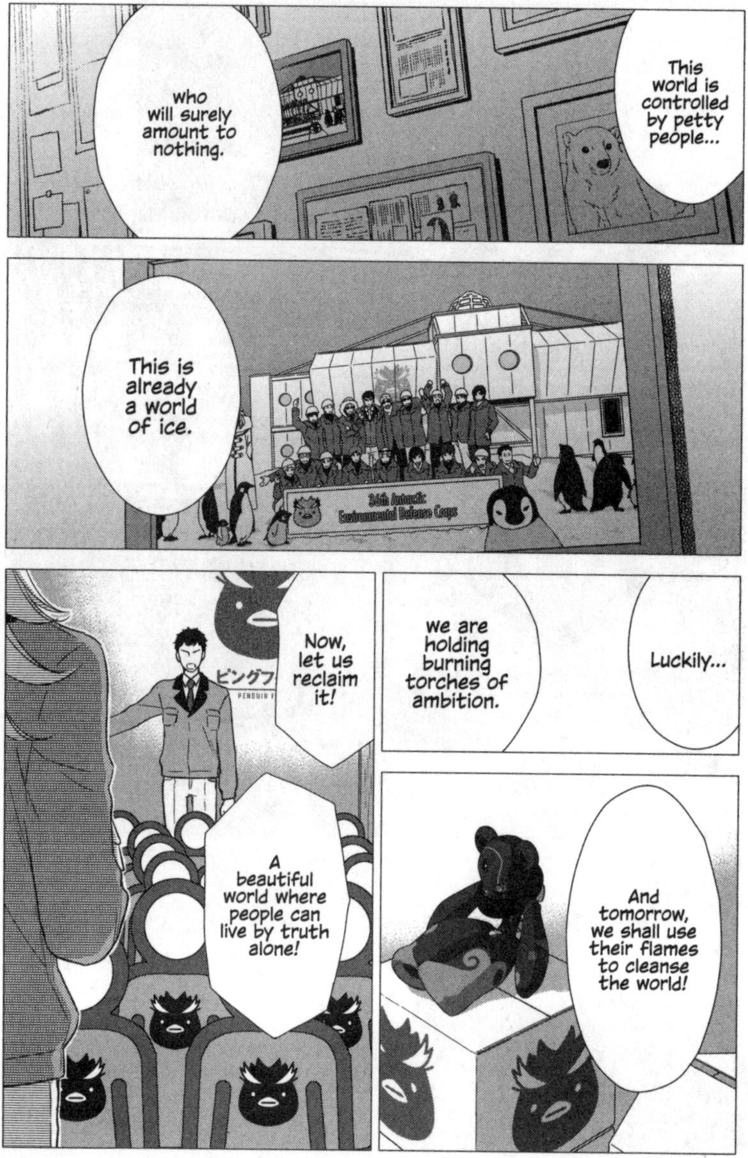
This world is controlled by petty people...
who will surely amount to nothing.
This is already a world of ice.
Luckily...
we are holding burning torches of ambition.
And tomorrow, we shall use their flames to cleanse the world!
Now, let us reclaim it!
A beautiful world where people can live by truth alone!

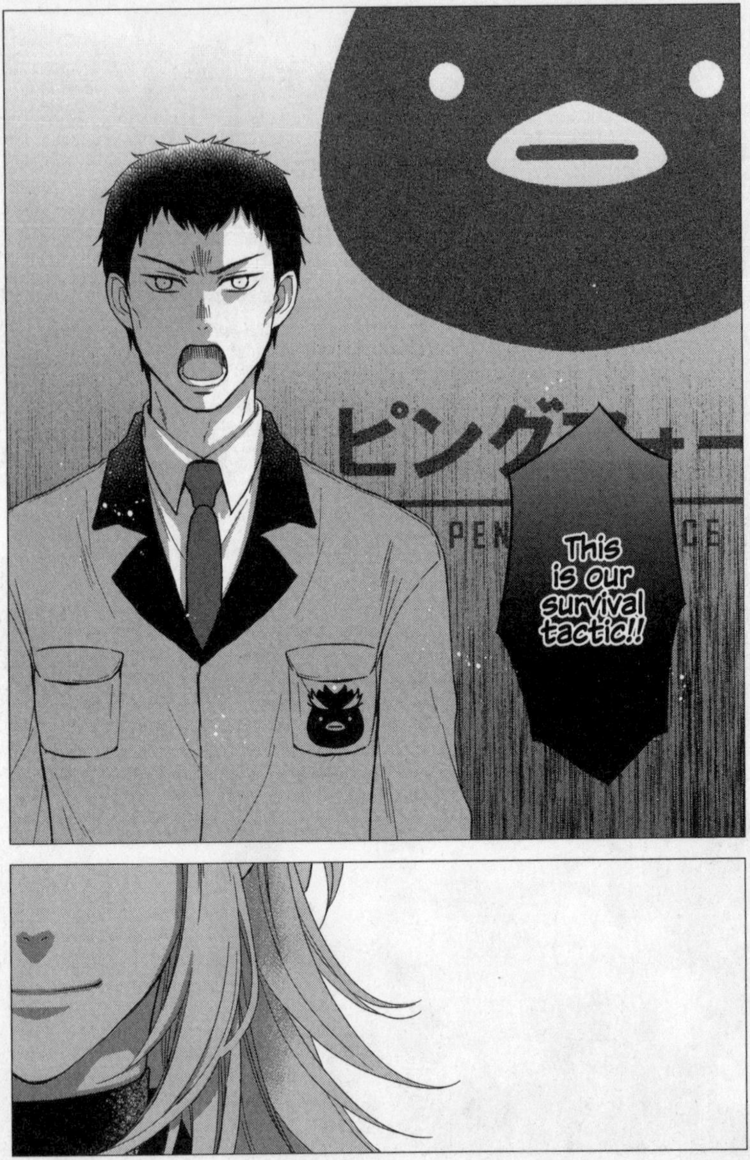
This is our survival tactic!!

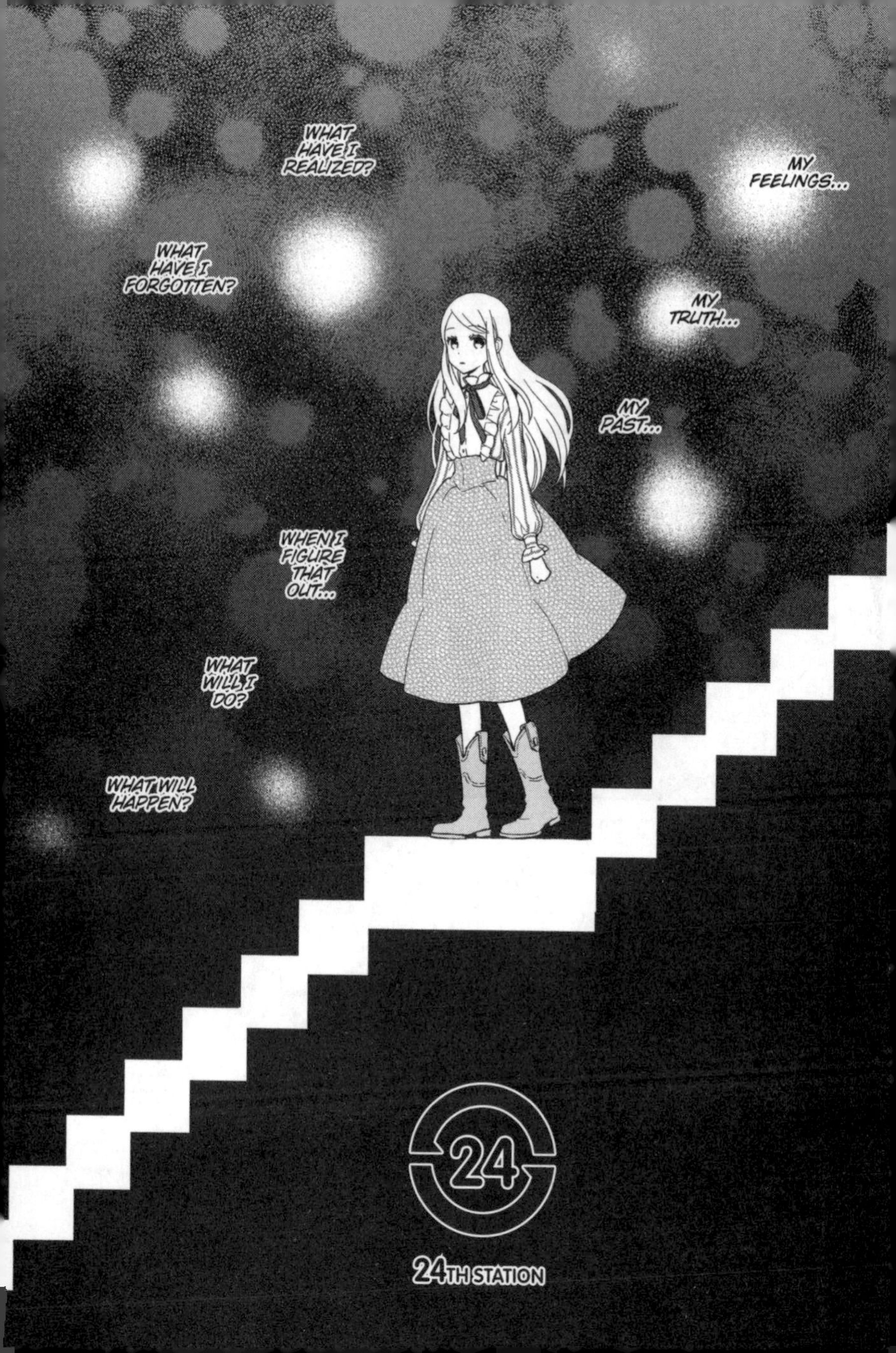
MY FEELINGS...
WHAT HAVE I REALIZED?
MY TRUTH...
WHAT HAVE I FORGOTTEN?
MY PAST...
WHEN I FIGURE THAT OUT...
WHAT WILL I DO?
WHAT WILL HAPPEN?
24
24TH STATION

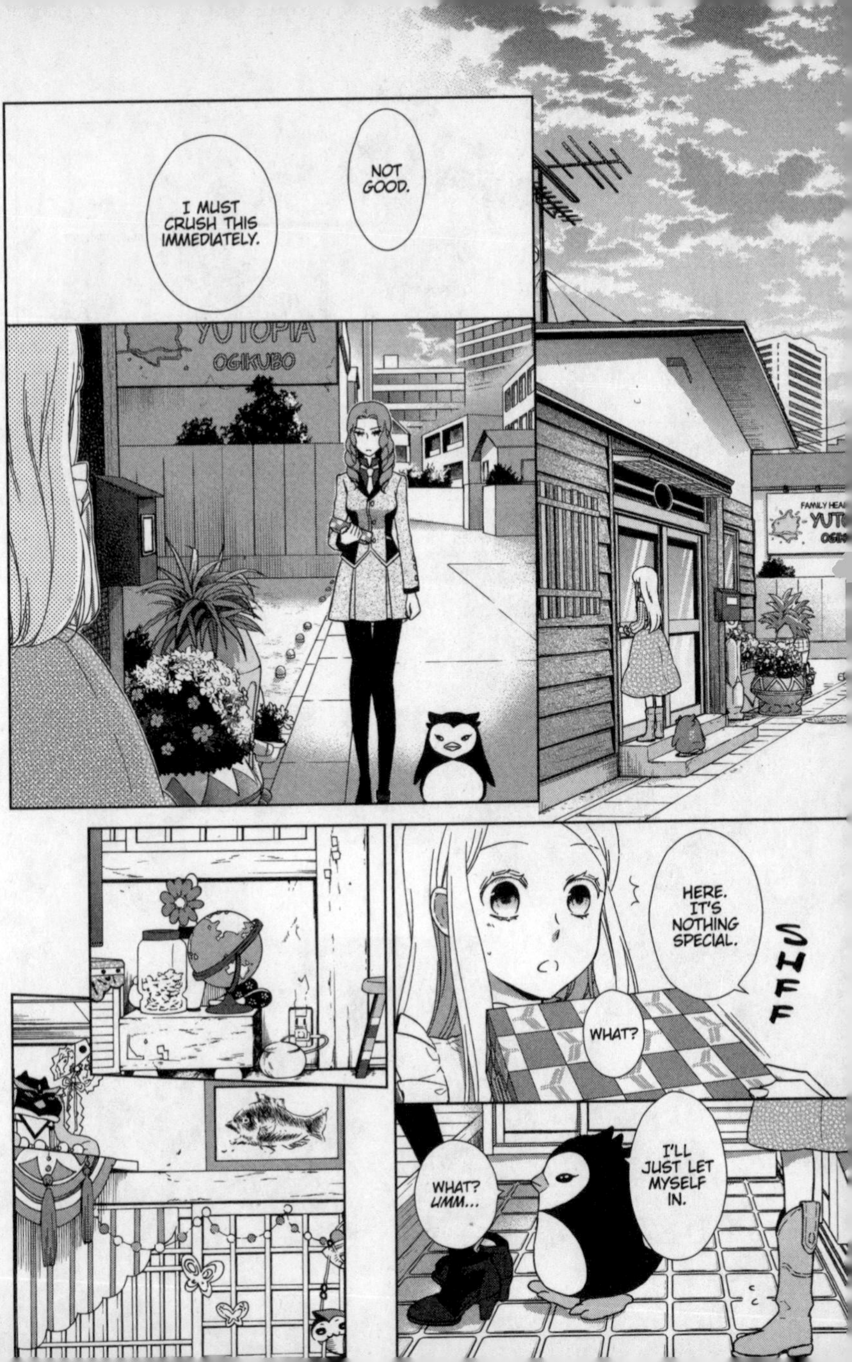
NOT GOOD.
I MUST CRUSH THIS IMMEDIATELY.
YUTOPIA
OGIKUBO
HERE. IT'S NOTHING SPECIAL.
SHFF
WHAT?
I'LL JUST LET MYSELF IN.
WHAT? UMM...

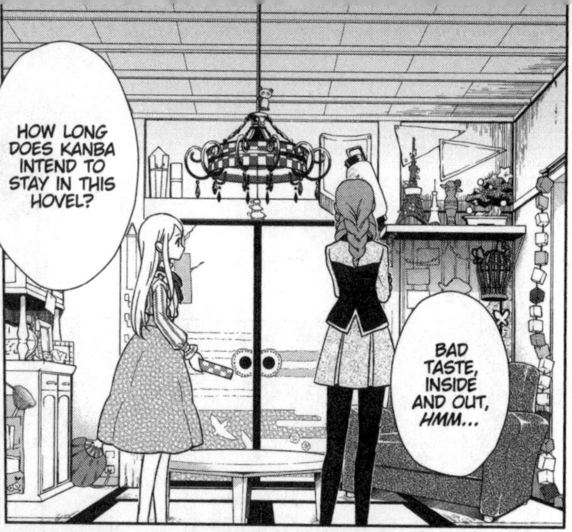
HOW LONG DOES KANBA INTEND TO STAY IN THIS HOVEL?
BAD TASTE, INSIDE AND OUT, HMM...

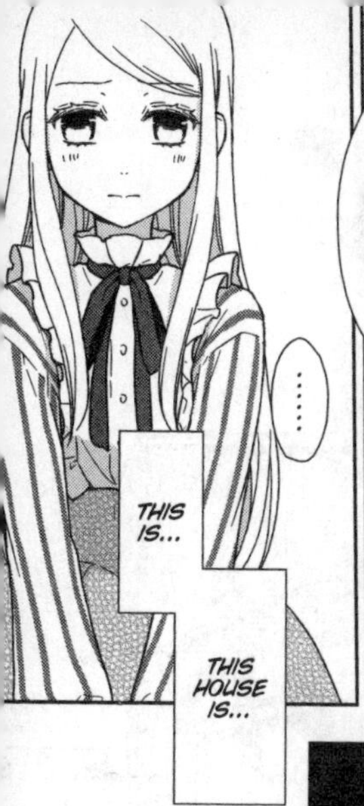
......
THIS IS...
THIS HOUSE IS...

Flashback

Himari

3 Years Ago

Mother and Father are gone.

※ *What they did for me, someone who could do nothing but cry every day...*

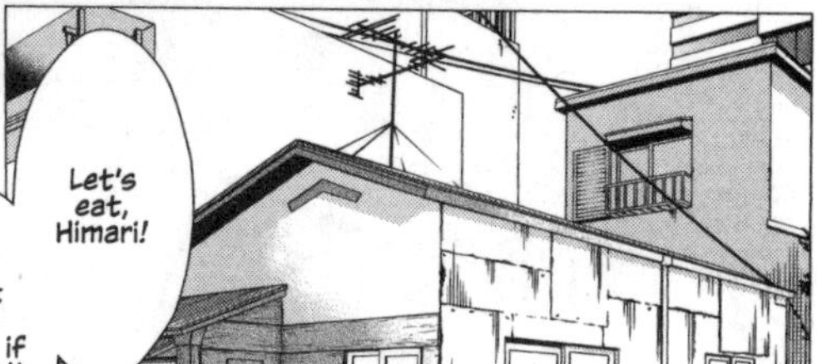
Let's eat, Himari!

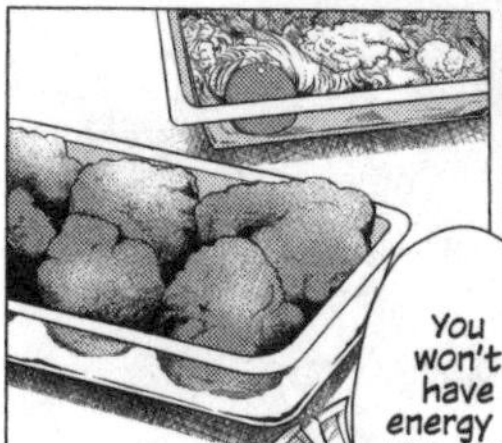
You won't have energy if you don't eat, you know.
Miso Soup

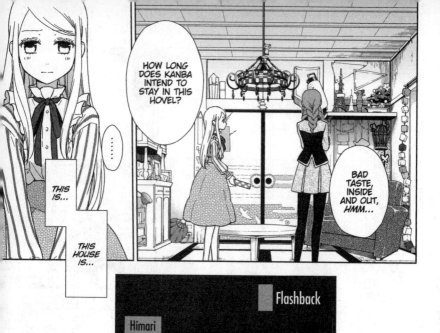

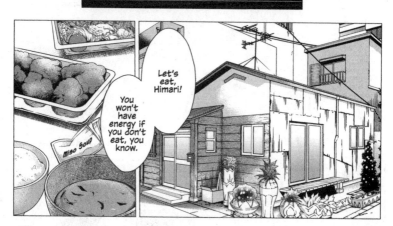

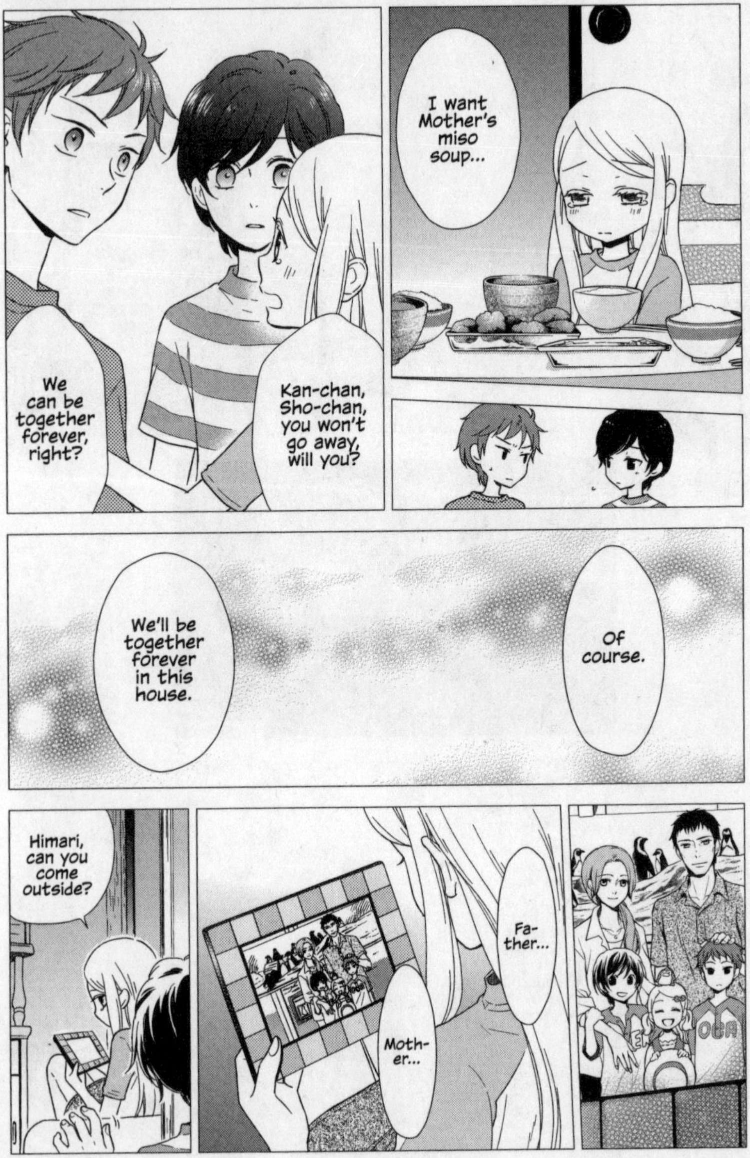
I want Mother's miso soup...
Kan-chan, Sho-chan, you won't go away, will you?
We can be together forever, right?
Of course.
We'll be together forever in this house.
Fa-ther...
Moth-er...
Himari, can you come outside?

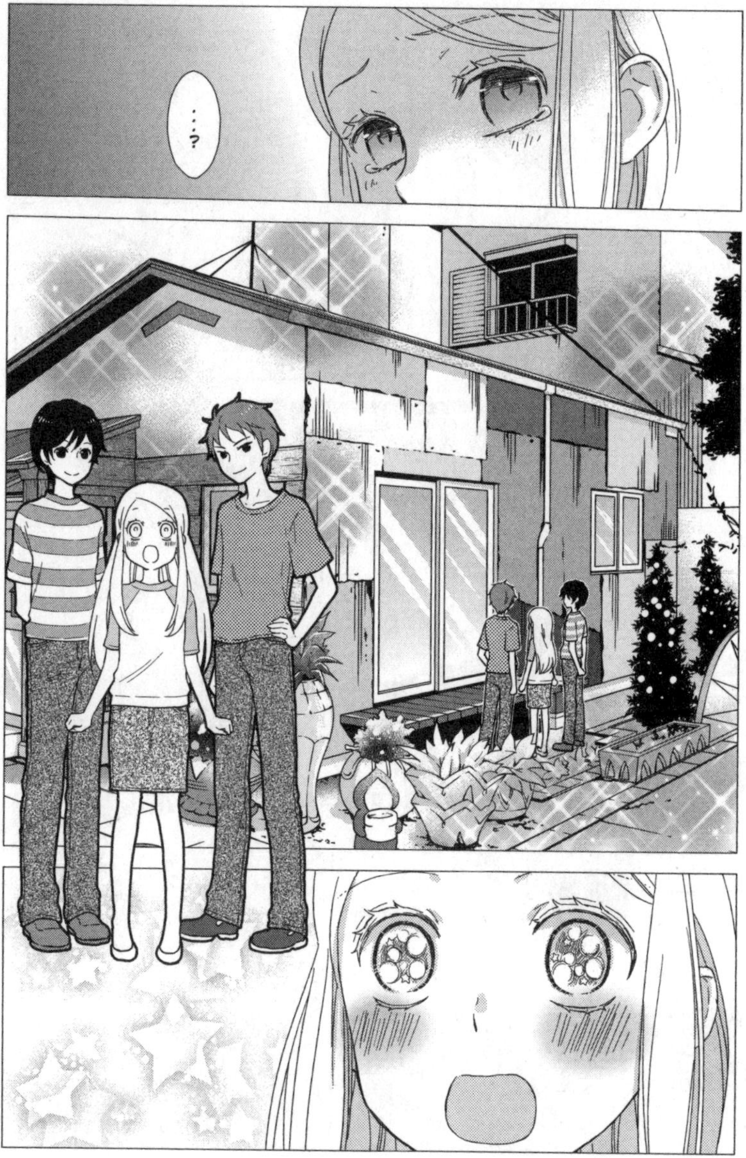
…?

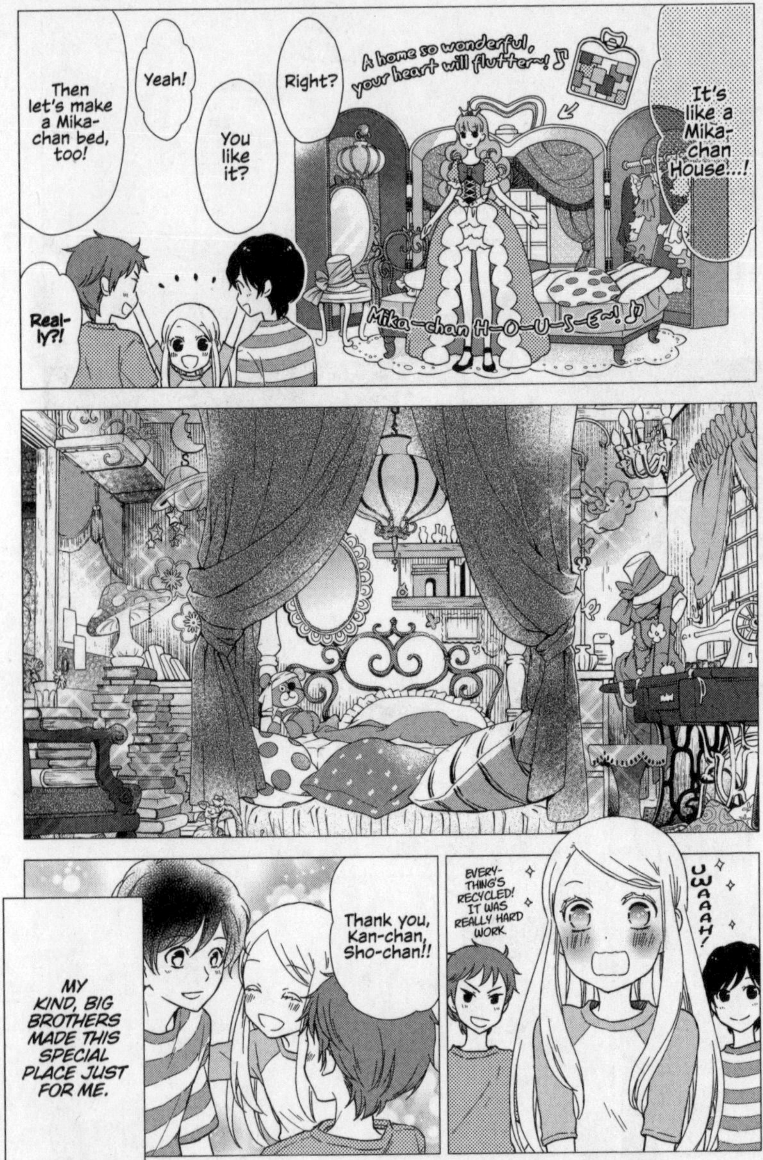
It's like a Mika-chan House...!
A home so wonderful, your heart will flutter~! ♪
Mika-chan H-O-U-S-E~! ♪
Right?
You like it?
Yeah!
Then let's make a Mika-chan bed, too!
Really?!
UWAAAH!
EVERYTHING'S RECYCLED! IT WAS REALLY HARD WORK
Thank you, Kan-chan, Sho-chan!!
MY KIND, BIG BROTHERS MADE THIS SPECIAL PLACE JUST FOR ME.

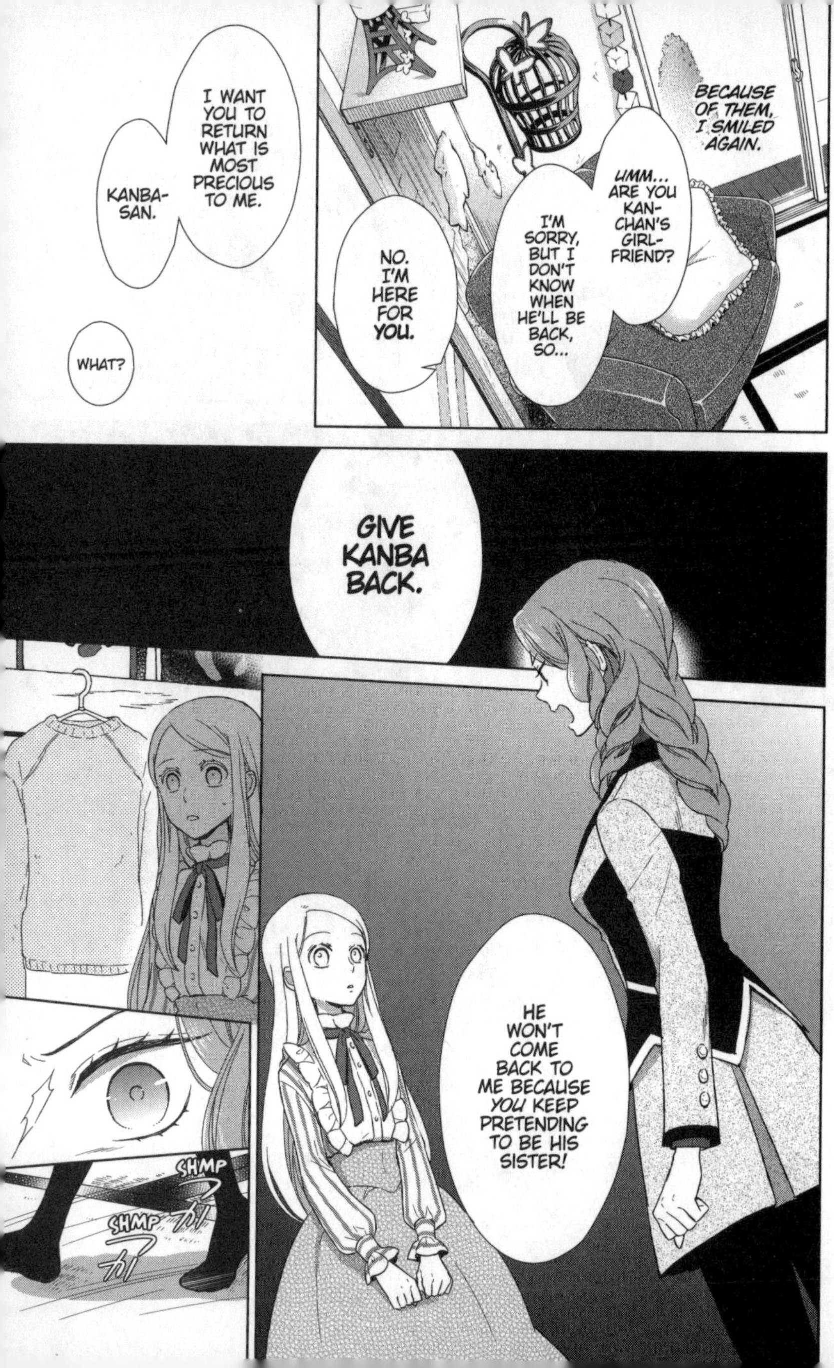
BECAUSE OF THEM, I SMILED AGAIN.
UMM... ARE YOU KAN-CHAN'S GIRL-FRIEND?
I'M SORRY, BUT I DON'T KNOW WHEN HE'LL BE BACK, SO...
NO. I'M HERE FOR YOU.
I WANT YOU TO RETURN WHAT IS MOST PRECIOUS TO ME.
KANBA-SAN.
WHAT?
GIVE KANBA BACK.
HE WON'T COME BACK TO ME BECAUSE YOU KEEP PRETENDING TO BE HIS SISTER!
SHMP
SHMP

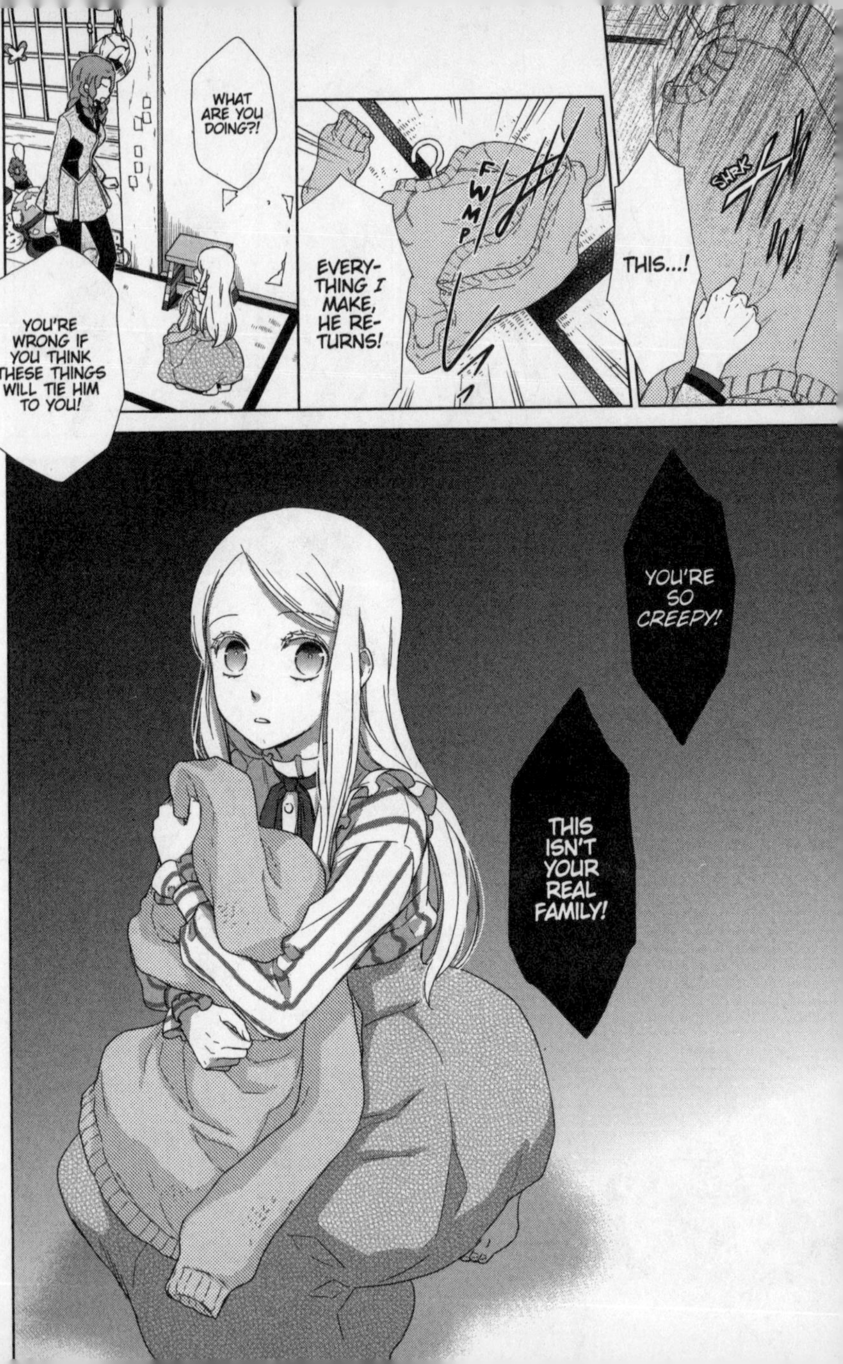
SHRK
THIS...!
FWMP
EVERY-THING I MAKE, HE RE-TURNS!
WHAT ARE YOU DOING?!
YOU'RE WRONG IF YOU THINK THESE THINGS WILL TIE HIM TO YOU!
YOU'RE SO CREEPY!
THIS ISN'T YOUR REAL FAMILY!

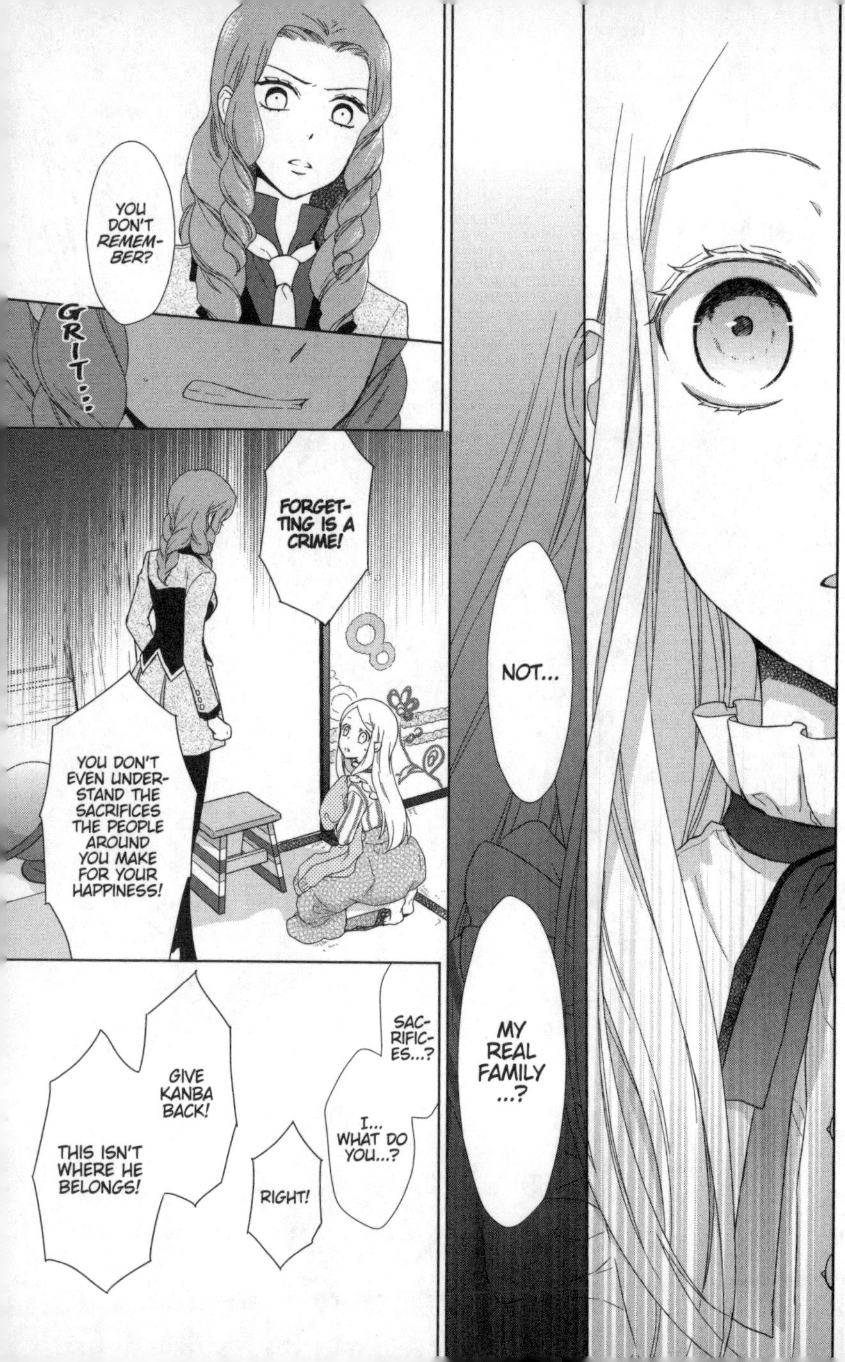
NOT...
MY REAL FAMILY...?
YOU DON'T REMEMBER?
GRIT...
FORGETTING IS A CRIME!
YOU DON'T EVEN UNDERSTAND THE SACRIFICES THE PEOPLE AROUND YOU MAKE FOR YOUR HAPPINESS!
SACRIFICES...?
I... WHAT DO YOU...?
RIGHT!
GIVE KANBA BACK!
THIS ISN'T WHERE HE BELONGS!

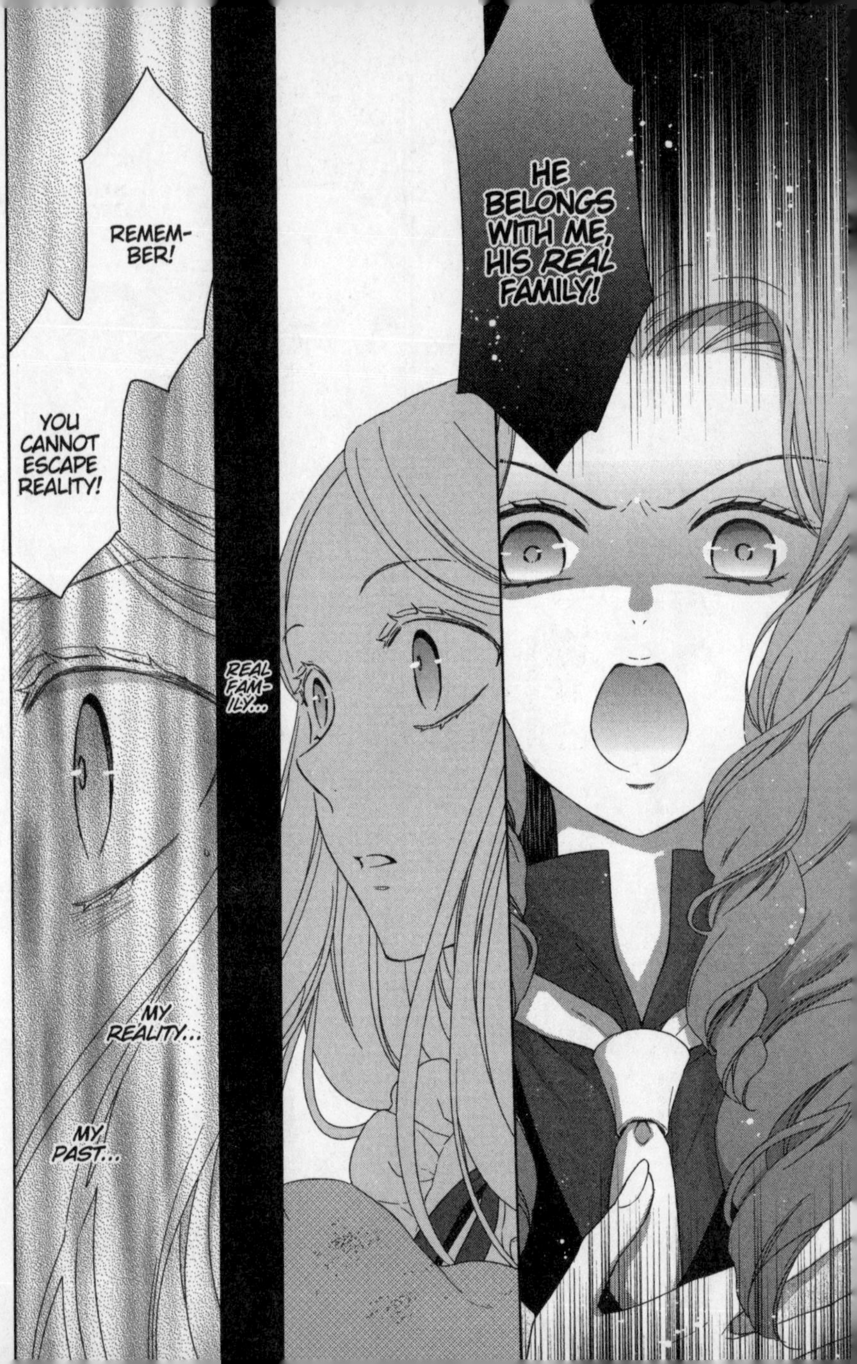
HE BELONGS WITH ME, HIS *REAL* FAMILY!
REAL FAMILY...
REMEMBER!
YOU CANNOT ESCAPE REALITY!
MY REALITY...
MY PAST...

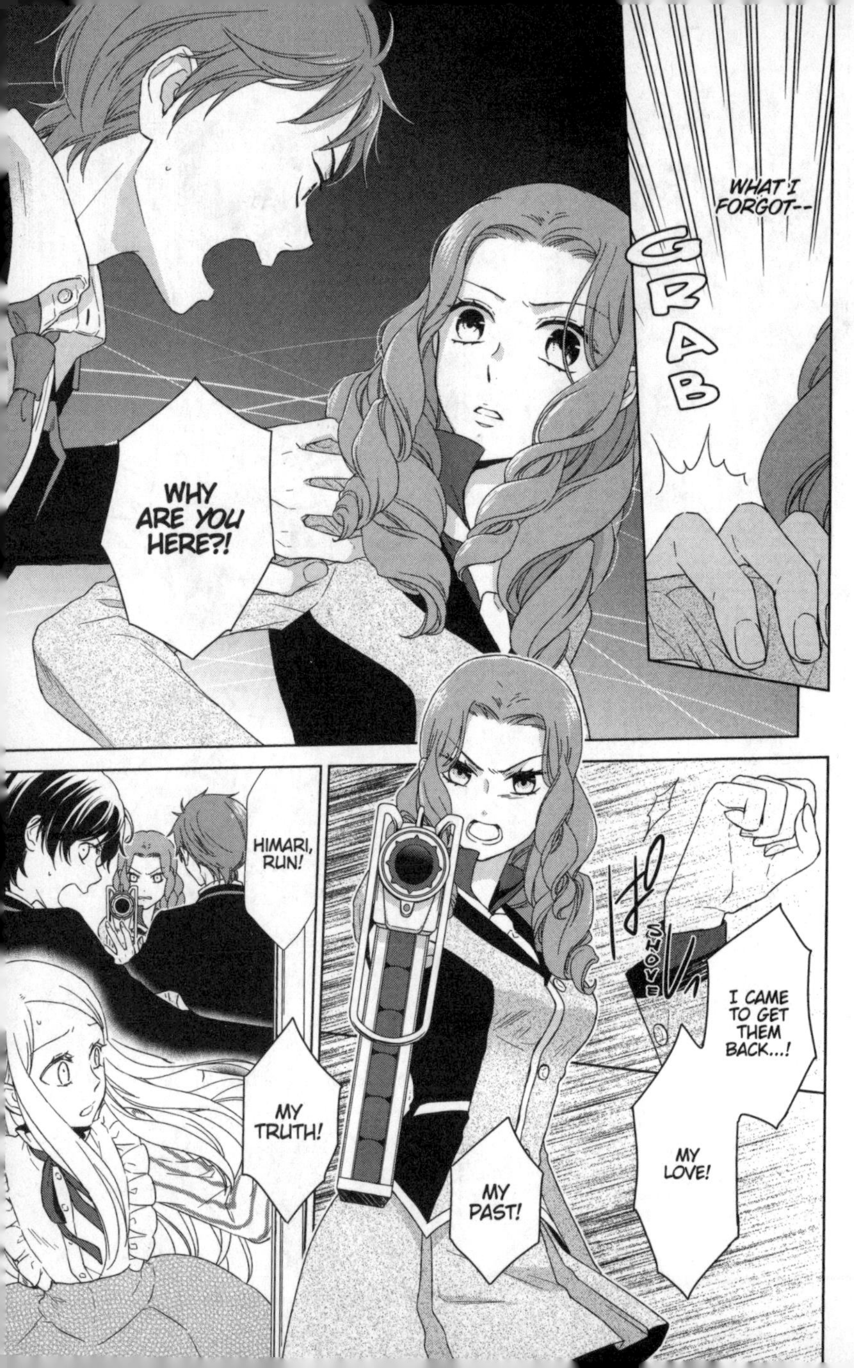

WHAT I FORGOT--
GRAB
WHY ARE YOU HERE?!
SHOVE
I CAME TO GET THEM BACK...!
MY LOVE!
MY PAST!
MY TRUTH!
HIMARI, RUN!

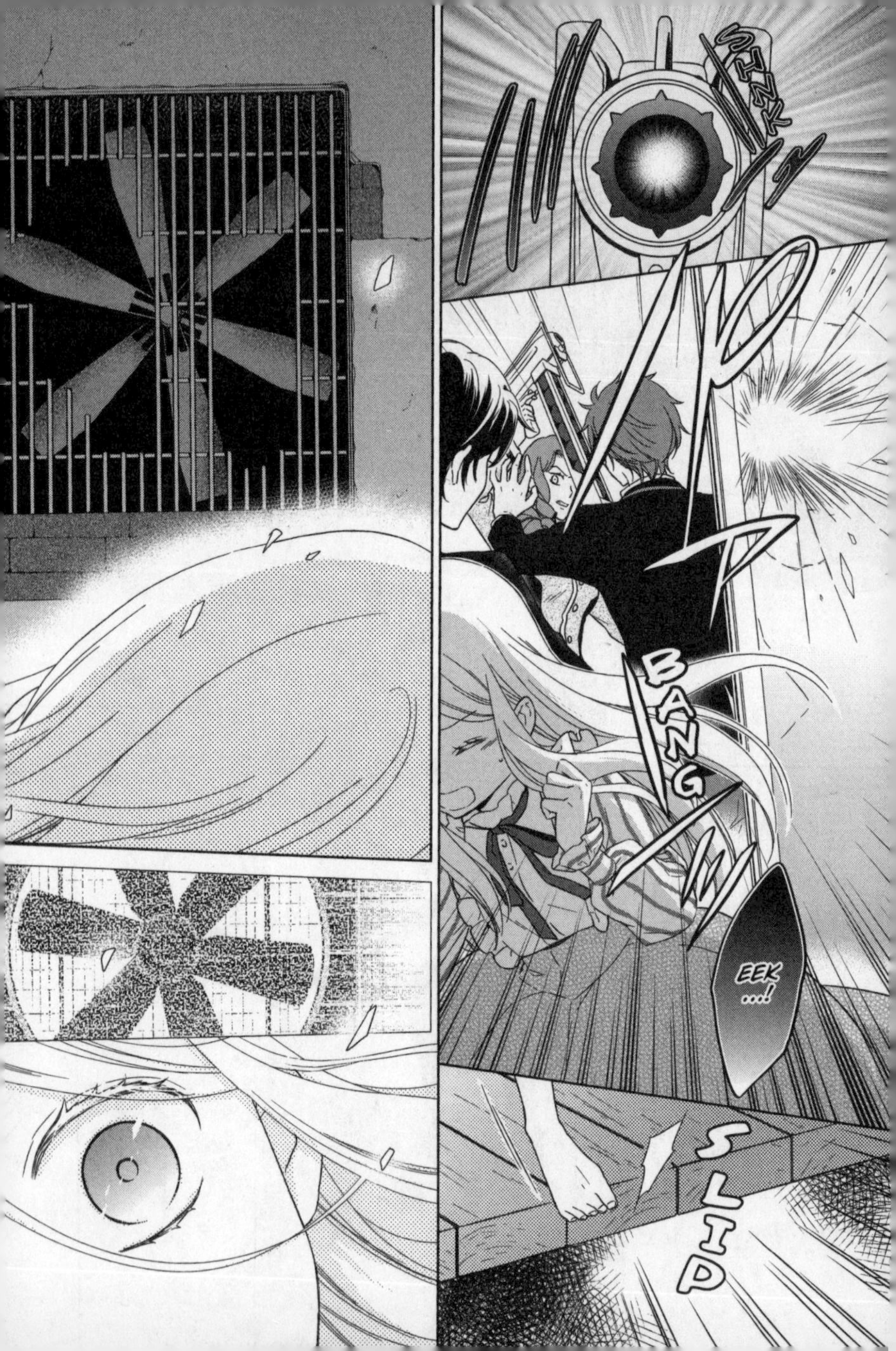
SHNK
BANG
EEK ...!
SLIP

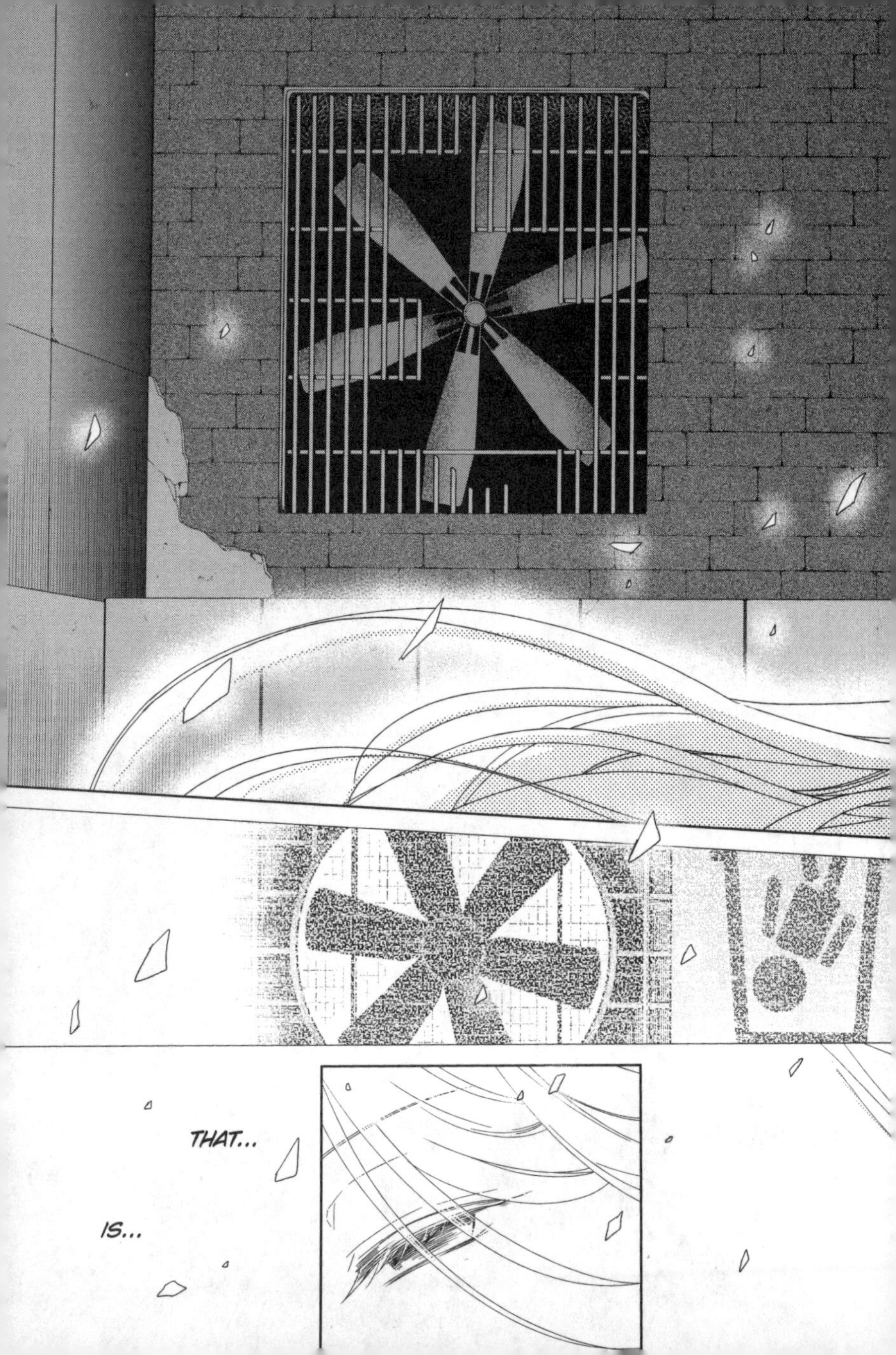
THAT...
IS...

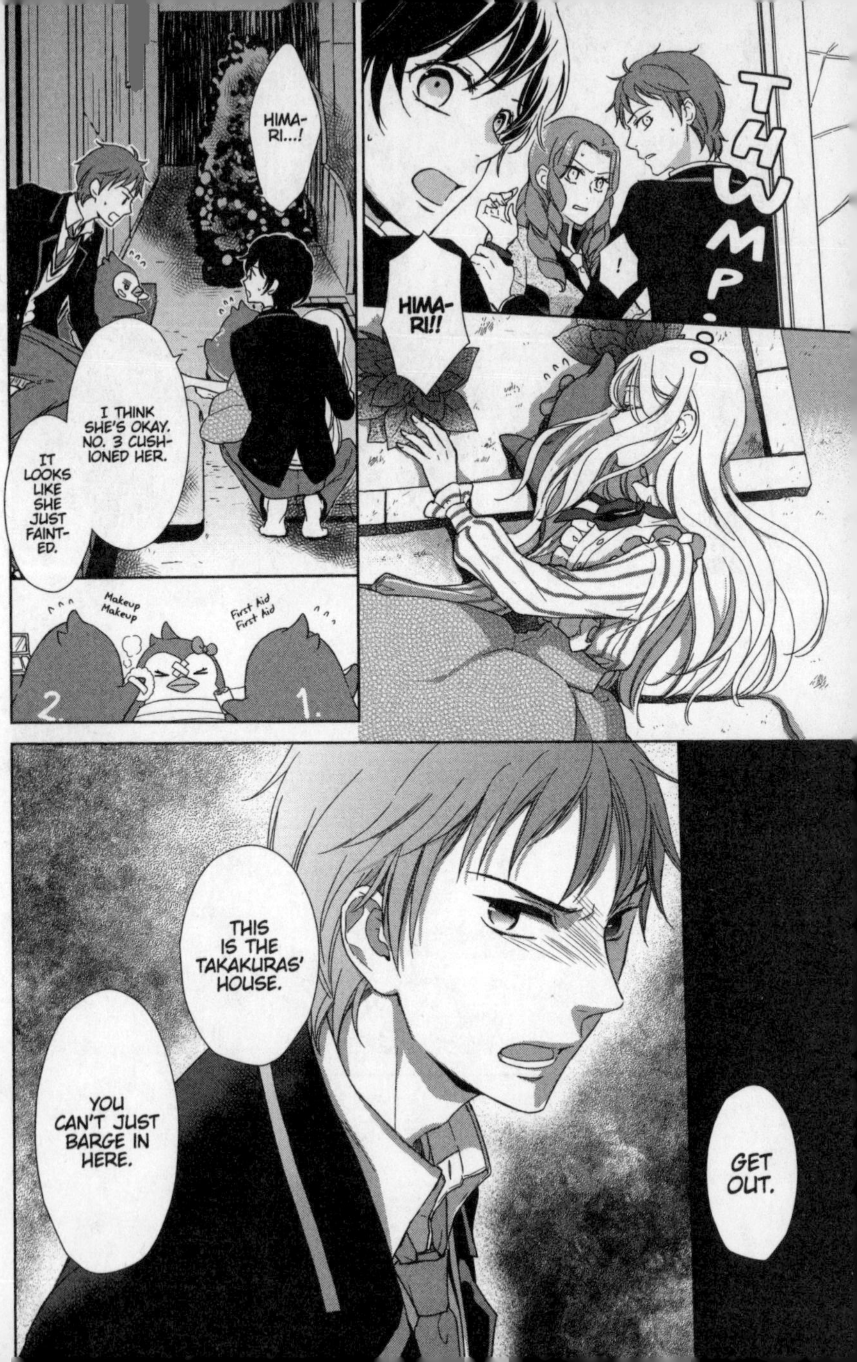
THWUMP...
HIMA-RI!!
!
HIMA-RI...!
I THINK SHE'S OKAY. NO. 3 CUSHIONED HER.
IT LOOKS LIKE SHE JUST FAINTED.
First Aid First Aid
Makeup Makeup
1.
2.
THIS IS THE TAKAKURAS' HOUSE.
YOU CAN'T JUST BARGE IN HERE.
GET OUT.

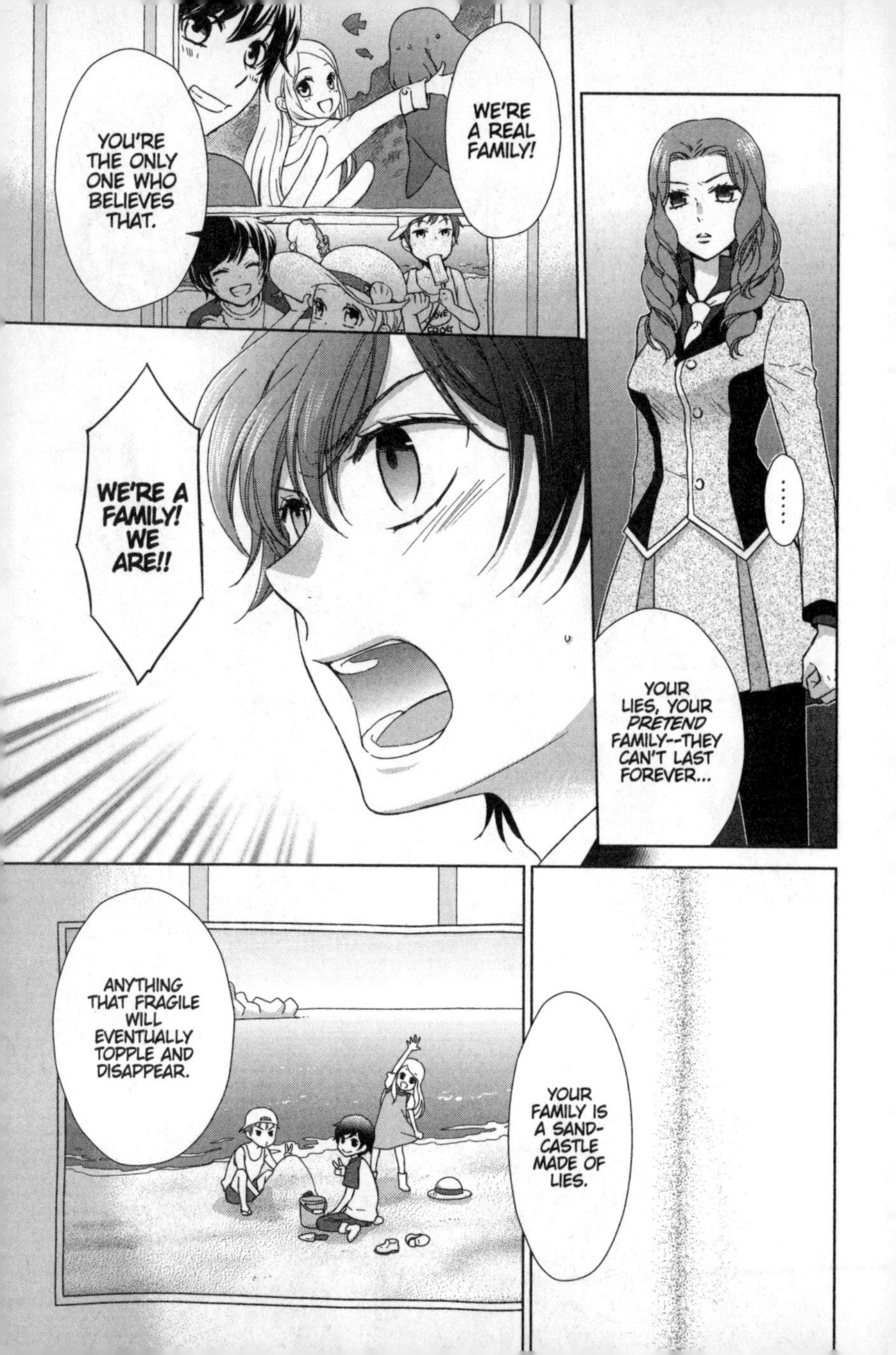
......
YOUR LIES, YOUR *PRETEND* FAMILY--THEY CAN'T LAST FOREVER...
WE'RE A REAL FAMILY!
YOU'RE THE ONLY ONE WHO BELIEVES THAT.
WE'RE A FAMILY! WE ARE!!
YOUR FAMILY IS A SAND-CASTLE MADE OF LIES.
ANYTHING THAT FRAGILE WILL EVENTUALLY TOPPLE AND DISAPPEAR.

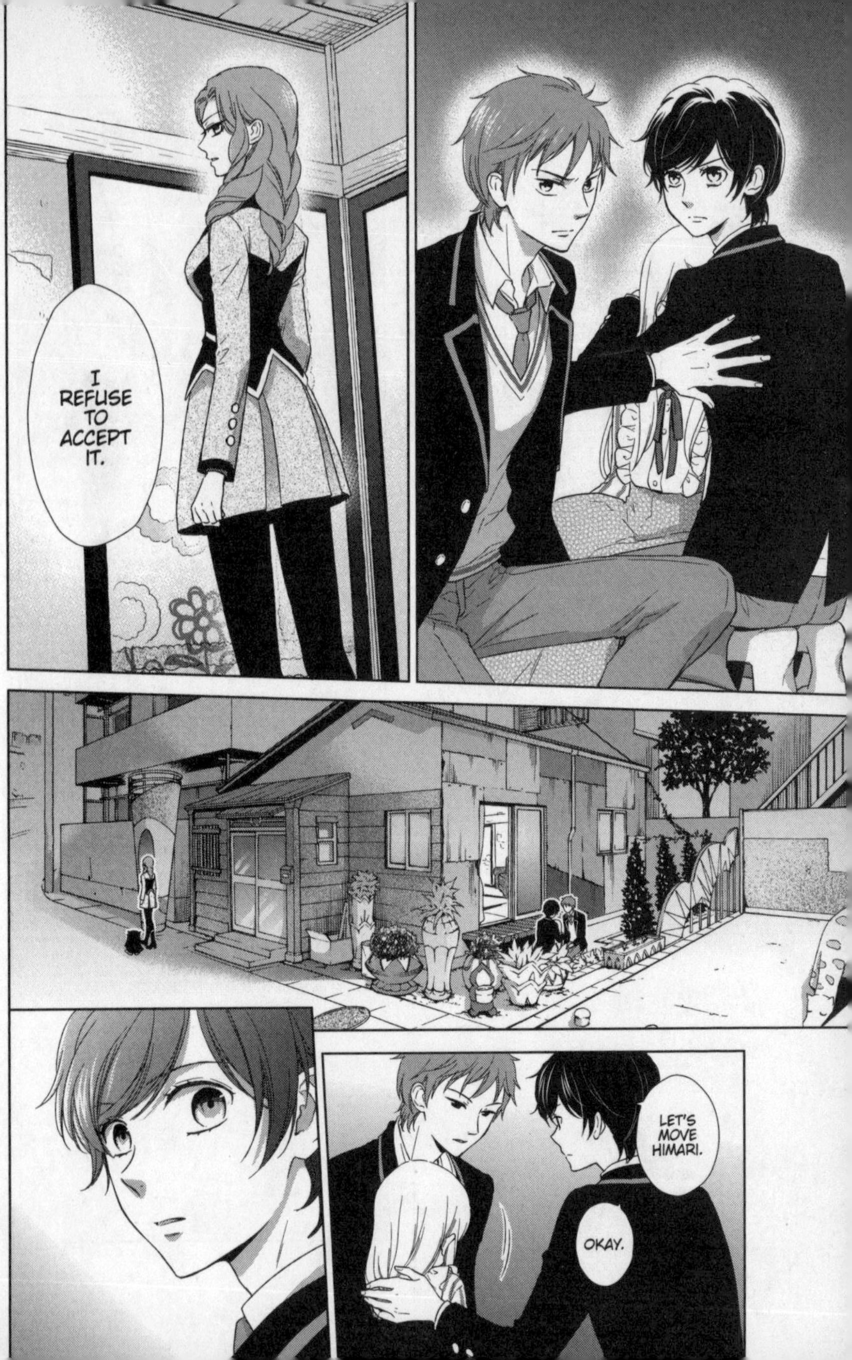
I REFUSE TO ACCEPT IT.
LET'S MOVE HIMARI.
OKAY.

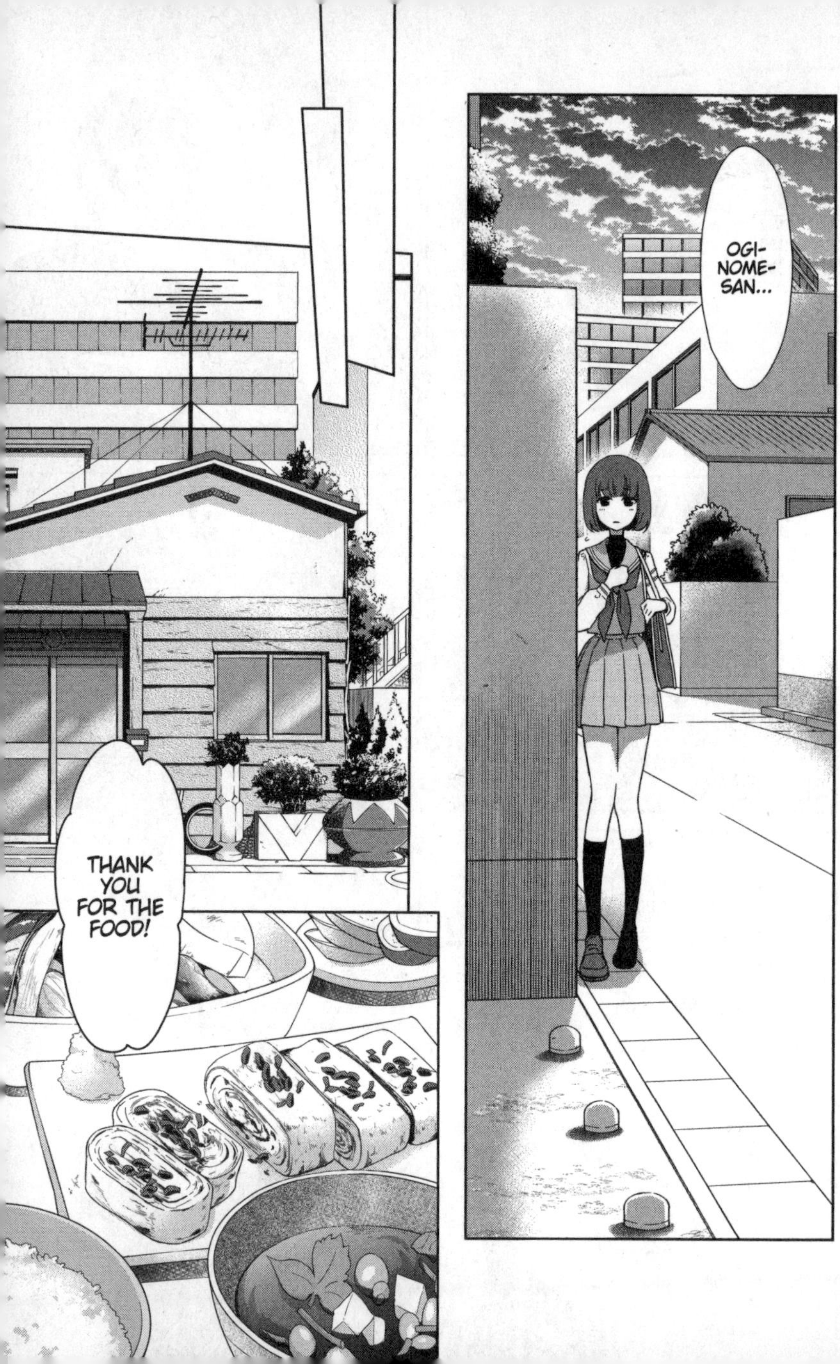
OGI-NOME-SAN...
THANK YOU FOR THE FOOD!

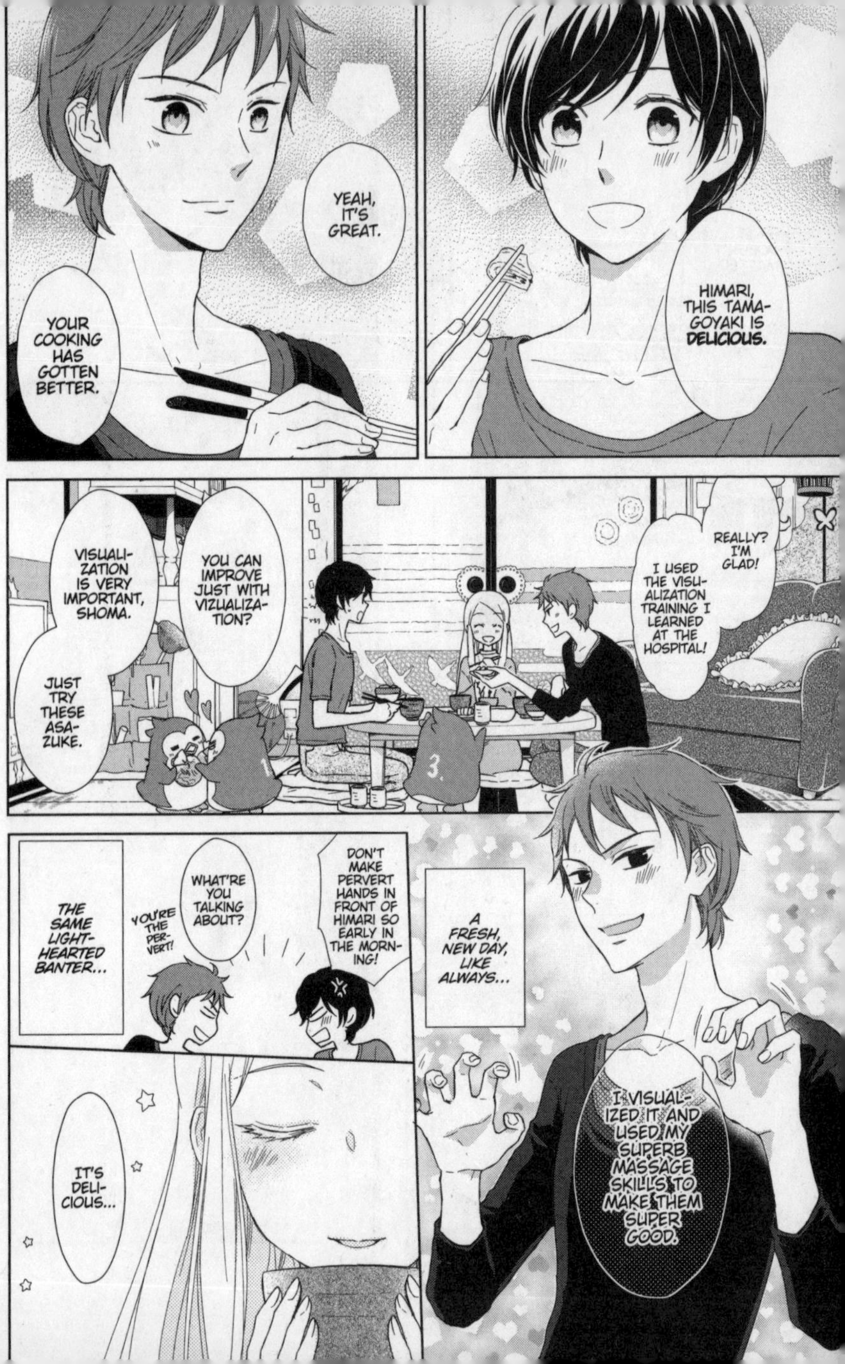
HIMARI, THIS TAMA-GOYAKI IS **DELICIOUS.**
YEAH, IT'S GREAT.
YOUR COOKING HAS GOTTEN BETTER.
REALLY? I'M GLAD!
I USED THE VISU-ALIZATION TRAINING I LEARNED AT THE HOSPITAL!
YOU CAN IMPROVE JUST WITH VIZUALIZA-TION?
VISUALI-ZATION IS VERY IMPORTANT, SHOMA.
JUST TRY THESE ASA-ZUKE.
A FRESH, NEW DAY, LIKE ALWAYS...
I VISUAL-IZED IT AND USED MY SUPERB MASSAGE SKILLS TO MAKE THEM SUPER GOOD.
DON'T MAKE PERVERT HANDS IN FRONT OF HIMARI SO EARLY IN THE MORN-ING!
WHAT'RE YOU TALKING ABOUT?
YOU'RE THE PER-VERT!
THE SAME LIGHT-HEARTED BANTER...
IT'S DELI-CIOUS...

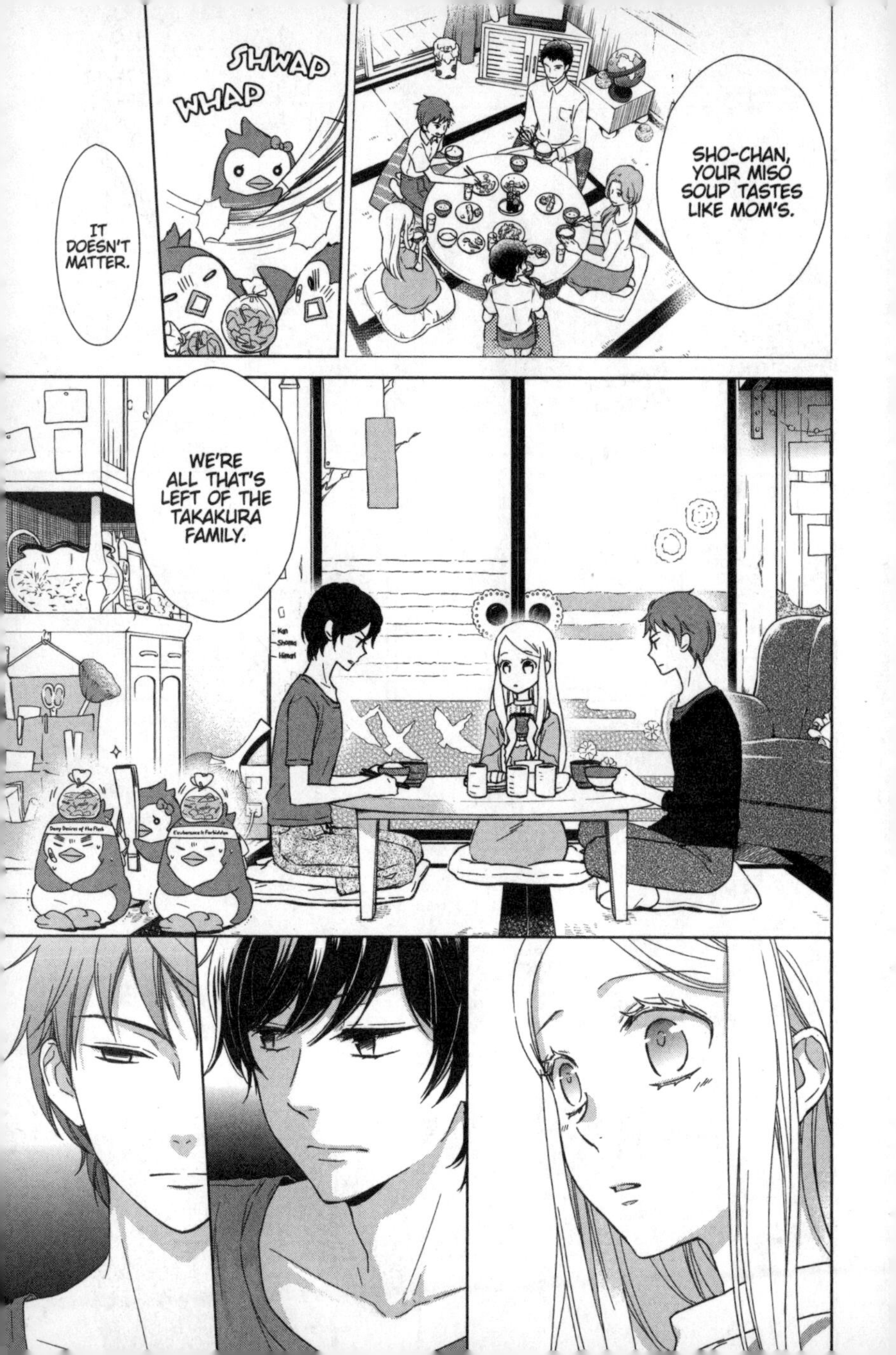
SHO-CHAN, YOUR MISO SOUP TASTES LIKE MOM'S.
SHWAP
WHAP
IT DOESN'T MATTER.
WE'RE ALL THAT'S LEFT OF THE TAKAKURA FAMILY.
Ken
Shoma
Himari
Exuberance Is Forbidden
Deny Desires of the Flesh

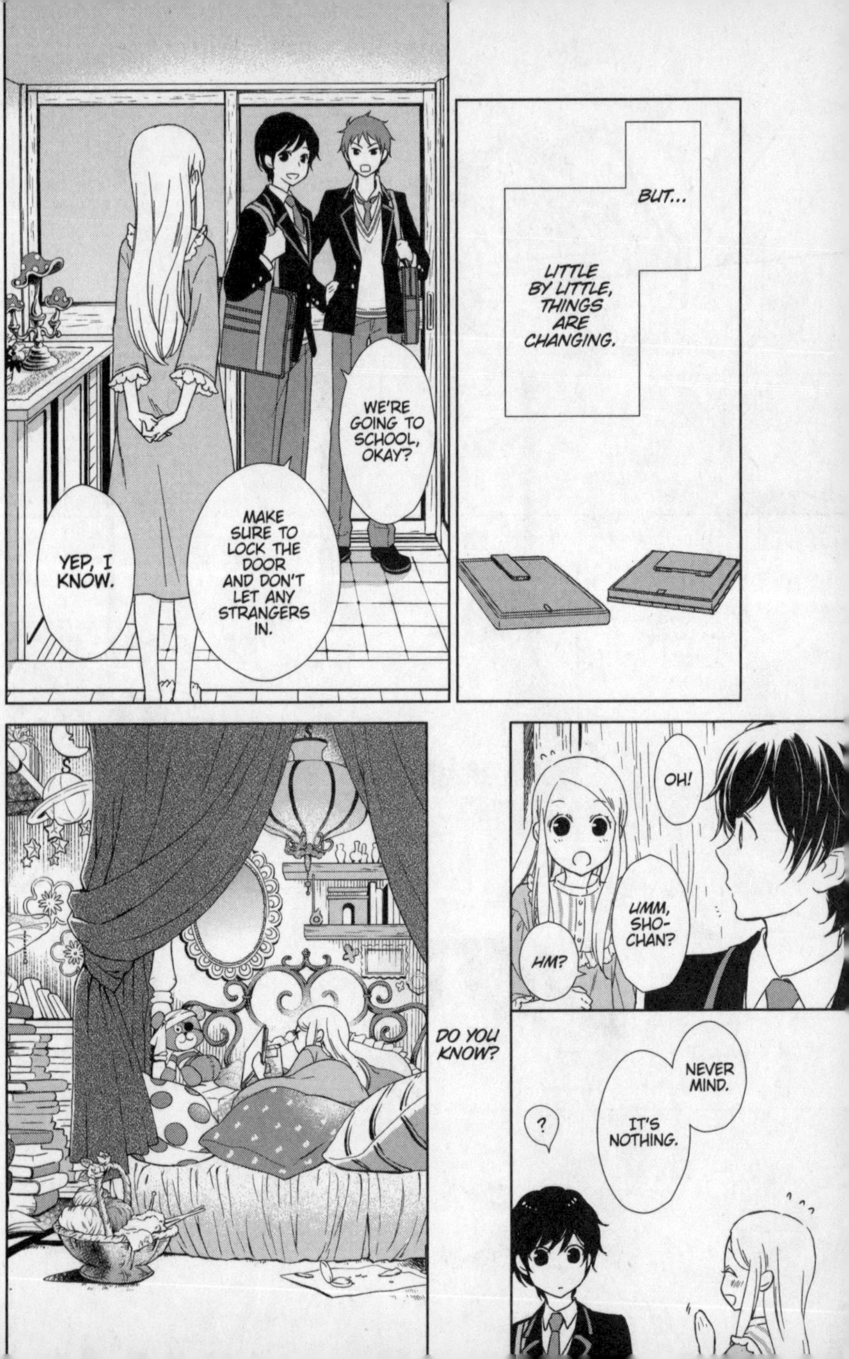
BUT...
LITTLE BY LITTLE, THINGS ARE CHANGING.
WE'RE GOING TO SCHOOL, OKAY?
MAKE SURE TO LOCK THE DOOR AND DON'T LET ANY STRANGERS IN.
YEP, I KNOW.
OH!
UMM, SHO-CHAN?
HM?
NEVER MIND.
IT'S NOTHING.
?
DO YOU KNOW?

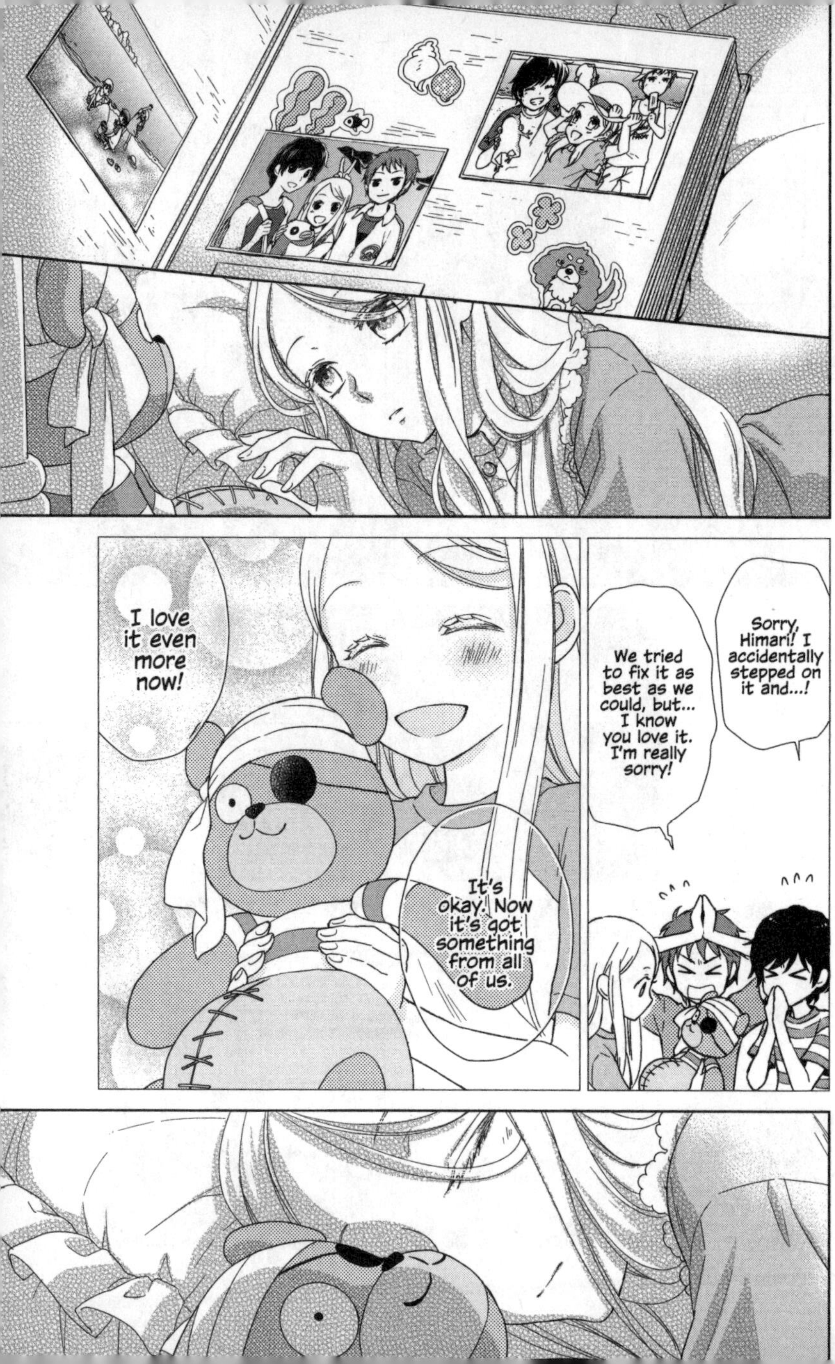
Sorry, Himari! I accidentally stepped on it and...!
We tried to fix it as best as we could, but... I know you love it. I'm really sorry!
It's okay. Now it's got something from all of us.
I love it even more now!

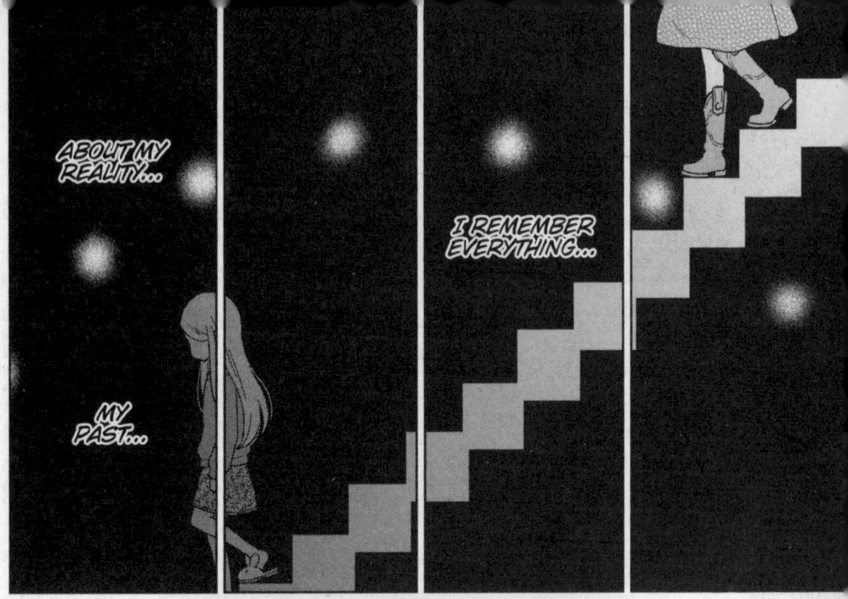
I REMEMBER EVERYTHING...
ABOUT MY REALITY...
MY PAST...

Flashback

Himari

10 Years Ago

The apartment I lived in.

※ *I waited for Mama there, alone.*

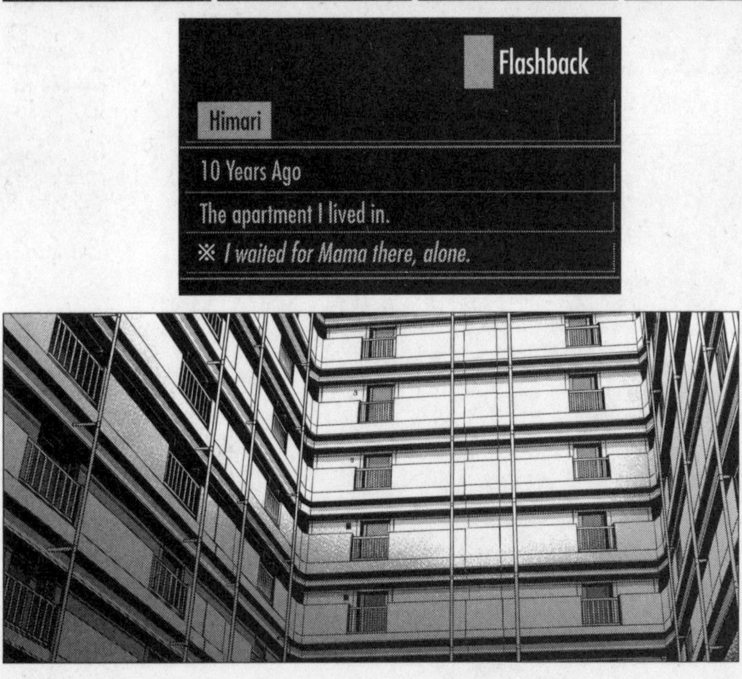

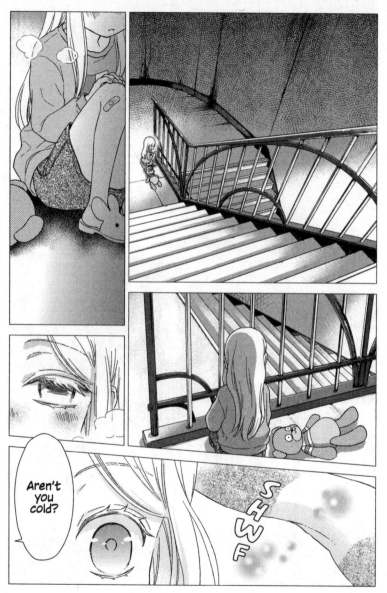

Aren't you cold?

SHWF

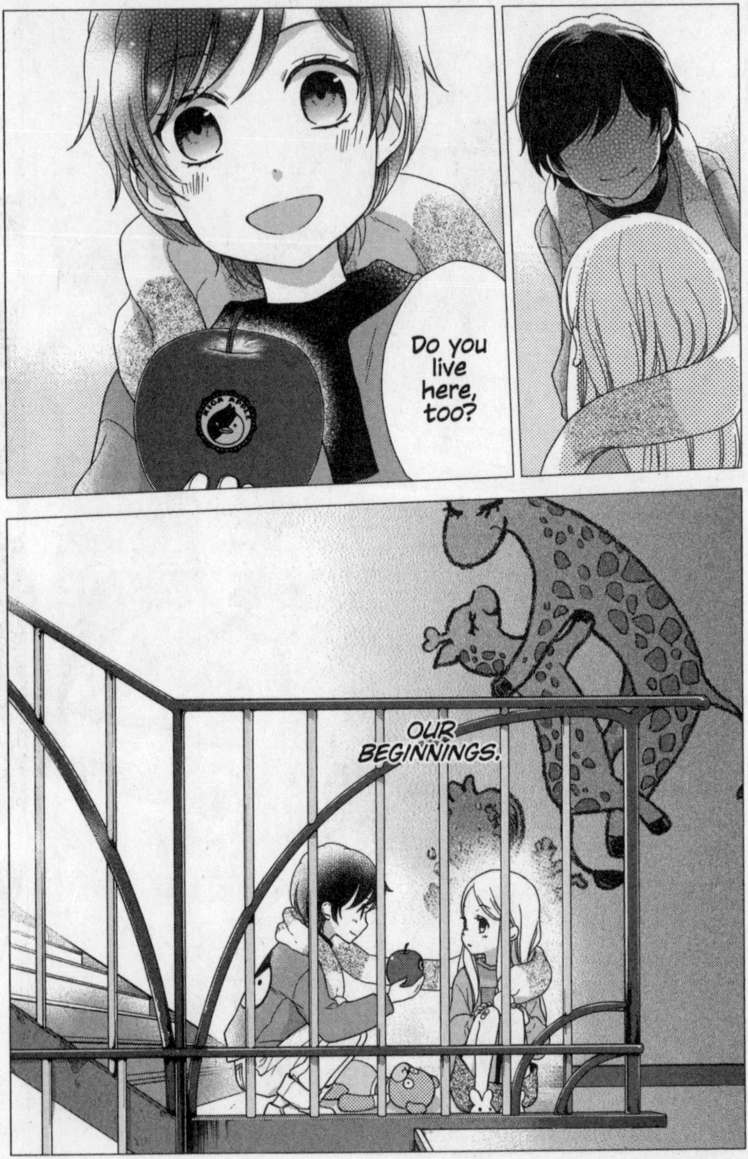
Do you live here, too?
OUR BEGINNINGS.

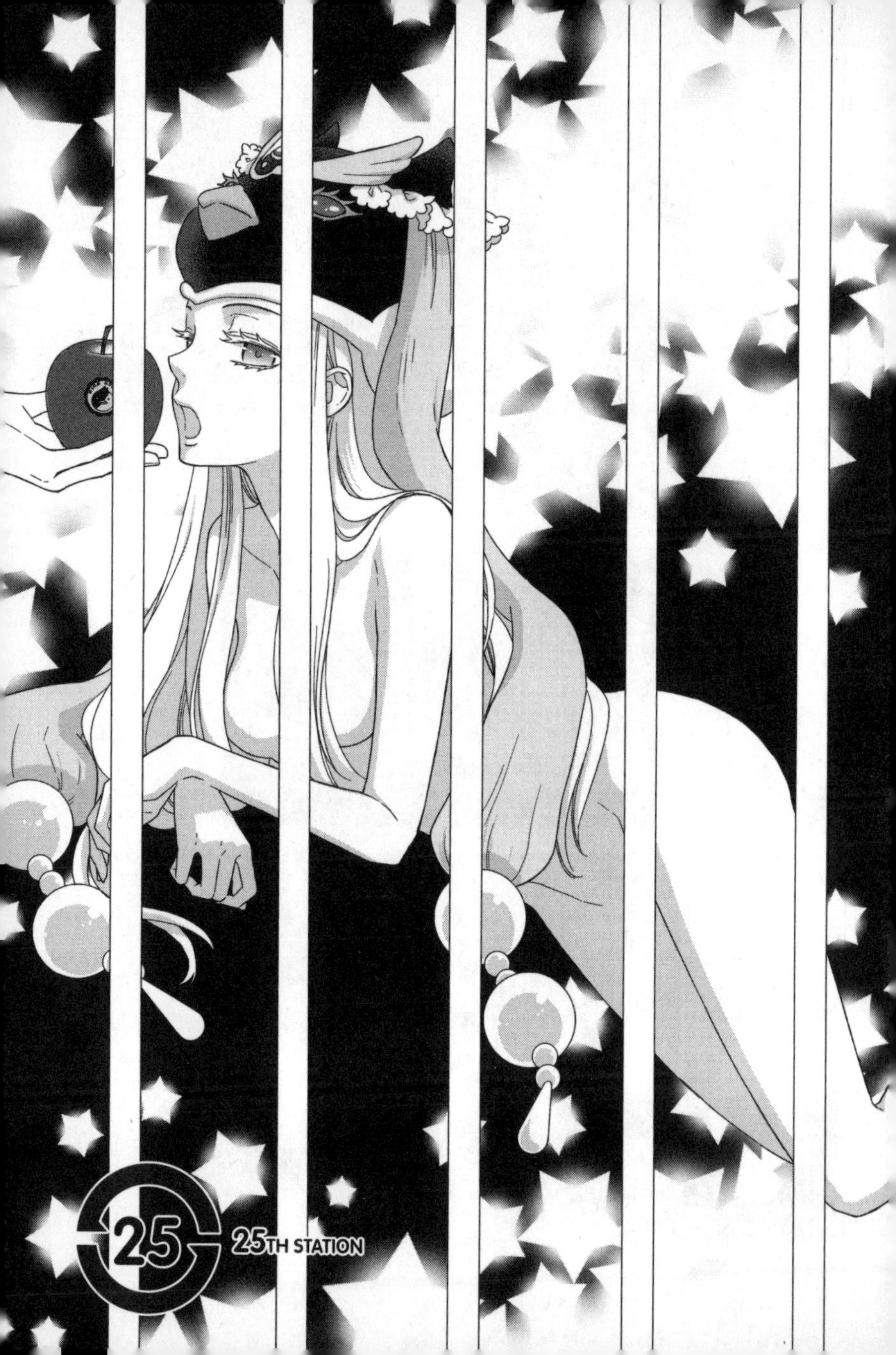

25
25TH STATION

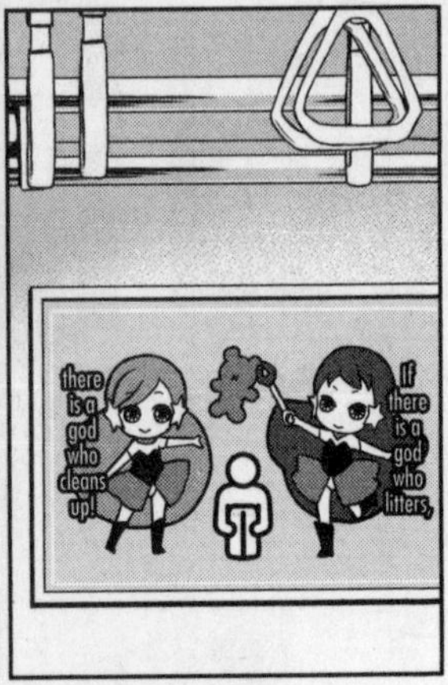
If there is a god who litters,
there is a god who cleans up!

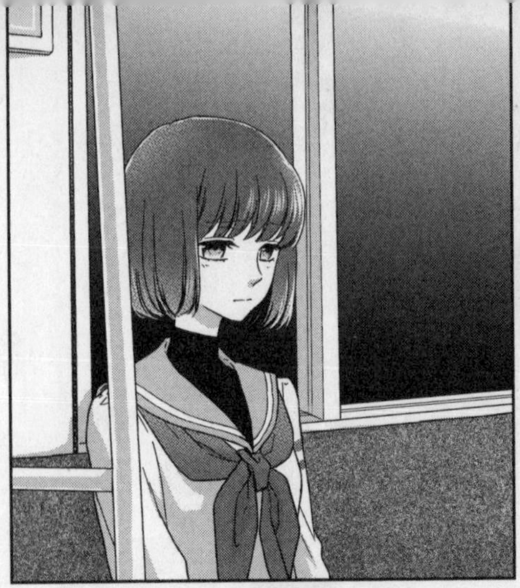

Flashback

Ringo

The Other Day

The Park Near the Takakura Home

※ *I didn't know about the secret those three kept...*

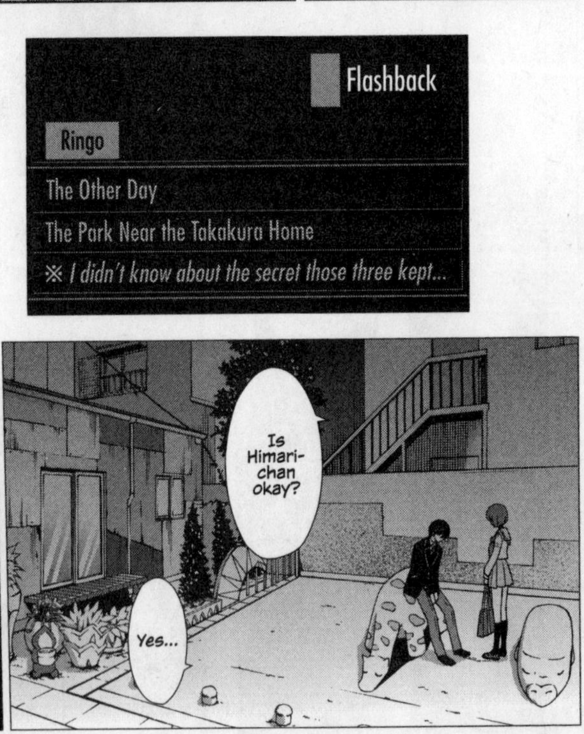
Is Himari-chan okay?
Yes...

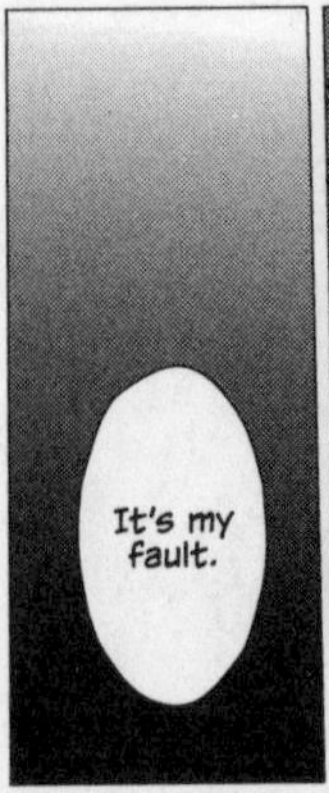
It's my fault.

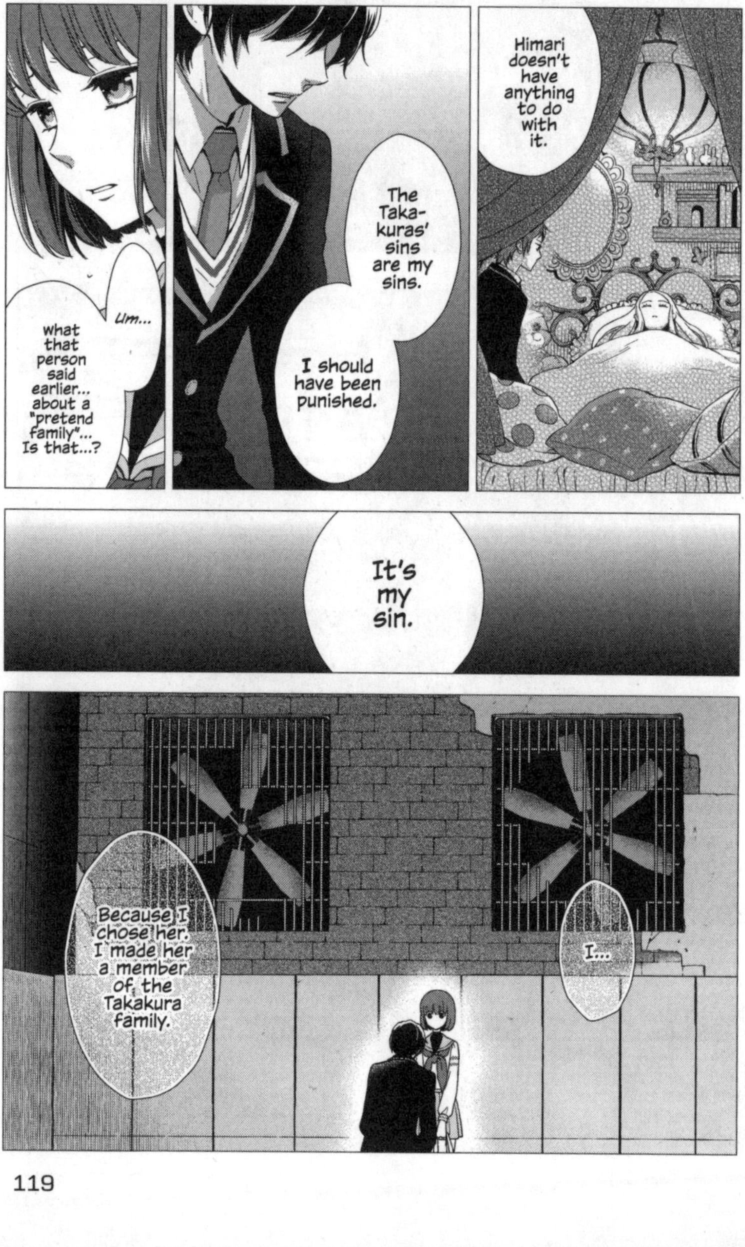

Himari doesn't have anything to do with it.
The Takakuras' sins are my sins.
I should have been punished.
Um...
what that person said earlier... about a "pretend family"... Is that...?
It's my sin.
I...
Because I chose her. I made her a member of the Takakura family.

Flashback

Shoma

10 Years Ago

Kiga Association · Hideout

※ *Where I met Himari all by myself.*

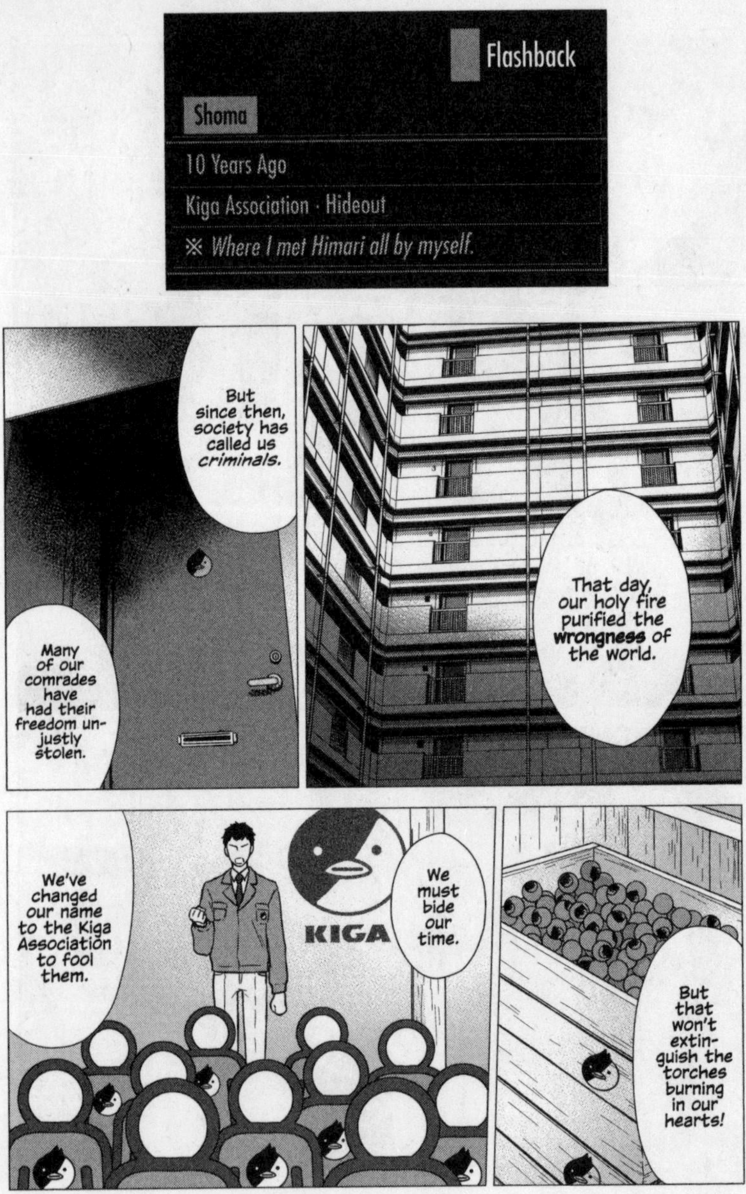
That day, our holy fire purified the **wrongness** of the world.
But since then, society has called us *criminals.*
Many of our comrades have had their freedom unjustly stolen.
But that won't extinguish the torches burning in our hearts!
We must bide our time.
KIGA
We've changed our name to the Kiga Association to fool them.

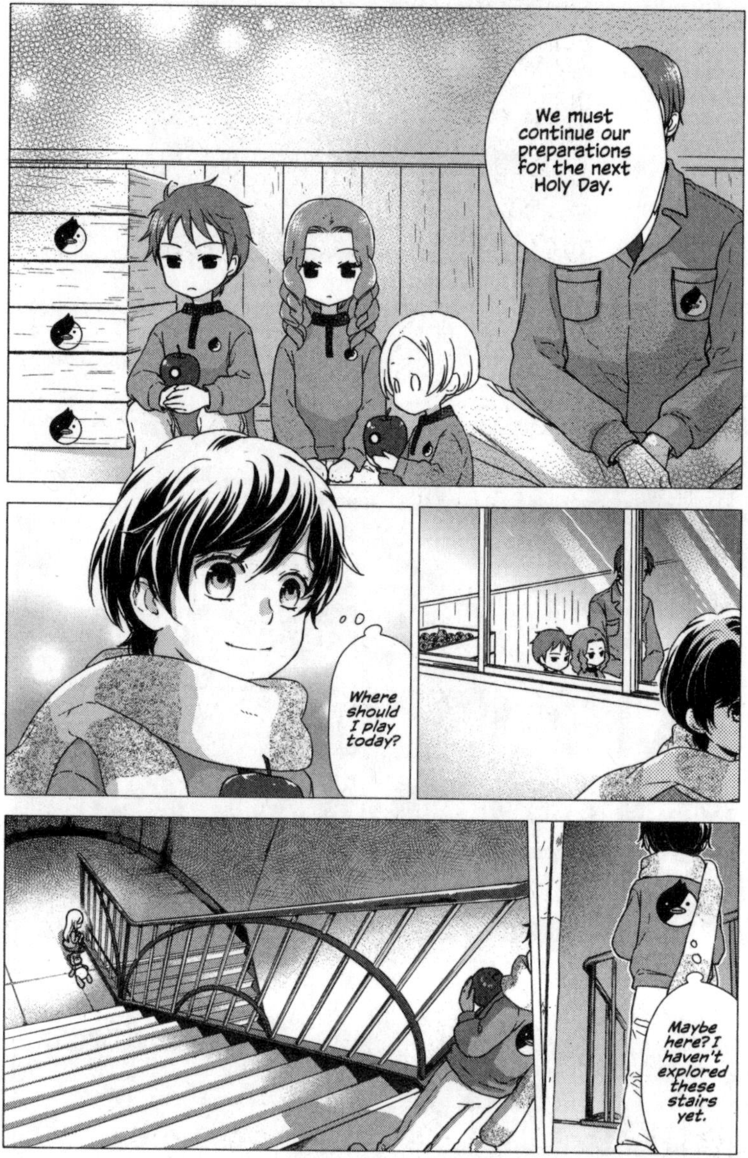
We must continue our preparations for the next Holy Day.
Where should I play today?
Maybe here? I haven't explored these stairs yet.

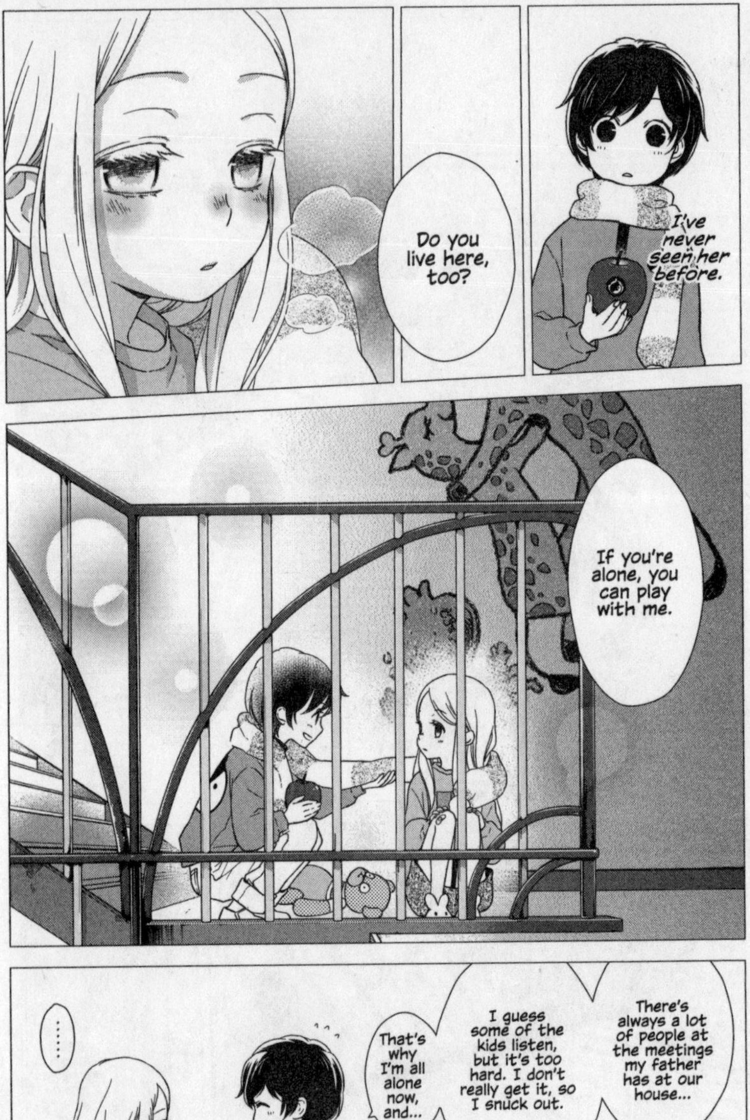
I've never seen her before.
Do you live here, too?
If you're alone, you can play with me.
There's always a lot of people at the meetings my father has at our house...
I guess some of the kids listen, but it's too hard. I don't really get it, so I snuck out.
That's why I'm all alone now, and...
......

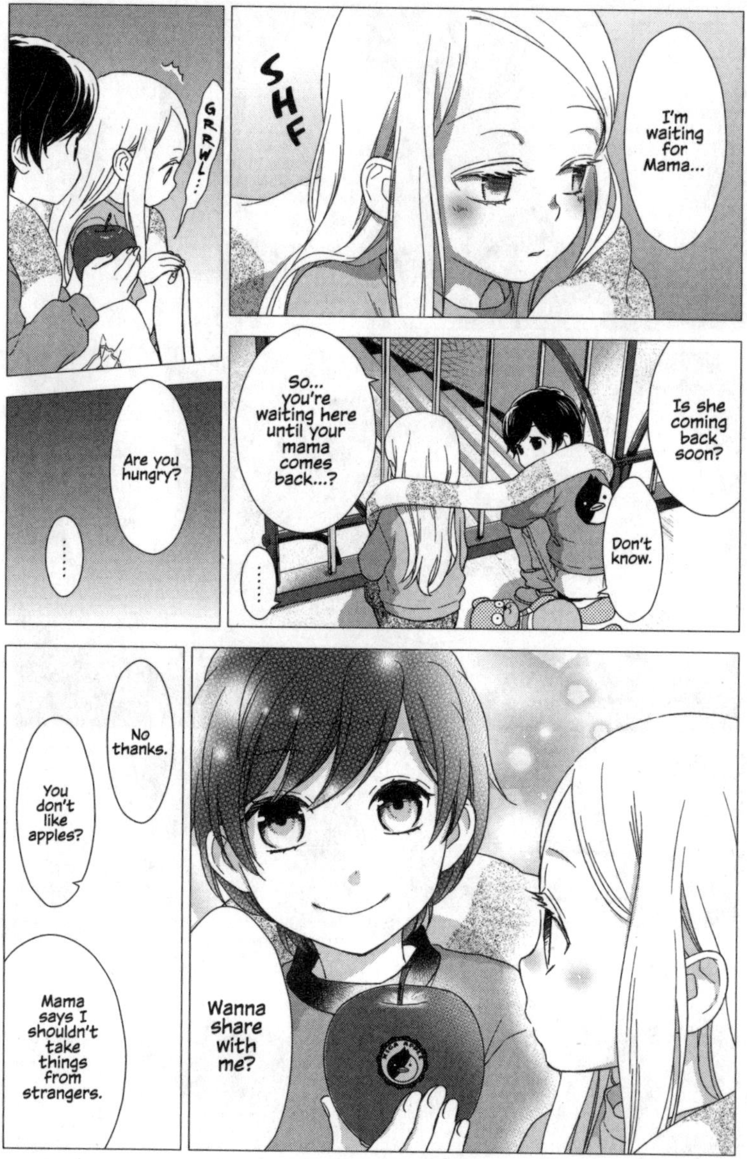
SHF
I'm waiting for Mama...
GRRWL...
So... you're waiting here until your mama comes back...?
......
Is she coming back soon?
Don't know.
Are you hungry?
......
Wanna share with me?
No thanks.
You don't like apples?
Mama says I shouldn't take things from strangers.

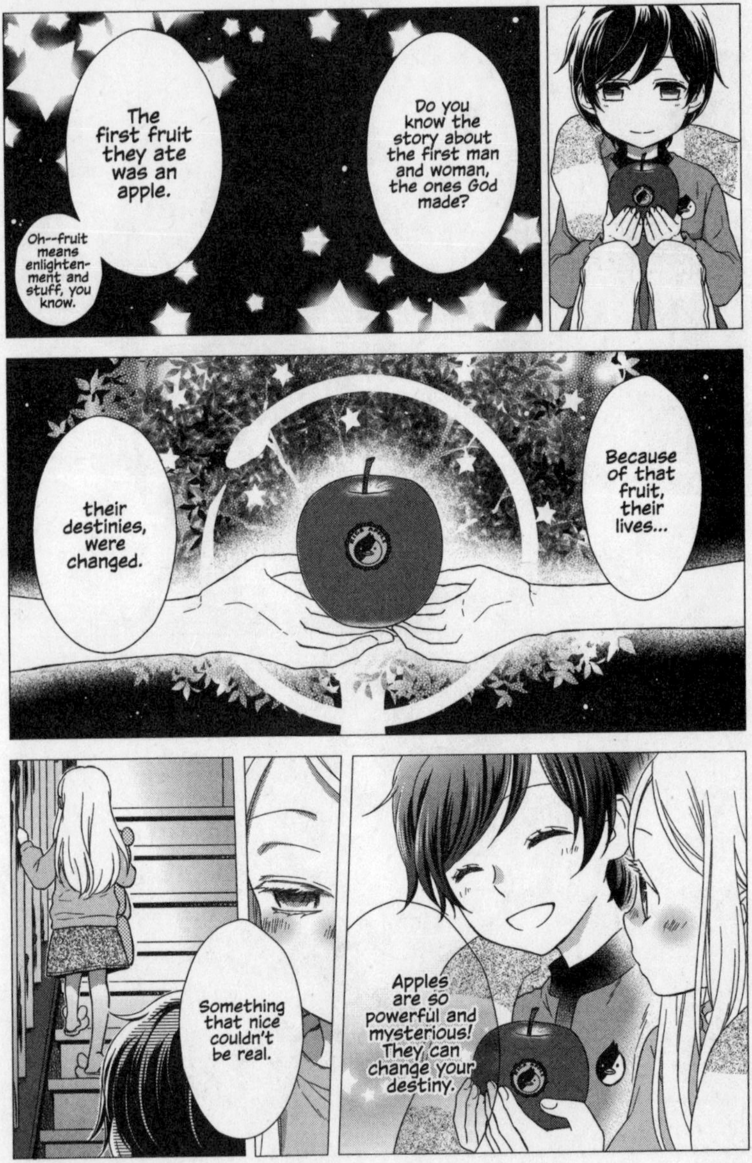
Do you know the story about the first man and woman, the ones God made?
The first fruit they ate was an apple.
Oh--fruit means enlighten-ment and stuff, you know.
Because of that fruit, their lives...
their destinies, were changed.
Apples are so powerful and mysterious! They can change your destiny.
Something that nice couldn't be real.

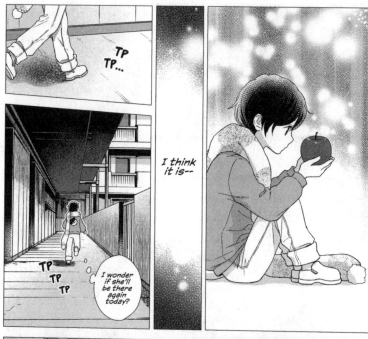

I think it is--
TP TP...
TP TP TP
I wonder if she'll be there again today?
Disappointed...
I GUESS I'LL EXPLORE SOMEPLACE ELSE...
No littering!

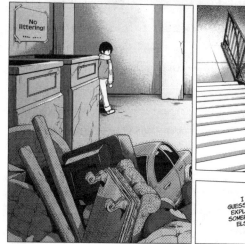

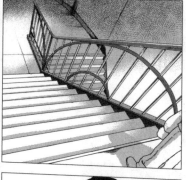

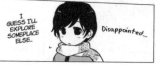

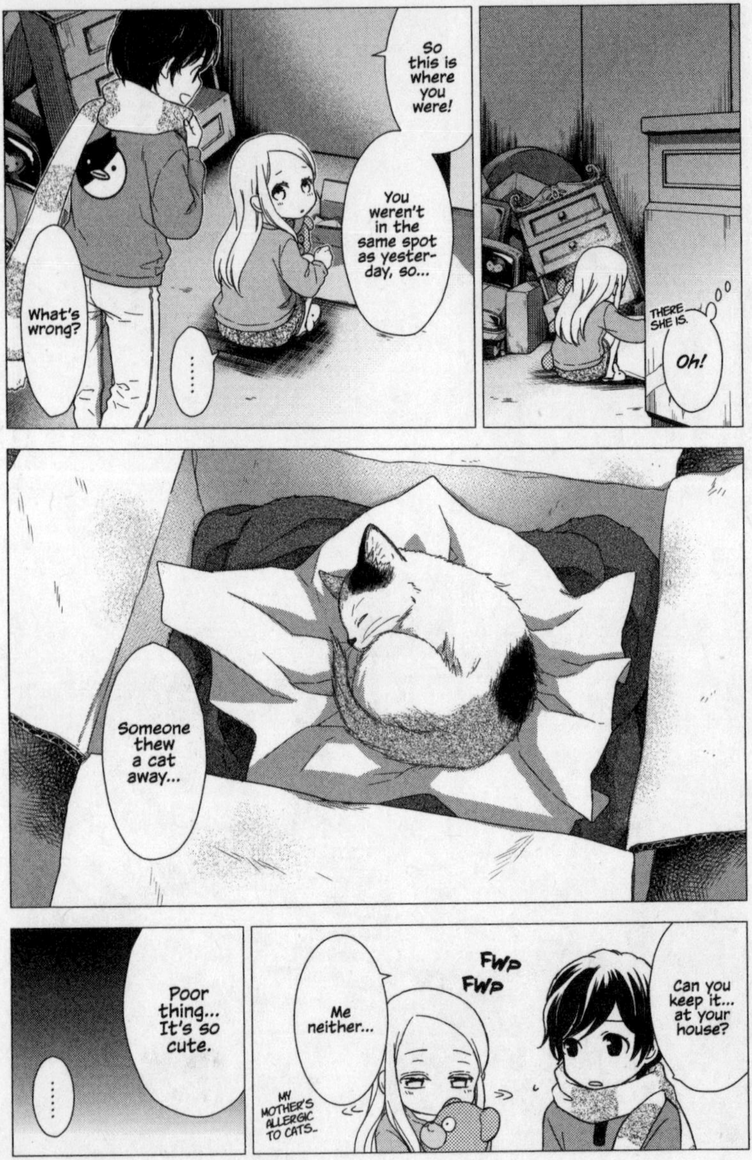
Oh!
THERE SHE IS.
So this is where you were!
You weren't in the same spot as yesterday, so...
......
What's wrong?
Someone thew a cat away...
Can you keep it... at your house?
FWP
FWP
Me neither...
MY MOTHER'S ALLERGIC TO CATS...
Poor thing... It's so cute.
......

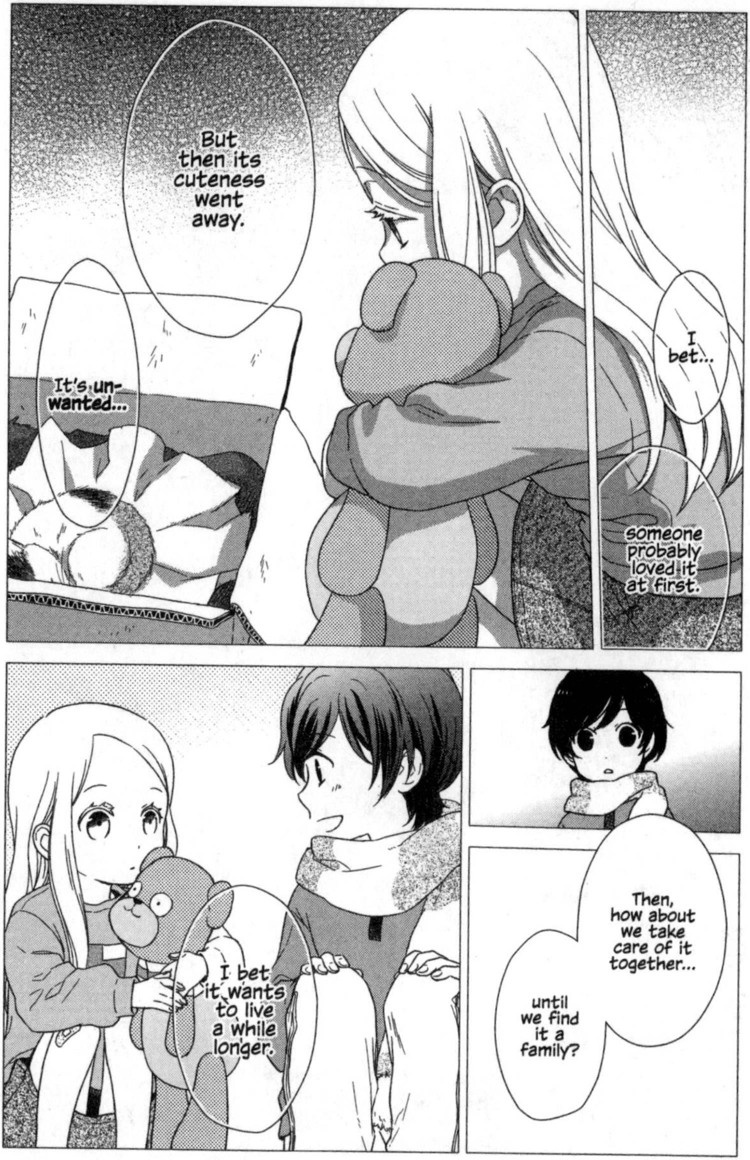
I bet...
someone probably loved it at first.
But then its cuteness went away.
It's un-wanted...
Then, how about we take care of it together...
until we find it a family?
I bet it wants to live a while longer.

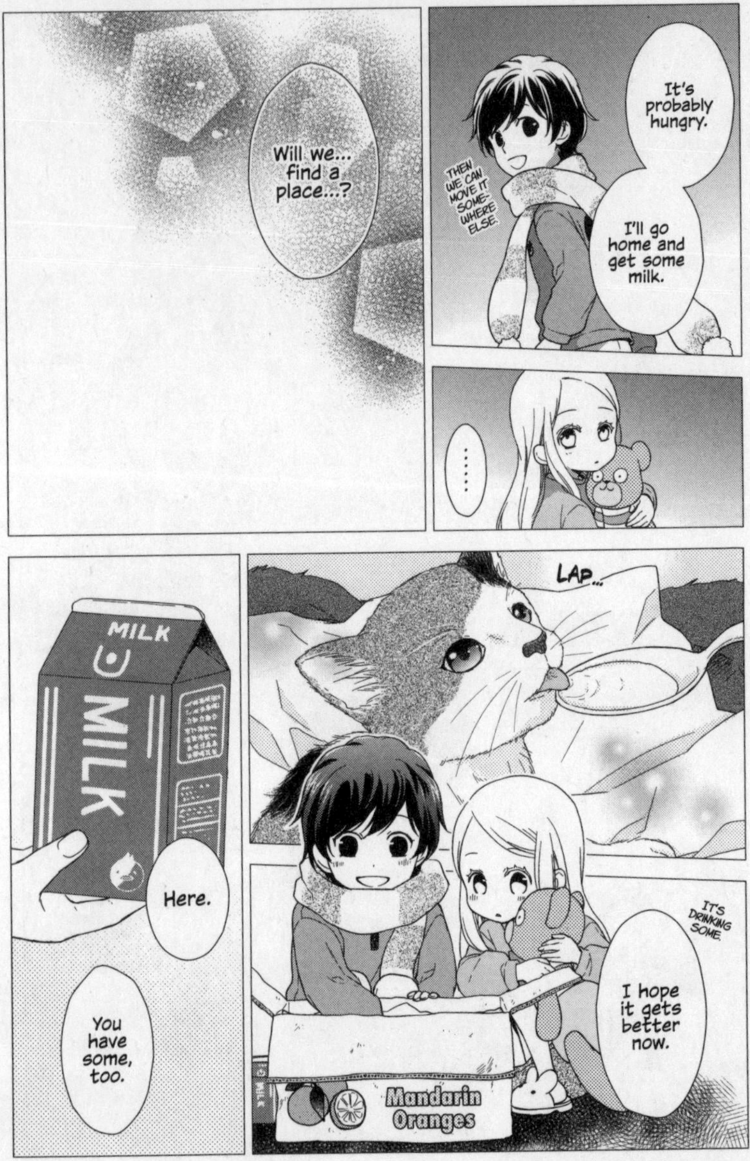
It's probably hungry.
I'll go home and get some milk.
THEN WE CAN MOVE IT SOME-WHERE ELSE.
......
Will we... find a place...?
LAP...
IT'S DRINKING SOME.
I hope it gets better now.
Mandarin Oranges
MILK
MILK
MILK
Here.
You have some, too.

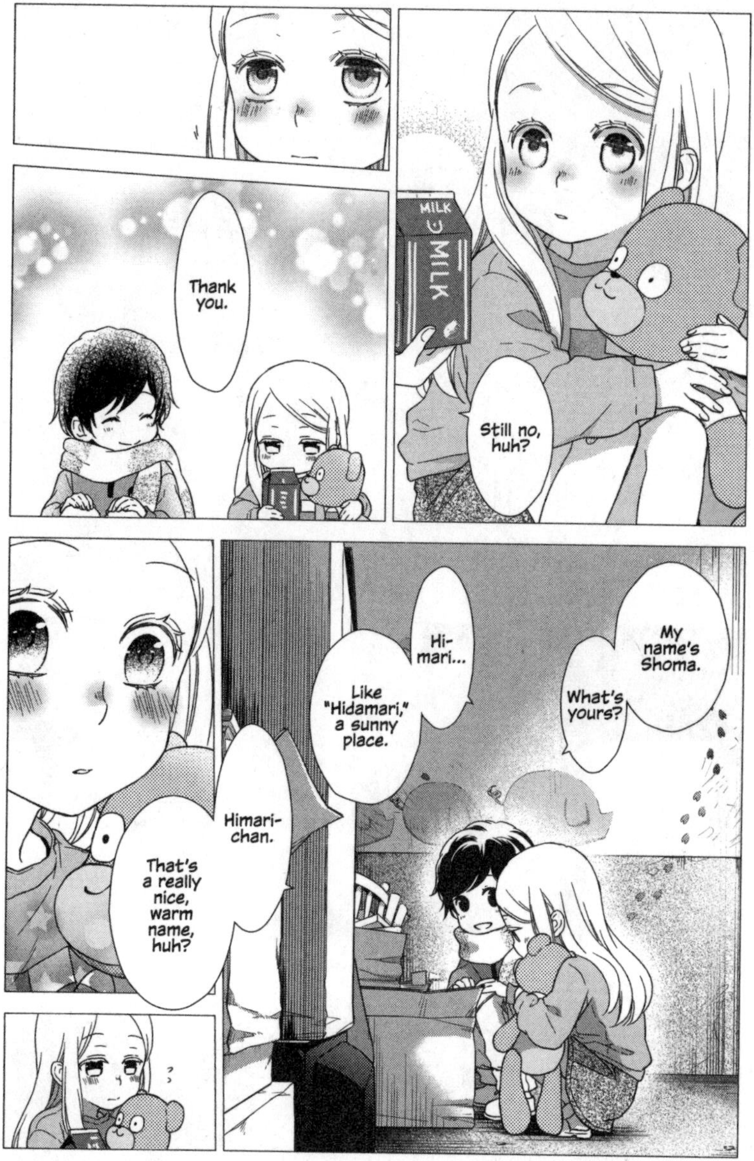
MILK
MILK
Still no, huh?
Thank you.
My name's Shoma.
What's yours?
Hi-mari...
Like "Hidamari," a sunny place.
Himari-chan.
That's a really nice, warm name, huh?

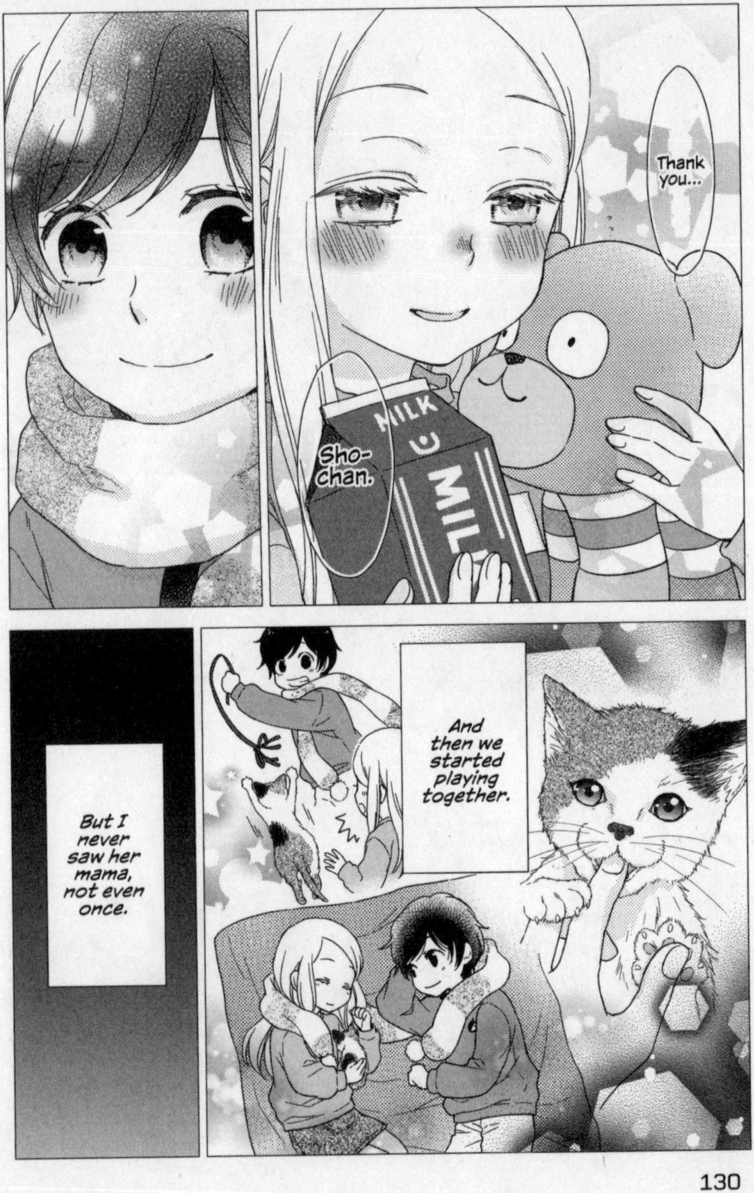
Thank you...
Sho-chan.
And then we started playing together.
But I never saw her mama, not even once.

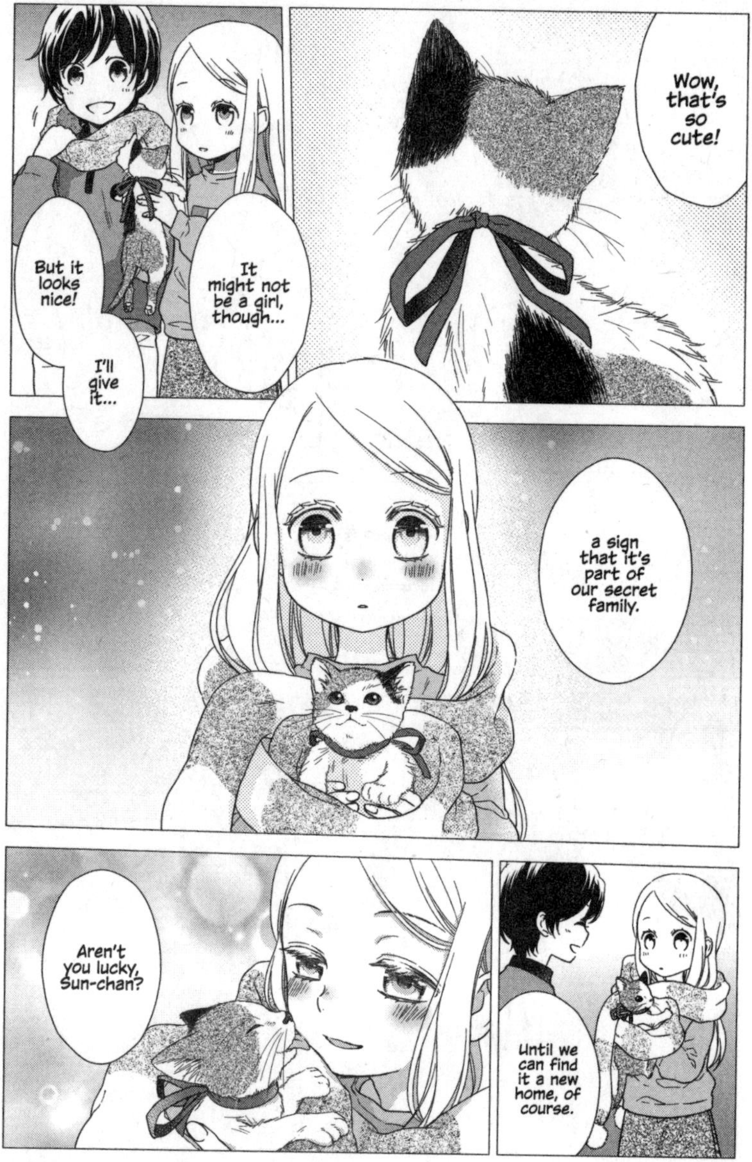
Wow, that's so cute!
It might not be a girl, though...
But it looks nice!
I'll give it...
a sign that it's part of our secret family.
Until we can find it a new home, of course.
Aren't you lucky, Sun-chan?

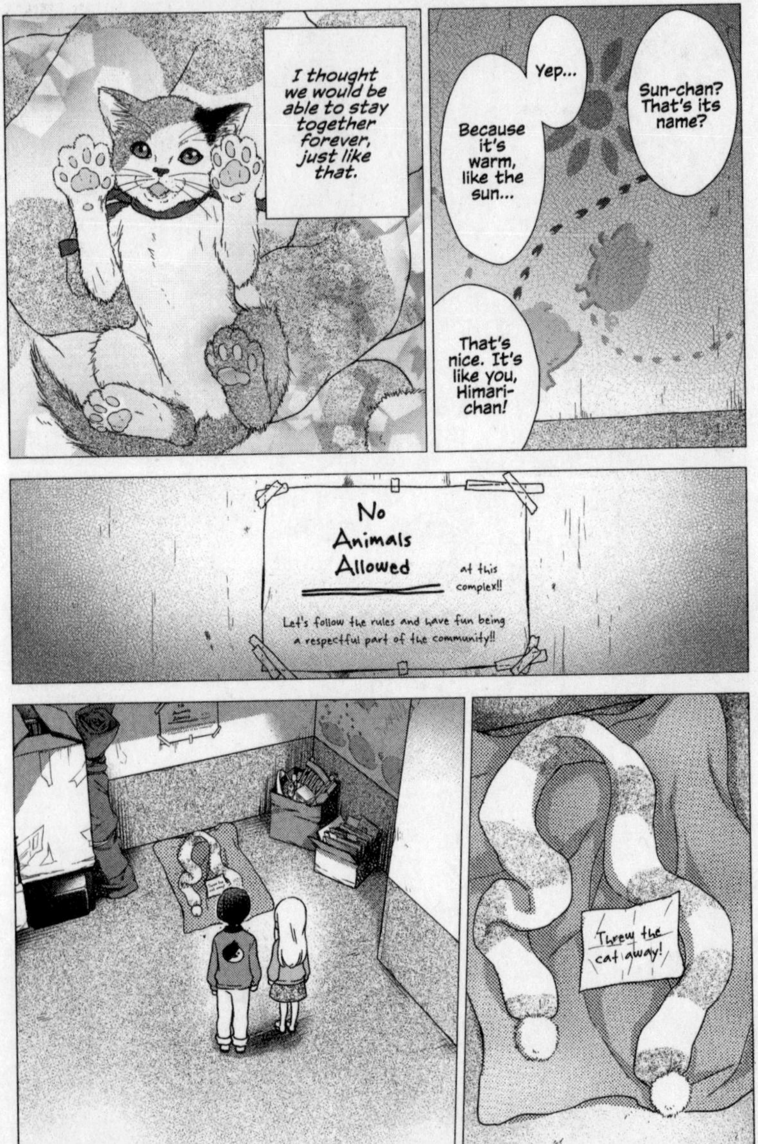
Sun-chan? That's its name?
Yep...
Because it's warm, like the sun...
That's nice. It's like you, Himari-chan!
I thought we would be able to stay together forever, just like that.
No Animals Allowed at this complex!!
Let's follow the rules and have fun being a respectful part of the community!!
Threw the cat away!

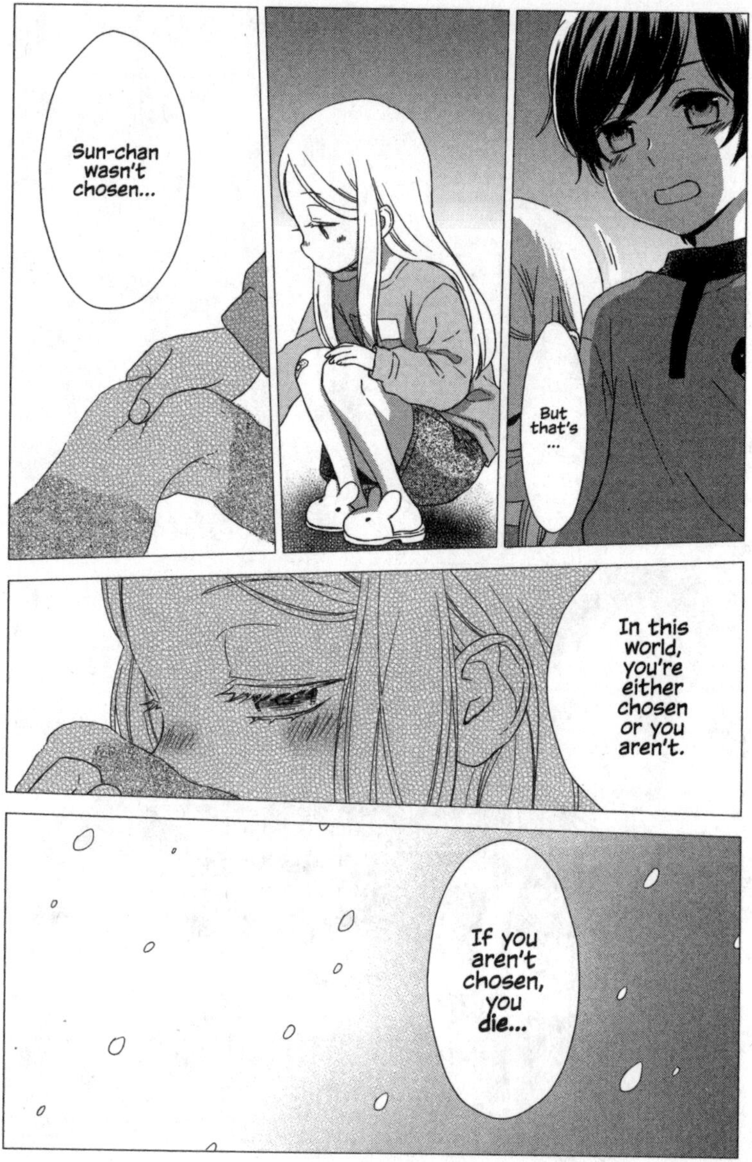
But that's ...
Sun-chan wasn't chosen...
In this world, you're either chosen or you aren't.
If you aren't chosen, you die...

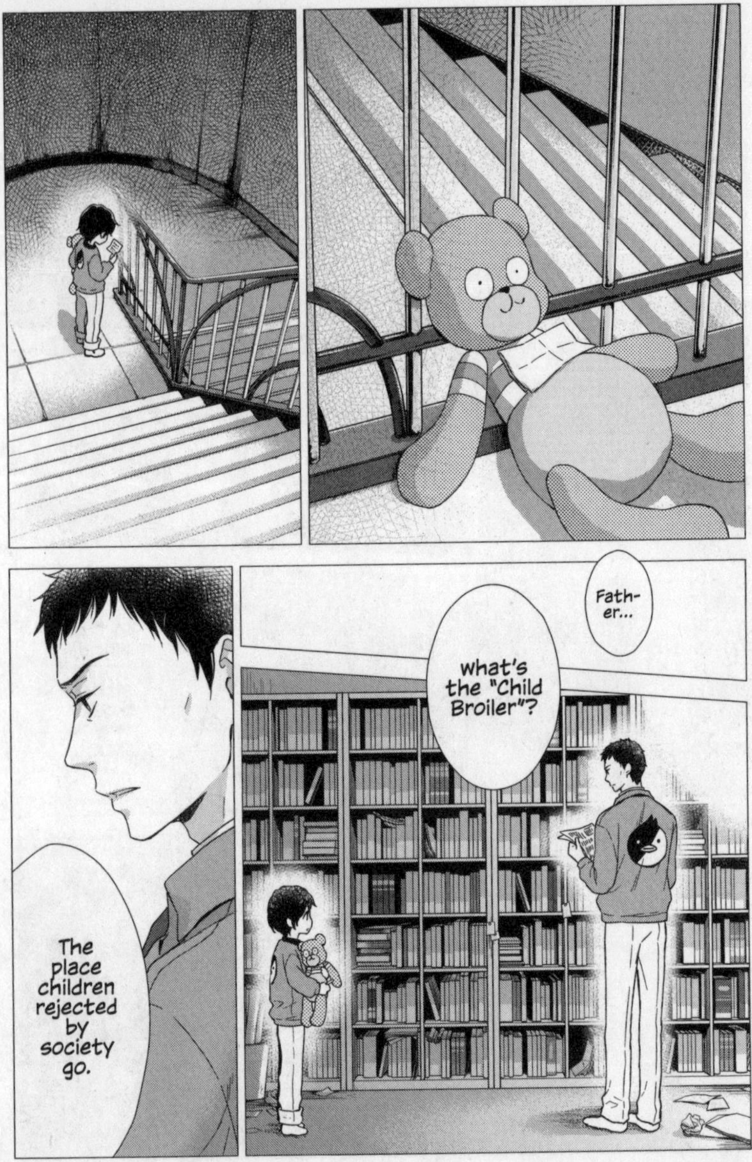
Father...
What's the "Child Broiler"?
The place children rejected by society go.

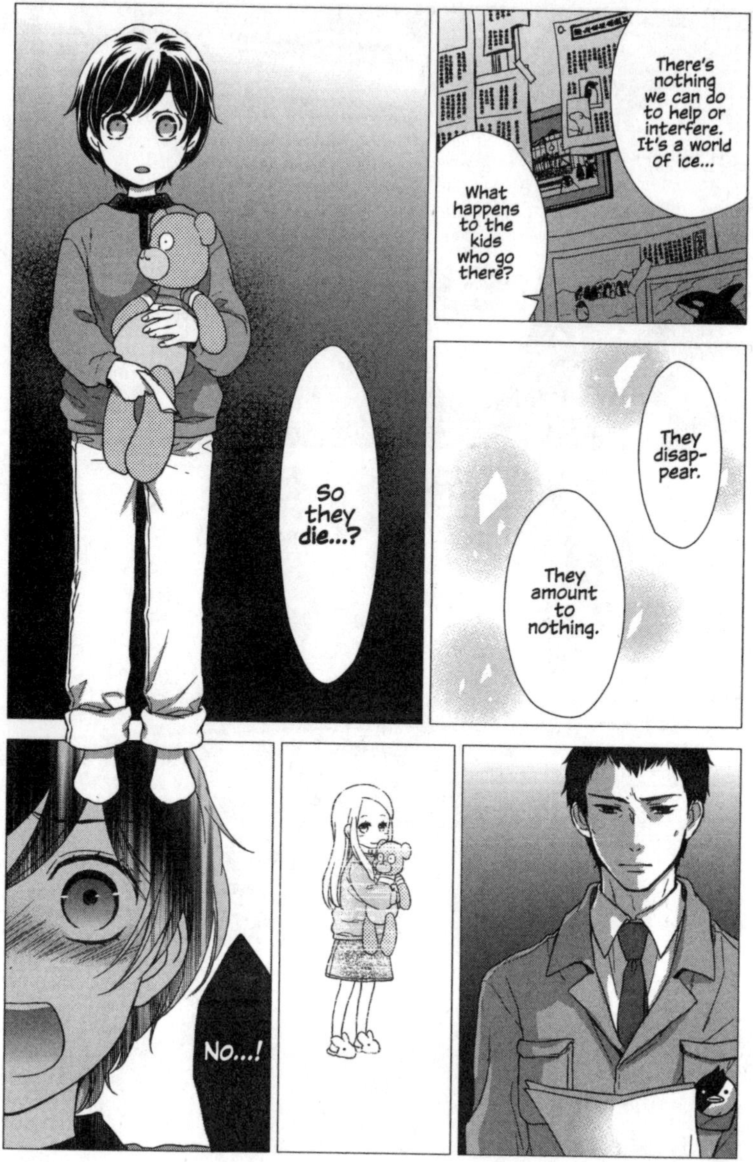
There's nothing we can do to help or interfere. It's a world of ice...
What happens to the kids who go there?
They disappear.
They amount to nothing.
So they die...?
No...!

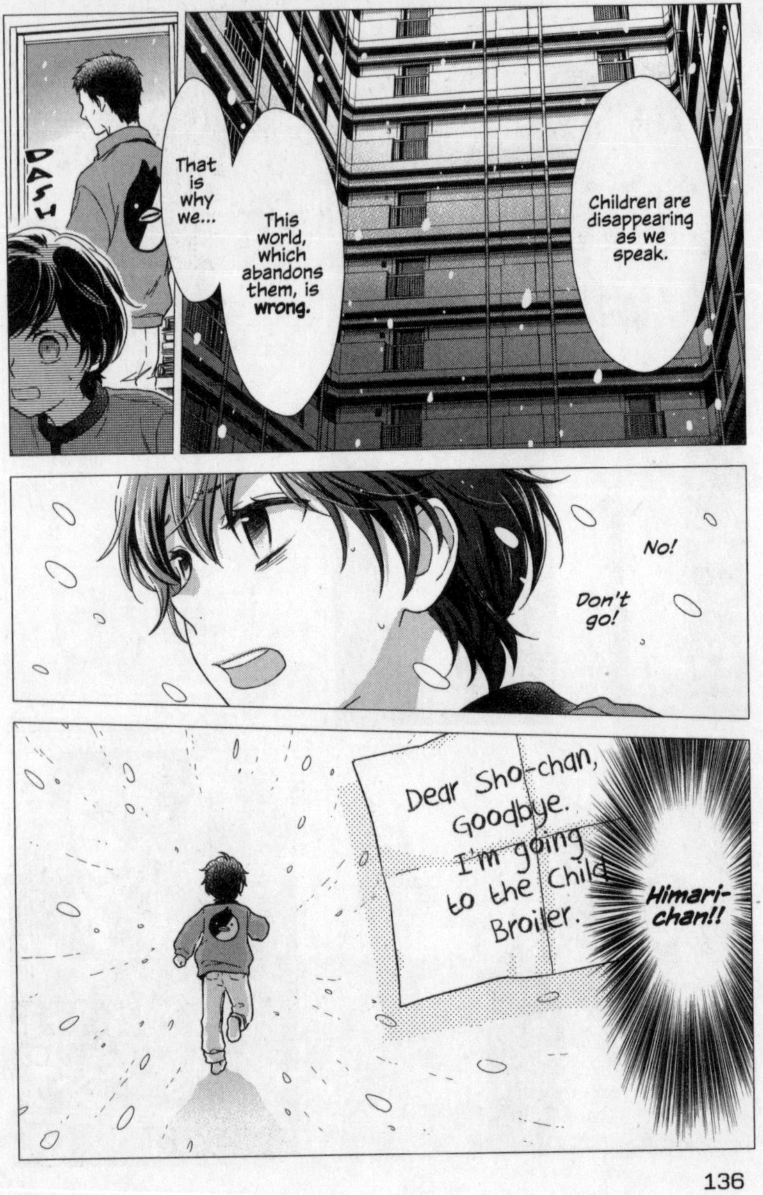

Children are disappearing as we speak.
This world, which abandons them, is wrong.
That is why we...
DASH
No!
Don't go!
Himari-chan!!
Dear Sho-chan, Goodbye. I'm going to the Child Broiler.

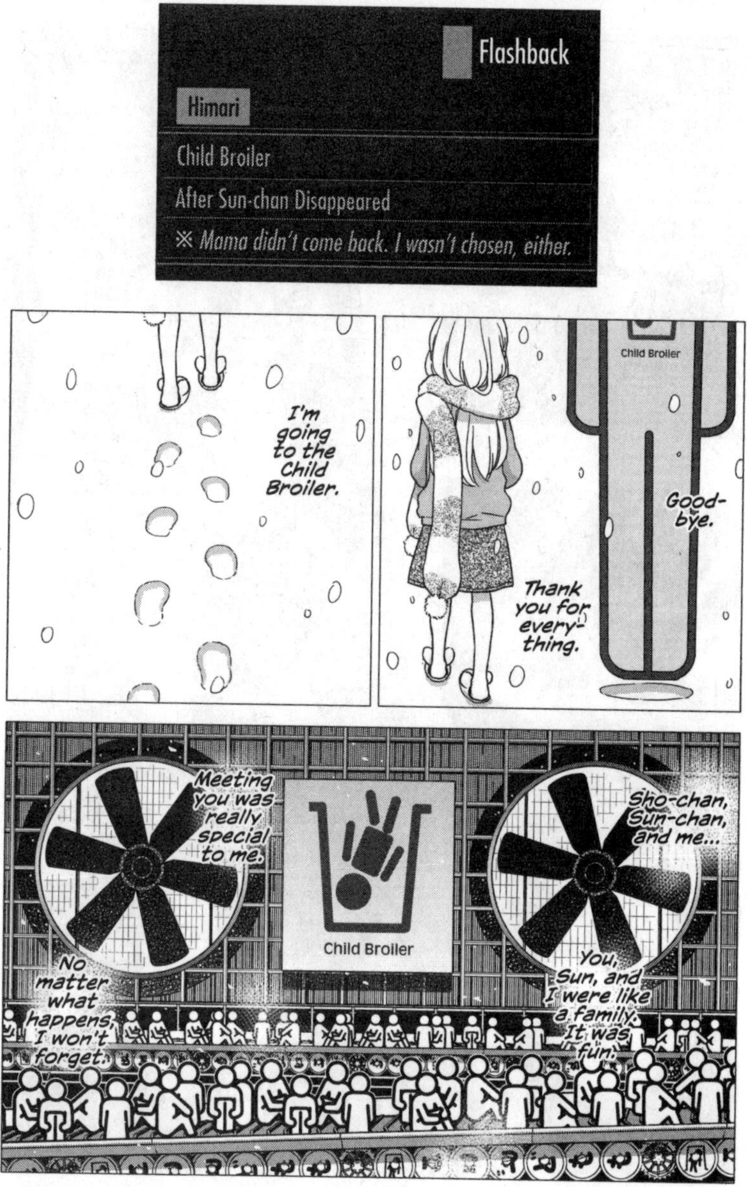
Flashback
Himari
Child Broiler
After Sun-chan Disappeared
※ Mama didn't come back. I wasn't chosen, either.
Child Broiler
Good-bye.
Thank you for everything.
I'm going to the Child Broiler.
Sho-chan, Sun-chan, and me...
Meeting you was really special to me.
Child Broiler
You, Sun, and I were like a family. It was fun.
No matter what happens, I won't forget.

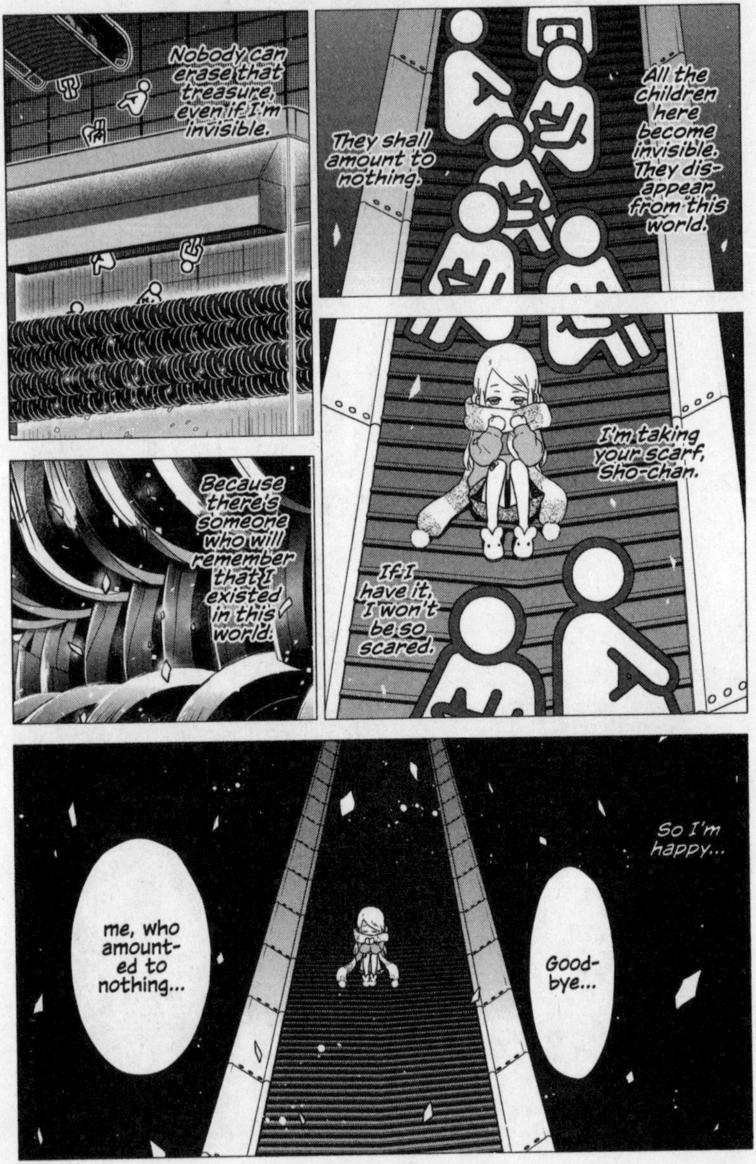
All the children here become invisible. They disappear from this world.
They shall amount to nothing.
Nobody can erase that treasure, even if I'm invisible.
I'm taking your scarf, Sho-chan.
If I have it, I won't be so scared.
Because there's someone who will remember that I existed in this world.
So I'm happy...
Good-bye...
me, who amounted to nothing...

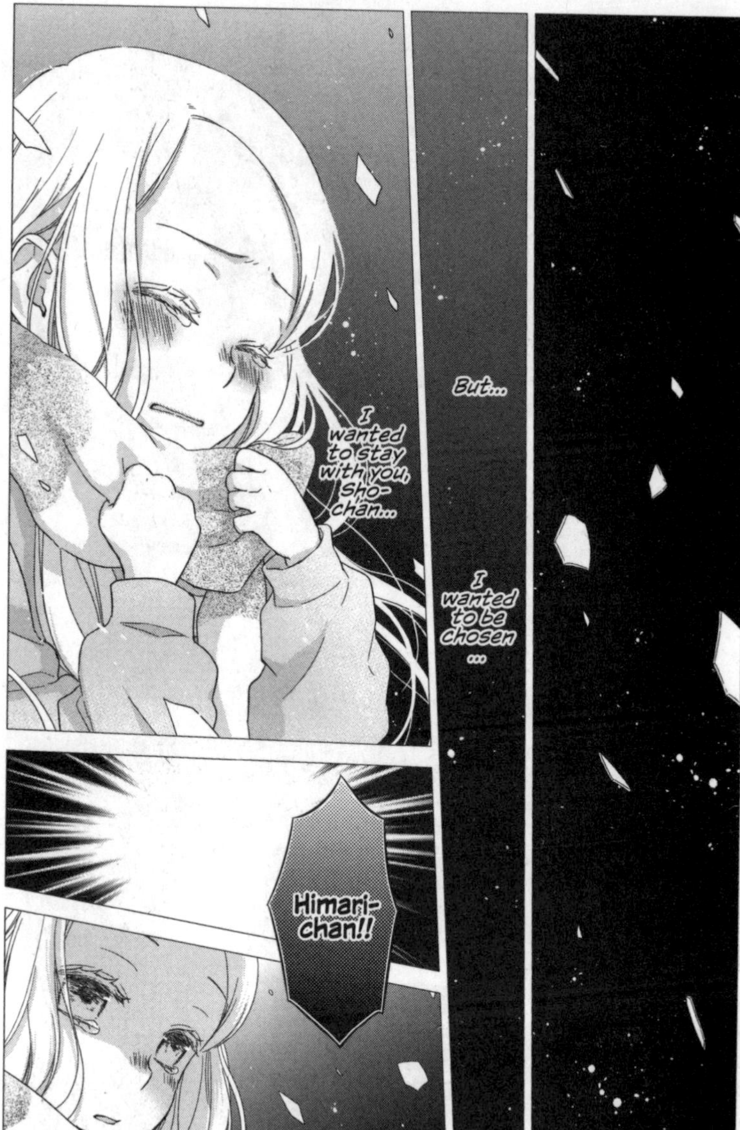
But...
I wanted to be chosen...
I wanted to stay with you, Sho-chan...
Himari-chan!!

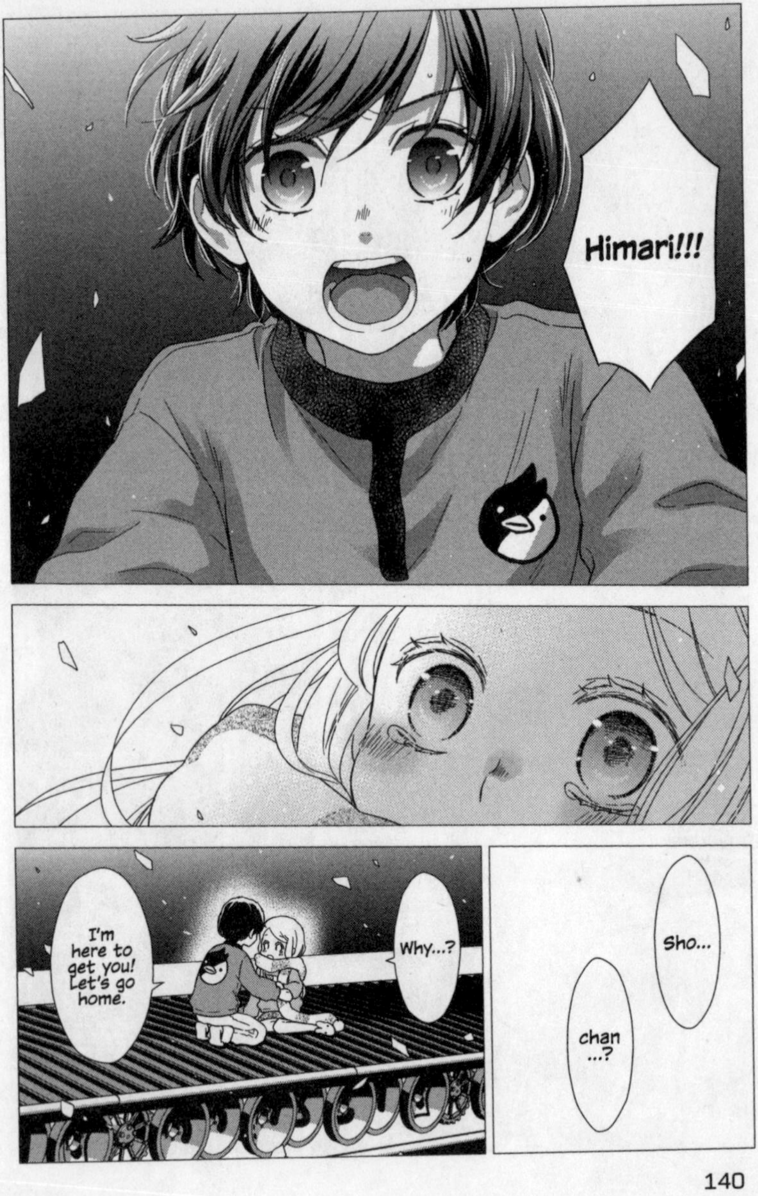
Himari!!!
Sho...
chan...?
Why...?
I'm here to get you! Let's go home.

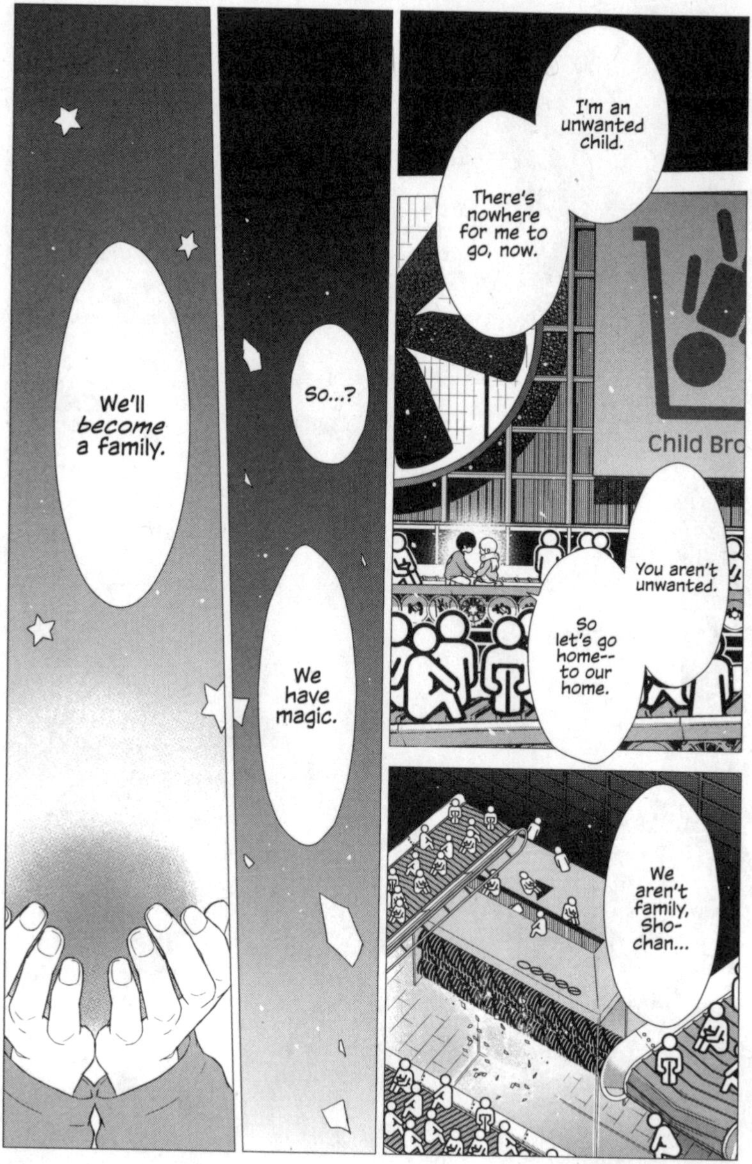
I'm an unwanted child.
There's nowhere for me to go, now.
Child Bro
You aren't unwanted.
So let's go home-- to our home.
We aren't family, Sho-chan...
So...?
We have magic.
We'll *become* a family.

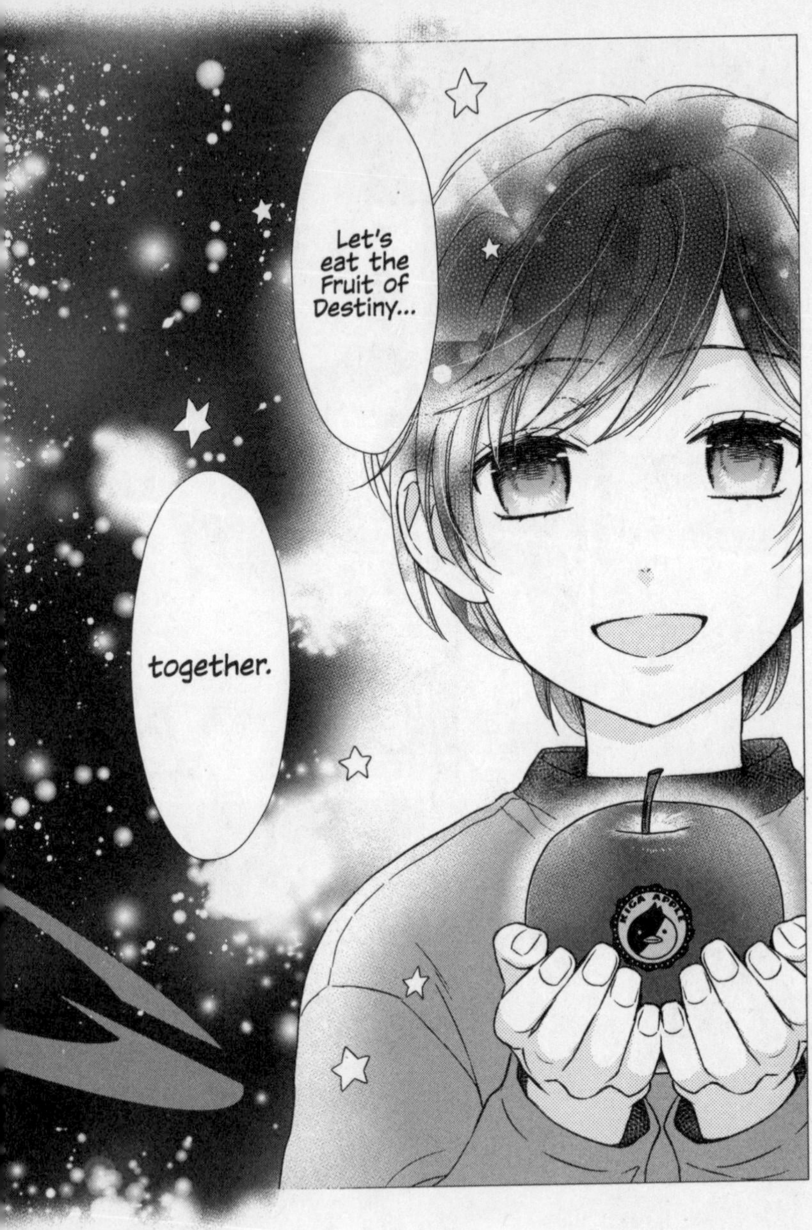
Let's eat the Fruit of Destiny...
together.

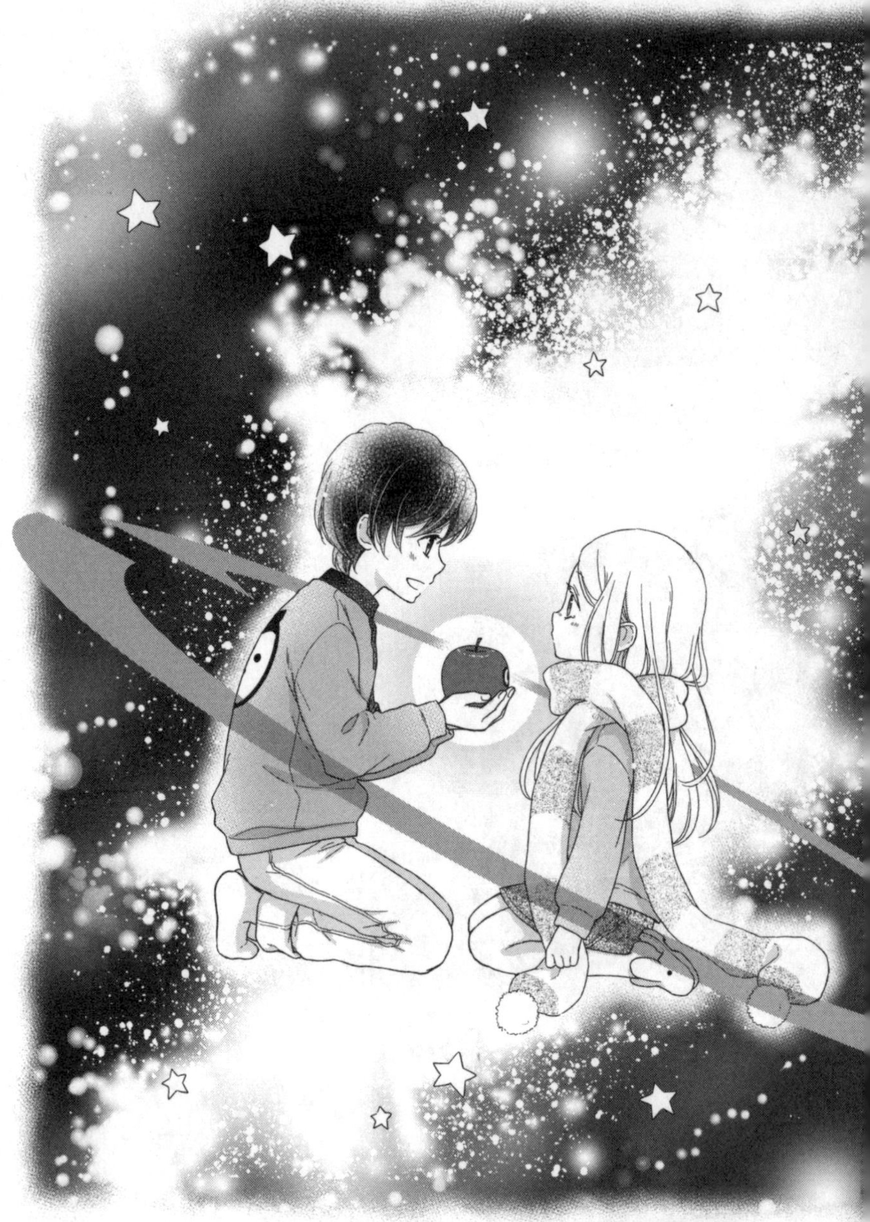

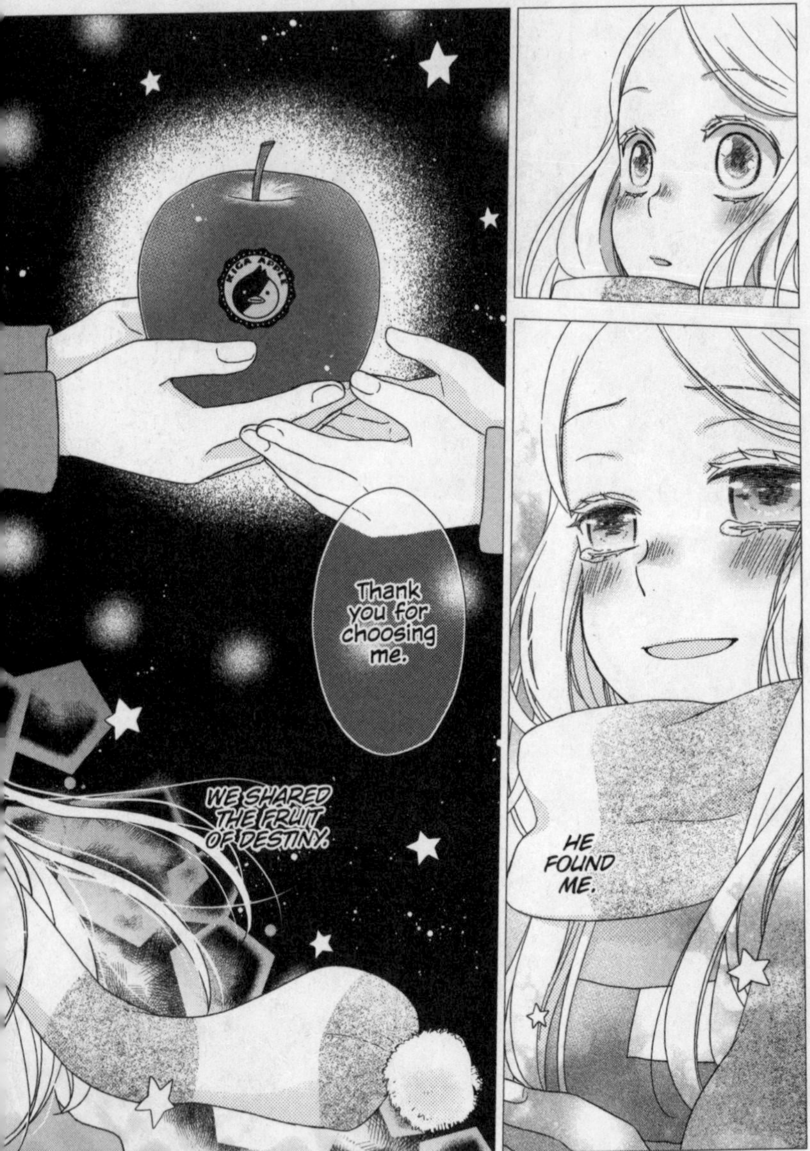
HE FOUND ME.
Thank you for choosing me.
WE SHARED THE FRUIT OF DESTINY.

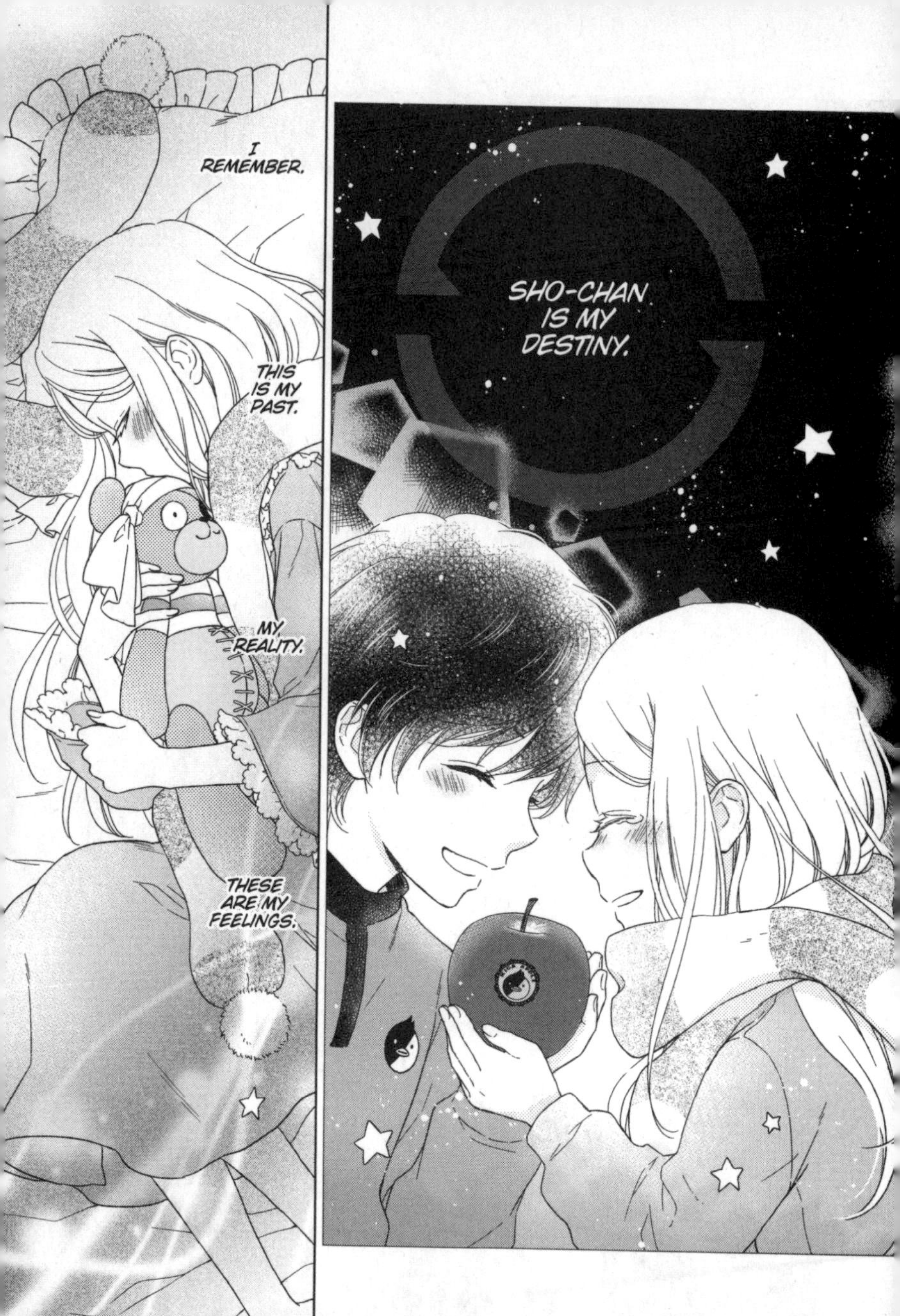
SHO-CHAN IS MY DESTINY.
I REMEMBER.
THIS IS MY PAST.
MY REALITY.
THESE ARE MY FEELINGS.

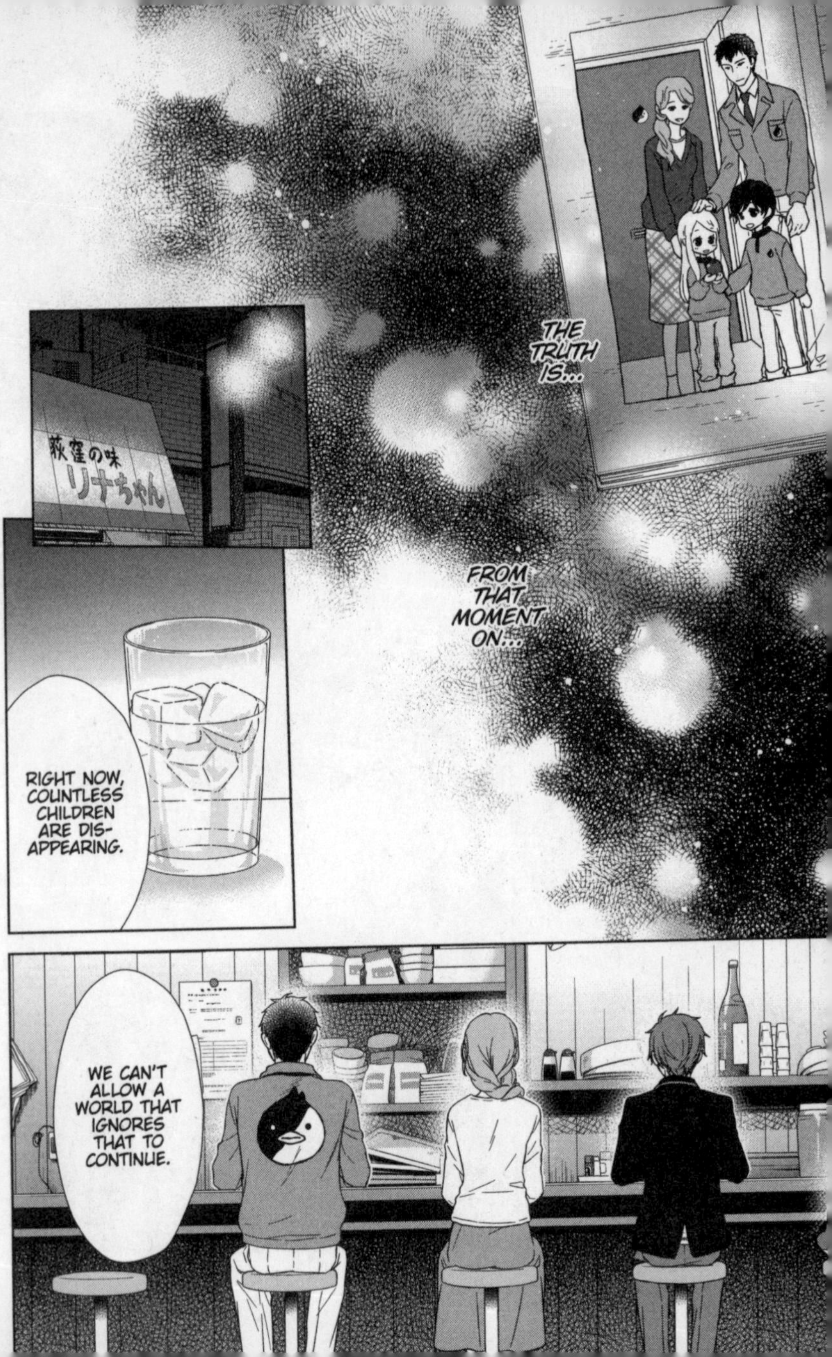
THE TRUTH IS...
FROM THAT MOMENT ON...
荻窪の味
リナちゃん
RIGHT NOW, COUNTLESS CHILDREN ARE DIS-APPEARING.
WE CAN'T ALLOW A WORLD THAT IGNORES THAT TO CONTINUE.

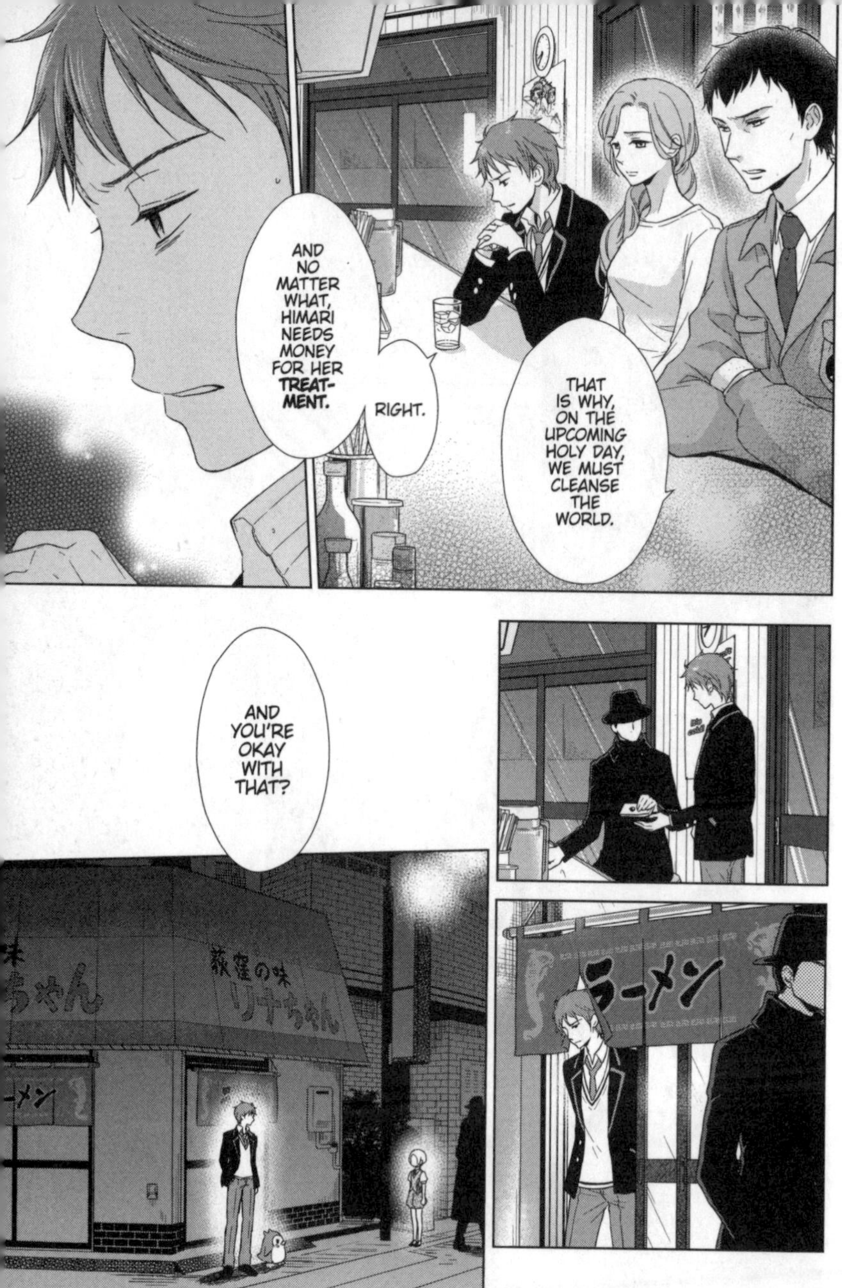
THAT IS WHY, ON THE UPCOMING HOLY DAY, WE MUST CLEANSE THE WORLD.
AND NO MATTER WHAT, HIMARI NEEDS MONEY FOR HER **TREATMENT.**
RIGHT.
AND YOU'RE OKAY WITH THAT?
ラーメン
荻窪の味
リナちゃん

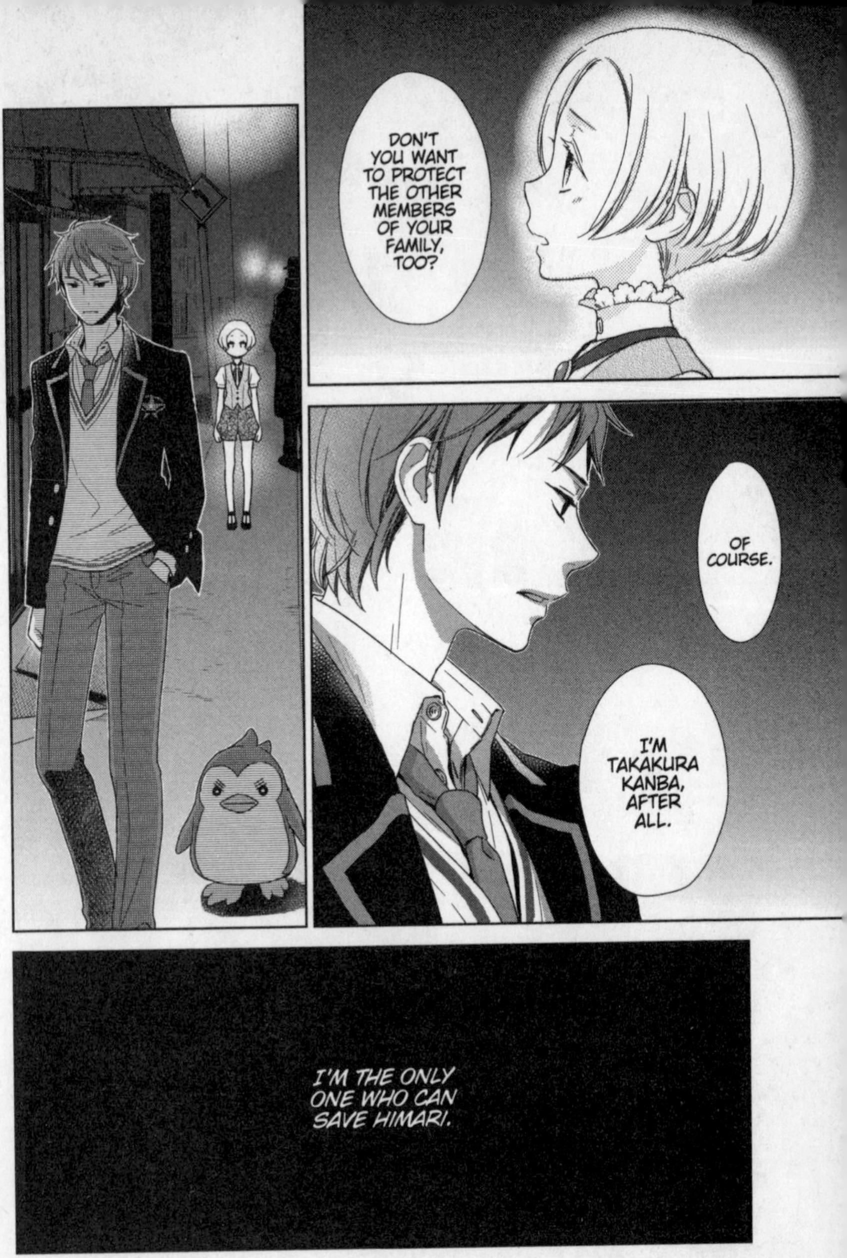
DON'T YOU WANT TO PROTECT THE OTHER MEMBERS OF YOUR FAMILY, TOO?
OF COURSE.
I'M TAKAKURA KANBA, AFTER ALL.
I'M THE ONLY ONE WHO CAN SAVE HIMARI.

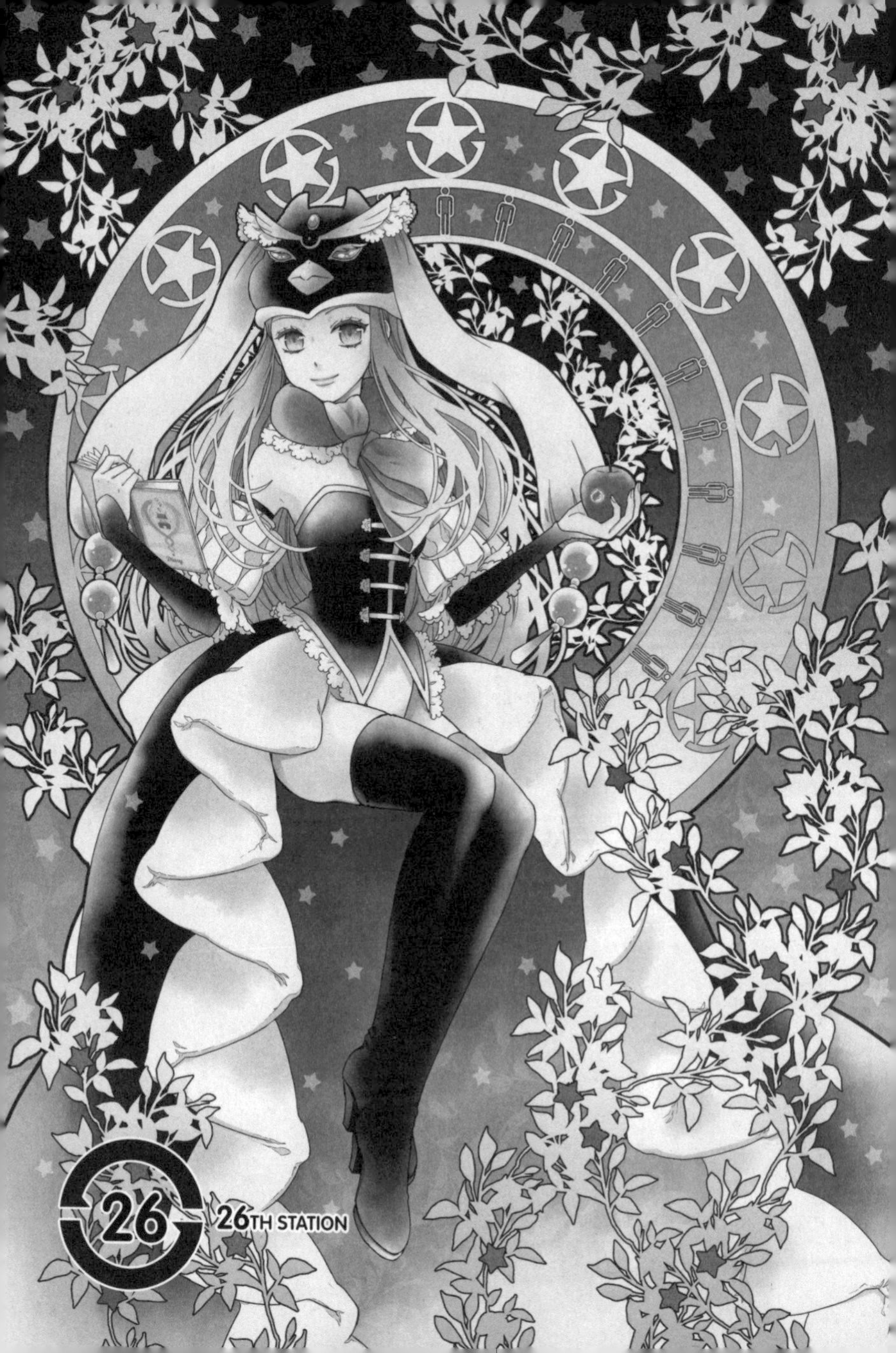
26
26TH STATION

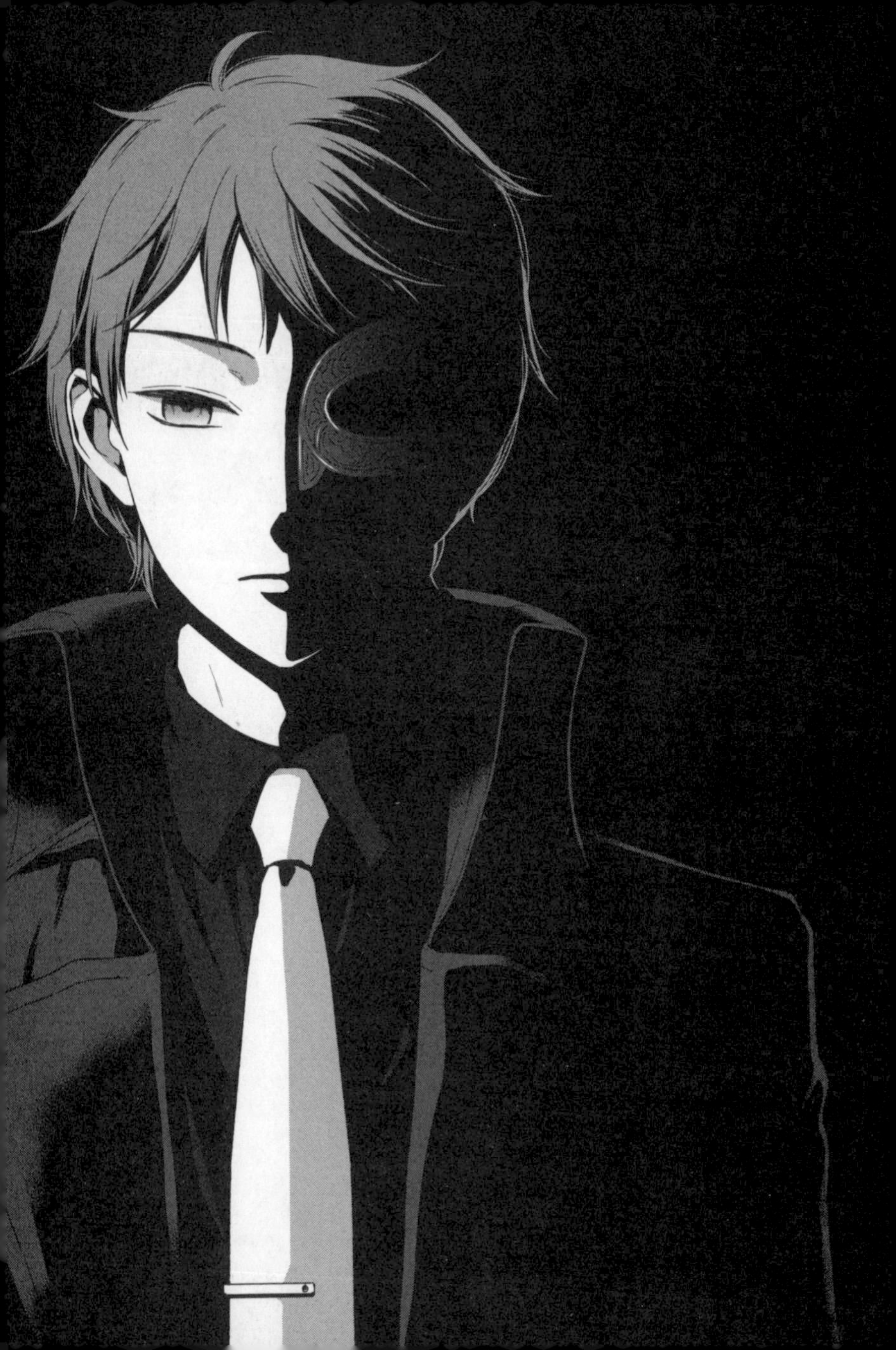

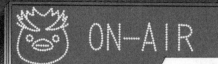

ON-AIR
Penguin-WAVE.
WELCOME TO MY EXAMINATION ROOM.
I'M THE HEAD DOCTOR, SANETOSHI.
I'M HIS ASSISTANT, SHIRASE.
I'M SOUYA.
BY THE WAY, I LOVE THE NECTAR OF SWEET APPLES...
BUT THE ONES I HAD TODAY DIDN'T HAVE ANY.
I GUESS THOSE APPLES DIDN'T CHOOSE ME. TOO BAD.
WELL NOW, LET'S START OUR OPENING SEGMENT.
"TELL US, DR. SANETOSHI!"
TO BEGIN, WE'D LIKE TO WELCOME A VERY SPECIAL GUEST.
THIS IS H-SAN. SHE'S A PATIENT OF MINE.
THANK YOU FOR HAVING ME.
TODAY'S THEME IS "FAMILY."
H-SAN, DO YOU HAVE ANYTHING YOU'D LIKE TO SHARE WITH US?
......

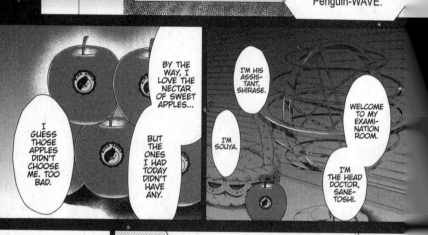

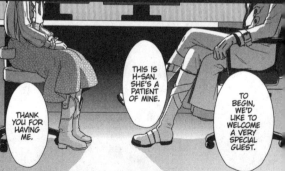

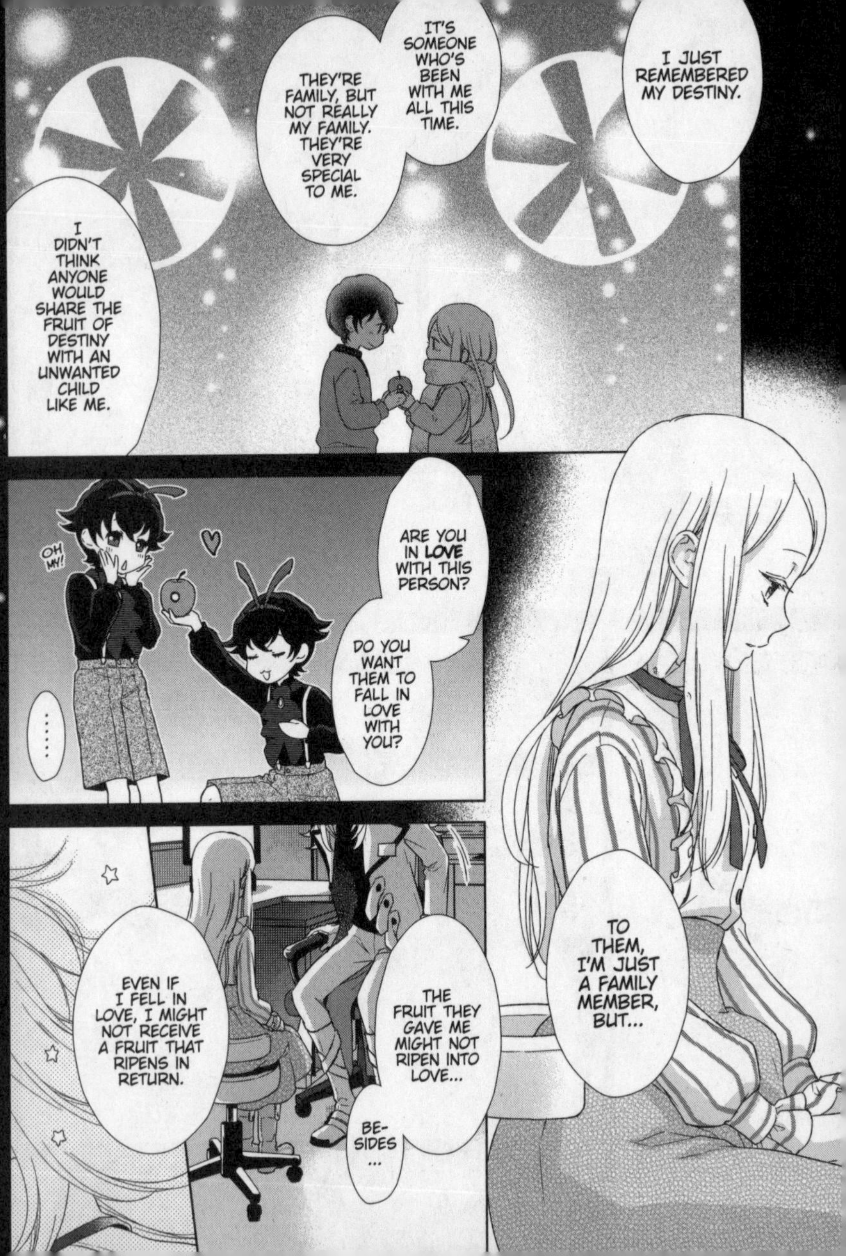
I JUST REMEMBERED MY DESTINY.
IT'S SOMEONE WHO'S BEEN WITH ME ALL THIS TIME.
THEY'RE FAMILY, BUT NOT REALLY MY FAMILY. THEY'RE VERY SPECIAL TO ME.
I DIDN'T THINK ANYONE WOULD SHARE THE FRUIT OF DESTINY WITH AN UNWANTED CHILD LIKE ME.
ARE YOU IN LOVE WITH THIS PERSON?
DO YOU WANT THEM TO FALL IN LOVE WITH YOU?
OH MY!
......
TO THEM, I'M JUST A FAMILY MEMBER, BUT...
THE FRUIT THEY GAVE ME MIGHT NOT RIPEN INTO LOVE...
BE-SIDES...
EVEN IF I FELL IN LOVE, I MIGHT NOT RECEIVE A FRUIT THAT RIPENS IN RETURN.

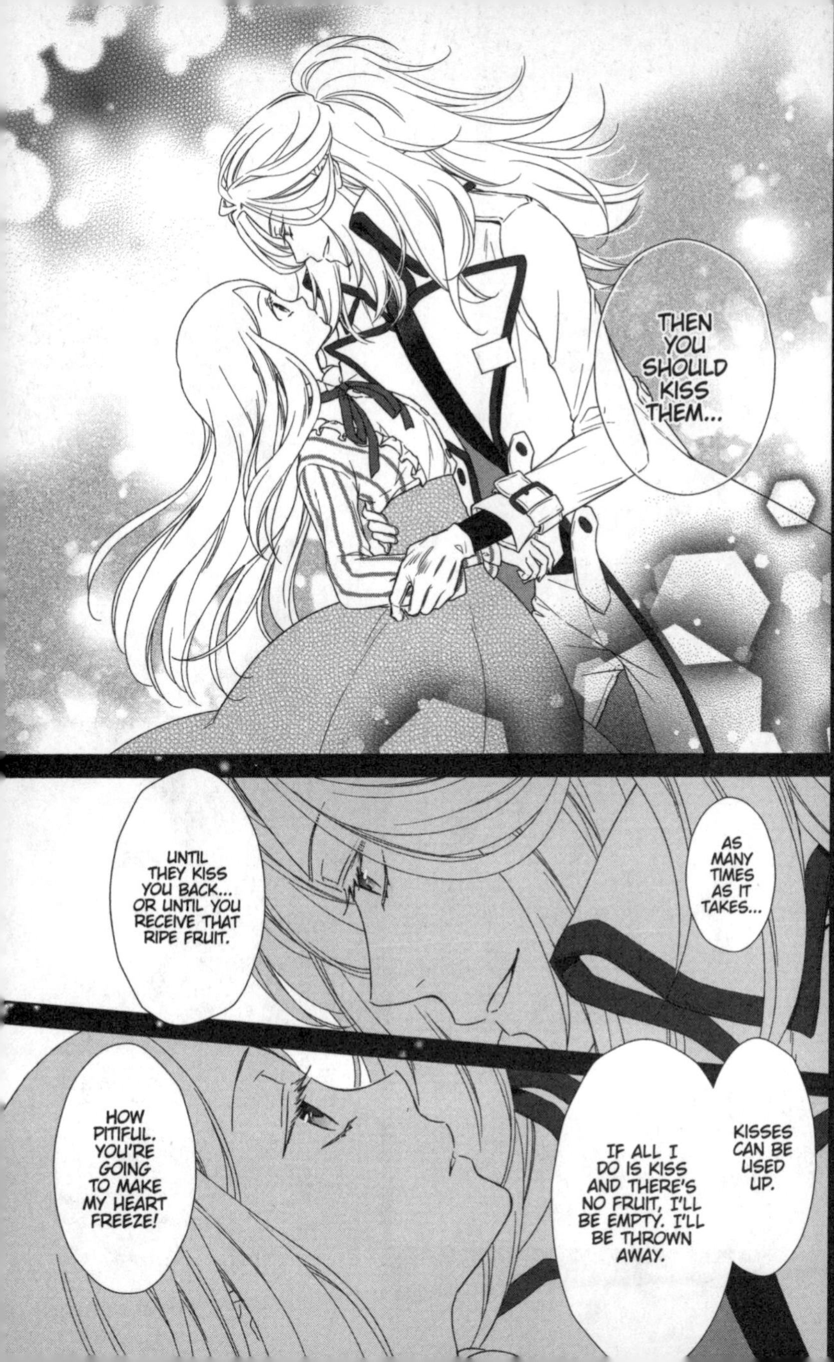
THEN YOU SHOULD KISS THEM...
AS MANY TIMES AS IT TAKES...
UNTIL THEY KISS YOU BACK... OR UNTIL YOU RECEIVE THAT RIPE FRUIT.
KISSES CAN BE USED UP.
IF ALL I DO IS KISS AND THERE'S NO FRUIT, I'LL BE EMPTY. I'LL BE THROWN AWAY.
HOW PITIFUL. YOU'RE GOING TO MAKE MY HEART FREEZE!

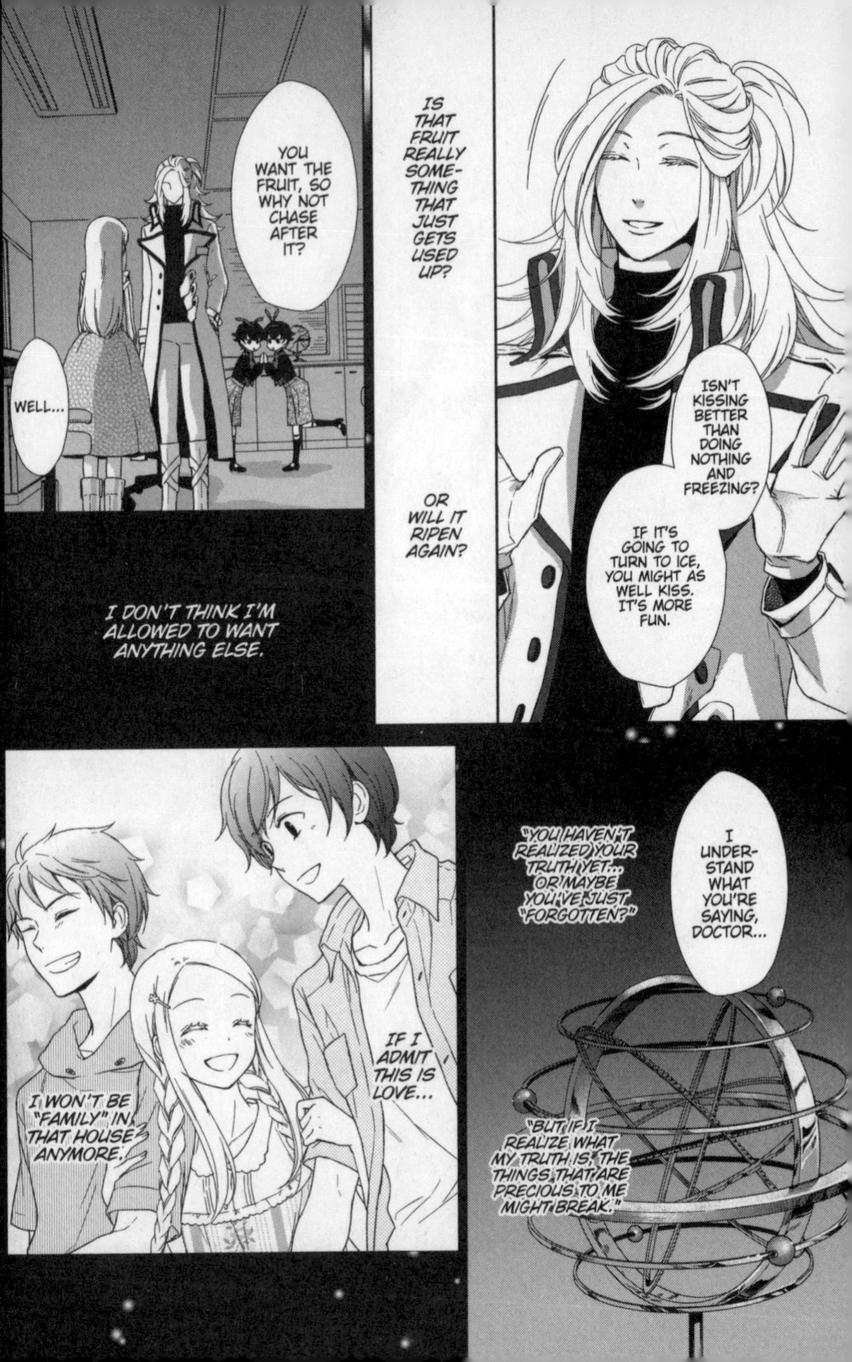

ISN'T KISSING BETTER THAN DOING NOTHING AND FREEZING?
IF IT'S GOING TO TURN TO ICE, YOU MIGHT AS WELL KISS. IT'S MORE FUN.
IS THAT FRUIT REALLY SOMETHING THAT JUST GETS USED UP?
OR WILL IT RIPEN AGAIN?
YOU WANT THE FRUIT, SO WHY NOT CHASE AFTER IT?
WELL...
I DON'T THINK I'M ALLOWED TO WANT ANYTHING ELSE.
I UNDERSTAND WHAT YOU'RE SAYING, DOCTOR...
"YOU HAVEN'T REALIZED YOUR TRUTH YET... OR MAYBE YOU'VE JUST "FORGOTTEN?"
"BUT IF I REALIZE WHAT MY TRUTH IS, THE THINGS THAT ARE PRECIOUS TO ME MIGHT BREAK."
IF I ADMIT THIS IS LOVE...
I WON'T BE "FAMILY" IN THAT HOUSE ANYMORE.

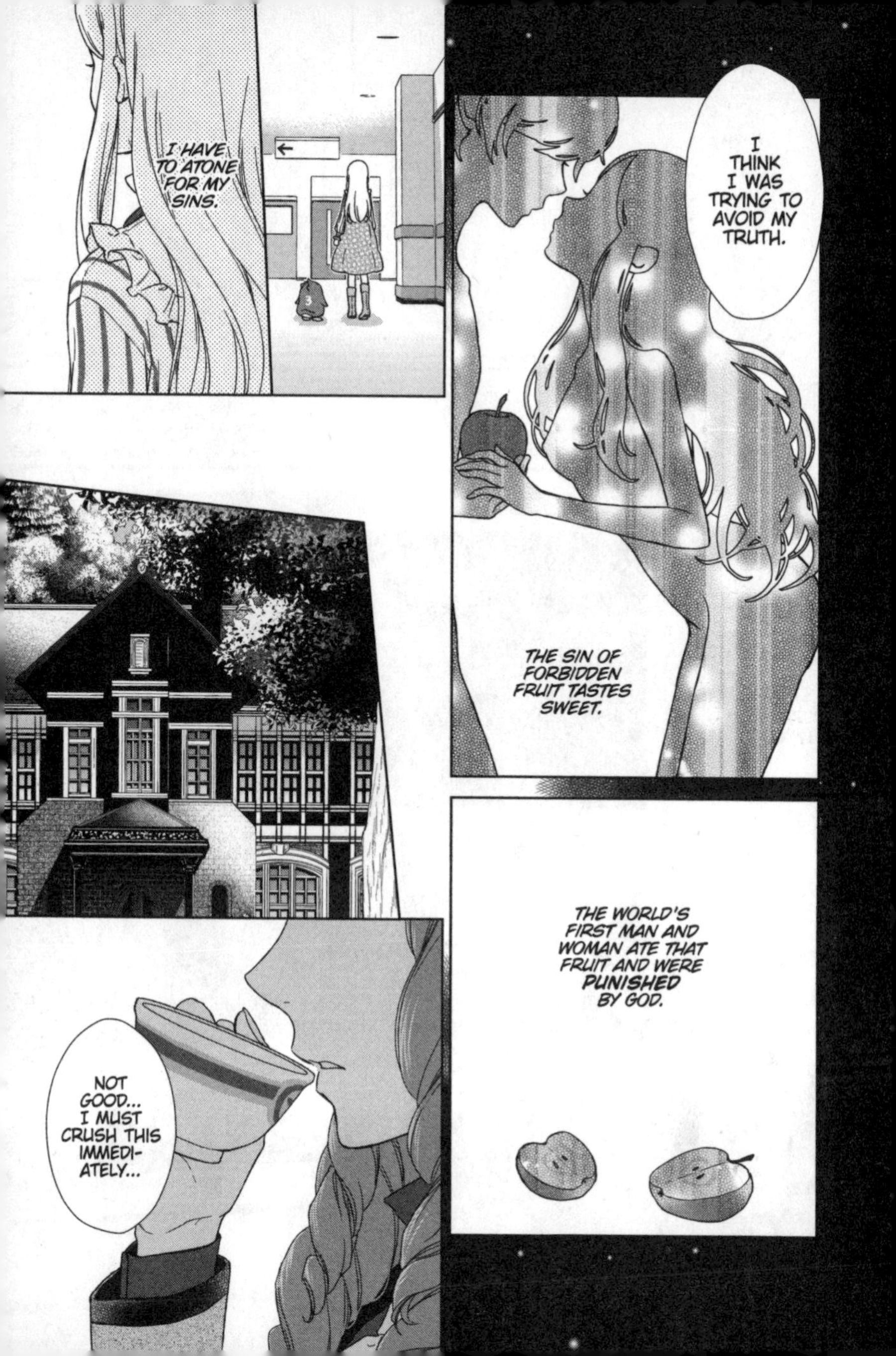
I THINK I WAS TRYING TO AVOID MY TRUTH.
THE SIN OF FORBIDDEN FRUIT TASTES SWEET.
THE WORLD'S FIRST MAN AND WOMAN ATE THAT FRUIT AND WERE PUNISHED BY GOD.
I HAVE TO ATONE FOR MY SINS.
NOT GOOD... I MUST CRUSH THIS IMMEDI-ATELY...

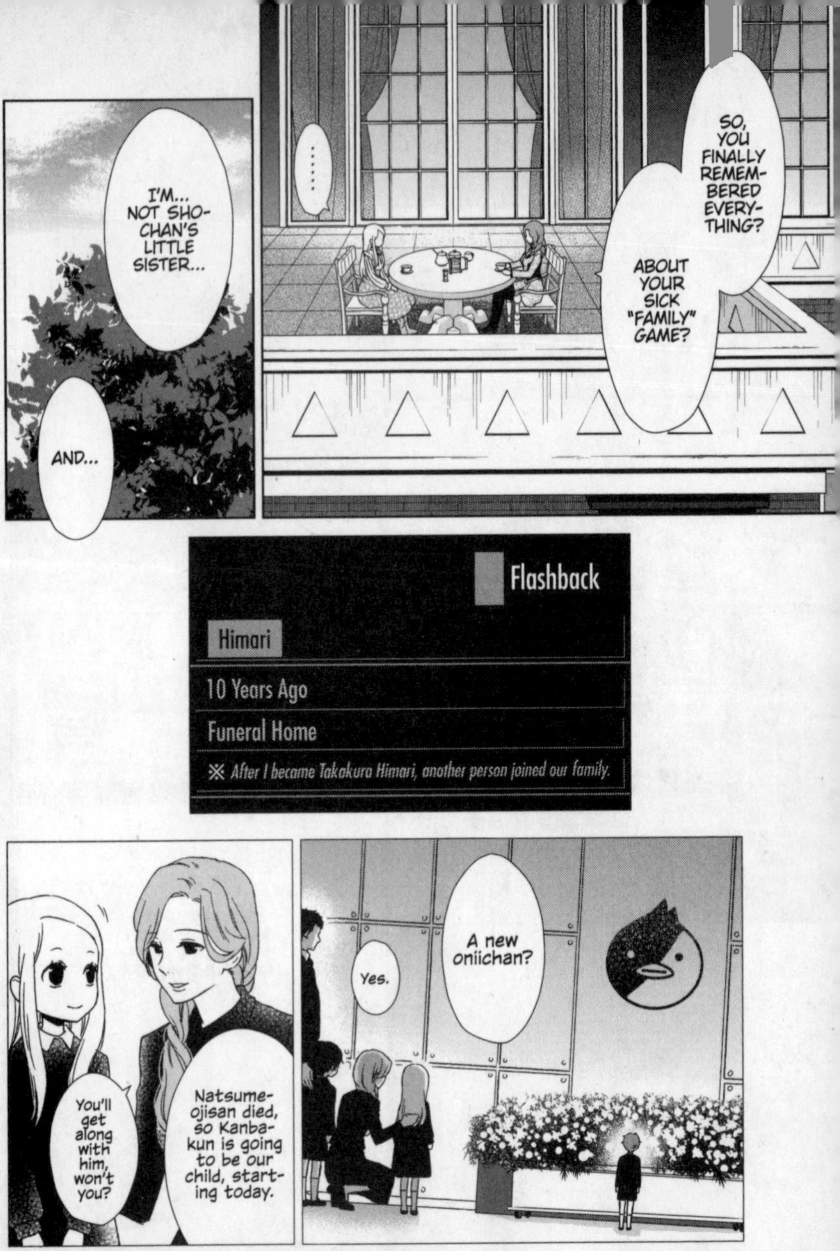
SO, YOU FINALLY REMEMBERED EVERYTHING?
ABOUT YOUR SICK "FAMILY" GAME?
......
I'M... NOT SHO-CHAN'S LITTLE SISTER...
AND...
Flashback
Himari
10 Years Ago
Funeral Home
※ After I became Takakura Himari, another person joined our family.
A new oniichan?
Yes.
Natsume-ojisan died, so Kanba-kun is going to be our child, starting today.
You'll get along with him, won't you?

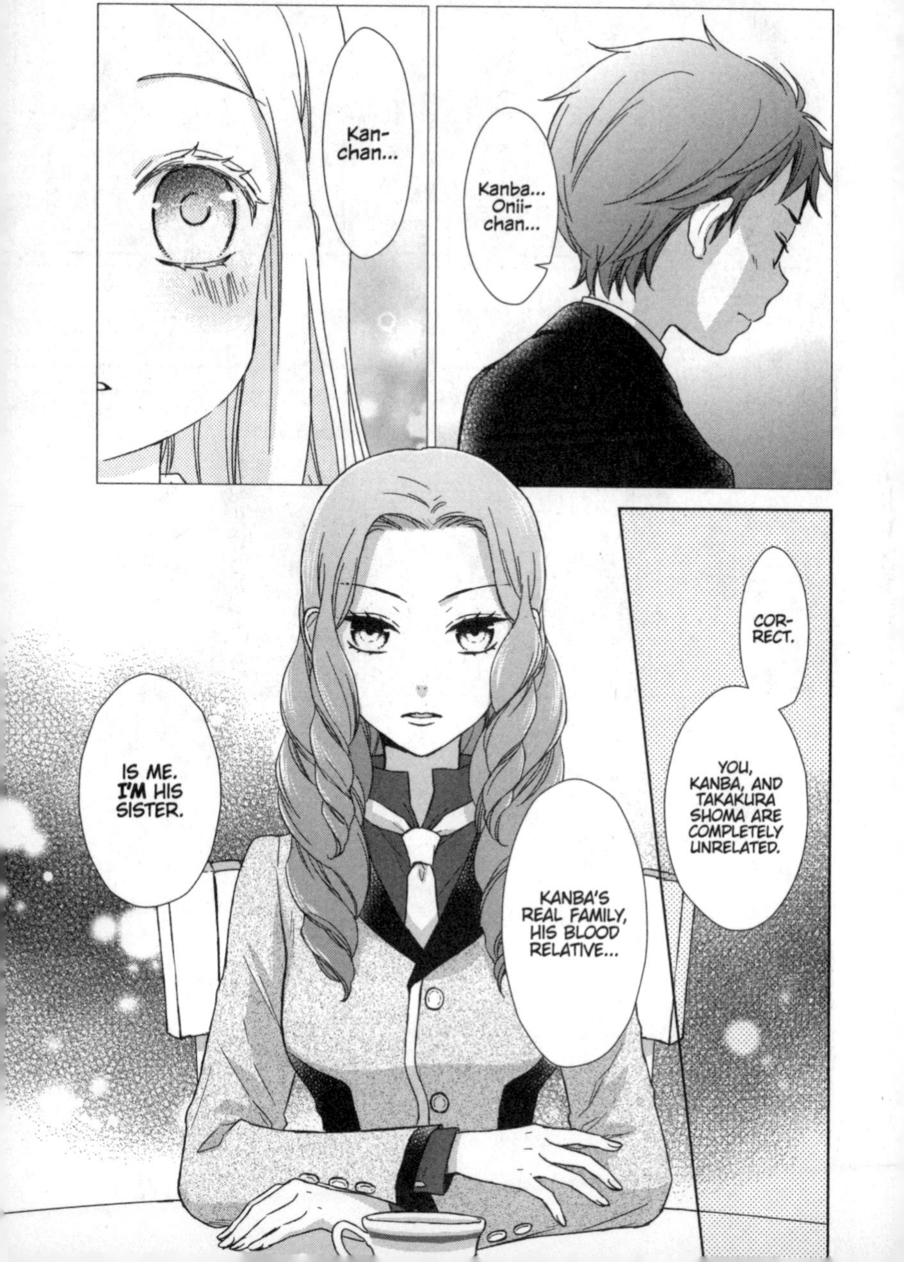
Kanba... Onii-chan...
Kan-chan...
COR-RECT.
YOU, KANBA, AND TAKAKURA SHOMA ARE COMPLETELY UNRELATED.
KANBA'S REAL FAMILY, HIS BLOOD RELATIVE...
IS ME. **I'M** HIS SISTER.

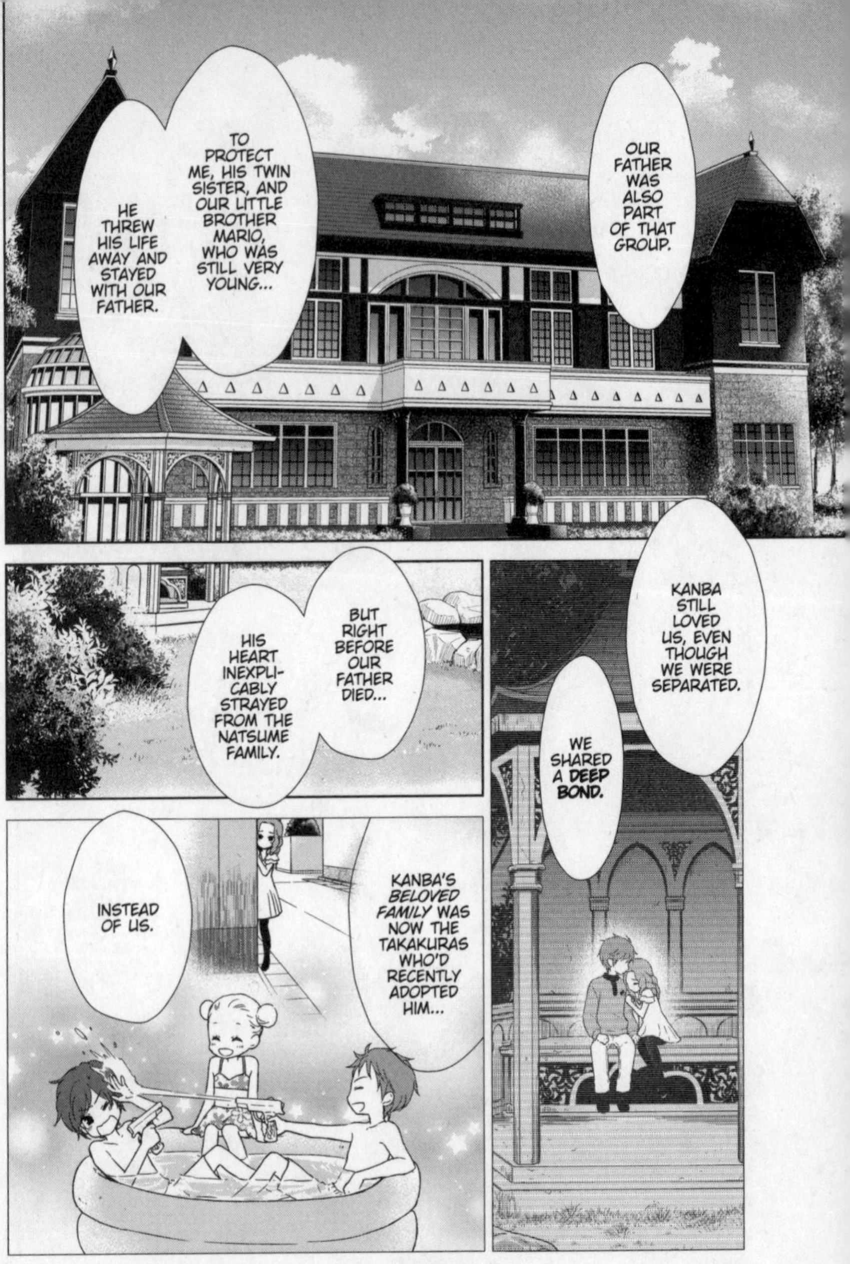
OUR FATHER WAS ALSO PART OF THAT GROUP.
TO PROTECT ME, HIS TWIN SISTER, AND OUR LITTLE BROTHER MARIO, WHO WAS STILL VERY YOUNG...
HE THREW HIS LIFE AWAY AND STAYED WITH OUR FATHER.
KANBA STILL LOVED US, EVEN THOUGH WE WERE SEPARATED.
WE SHARED A **DEEP BOND.**
BUT RIGHT BEFORE OUR FATHER DIED...
HIS HEART INEXPLI-CABLY STRAYED FROM THE NATSUME FAMILY.
KANBA'S *BELOVED FAMILY* WAS NOW THE TAKAKURAS WHO'D RECENTLY ADOPTED HIM...
INSTEAD OF US.

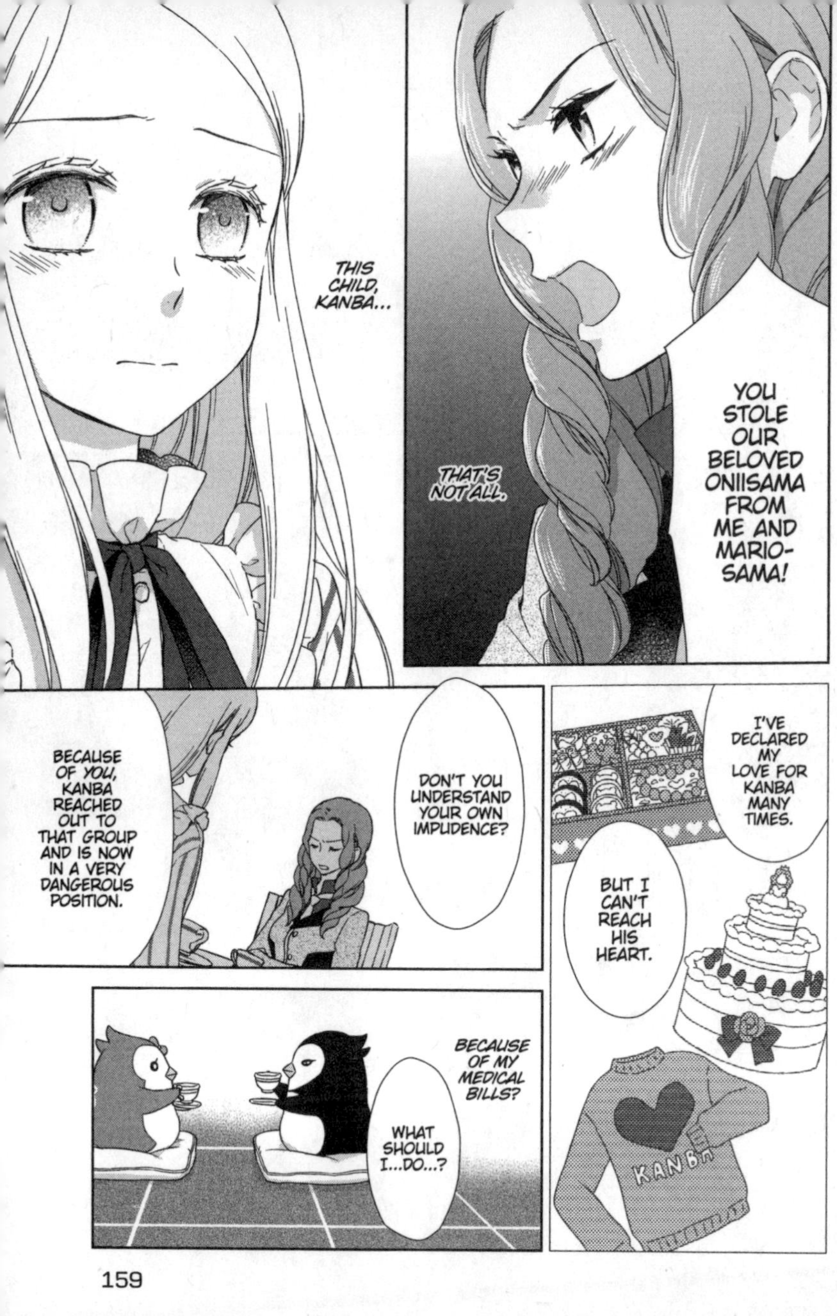
YOU STOLE OUR BELOVED ONIISAMA FROM ME AND MARIO-SAMA!
THAT'S NOT ALL.
THIS CHILD, KANBA...
I'VE DECLARED MY LOVE FOR KANBA MANY TIMES.
BUT I CAN'T REACH HIS HEART.
KANBA
DON'T YOU UNDERSTAND YOUR OWN IMPUDENCE?
BECAUSE OF YOU, KANBA REACHED OUT TO THAT GROUP AND IS NOW IN A VERY DANGEROUS POSITION.
BECAUSE OF MY MEDICAL BILLS?
WHAT SHOULD I...DO...?

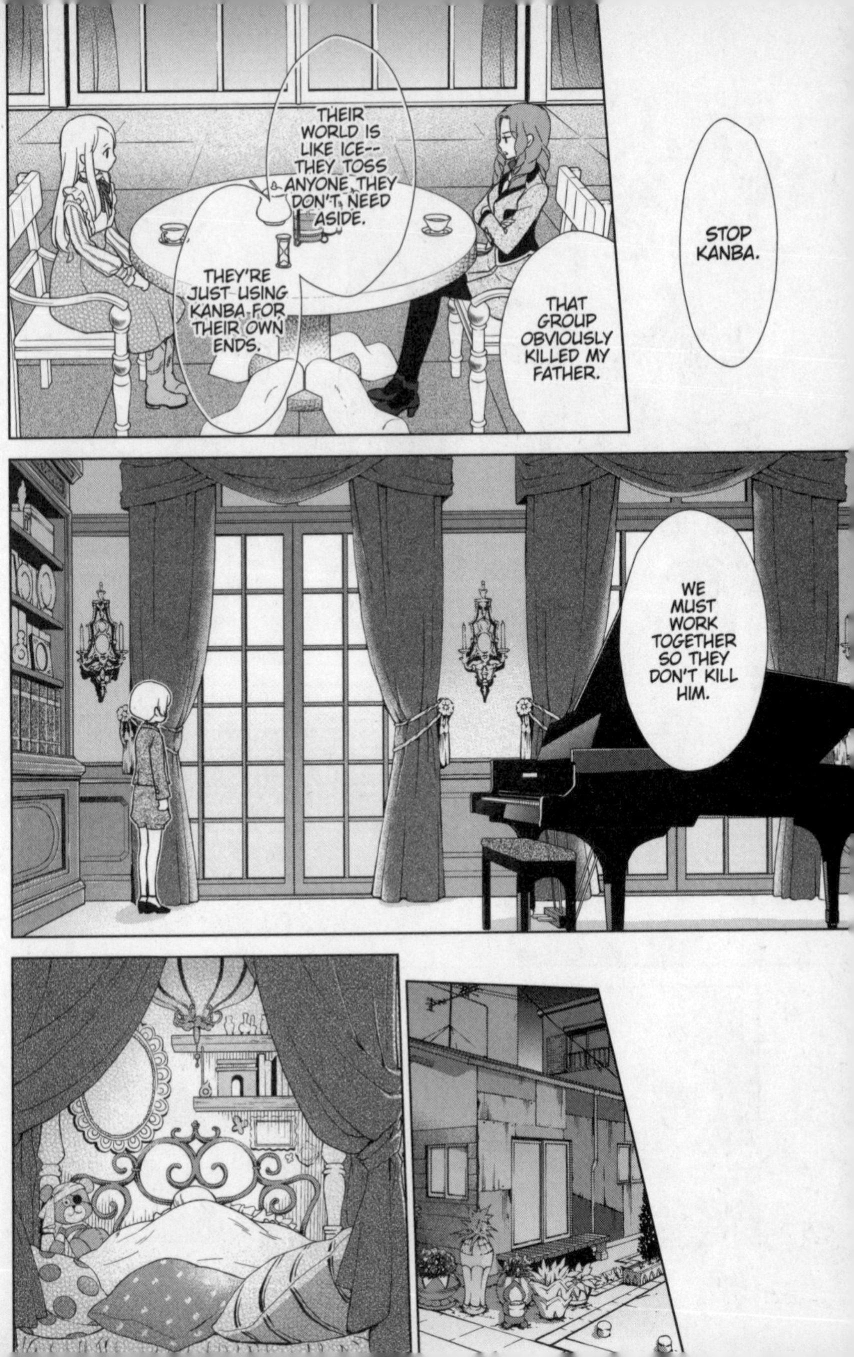
STOP KANBA.
THAT GROUP OBVIOUSLY KILLED MY FATHER.
THEIR WORLD IS LIKE ICE-- THEY TOSS ANYONE THEY DON'T NEED ASIDE.
THEY'RE JUST USING KANBA FOR THEIR OWN ENDS.
WE MUST WORK TOGETHER SO THEY DON'T KILL HIM.

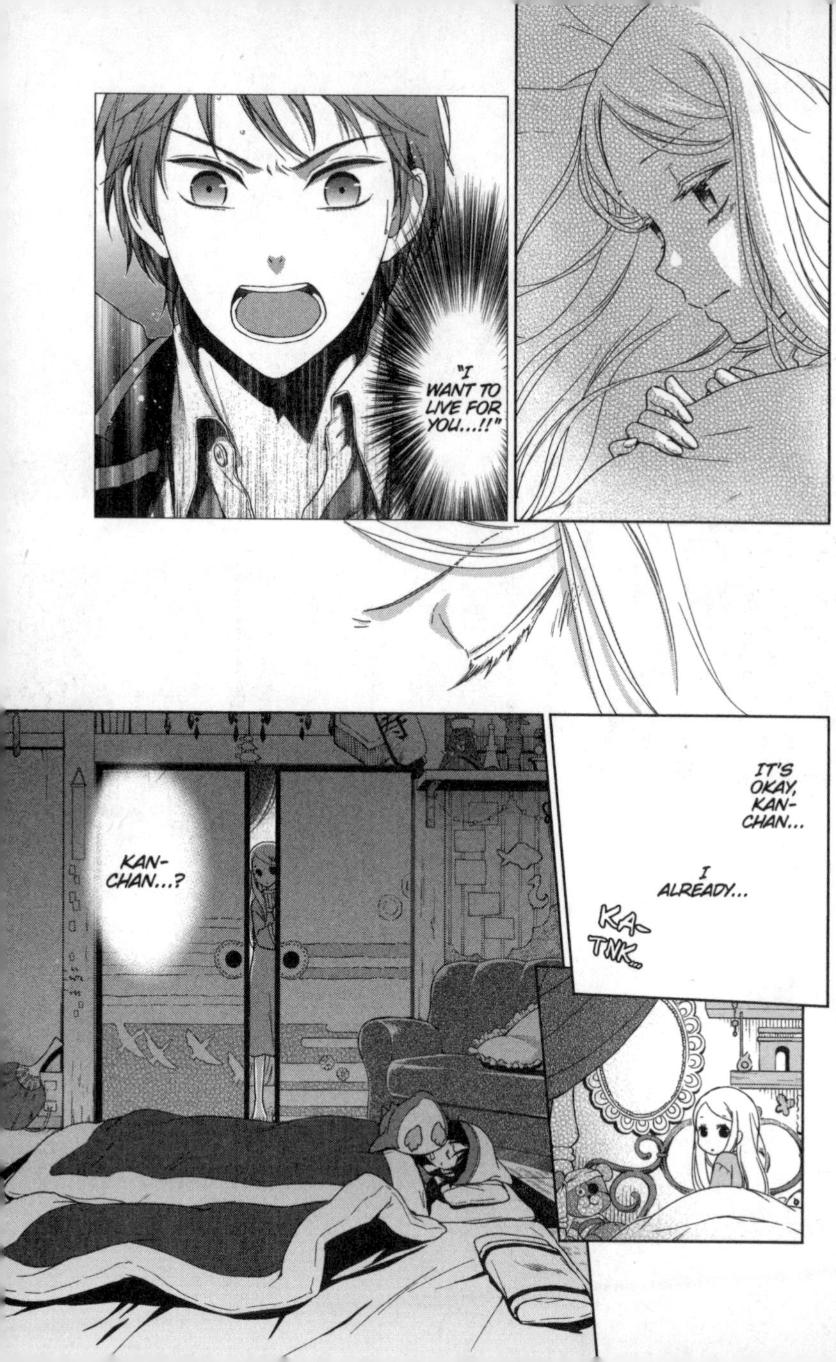
"I WANT TO LIVE FOR YOU...!!"
IT'S OKAY, KAN-CHAN...
I ALREADY...
KA-TNK..
KAN-CHAN...?

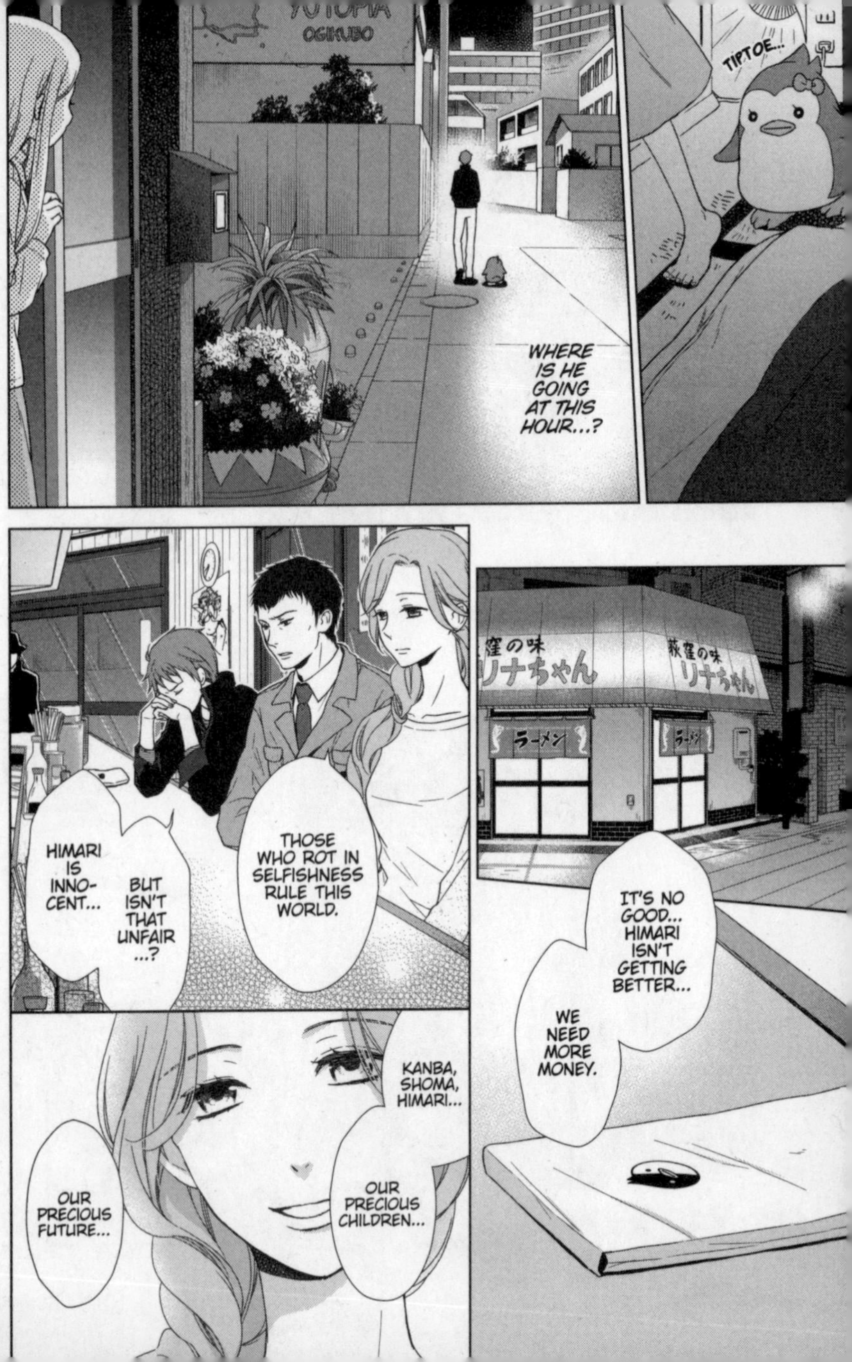
TIPTOE...
OGIKUBO
WHERE IS HE GOING AT THIS HOUR...?
荻窪の味 リナちゃん
ラーメン
IT'S NO GOOD... HIMARI ISN'T GETTING BETTER...
WE NEED MORE MONEY.
THOSE WHO ROT IN SELFISHNESS RULE THIS WORLD.
HIMARI IS INNO-CENT...
BUT ISN'T THAT UNFAIR ...?
KANBA, SHOMA, HIMARI...
OUR PRECIOUS CHILDREN...
OUR PRECIOUS FUTURE...

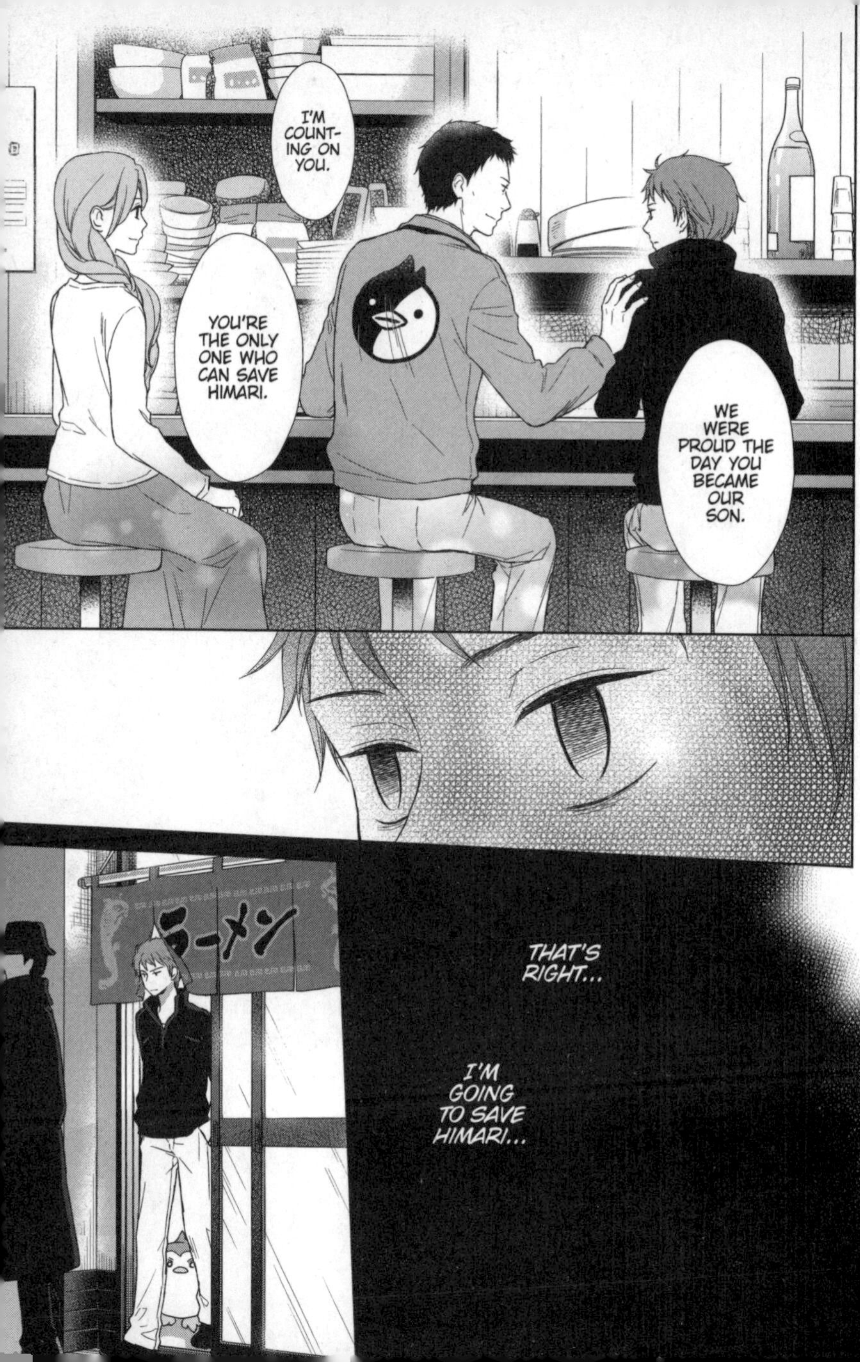
WE WERE PROUD THE DAY YOU BECAME OUR SON.
YOU'RE THE ONLY ONE WHO CAN SAVE HIMARI.
I'M COUNTING-ING ON YOU.
ラーメン
THAT'S RIGHT...
I'M GOING TO SAVE HIMARI...

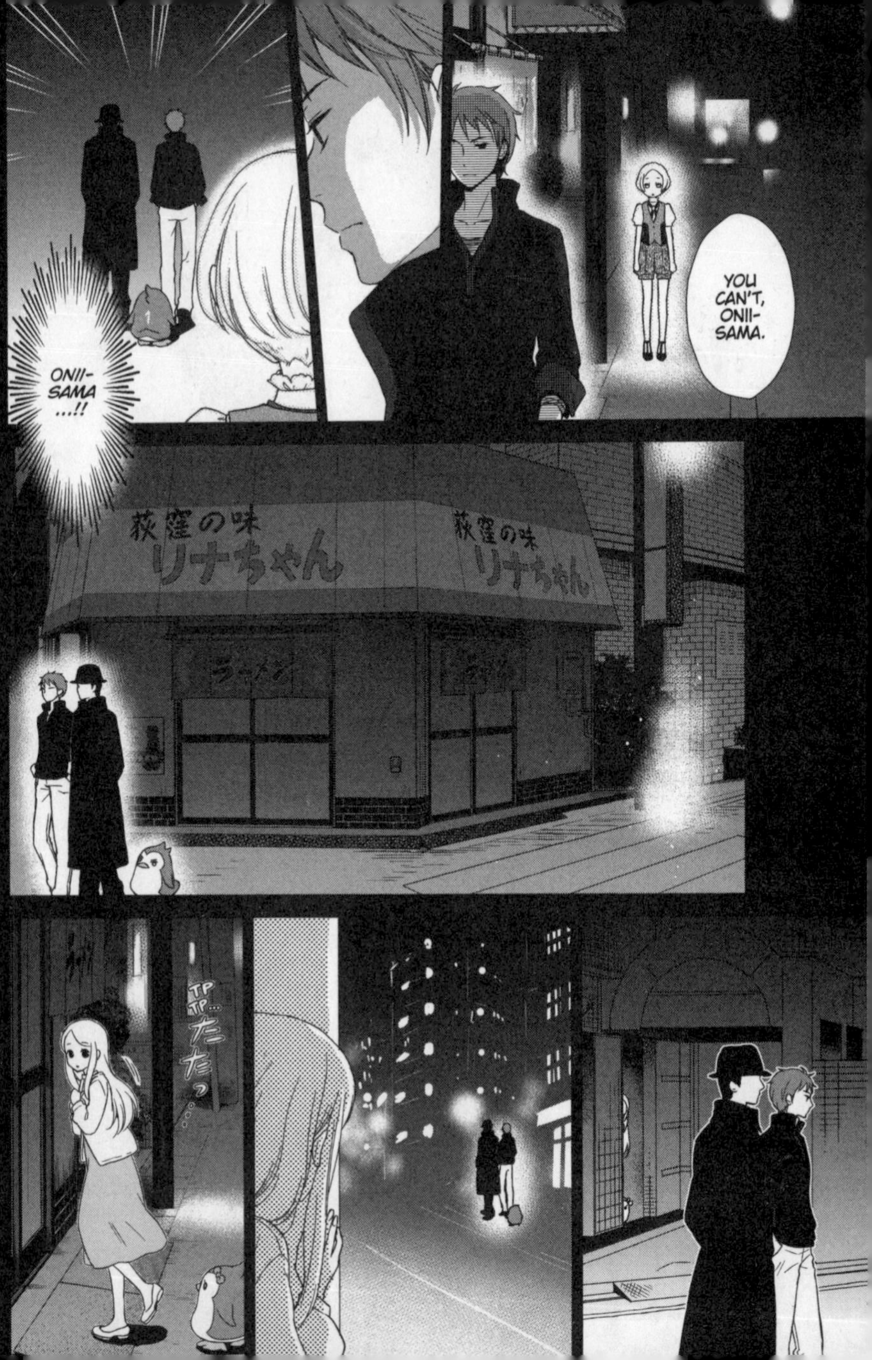
YOU CAN'T, ONII-SAMA.
ONII-SAMA ...!!
荻窪の味 リナちゃん
荻窪の味 リナちゃん
TP TP...
たたっ...

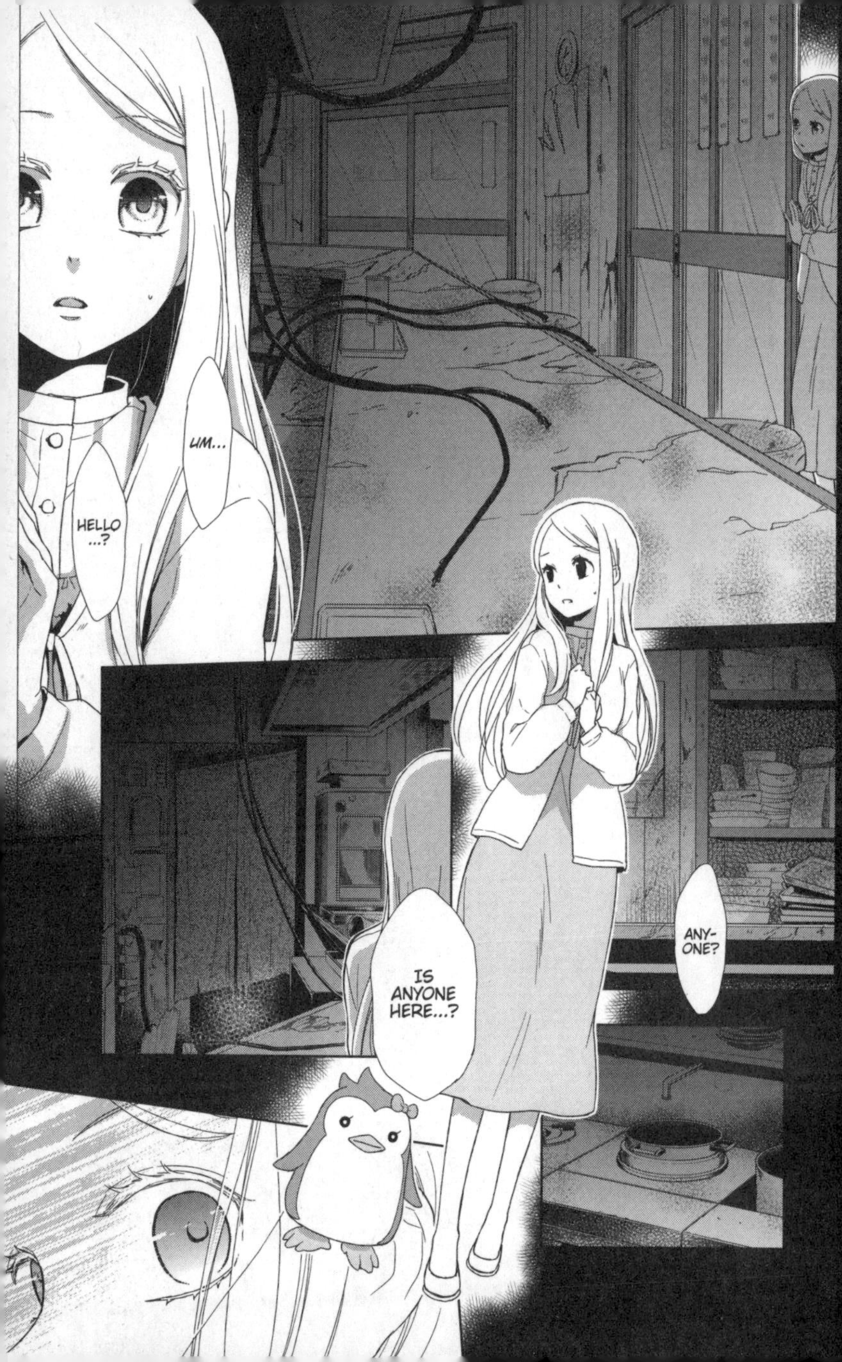
UM...
HELLO ...?
ANY-ONE?
IS ANYONE HERE...?

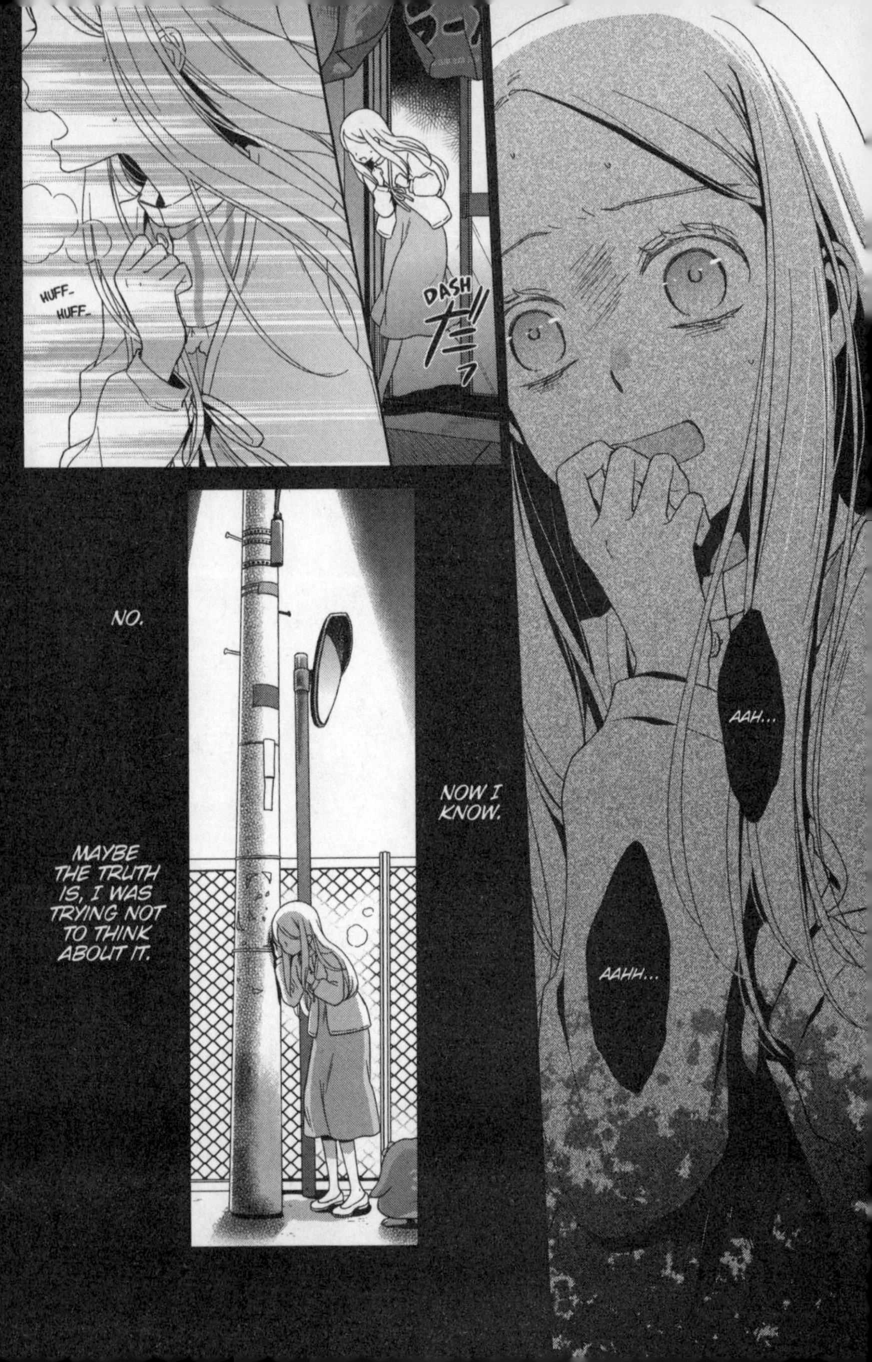
AAH...
AAHH...
DASH
HUFF-
HUFF-
NO.
NOW I KNOW.
MAYBE THE TRUTH IS, I WAS TRYING NOT TO THINK ABOUT IT.

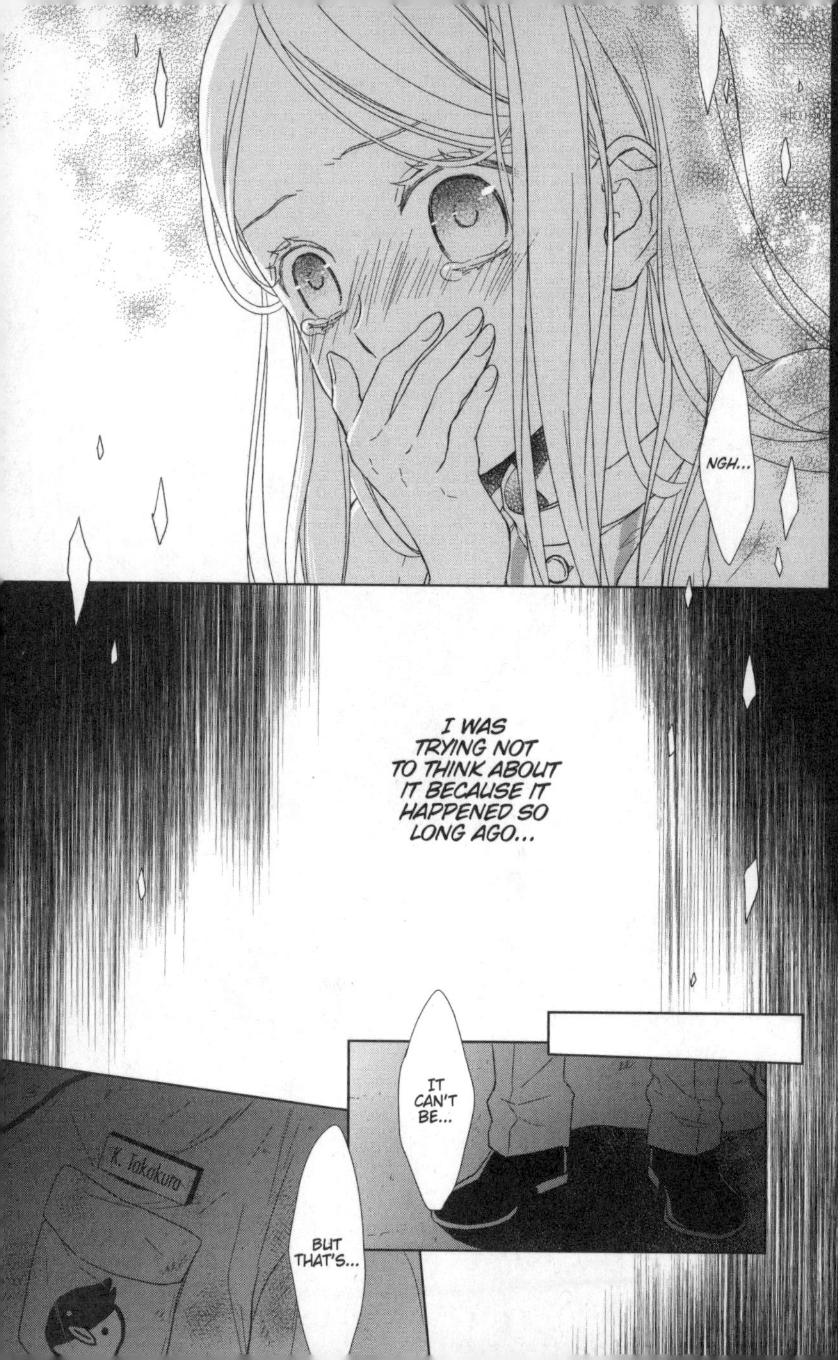
NGH...
I WAS TRYING NOT TO THINK ABOUT IT BECAUSE IT HAPPENED SO LONG AGO...
IT CAN'T BE...
K. Takakura
BUT THAT'S...

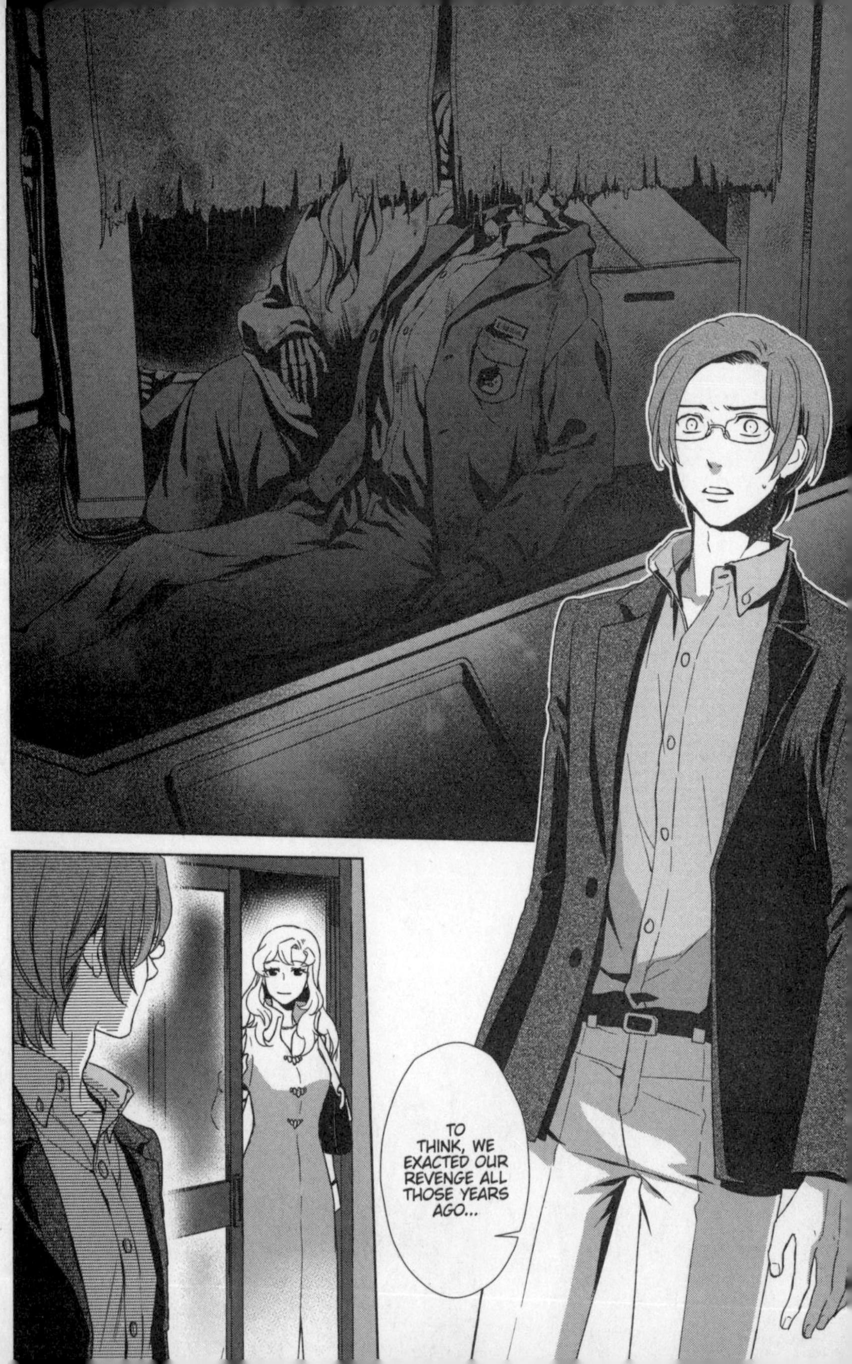
TO THINK, WE EXACTED OUR REVENGE ALL THOSE YEARS AGO...

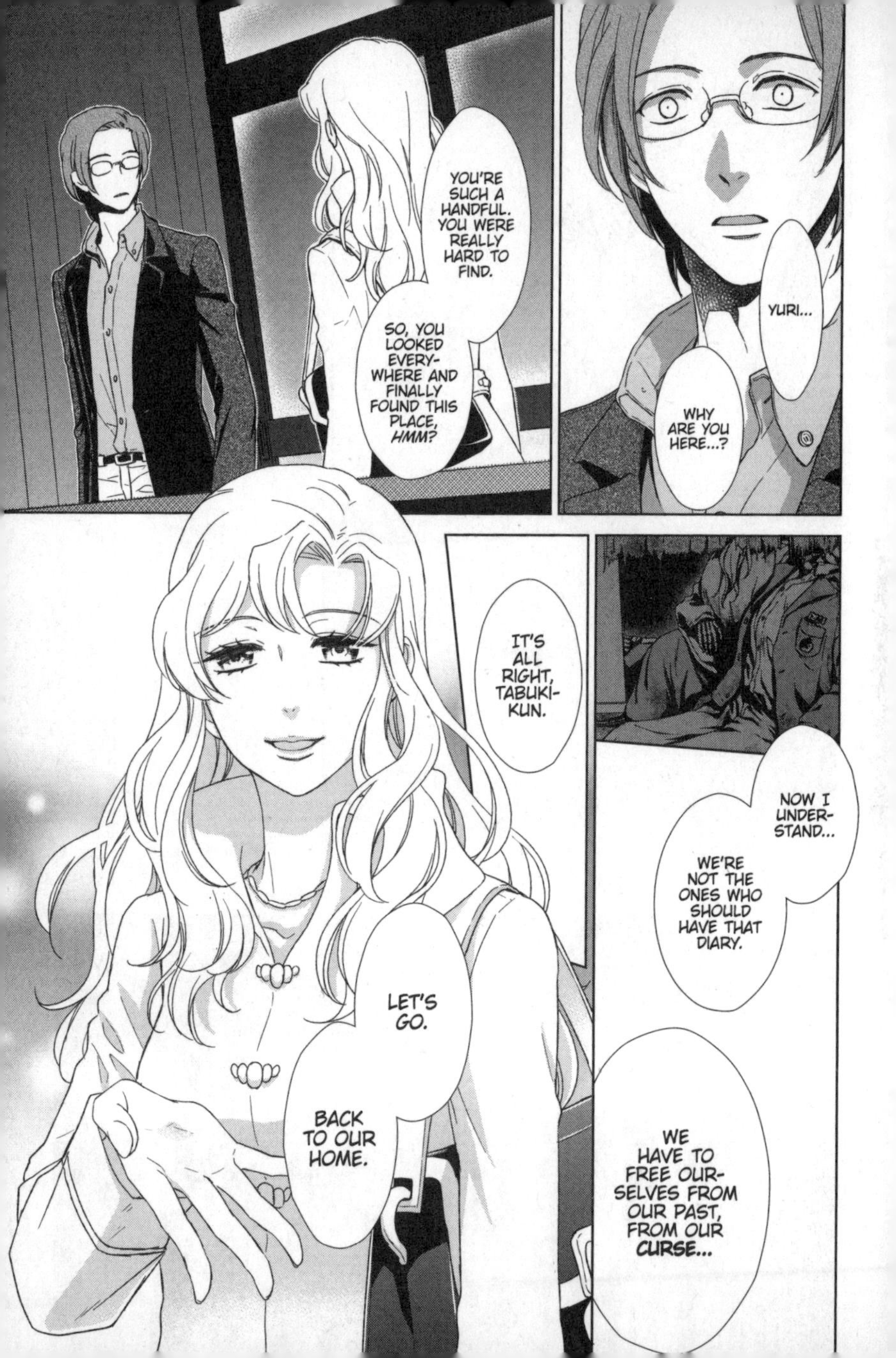
YURI...
WHY ARE YOU HERE...?
YOU'RE SUCH A HANDFUL. YOU WERE REALLY HARD TO FIND.
SO, YOU LOOKED EVERY-WHERE AND FINALLY FOUND THIS PLACE, *HMM?*
IT'S ALL RIGHT, TABUKI-KUN.
NOW I UNDER-STAND...
WE'RE NOT THE ONES WHO SHOULD HAVE THAT DIARY.
WE HAVE TO FREE OUR-SELVES FROM OUR PAST, FROM OUR **CURSE...**
LET'S GO.
BACK TO OUR HOME.

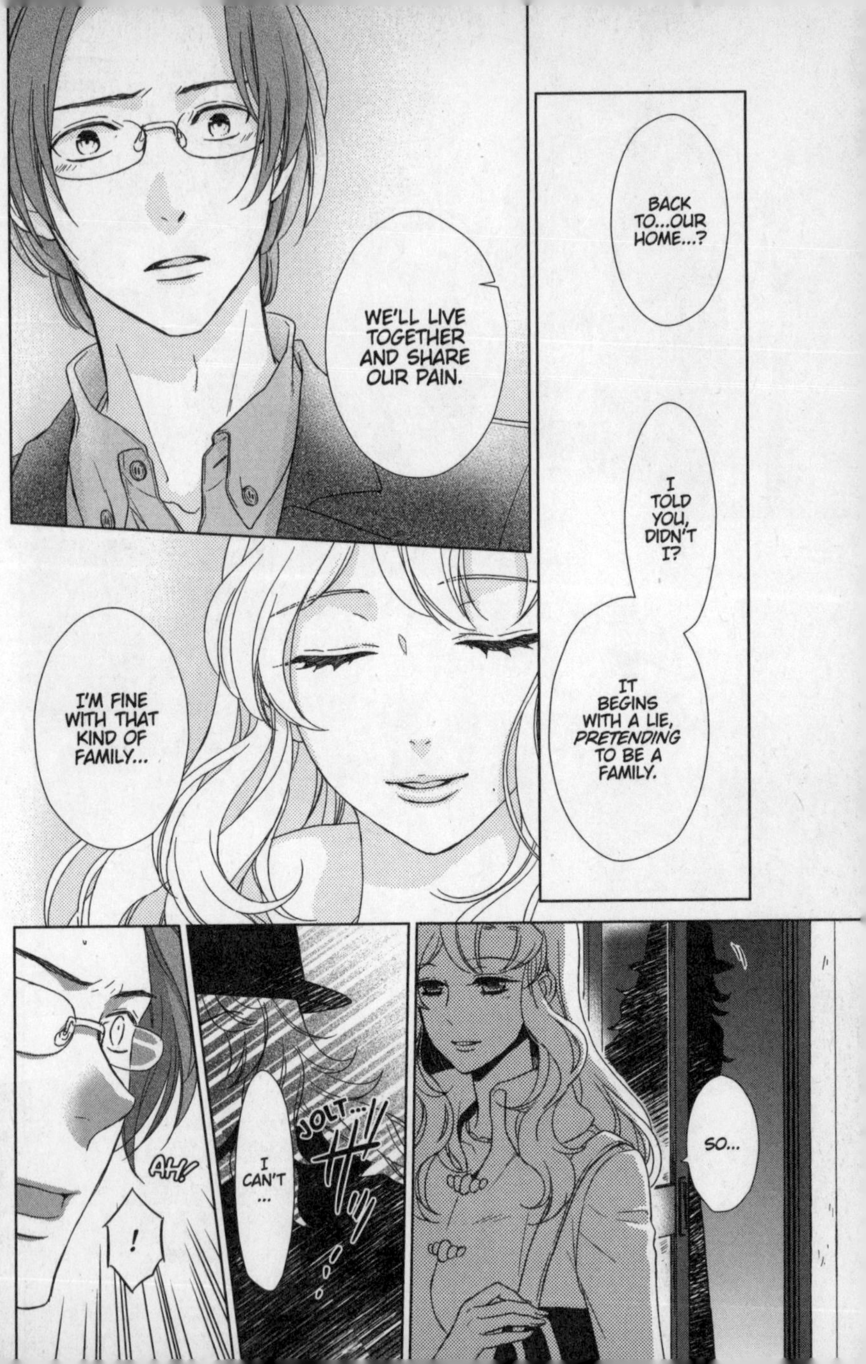
BACK TO...OUR HOME...?
I TOLD YOU, DIDN'T I?
IT BEGINS WITH A LIE, *PRETENDING* TO BE A FAMILY.
WE'LL LIVE TOGETHER AND SHARE OUR PAIN.
I'M FINE WITH THAT KIND OF FAMILY...
SO...
JOLT...
I CAN'T ...
AH!
!

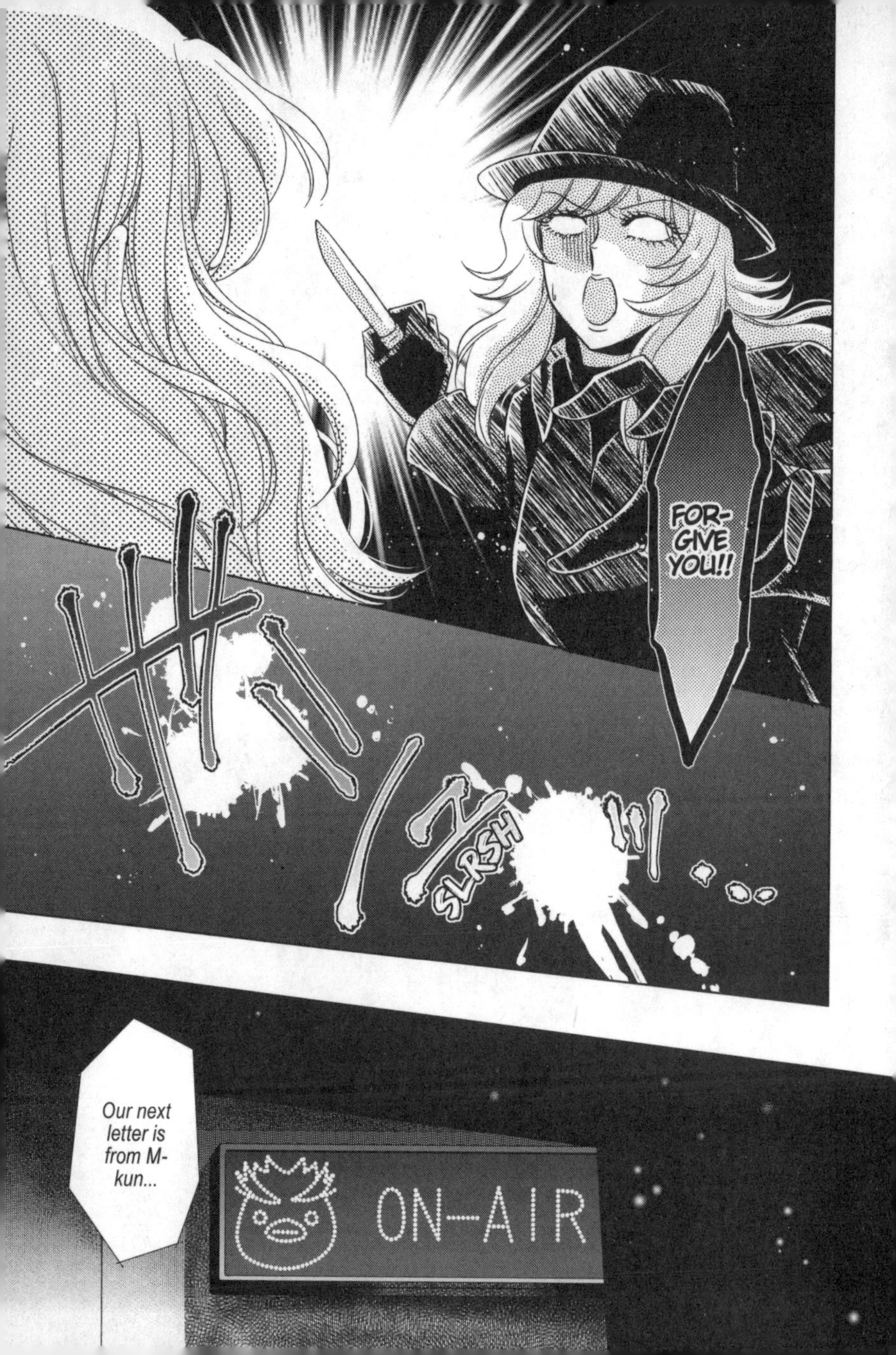
FOR-GIVE YOU!!
SLASH
Our next letter is from M-kun...
ON-AIR

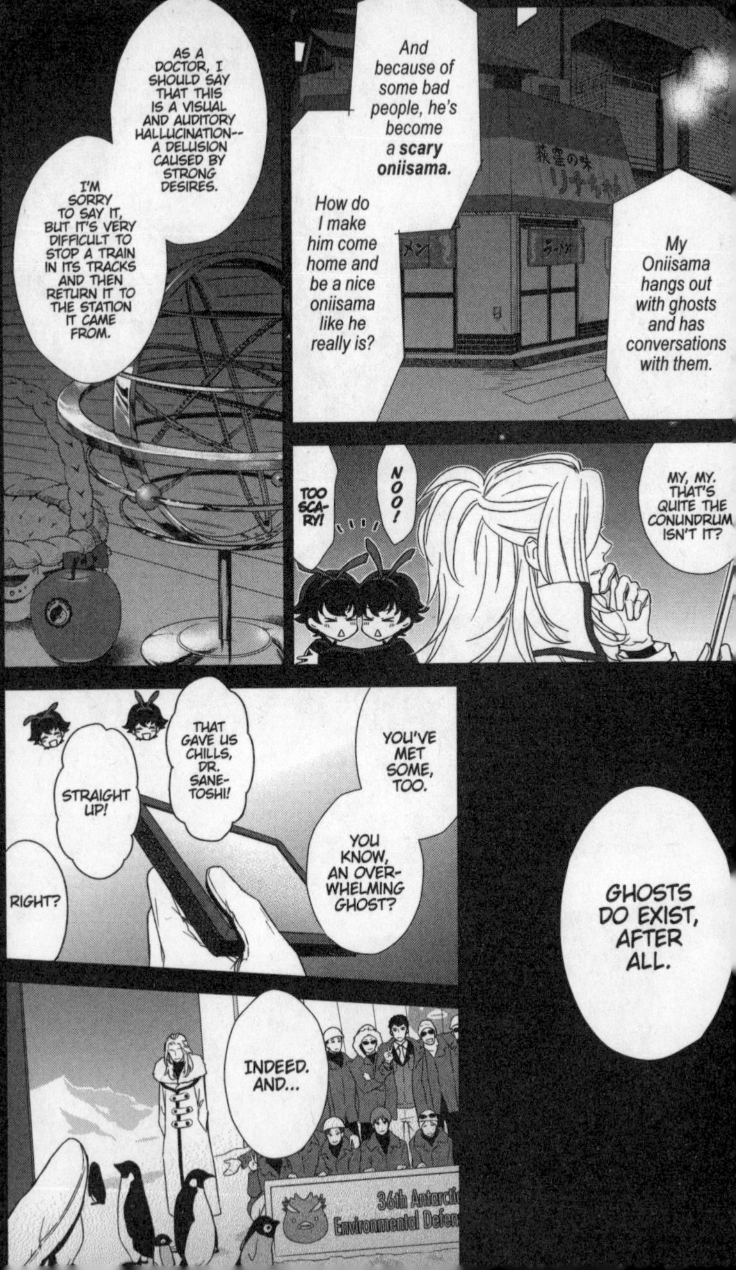

My Oniisama hangs out with ghosts and has conversations with them.
And because of some bad people, he's become a **scary oniisama.**
How do I make him come home and be a nice oniisama like he really is?
MY, MY. THAT'S QUITE THE CONUNDRUM ISN'T IT?
NOO!
TOO SCARY!
AS A DOCTOR, I SHOULD SAY THAT THIS IS A VISUAL AND AUDITORY HALLUCINATION-- A DELUSION CAUSED BY STRONG DESIRES.
I'M SORRY TO SAY IT, BUT IT'S VERY DIFFICULT TO STOP A TRAIN IN ITS TRACKS AND THEN RETURN IT TO THE STATION IT CAME FROM.
GHOSTS DO EXIST, AFTER ALL.
YOU'VE MET SOME, TOO.
YOU KNOW, AN OVERWHELMING GHOST?
THAT GAVE US CHILLS, DR. SANETOSHI!
STRAIGHT UP!
RIGHT?
INDEED. AND...

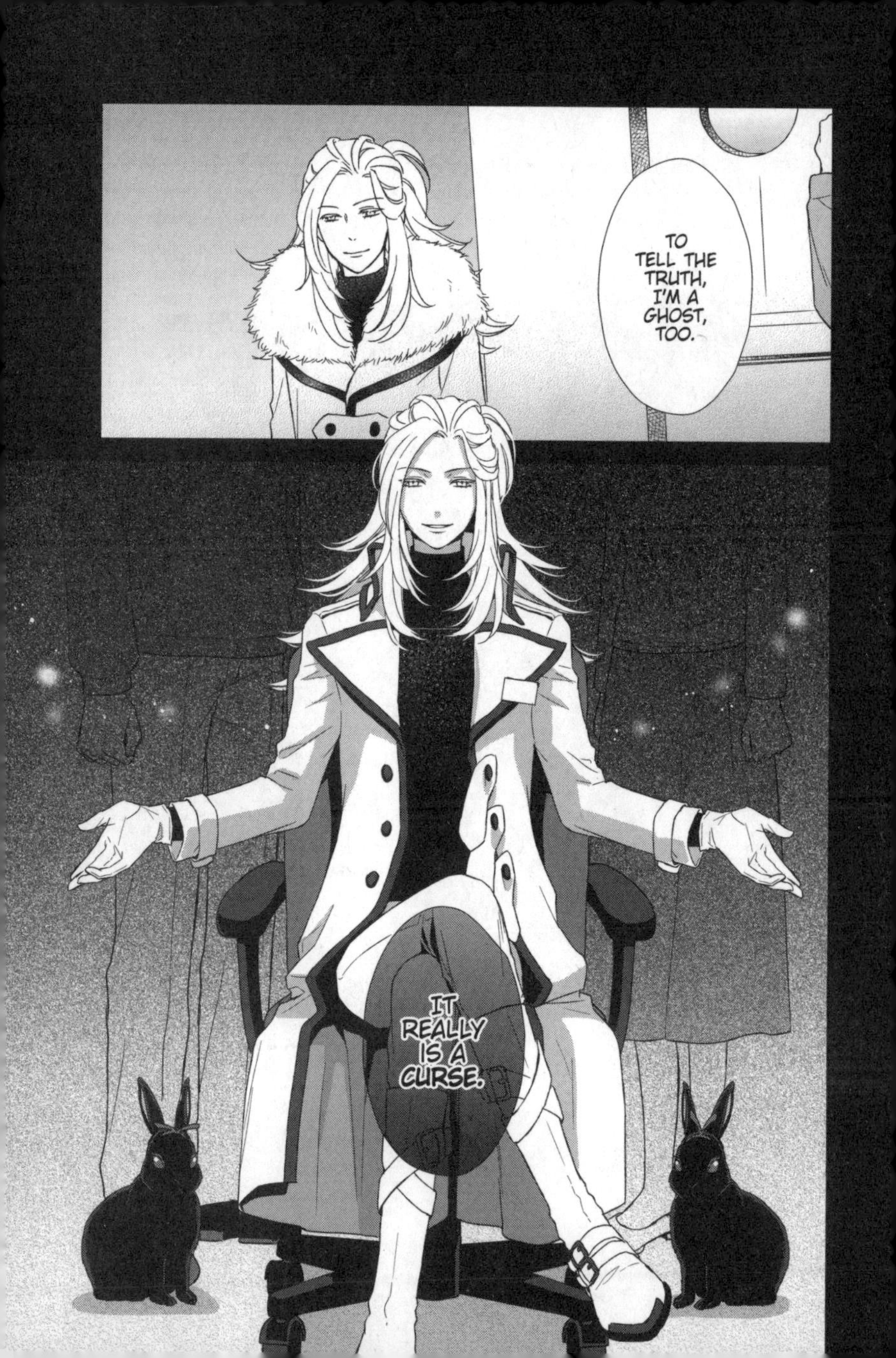
TO TELL THE TRUTH, I'M A GHOST, TOO.
IT REALLY IS A CURSE.

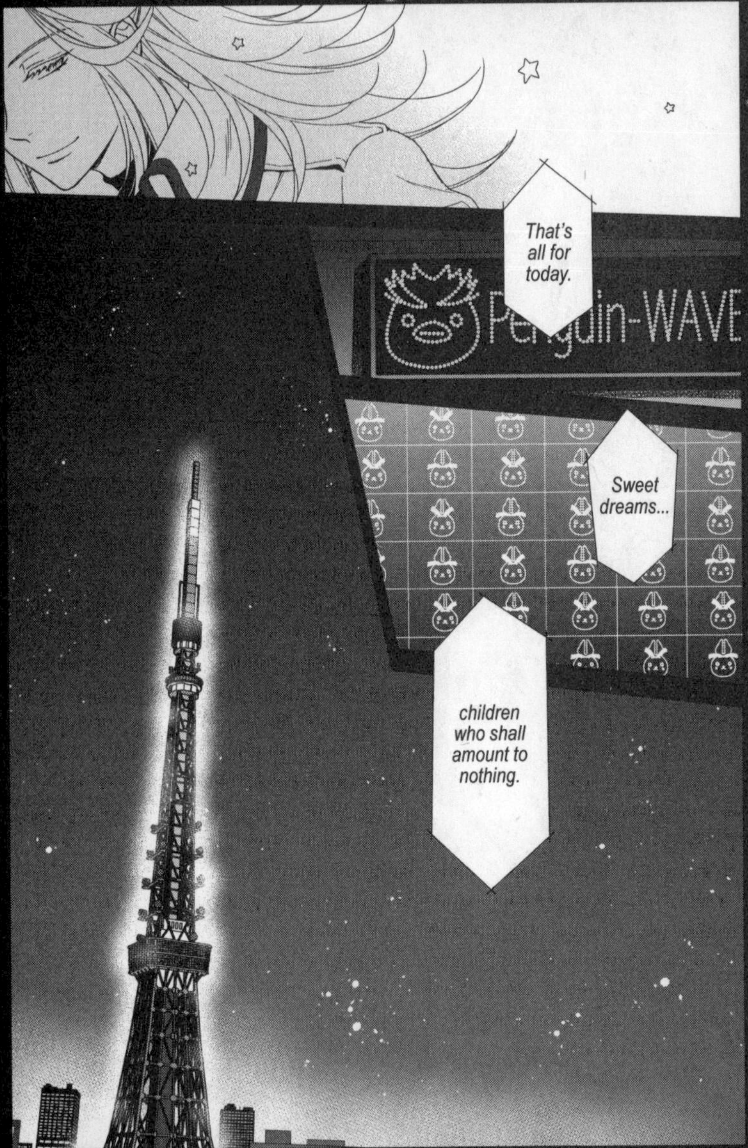
That's all for today.
Sweet dreams...
children who shall amount to nothing.

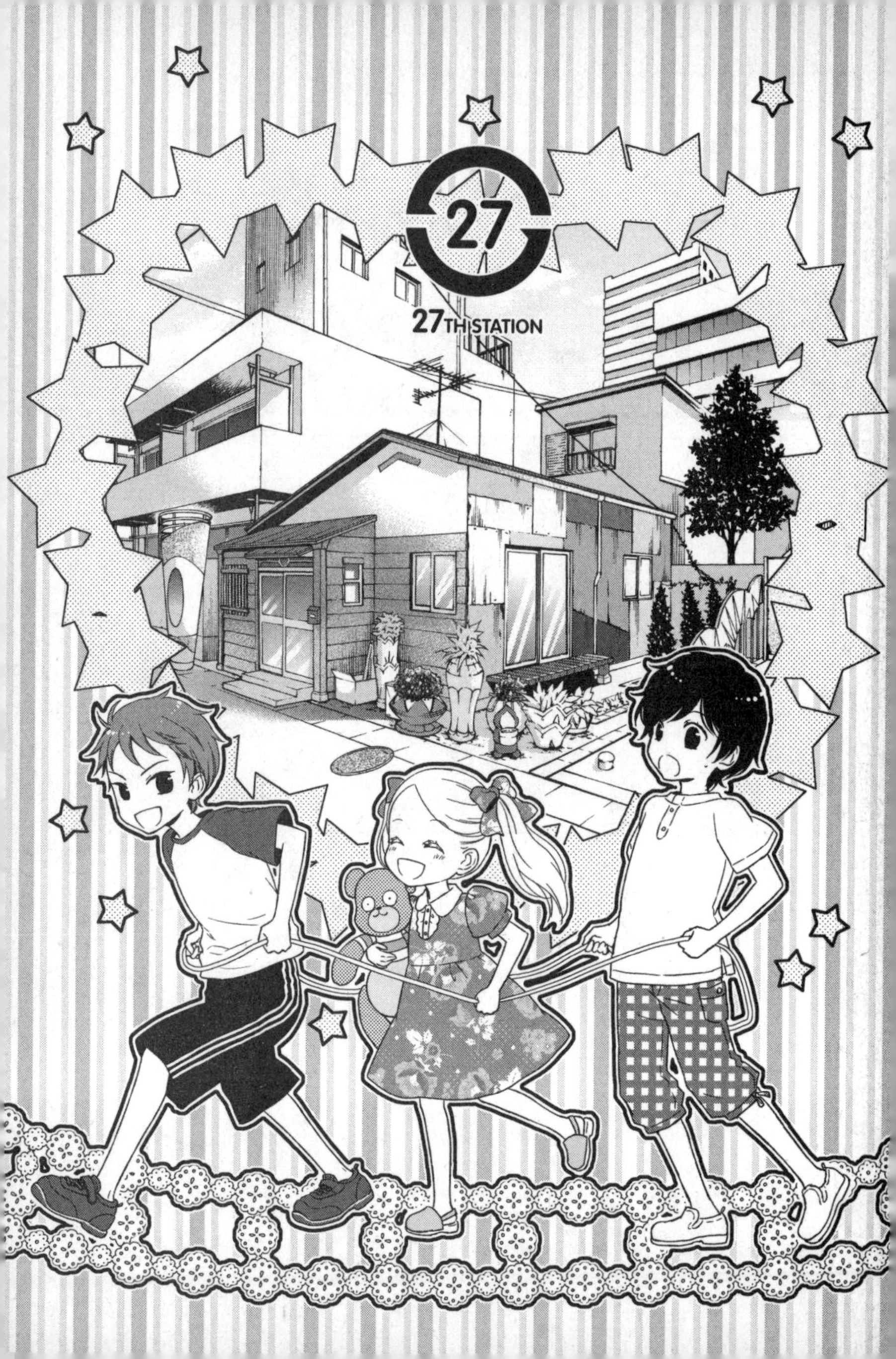
27
27TH STATION

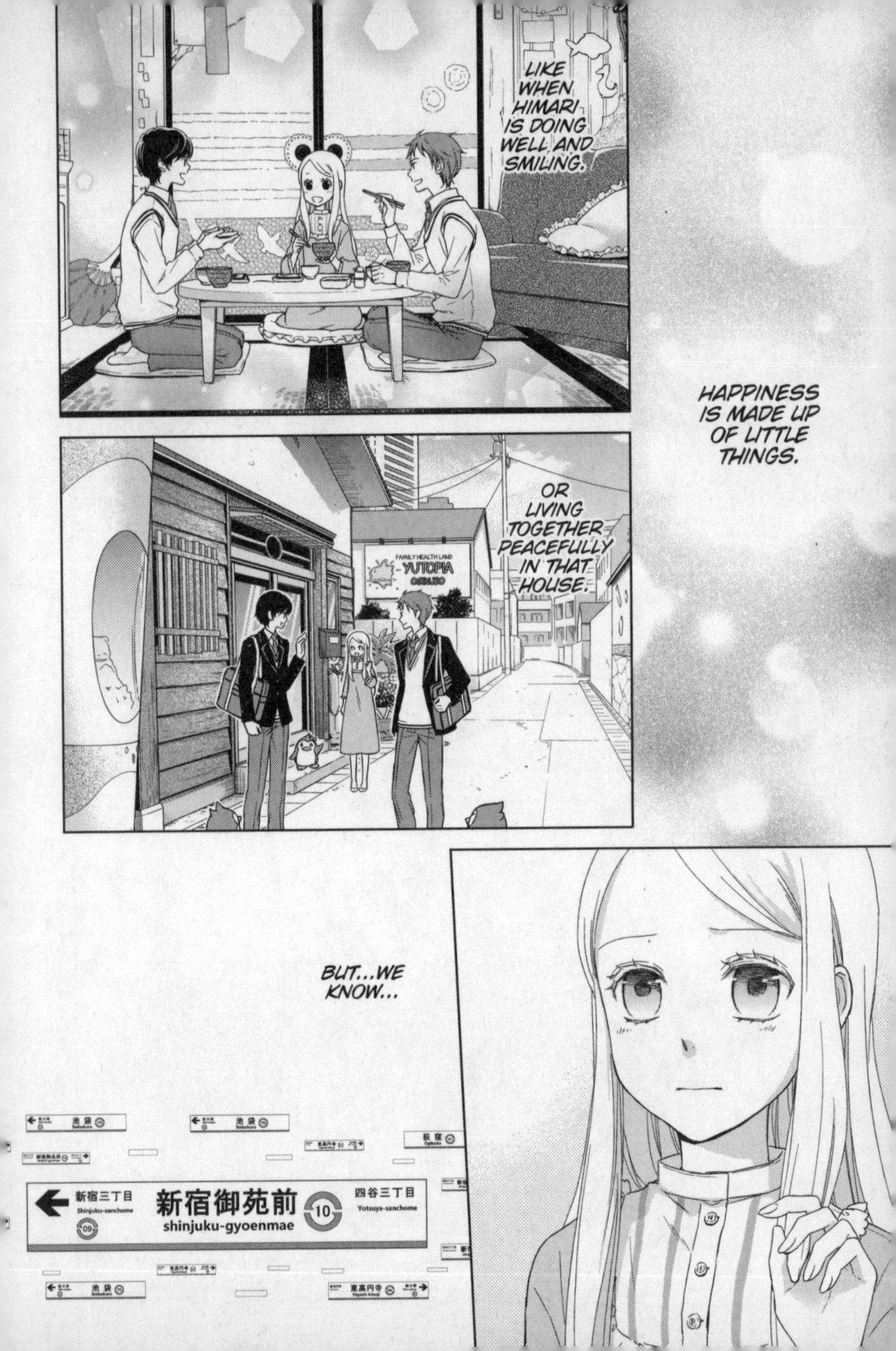
HAPPINESS IS MADE UP OF LITTLE THINGS.
LIKE WHEN HIMARI IS DOING WELL AND SMILING.
OR LIVING TOGETHER PEACEFULLY IN THAT HOUSE.
FAMILY HEALTH LAND
YUTOPIA
BUT...WE KNOW...
新宿三丁目
Shinjuku-sanchome
09
新宿御苑前
shinjuku-gyoenmae
10
四谷三丁目
Yotsuya-sanchome

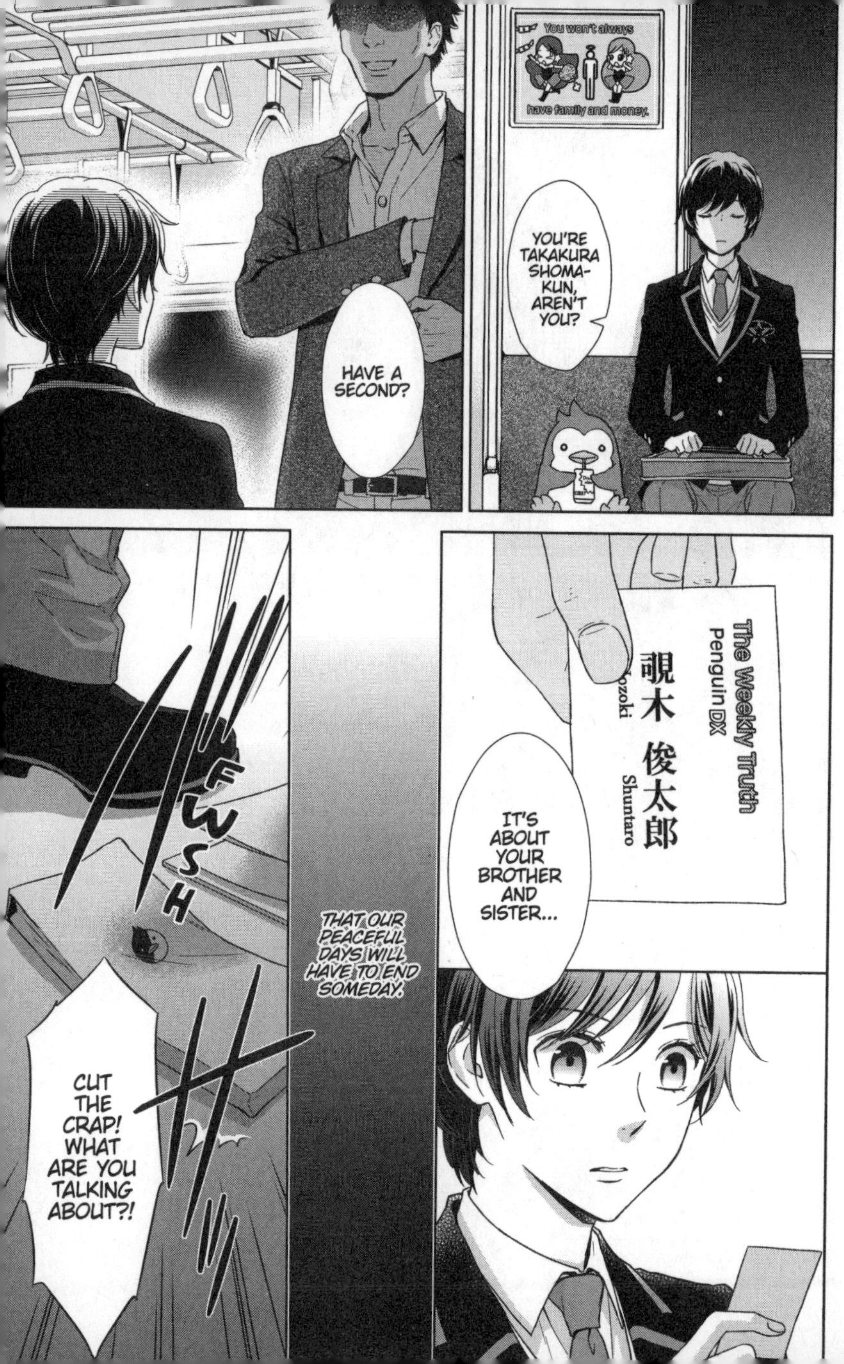
You won't always
have family and money.
YOU'RE TAKAKURA SHOMA-KUN, AREN'T YOU?
HAVE A SECOND?
The Weekly Truth
Penguin DX
覗木 俊太郎
ozoki Shuntaro
IT'S ABOUT YOUR BROTHER AND SISTER...
THAT OUR PEACEFUL DAYS WILL HAVE TO END SOMEDAY.
FWSH
CUT THE CRAP! WHAT ARE YOU TALKING ABOUT?!

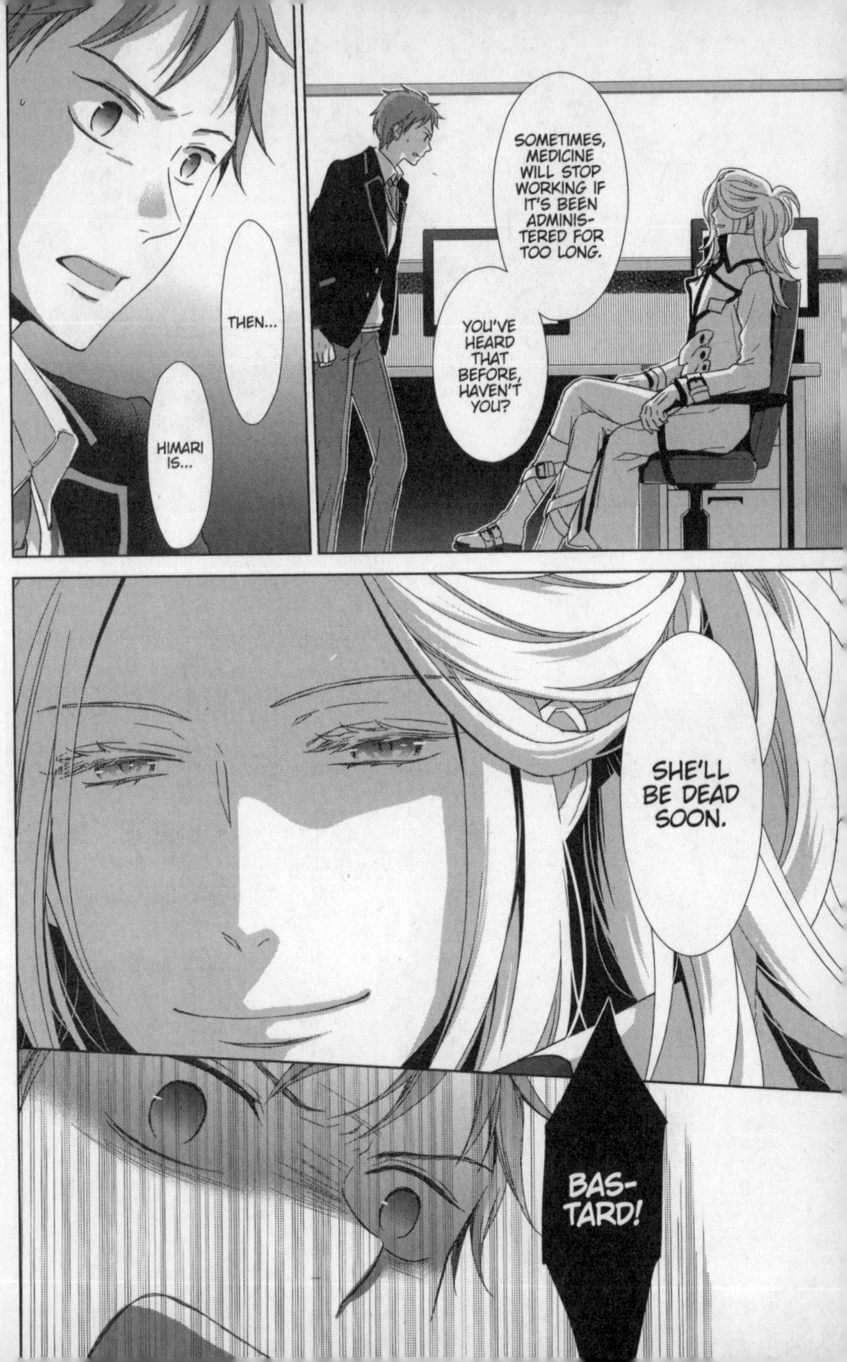
SOMETIMES, MEDICINE WILL STOP WORKING IF IT'S BEEN ADMINIS-TERED FOR TOO LONG.
YOU'VE HEARD THAT BEFORE, HAVEN'T YOU?
THEN...
HIMARI IS...
SHE'LL BE DEAD SOON.
BAS-TARD!

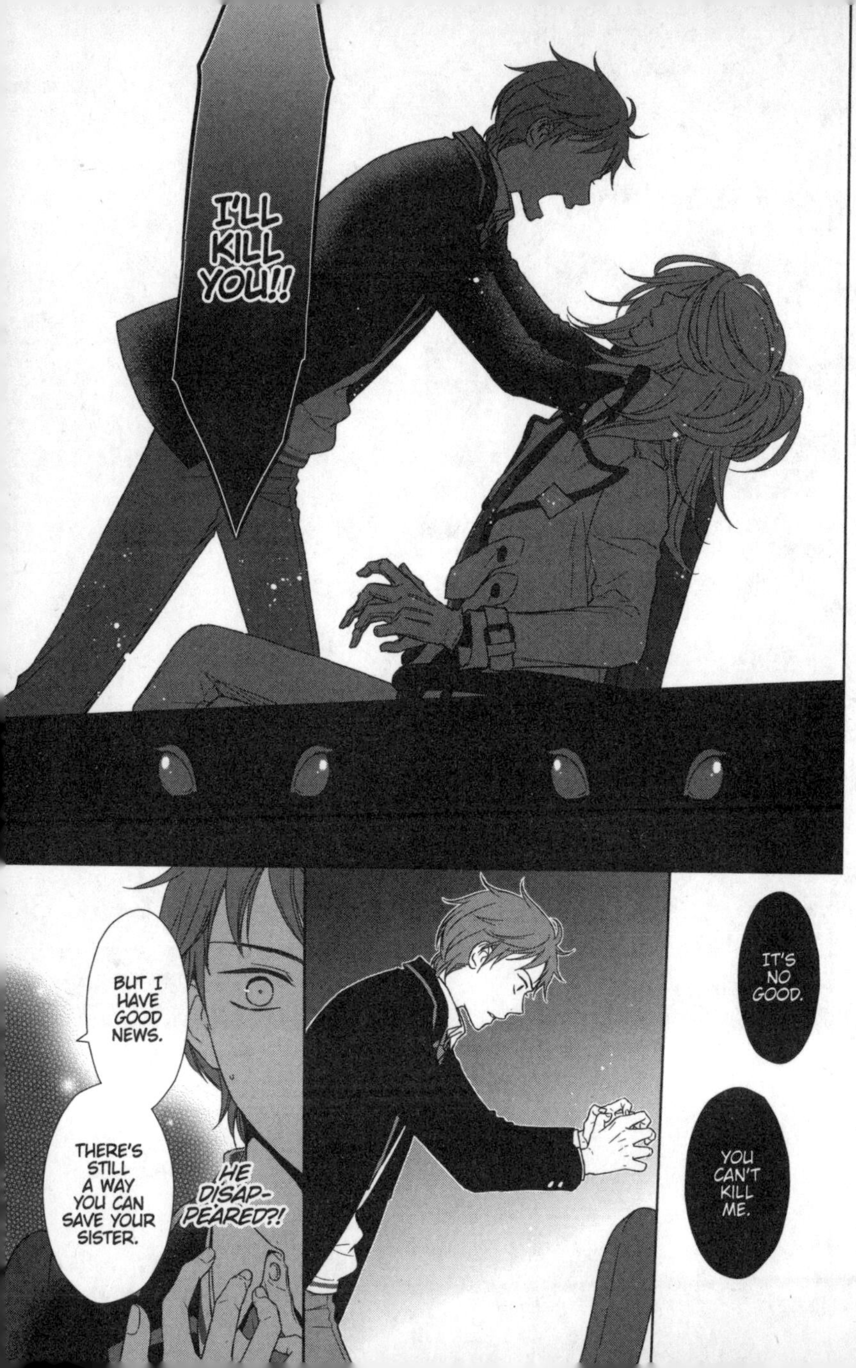
I'LL KILL YOU!!
IT'S NO GOOD.
YOU CAN'T KILL ME.
HE DISAP-PEARED?!
BUT I HAVE GOOD NEWS.
THERE'S STILL A WAY YOU CAN SAVE YOUR SISTER.

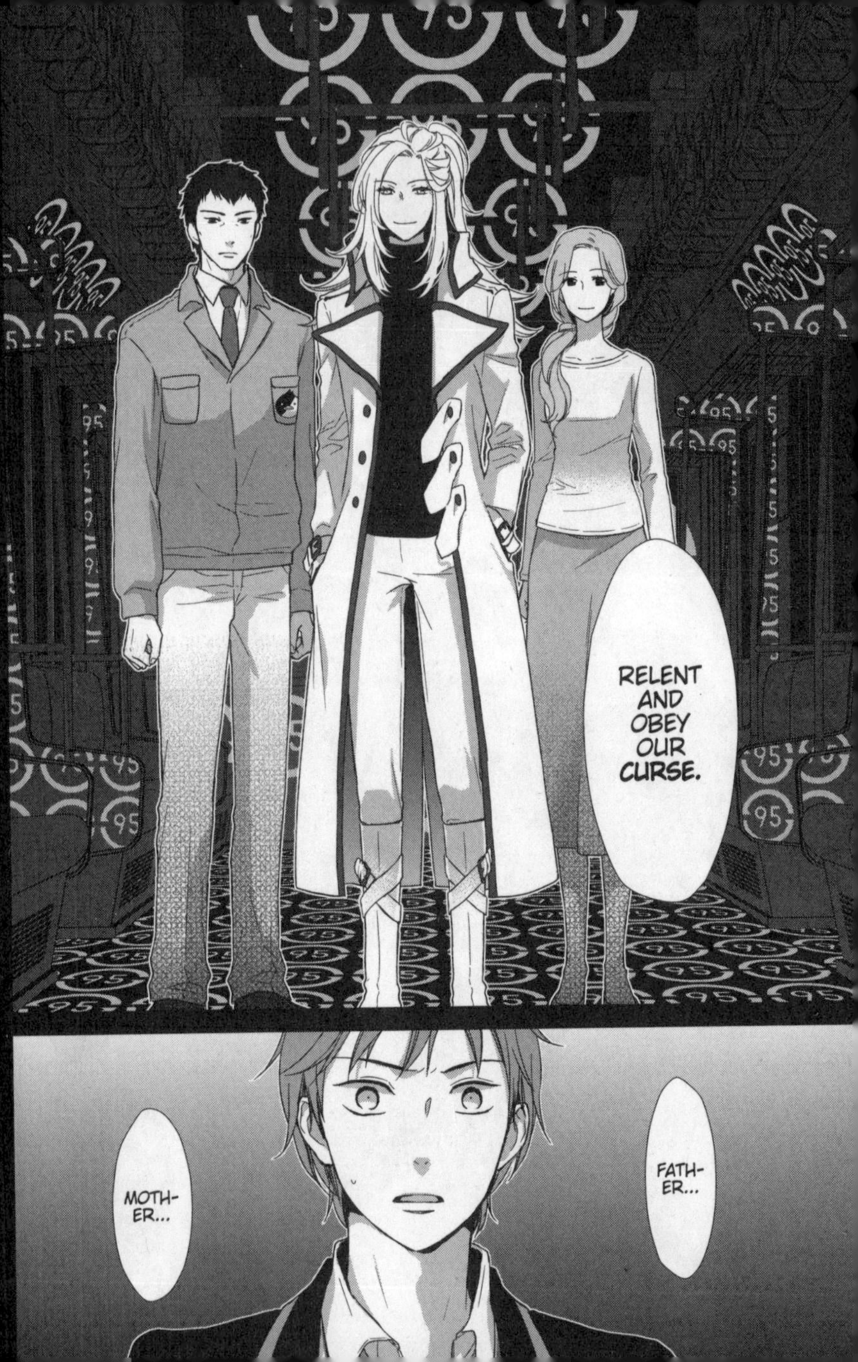
RELENT AND OBEY OUR CURSE.
FATH-ER...
MOTH-ER...

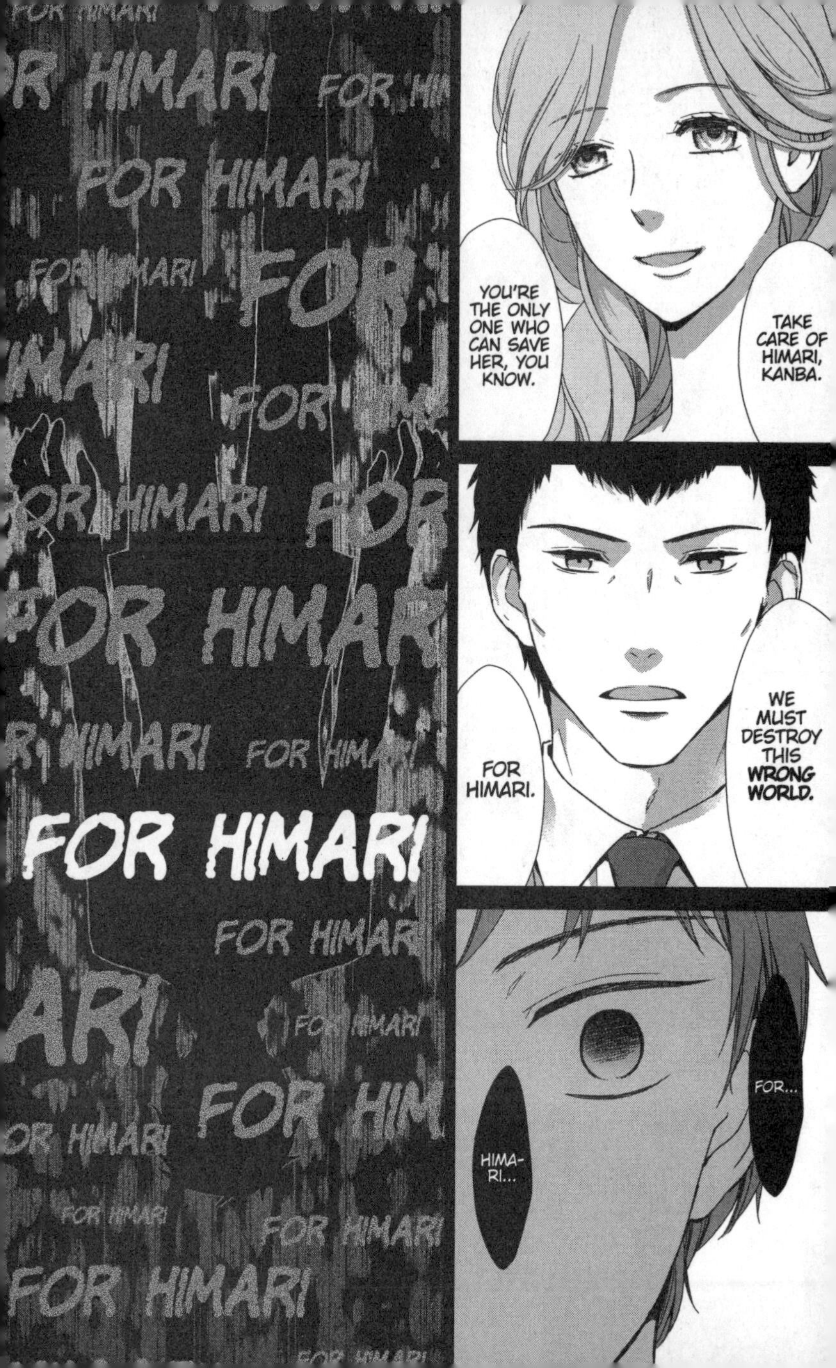
TAKE CARE OF HIMARI, KANBA.
YOU'RE THE ONLY ONE WHO CAN SAVE HER, YOU KNOW.
WE MUST DESTROY THIS WRONG WORLD.
FOR HIMARI.
FOR...
HIMA-RI...
FOR HIMARI
FOR HIMARI
FOR HIMARI
FOR HIMARI
FOR HIMARI
FOR HIMARI

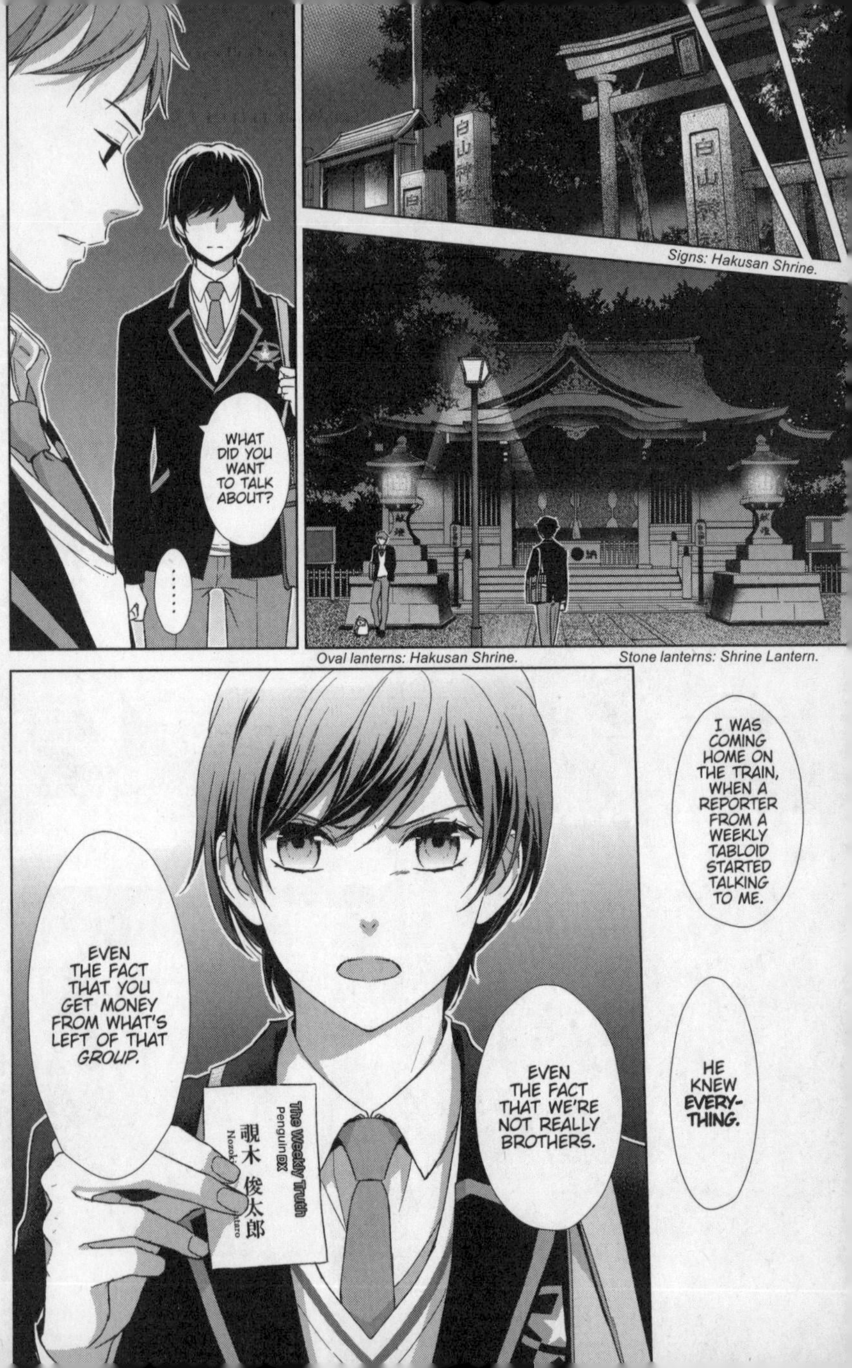
Signs: Hakusan Shrine.
Oval lanterns: Hakusan Shrine.
Stone lanterns: Shrine Lantern.
WHAT DID YOU WANT TO TALK ABOUT?
......
I WAS COMING HOME ON THE TRAIN, WHEN A REPORTER FROM A WEEKLY TABLOID STARTED TALKING TO ME.
HE KNEW **EVERYTHING.**
EVEN THE FACT THAT WE'RE NOT REALLY BROTHERS.
EVEN THE FACT THAT YOU GET MONEY FROM WHAT'S LEFT OF THAT *GROUP.*
The Weekly Truth
Penguin DX
覗木 俊太郎

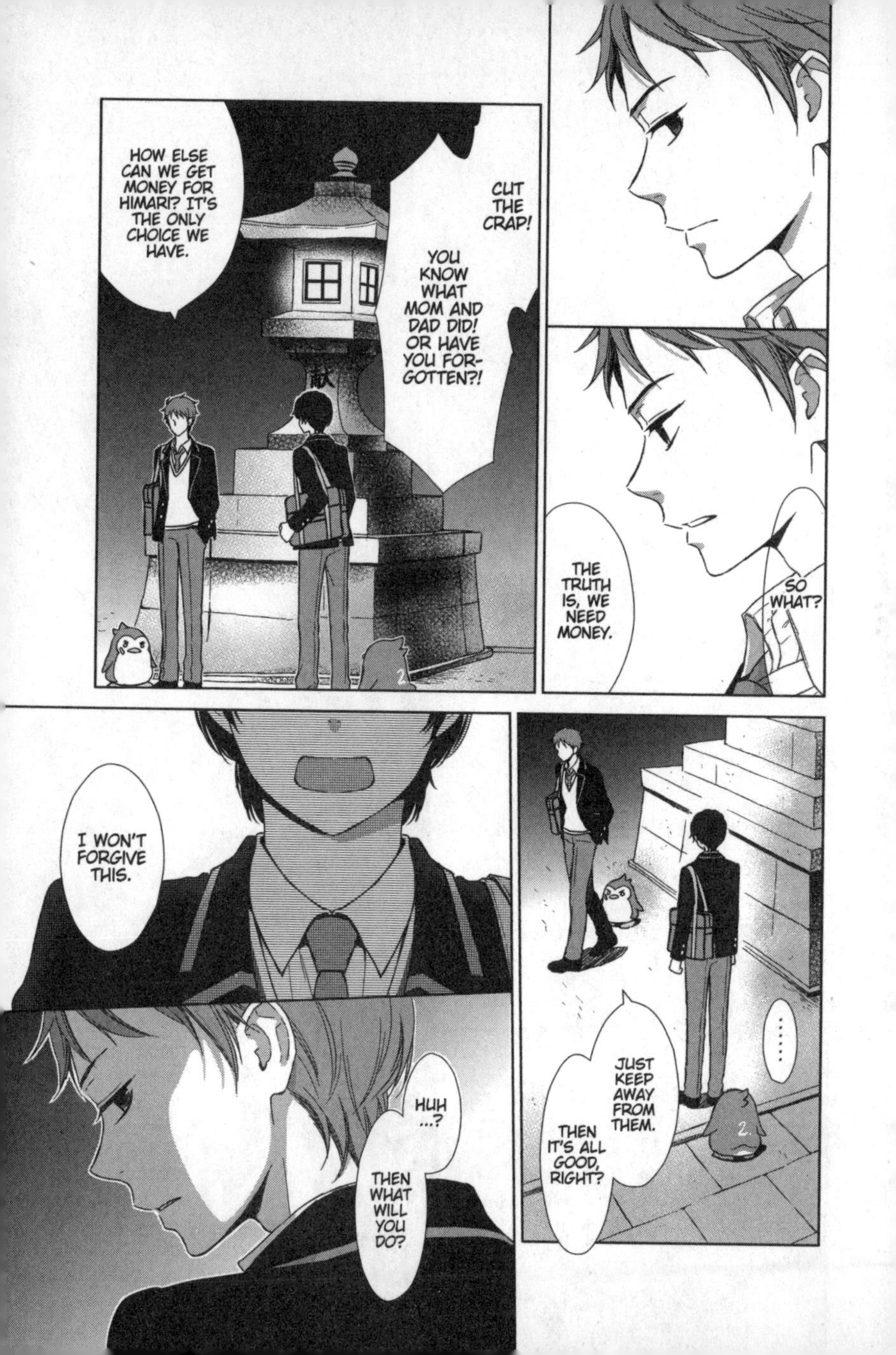

THE TRUTH IS, WE NEED MONEY.
SO WHAT?
CUT THE CRAP!
YOU KNOW WHAT MOM AND DAD DID! OR HAVE YOU FOR-GOTTEN?!
HOW ELSE CAN WE GET MONEY FOR HIMARI? IT'S THE ONLY CHOICE WE HAVE.
......
JUST KEEP AWAY FROM THEM.
THEN IT'S ALL GOOD, RIGHT?
I WON'T FORGIVE THIS.
HUH ...?
THEN WHAT WILL YOU DO?

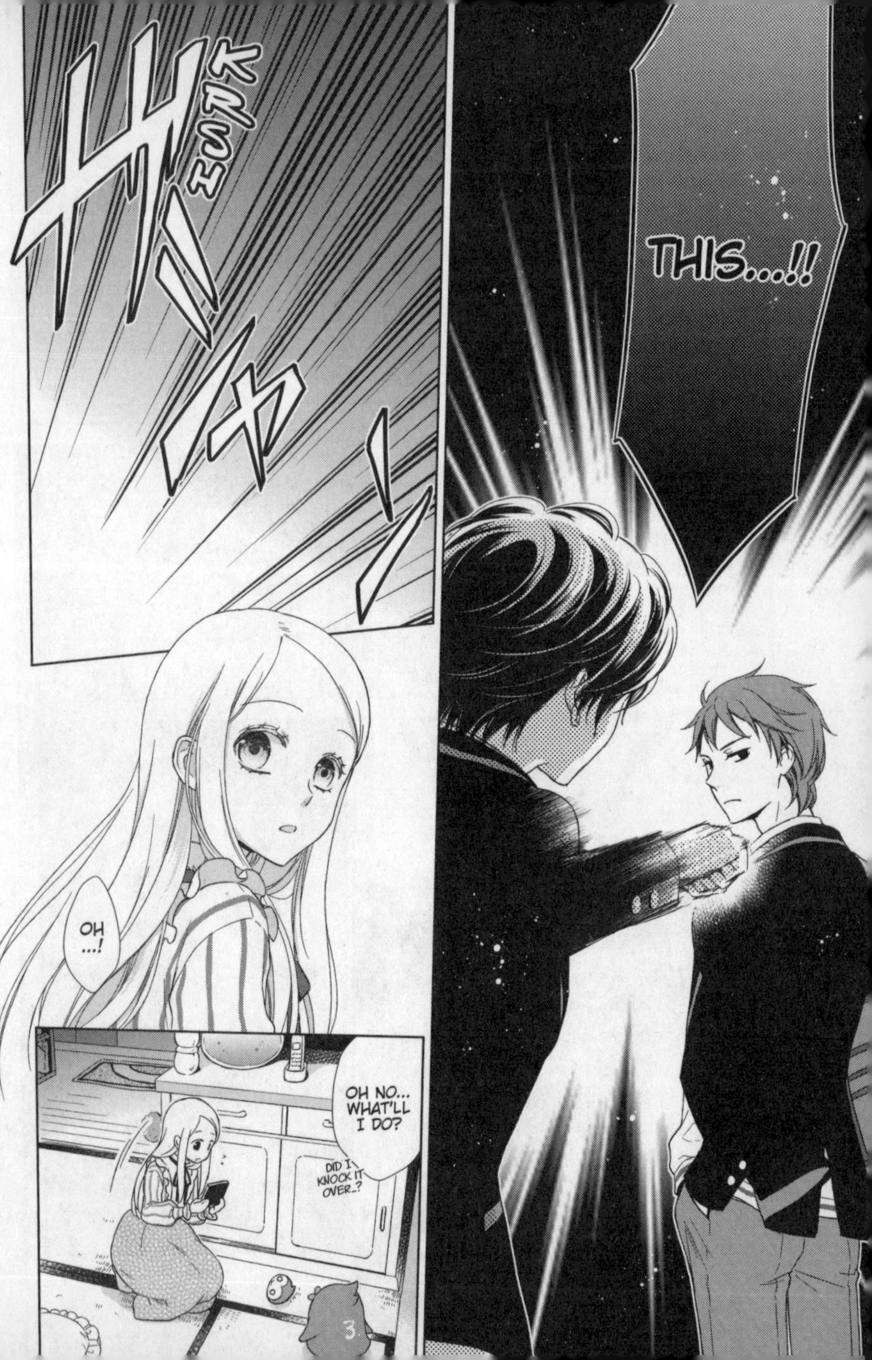
THIS...!!
KRSH
OH ...!
OH NO... WHAT'LL I DO?
DID I KNOCK IT OVER..?

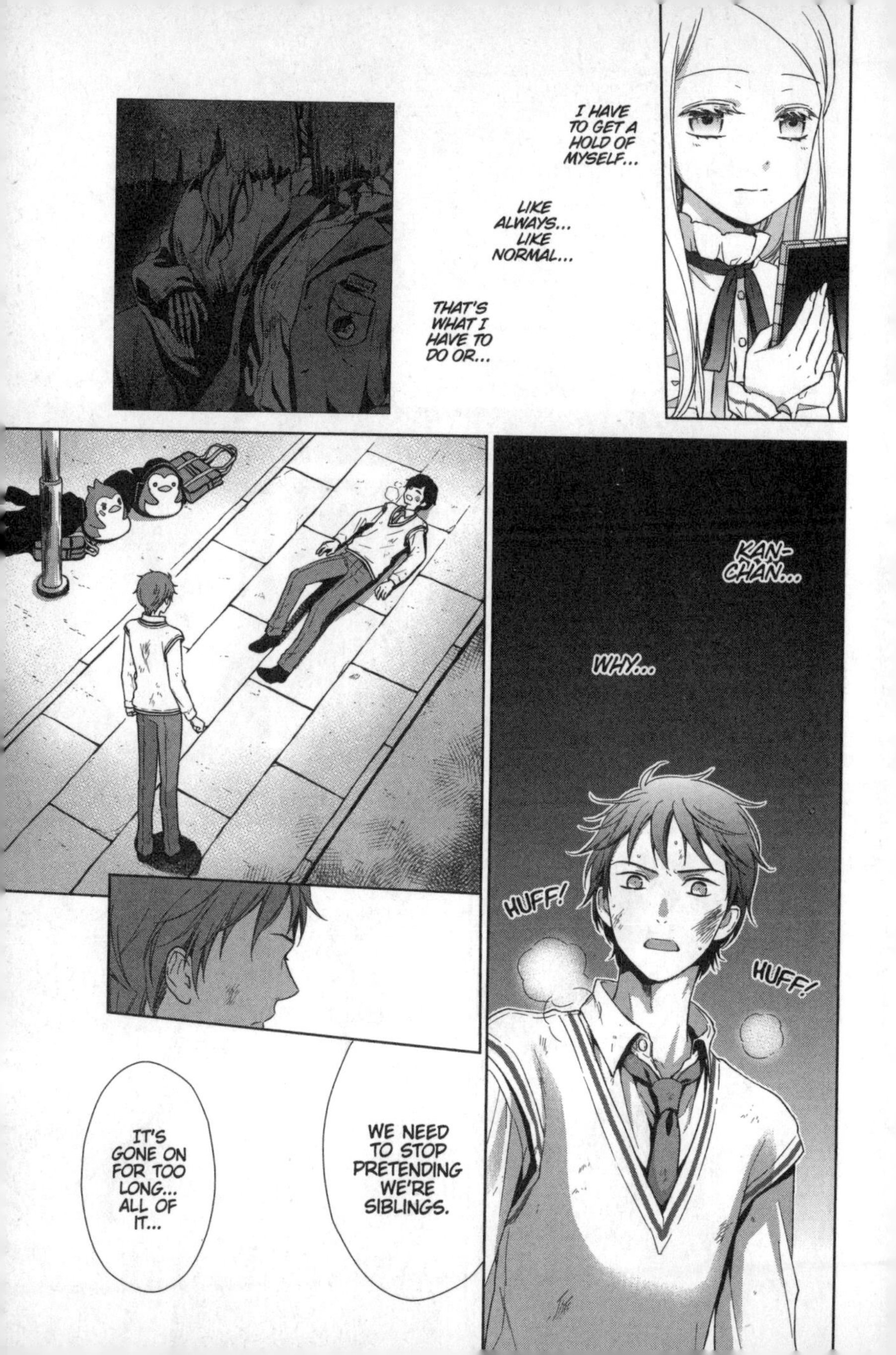
I HAVE TO GET A HOLD OF MYSELF...
LIKE ALWAYS... LIKE NORMAL...
THAT'S WHAT I HAVE TO DO OR...
KAN-CHAN...
WHY...
HUFF!
HUFF!
WE NEED TO STOP PRETENDING WE'RE SIBLINGS.
IT'S GONE ON FOR TOO LONG... ALL OF IT...

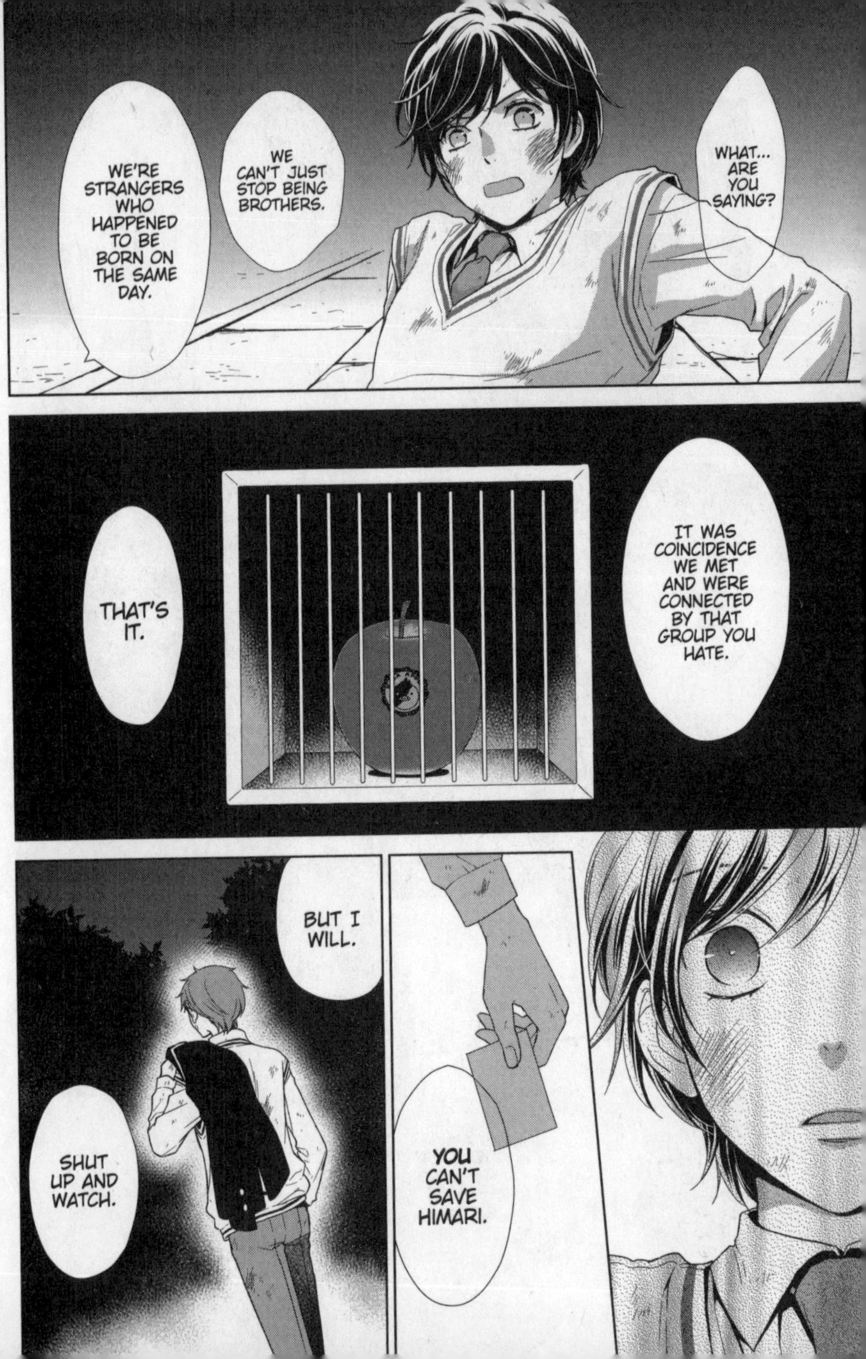
WHAT... ARE YOU SAYING?
WE CAN'T JUST STOP BEING BROTHERS.
WE'RE STRANGERS WHO HAPPENED TO BE BORN ON THE SAME DAY.
IT WAS COINCIDENCE WE MET AND WERE CONNECTED BY THAT GROUP YOU HATE.
THAT'S IT.
YOU CAN'T SAVE HIMARI.
BUT I WILL.
SHUT UP AND WATCH.

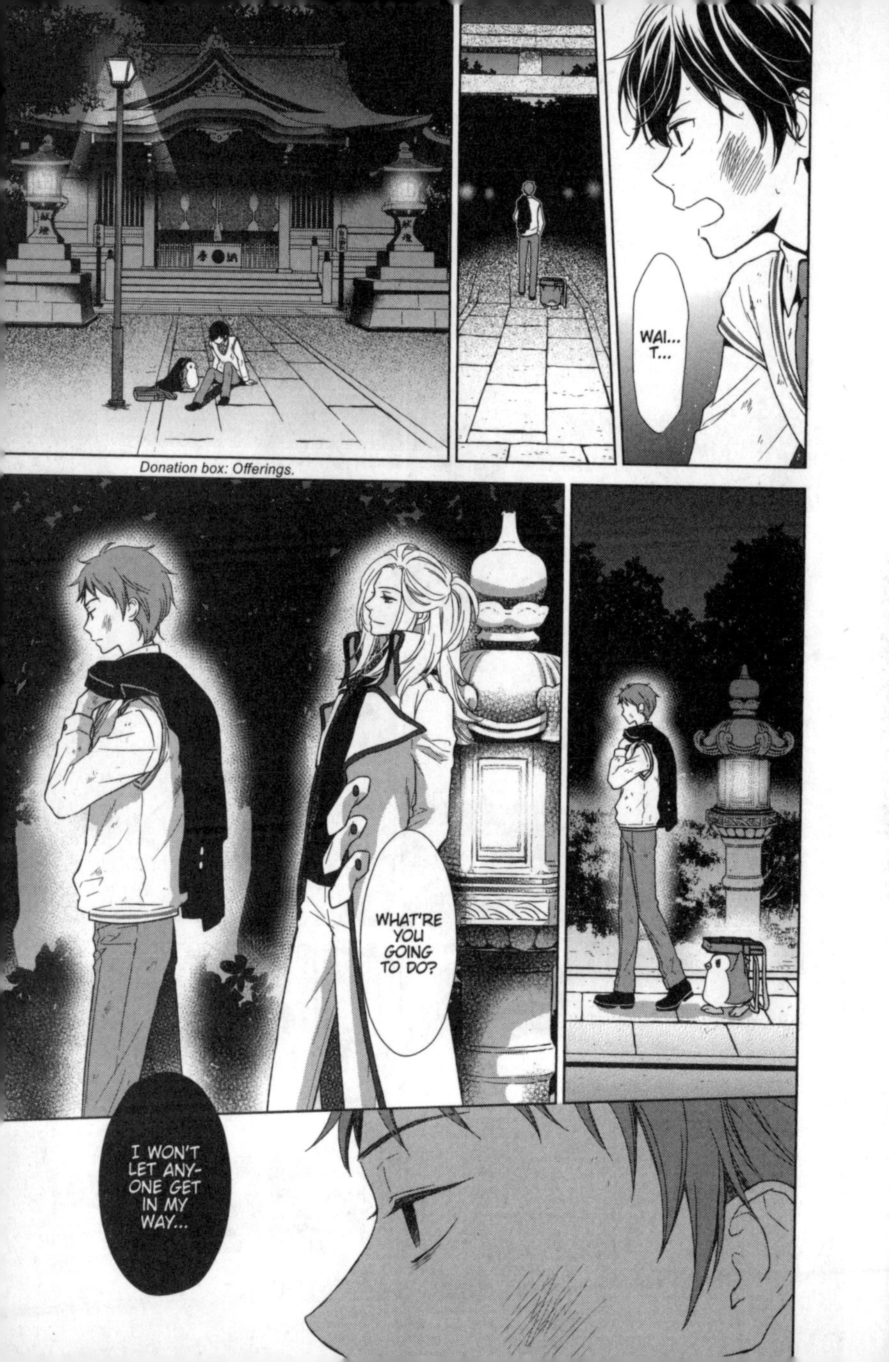
WAI... T...
Donation box: Offerings.
WHAT'RE YOU GOING TO DO?
I WON'T LET ANY-ONE GET IN MY WAY...

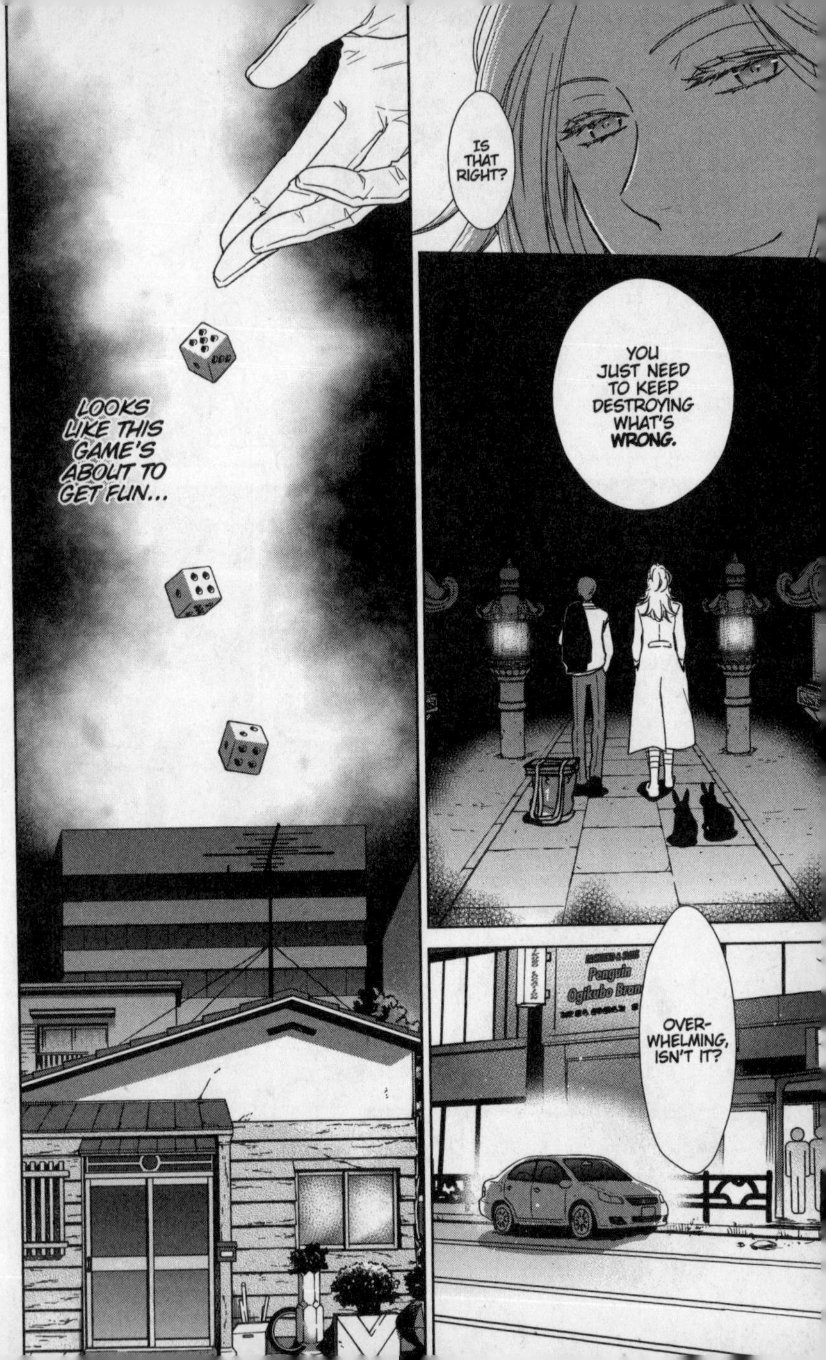
IS THAT RIGHT?
YOU JUST NEED TO KEEP DESTROYING WHAT'S WRONG.
OVER-WHELMING, ISN'T IT?
LOOKS LIKE THIS GAME'S ABOUT TO GET FUN...

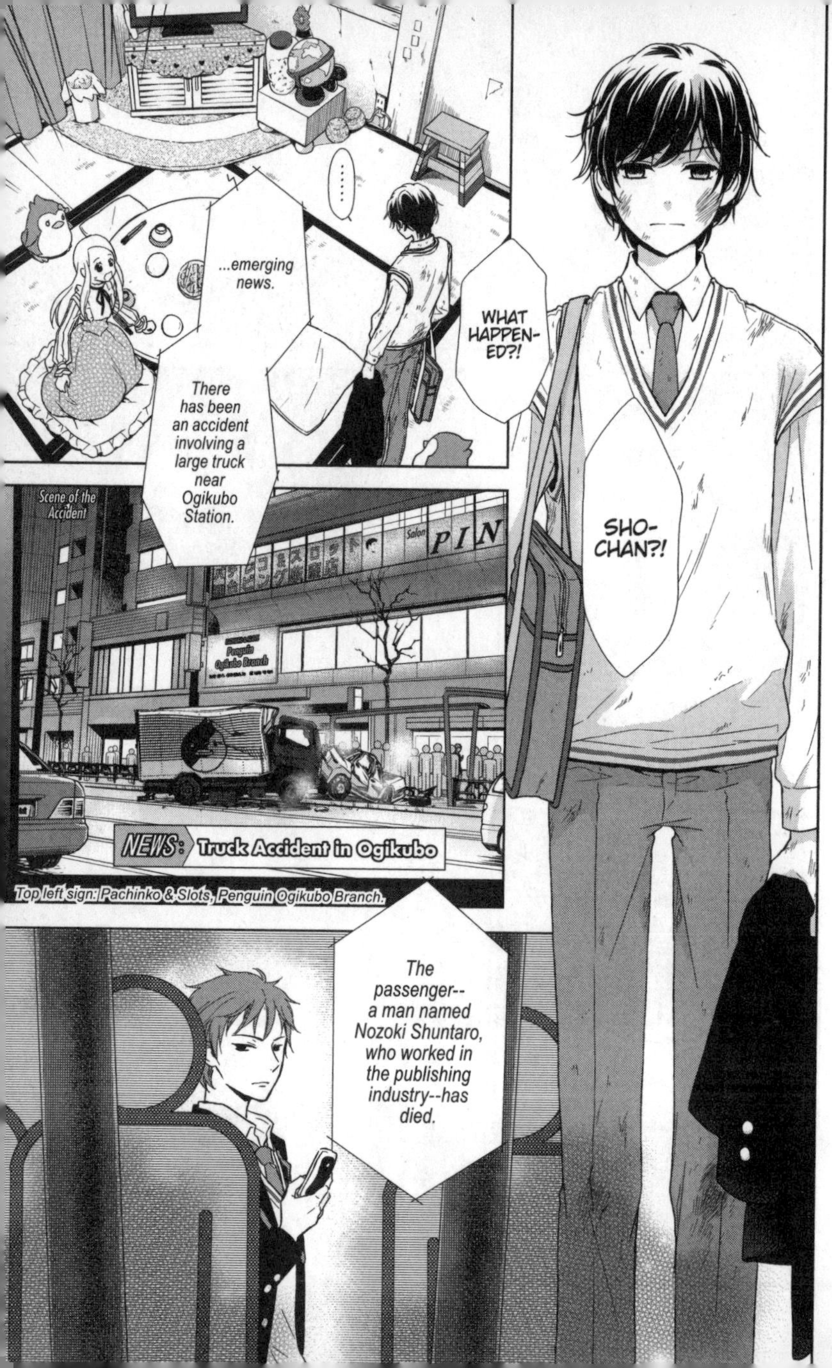
WHAT HAPPENED?!
SHO-CHAN?!
......
...emerging news.
There has been an accident involving a large truck near Ogikubo Station.
Scene of the Accident
Salon PIN
Penguin Ogikubo Branch
NEWS: Truck Accident in Ogikubo
Top left sign: Pachinko & Slots, Penguin Ogikubo Branch.
The passenger--a man named Nozoki Shuntaro, who worked in the publishing industry--has died.

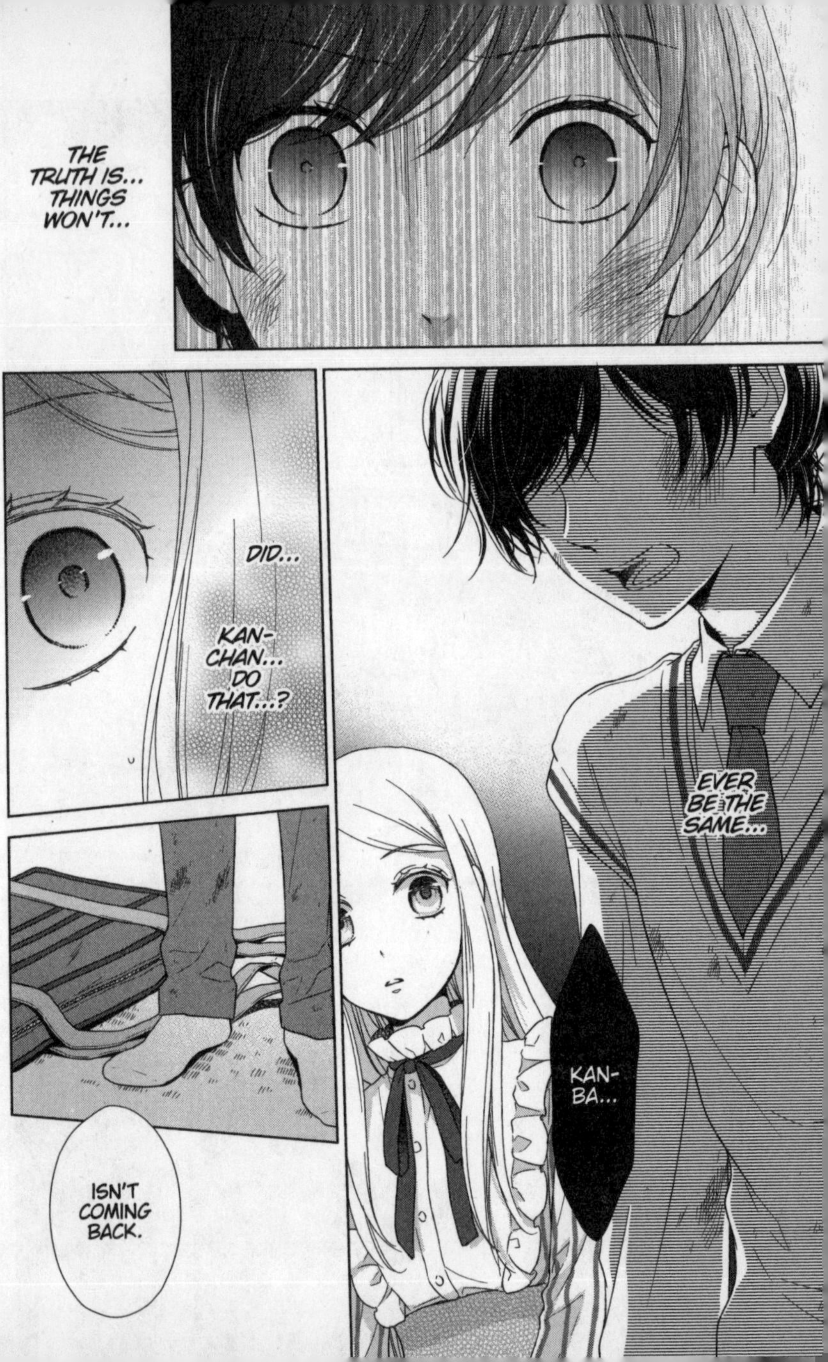
THE TRUTH IS... THINGS WON'T...
EVER BE THE SAME...
KAN-BA...
DID... KAN-CHAN... DO THAT...?
ISN'T COMING BACK.

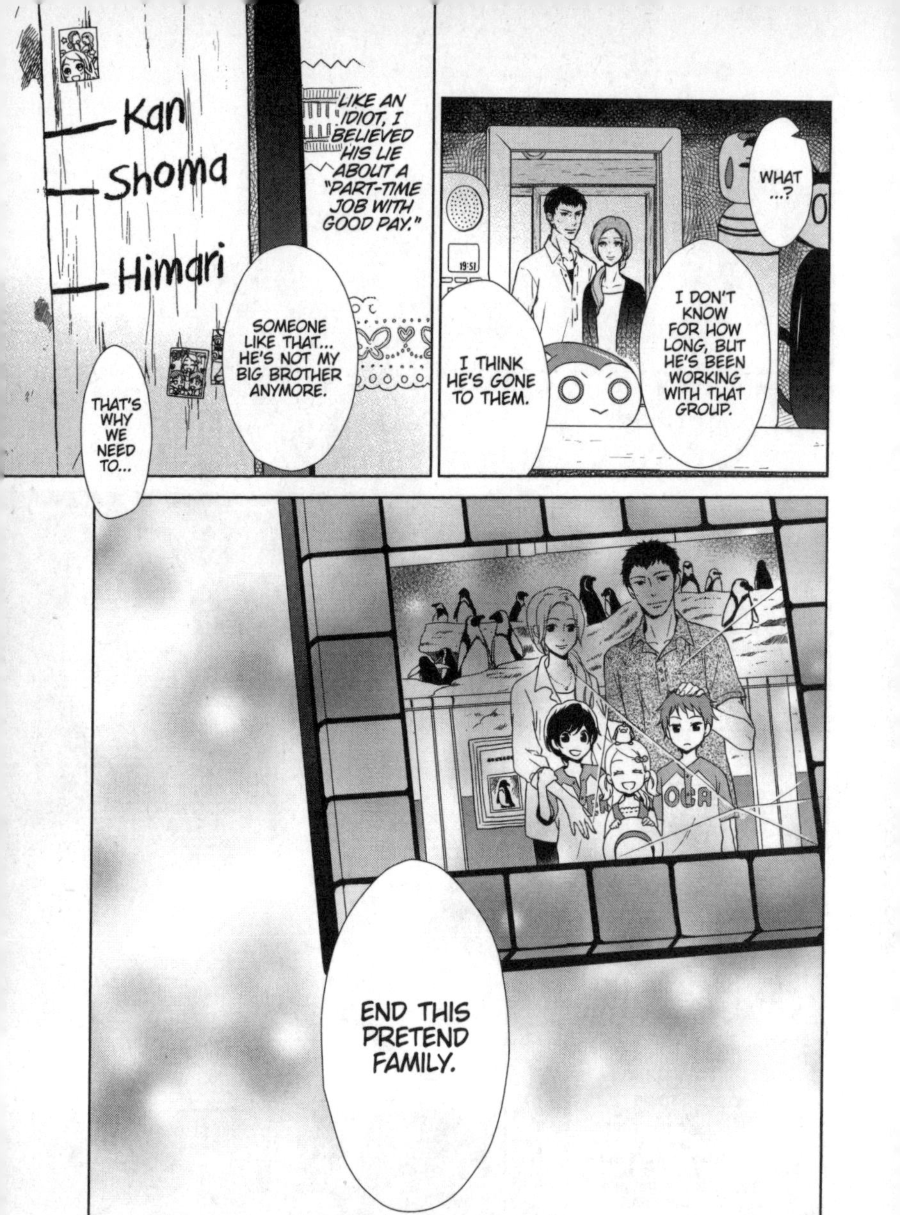
WHAT ...?
I DON'T KNOW FOR HOW LONG, BUT HE'S BEEN WORKING WITH THAT GROUP.
I THINK HE'S GONE TO THEM.
LIKE AN IDIOT, I BELIEVED HIS LIE ABOUT A "PART-TIME JOB WITH GOOD PAY."
Kan
Shoma
Himari
SOMEONE LIKE THAT... HE'S NOT MY BIG BROTHER ANYMORE.
THAT'S WHY WE NEED TO...
END THIS PRETEND FAMILY.

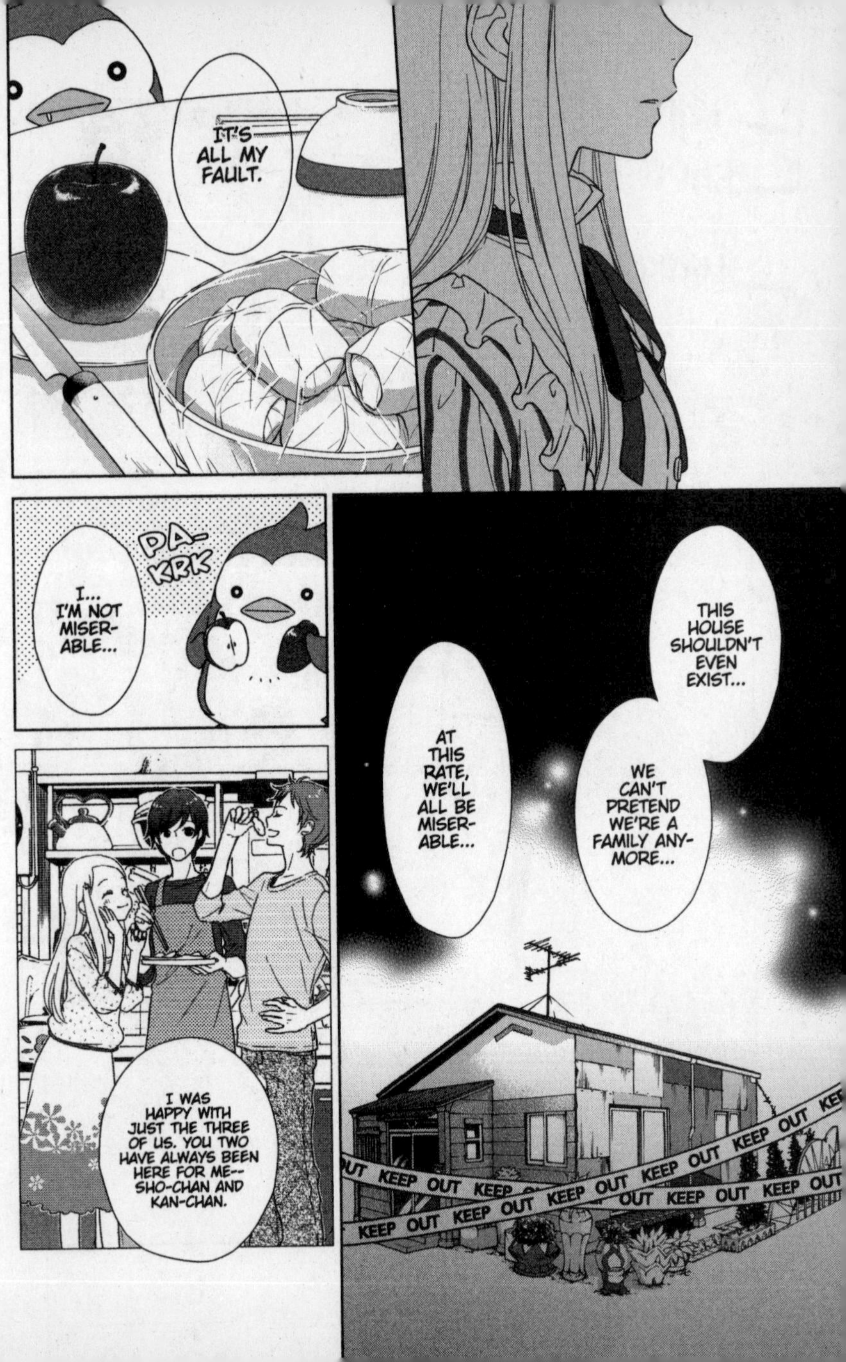
IT'S ALL MY FAULT.
THIS HOUSE SHOULDN'T EVEN EXIST...
WE CAN'T PRETEND WE'RE A FAMILY ANYMORE...
AT THIS RATE, WE'LL ALL BE MISERABLE...
KEEP OUT KEEP OUT KEEP OUT
PA-KRK
I... I'M NOT MISERABLE...
I WAS HAPPY WITH JUST THE THREE OF US. YOU TWO HAVE ALWAYS BEEN HERE FOR ME-- SHO-CHAN AND KAN-CHAN.

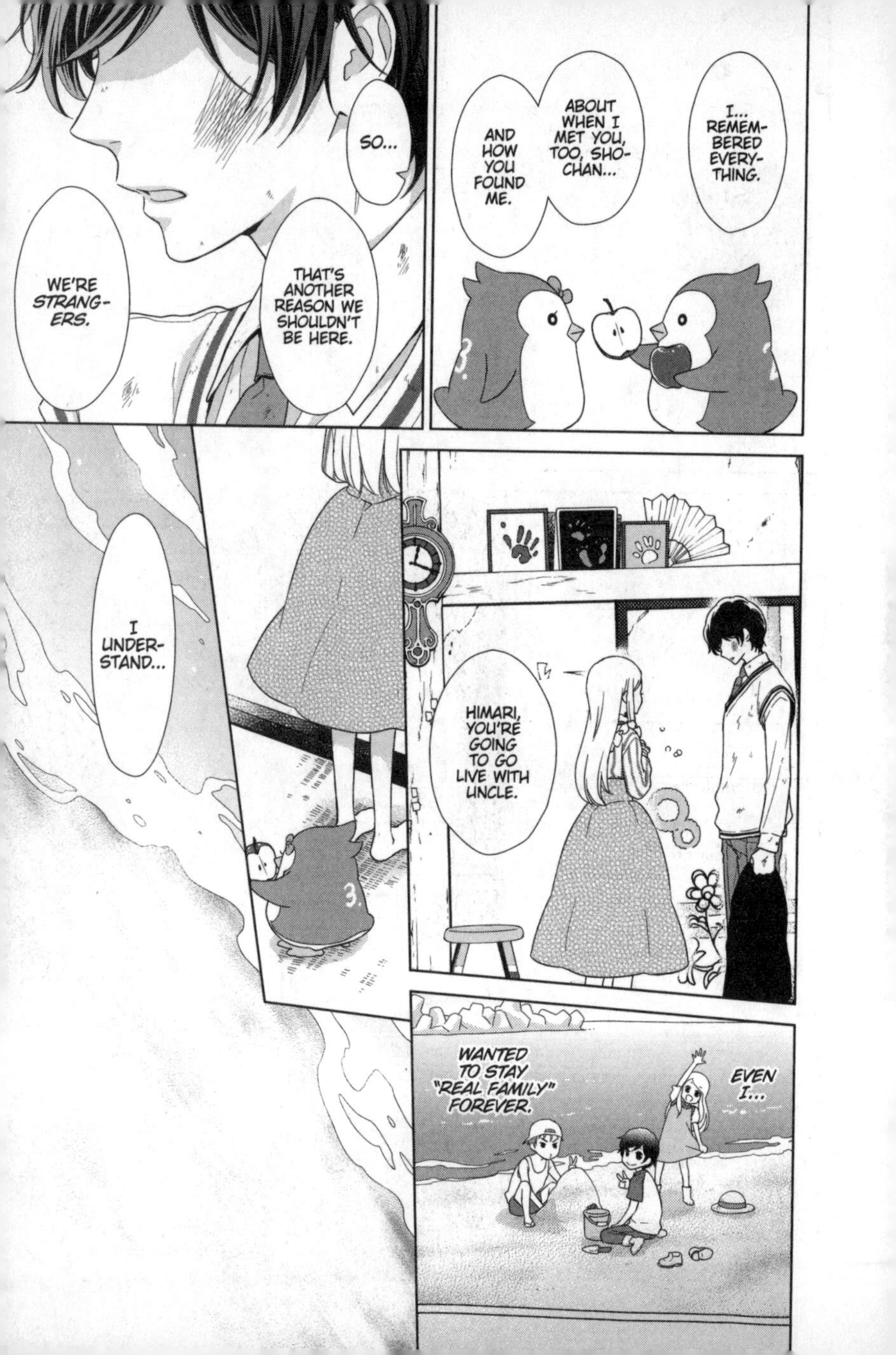

I... REMEMBERED EVERYTHING.
ABOUT WHEN I MET YOU, TOO, SHO-CHAN...
AND HOW YOU FOUND ME.
SO...
THAT'S ANOTHER REASON WE SHOULDN'T BE HERE.
WE'RE STRANGERS.
HIMARI, YOU'RE GOING TO GO LIVE WITH UNCLE.
EVEN I...
WANTED TO STAY "REAL FAMILY" FOREVER.
I UNDERSTAND...

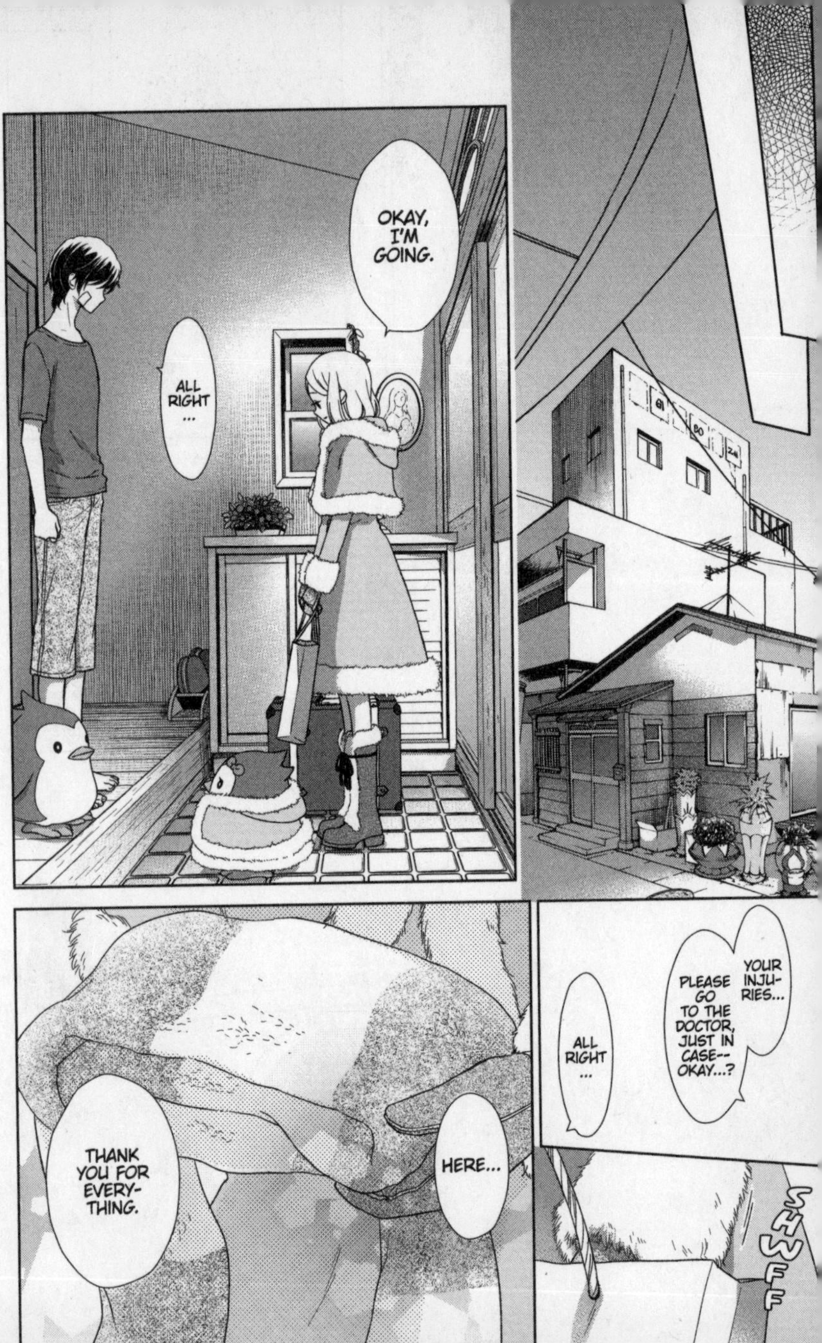
OKAY, I'M GOING.
ALL RIGHT ...
YOUR INJURIES...
PLEASE GO TO THE DOCTOR, JUST IN CASE-- OKAY...?
ALL RIGHT ...
SHWFF
HERE...
THANK YOU FOR EVERYTHING.

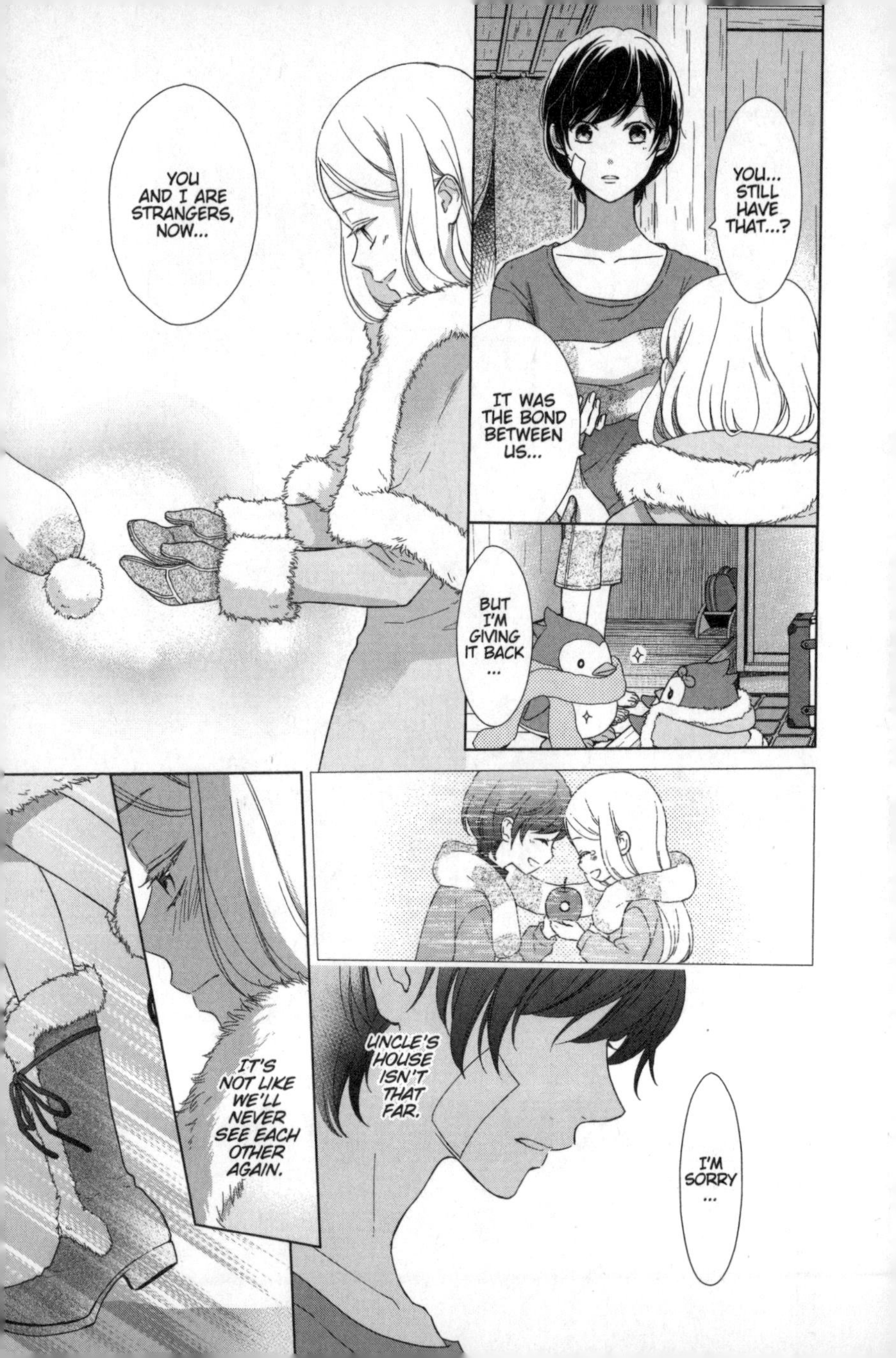

YOU... STILL HAVE THAT...?
IT WAS THE BOND BETWEEN US...
BUT I'M GIVING IT BACK ...
YOU AND I ARE STRANGERS, NOW...
I'M SORRY ...
UNCLE'S HOUSE ISN'T THAT FAR.
IT'S NOT LIKE WE'LL NEVER SEE EACH OTHER AGAIN.

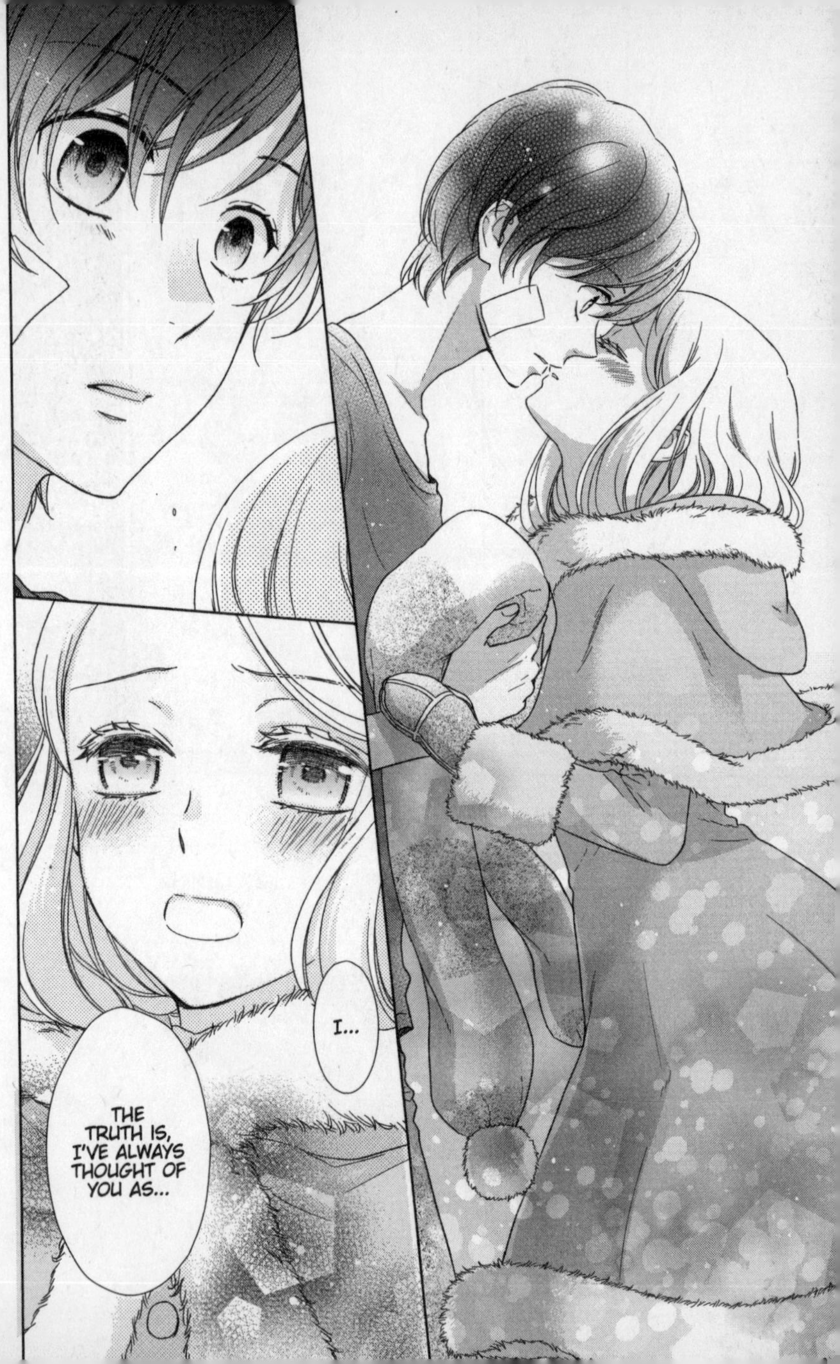
I...
THE TRUTH IS, I'VE ALWAYS THOUGHT OF YOU AS...

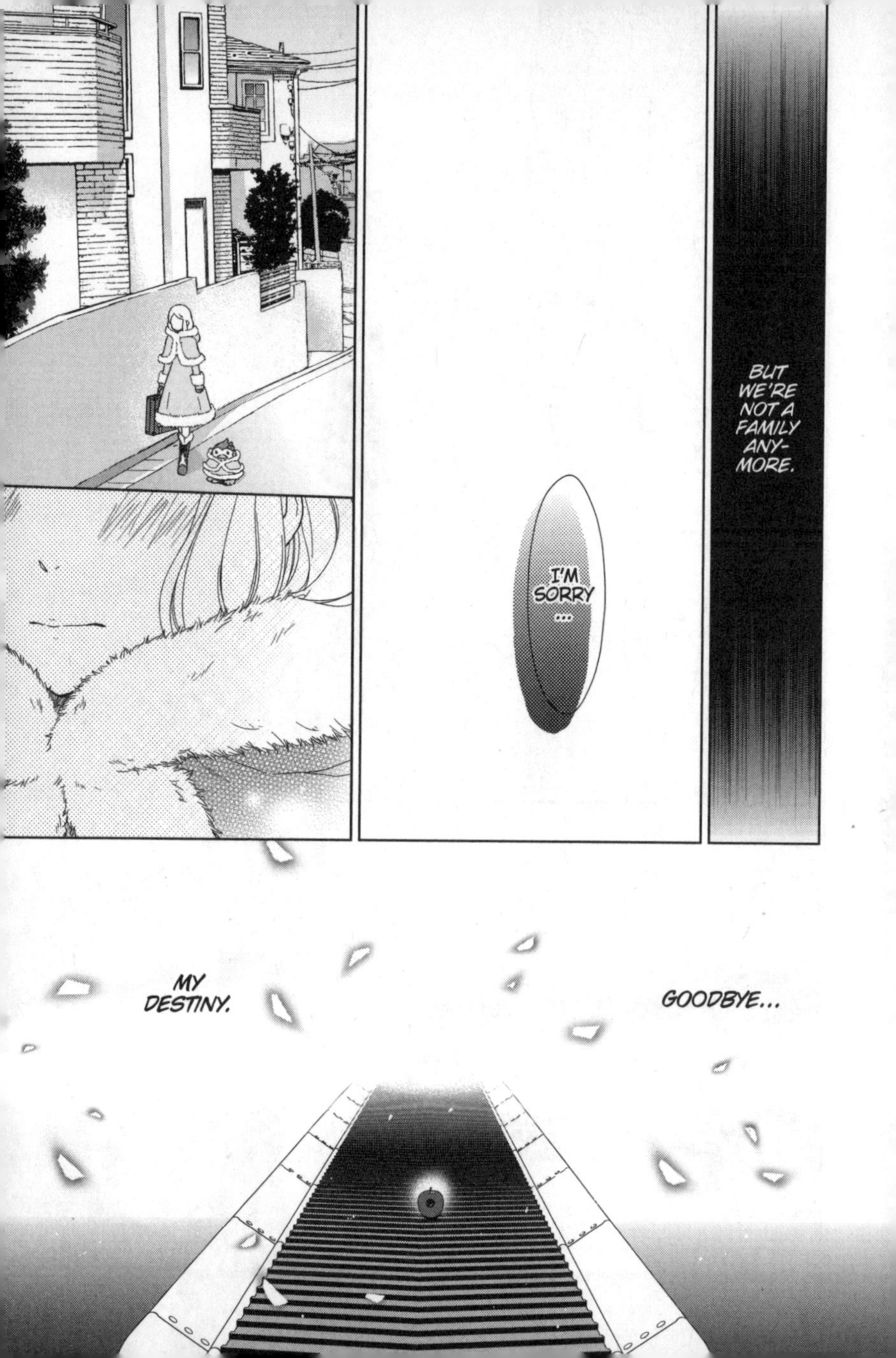
BUT WE'RE NOT A FAMILY ANYMORE.
I'M SORRY...
GOODBYE...
MY DESTINY.

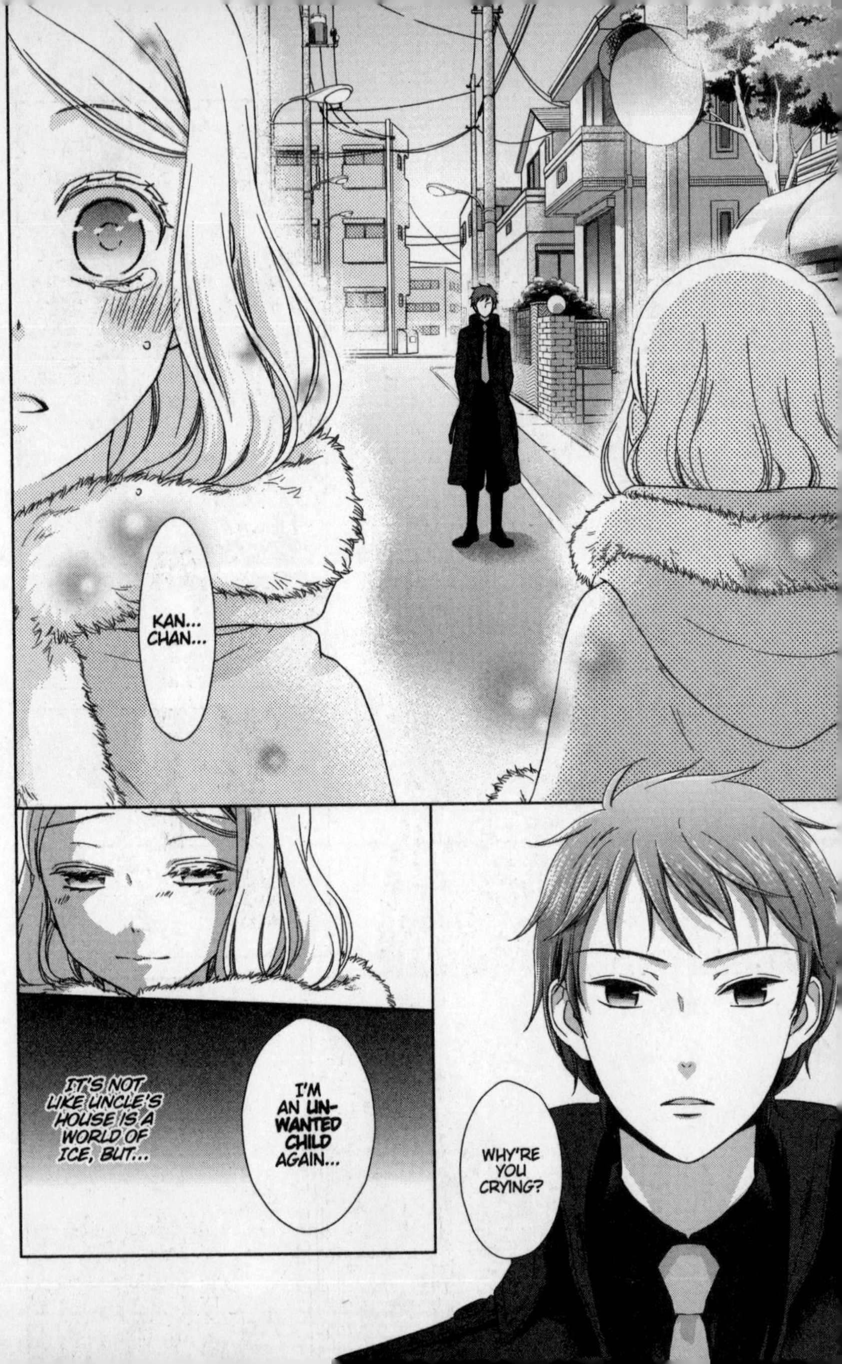
KAN... CHAN...
WHY'RE YOU CRYING?
I'M AN UN-WANTED CHILD AGAIN...
IT'S NOT LIKE UNCLE'S HOUSE IS A WORLD OF ICE, BUT...

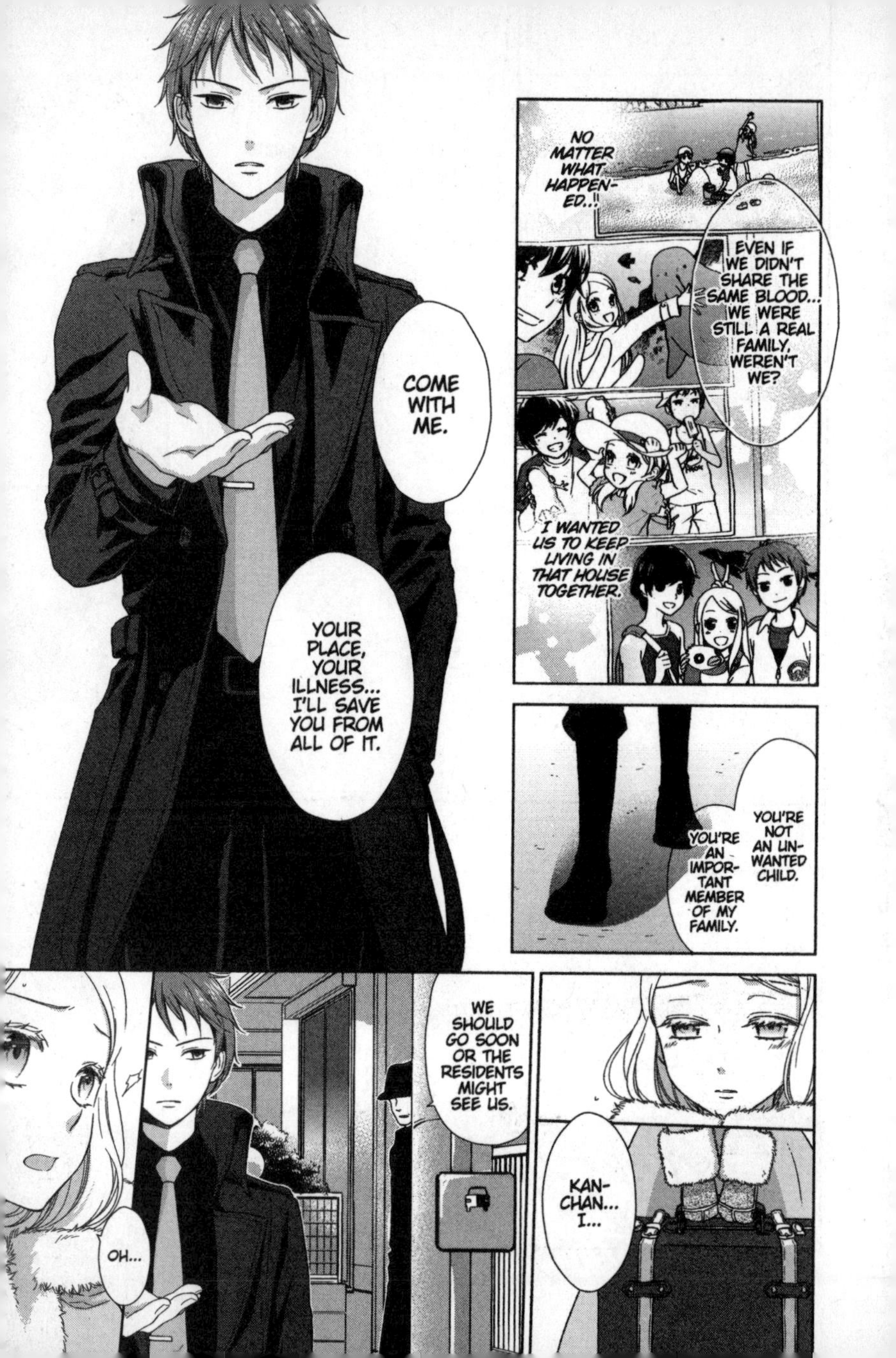
NO MATTER WHAT HAPPENED..!
EVEN IF WE DIDN'T SHARE THE SAME BLOOD... WE WERE STILL A REAL FAMILY, WEREN'T WE?
I WANTED US TO KEEP LIVING IN THAT HOUSE TOGETHER.
YOU'RE NOT AN UNWANTED CHILD.
YOU'RE AN IMPORTANT MEMBER OF MY FAMILY.
COME WITH ME.
YOUR PLACE, YOUR ILLNESS... I'LL SAVE YOU FROM ALL OF IT.
KAN-CHAN... I...
WE SHOULD GO SOON OR THE RESIDENTS MIGHT SEE US.
OH...

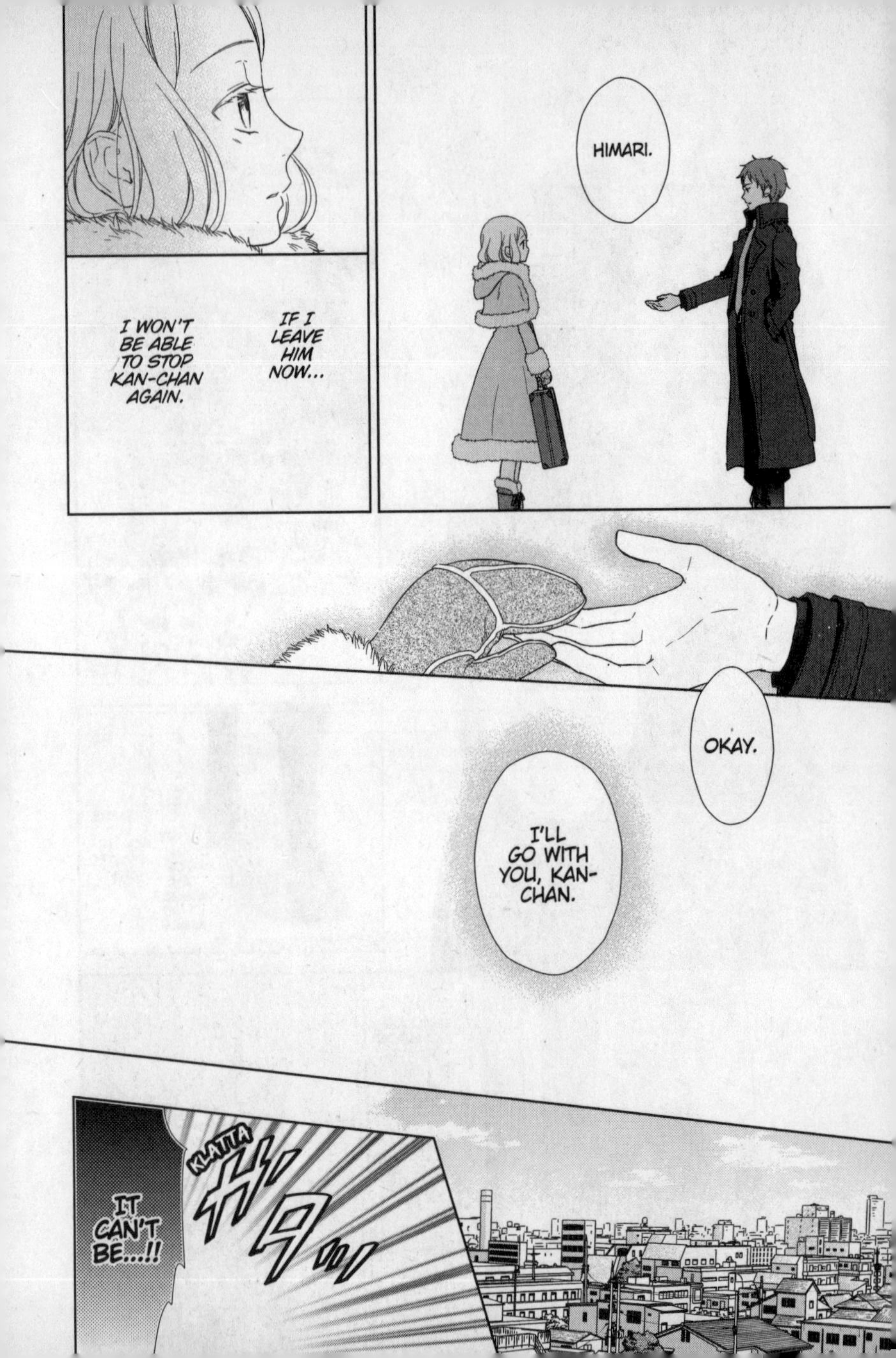
HIMARI.
IF I LEAVE HIM NOW...
I WON'T BE ABLE TO STOP KAN-CHAN AGAIN.
OKAY.
I'LL GO WITH YOU, KAN-CHAN.
KLATTA
IT CAN'T BE...!!

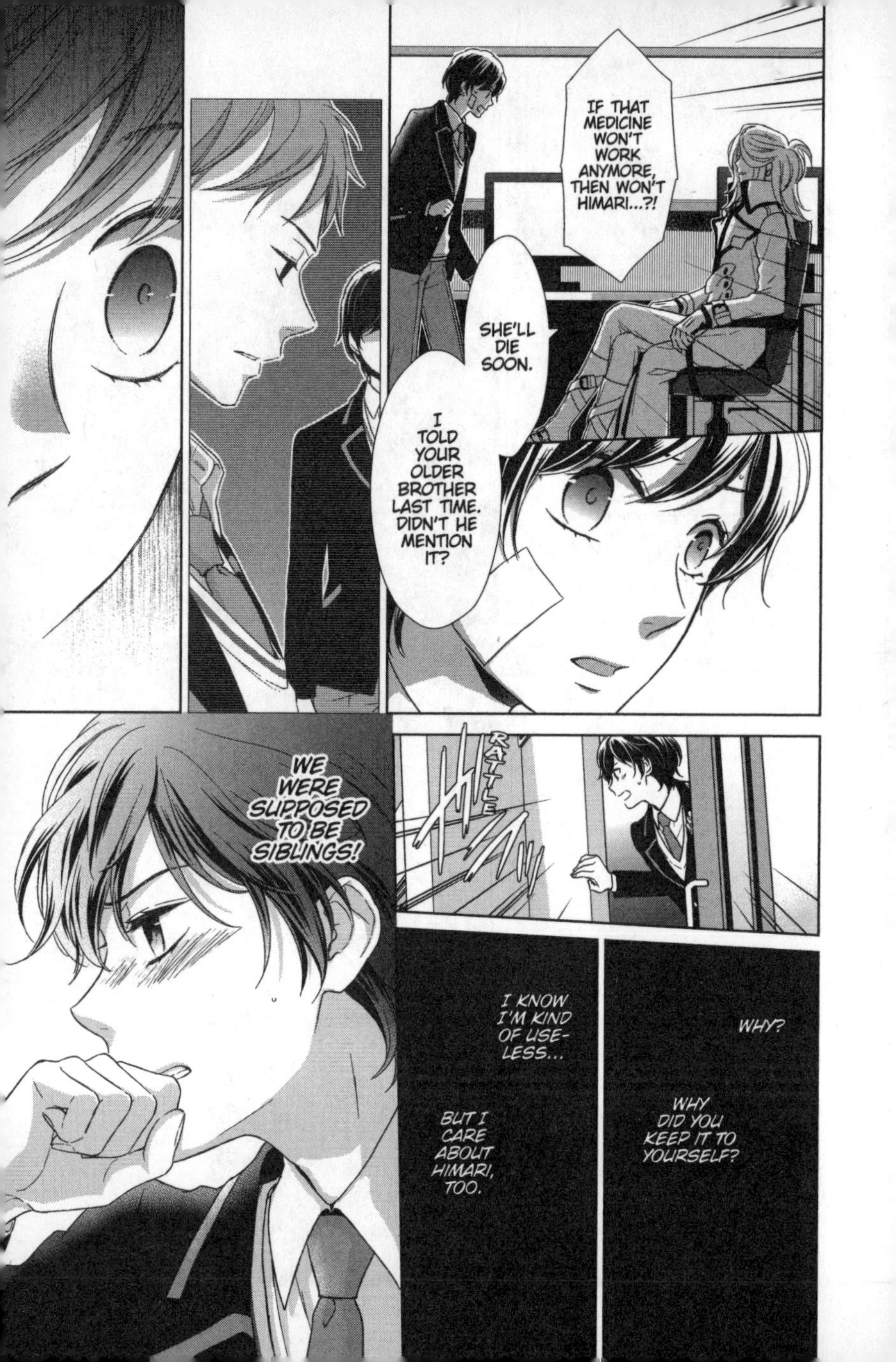
IF THAT MEDICINE WON'T WORK ANYMORE, THEN WON'T HIMARI...?!
SHE'LL DIE SOON.
I TOLD YOUR OLDER BROTHER LAST TIME. DIDN'T HE MENTION IT?
RATTLE
WHY?
WHY DID YOU KEEP IT TO YOURSELF?
I KNOW I'M KIND OF USE-LESS...
BUT I CARE ABOUT HIMARI, TOO.
WE WERE SUPPOSED TO BE SIBLINGS!

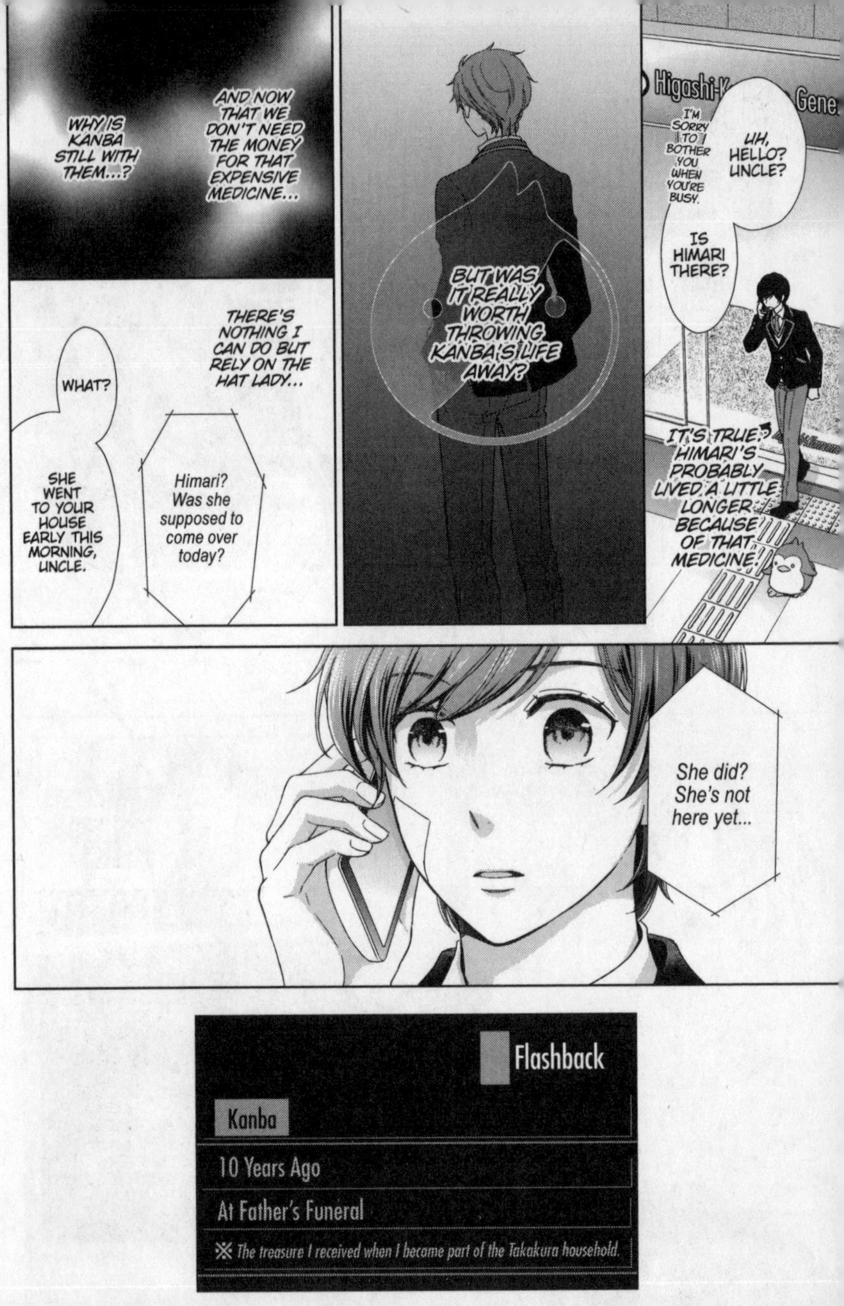
UH, HELLO? UNCLE?
I'M SORRY TO BOTHER YOU WHEN YOU'RE BUSY.
IS HIMARI THERE?
IT'S TRUE. HIMARI'S PROBABLY LIVED A LITTLE LONGER BECAUSE OF THAT MEDICINE.
BUT WAS IT REALLY WORTH THROWING KANBA'S LIFE AWAY?
AND NOW THAT WE DON'T NEED THE MONEY FOR THAT EXPENSIVE MEDICINE...
WHY IS KANBA STILL WITH THEM...?
THERE'S NOTHING I CAN DO BUT RELY ON THE HAT LADY...
Himari? Was she supposed to come over today?
WHAT?
SHE WENT TO YOUR HOUSE EARLY THIS MORNING, UNCLE.
She did? She's not here yet...

Flashback

Kanba

10 Years Ago

At Father's Funeral

※ *The treasure I received when I became part of the Takakura household.*

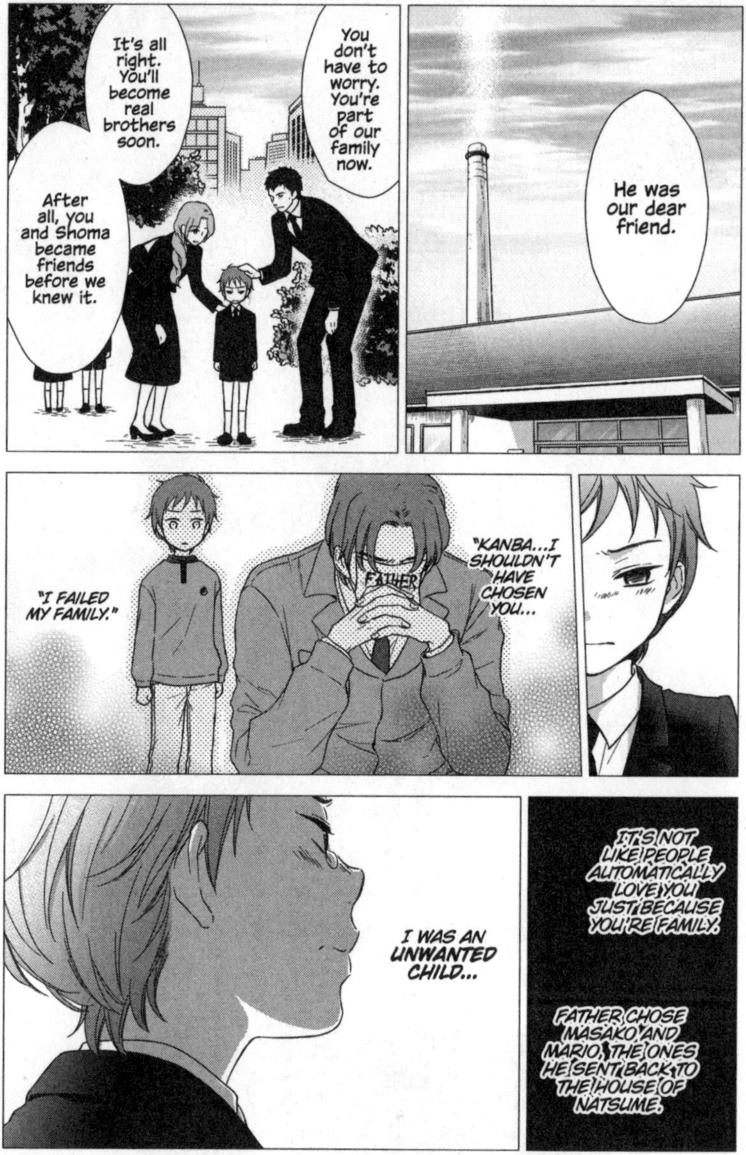
He was our dear friend.
You don't have to worry. You're part of our family now.
It's all right. You'll become real brothers soon.
After all, you and Shoma became friends before we knew it.
"KANBA...I SHOULDN'T HAVE CHOSEN YOU...
FATHER
"I FAILED MY FAMILY."
IT'S NOT LIKE PEOPLE AUTOMATICALLY LOVE YOU JUST BECAUSE YOU'RE FAMILY.
FATHER CHOSE MASAKO AND MARIO, THE ONES HE SENT BACK TO THE HOUSE OF NATSUME.
I WAS AN UNWANTED CHILD...

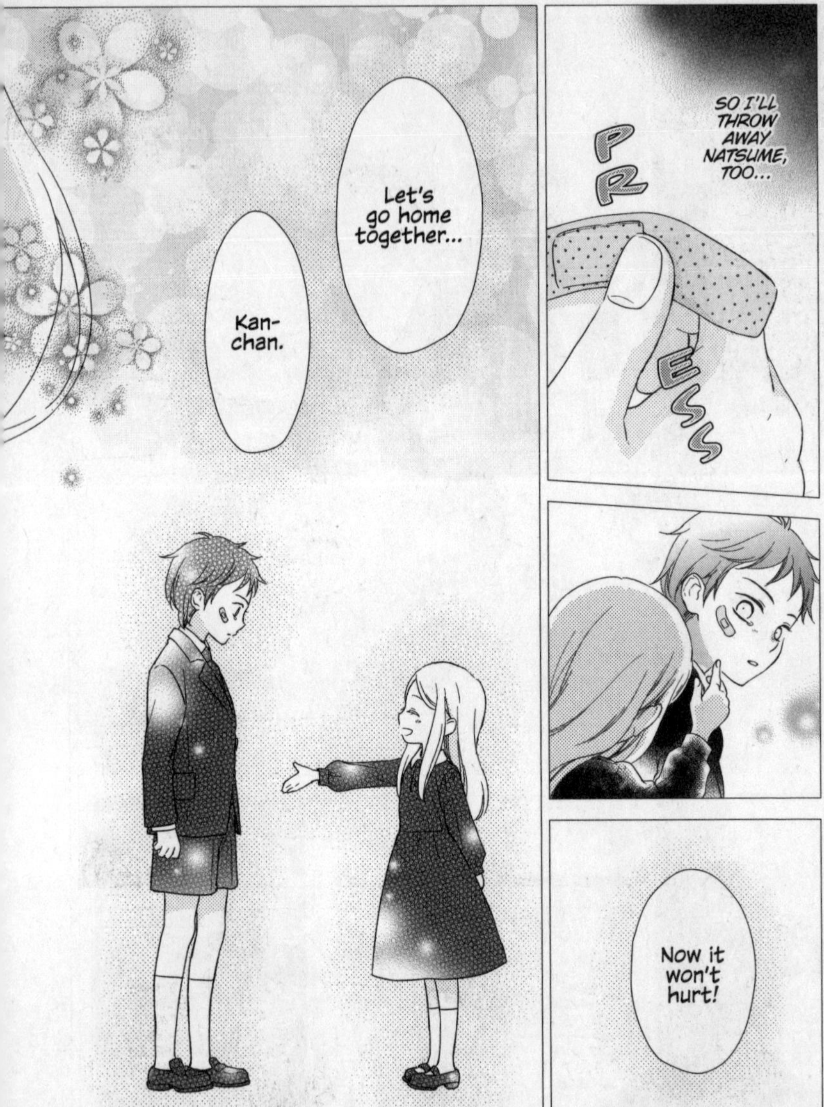
SO I'LL THROW AWAY NATSUME, TOO...
PRESS
Now it won't hurt!
Let's go home together...
Kan-chan.

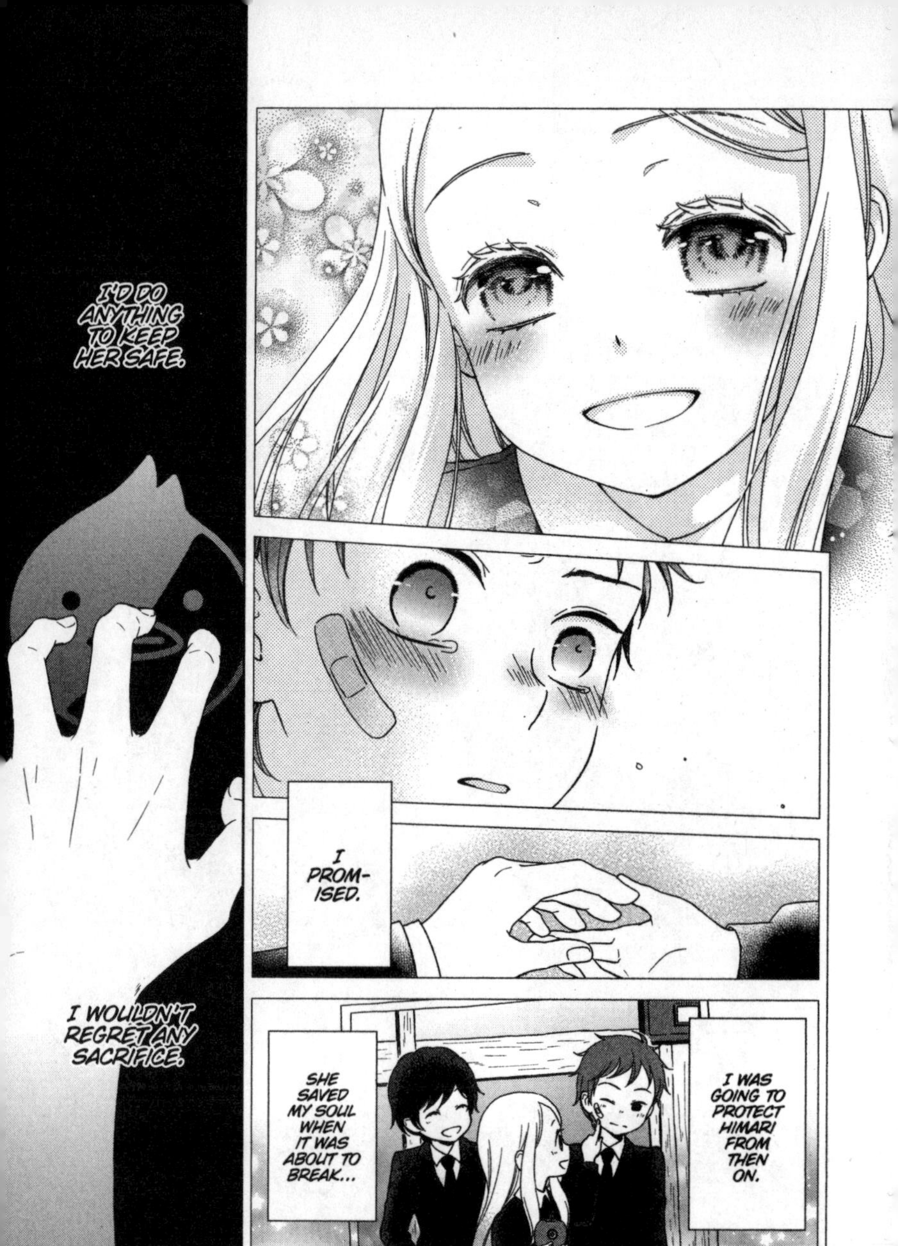
I PROMISED.
I WAS GOING TO PROTECT HIMARI FROM THEN ON.
SHE SAVED MY SOUL WHEN IT WAS ABOUT TO BREAK...
I'D DO ANYTHING TO KEEP HER SAFE.
I WOULDN'T REGRET ANY SACRIFICE.

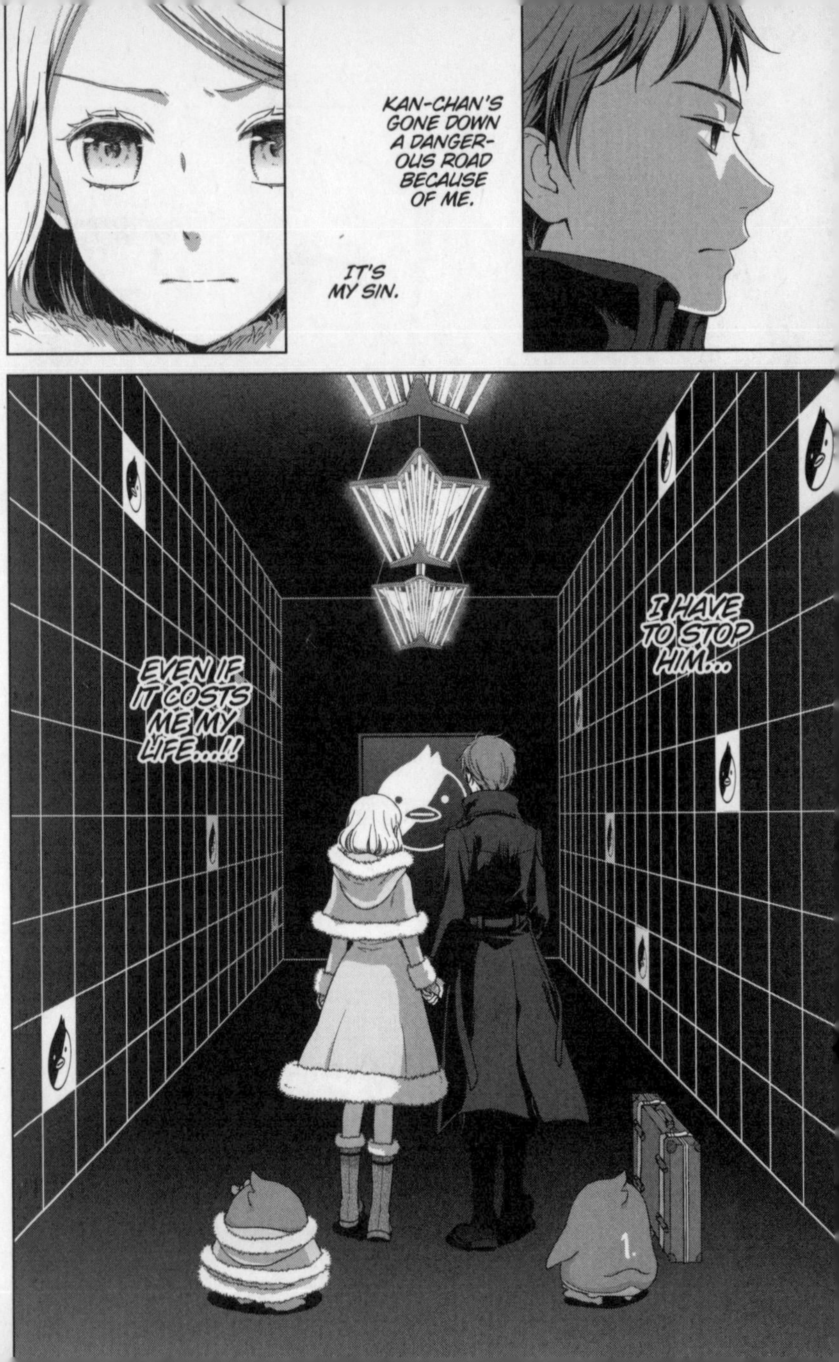
KAN-CHAN'S GONE DOWN A DANGEROUS ROAD BECAUSE OF ME.
IT'S MY SIN.
I HAVE TO STOP HIM...
EVEN IF IT COSTS ME MY LIFE...!!

END

NEXT STATION

PENGUINDRUM

volume

#5

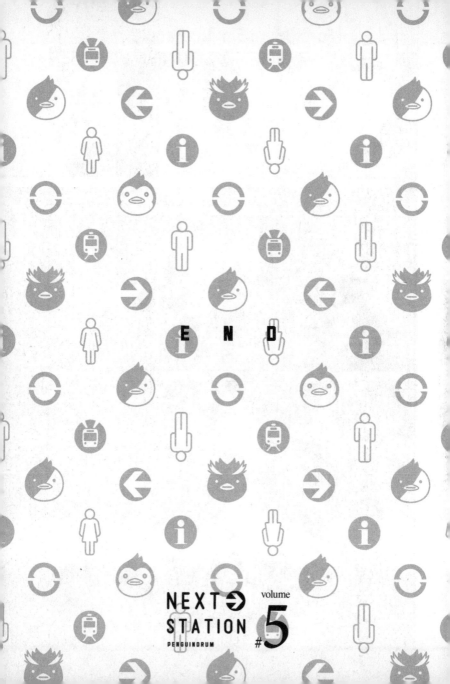

Forbidden: Similar People

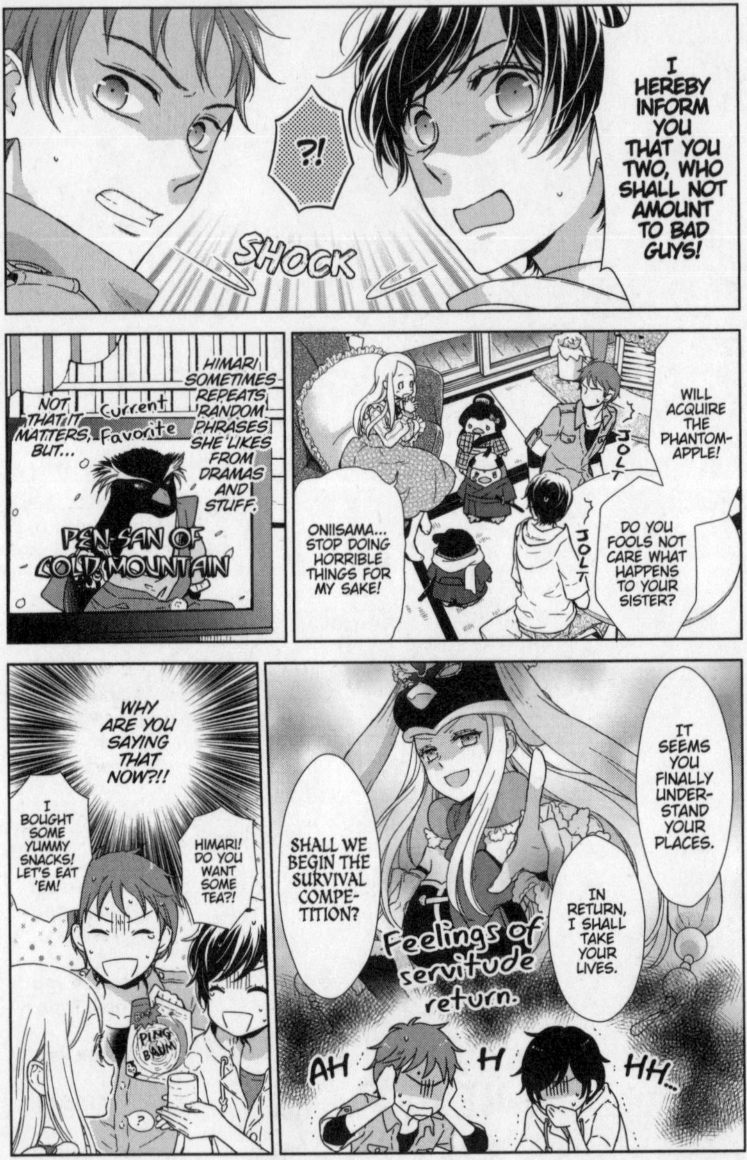
I HEREBY INFORM YOU THAT YOU TWO, WHO SHALL NOT AMOUNT TO BAD GUYS!
?!
SHOCK
WILL ACQUIRE THE PHANTOM-APPLE!
JOLT
JOLT
DO YOU FOOLS NOT CARE WHAT HAPPENS TO YOUR SISTER?
ONIISAMA... STOP DOING HORRIBLE THINGS FOR MY SAKE!
HIMARI SOMETIMES REPEATS RANDOM PHRASES SHE LIKES FROM DRAMAS AND STUFF.
NOT THAT IT MATTERS, BUT...
Current Favorite
PEN-SAN OF COLD MOUNTAIN
IT SEEMS YOU FINALLY UNDER-STAND YOUR PLACES.
SHALL WE BEGIN THE SURVIVAL COMPE-TITION?
IN RETURN, I SHALL TAKE YOUR LIVES.
Feelings of servitude return.
AH H HH...
WHY ARE YOU SAYING THAT NOW?!!
HIMARI! DO YOU WANT SOME TEA?!
I BOUGHT SOME YUMMY SNACKS! LET'S EAT 'EM!
PING BAUM
?

At this station, this
train will not arrive at
the same destination
as the previous cars.
Please be careful not to
take the wrong train.

Thank you to Kunihiko
Ikuhara, the director...
Lily Hoshino, the mangaka...
my editor, Fujimoto-san...
Kaneda-san...

Wataru Osakabe-san...
and everyone else involved.
Thanks also to
Touko Akiba-san,
my family, and
my readers...

I'd love to see you
on the next train.

Thank you.

2015.10.

Isuzu Shibata

SEVEN SEAS ENTERTAINMENT PRESENTS

PENGUINDRUM

art by **ISUZU SHIBATA**   story by **ikunichawder**   character designs by **LILY HOSHINO**   **VOL. 4**

TRANSLATION **Beni Axia Conrad**	MAWARU—PENGUINDRUM Vol. 4 by ikunichawder, Isuzu Shibata, & Lily Hoshino ©2016 ikunichawder / SHIBATA ISUZU / GENTOSHA COMICS INC. ©ikunichawder/pingroup All rights reserved.
ADAPTATION **Lora Gray**	
LETTERING **Jennifer Skarupa**	Original Japanese edition published in 2016 by GENTOSHA COMICS Inc. English translation rights arranged worldwide with GENTOSHA COMICS Inc. through Digital Catapult Inc., Tokyo.
COVER DESIGN **Kris Aubin**	
PROOFREADER **Dawn Davis** **Danielle King**	No portion of this book may be reproduced or transmitted in any form without written permission from the copyright holders. This is a work of fiction. Names, characters, places, and incidents are the products of the author's imagination or are used fictitiously. Any resemblance to actual events, locales, or persons, living or dead, is entirely coincidental.
EDITOR **Jenn Grunigen**	
PREPRESS TECHNICIAN **Rhiannon Rasmussen-Silverstein**	Seven Seas press and purchase enquiries can be sent to Marketing Manager Lianne Sentar at press@gomanga.com. Information regarding the distribution and purchase of digital editions is available from Digital Manager CK Russell at digital@gomanga.com.
PRODUCTION MANAGER **Lissa Pattillo**	
MANAGING EDITOR **Julie Davis**	Seven Seas and the Seven Seas logo are trademarks of Seven Seas Entertainment. All rights reserved.
ASSOCIATE PUBLISHER **Adam Arnold**	ISBN: 978-1-64505-779-6 Printed in Canada First Printing: April 2021
PUBLISHER **Jason DeAngelis**	10 9 8 7 6 5 4 3 2 1

FOLLOW US ONLINE: *www.sevenseasentertainment.com*

READING DIRECTIONS

This book reads from *right to left*, Japanese style. If this is your first time reading manga, you start reading from the top right panel on each page and take it from there. If you get lost, just follow the numbered diagram here. It may seem backwards at first, but you'll get the hang of it! Have fun!!

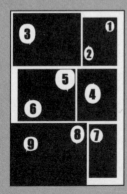